WITCHFINDER

...father has escaped from hell and walks
among us. his trident symbol branded into the earth
...appears all over the world. A scorching beacon.
...sign that war is coming. Jake is struggling
...grow used to his reputation as the
...youngest ever demon hunter. But now he must push
...to the extreme. To defeat his Demon Father Jake must
...and his mother he will embark on a treacherous
...that will take him into another dimension
...of fire and pain.

A place where innocent people
are tried and tortured.
A place where the law of the
witchfinder rules.
Let the rushes be lit for there will be
gall...

For Grace and Noah Lewis-Bettison
& Eleanor Bettison

WITCHFINDER
Gallows at Twilight

OXFORD
UNIVERSITY PRESS

Great Clarendon Street, Oxford OX2 6DP

Oxford University Press is a department of the University of Oxford.
It furthers the University's objective of excellence in research, scholarship,
and education by publishing worldwide in

Oxford   New York

Auckland   Cape Town   Dar es Salaam   Hong Kong   Karachi
Kuala Lumpur   Madrid   Melbourne   Mexico City   Nairobi
New Delhi   Shanghai   Taipei   Toronto

With offices in

Argentina   Austria   Brazil   Chile   Czech Republic   France   Greece
Guatemala   Hungary   Italy   Japan   Poland   Portugal   Singapore
South Korea   Switzerland   Thailand   Turkey   Ukraine   Vietnam

Oxford is a registered trade mark of Oxford University Press
in the UK and in certain other countries

British Library Cataloguing in Publication Data

Data available

ISBN: 978-0-19-273191-3

1 3 5 7 9 10 8 6 4 2

Printed in Great Britain
Paper used in the production of this book is a natural,
recyclable product made from wood grown in sustainable forests.
The manufacturing process conforms to the environmental
regulations of the country of origin.

WITCHFINDER
Gallows at Twilight

WILLIAM HUSSEY

OXFORD
UNIVERSITY PRESS

Contents

Then: 1645
The House of Bones

'She is coming, my sisters. The poor, doomed child . . . '

The witch's foot danced on the pedal of the spinning wheel.

'Her stomach is as empty as a leper's begging bowl and her feet are bare and bleeding,' the witch continued. 'Though she is but twelve years old she has cried all the tears of a long-lived life. And now, through heartache and hardship, she has come to *our* door. Death has found her at last.'

With her right hand the witch teased an invisible strand away from the hissing wheel. The magically woven thread passed from her fingers as a funnel of smoke. It spread out, coiling and condensing, until it had grown into a wall of cloud. Inside this foggy screen, a figure moved. A child, lost in a forest. The cloud crackled and the girl emerged from between the trees and stepped under the shadow of the manor house.

'She is here.'

Lizzie Redfern grasped the lion's head knocker. She tried to lift the heavy brass ring clasped between the lion's teeth, but the effort sapped the last of her strength. Her legs gave way and she tumbled down, smacking her face against the cold stone step. Lizzie felt no pain. She was beyond any sense or feeling now.

Dimly, she heard the rasp of a bolt and the weary grumble of the door. Candlelight dazzled. A figure stooped down, its ivory face pinched with concern. Arms encircled Lizzie and picked her from the ground. A rush of words wafted into her ear—

'Here you are, my dear, just as my clever sister foretold. But you are such a little thing! Come now, into the warmth and the light.'

The sound of the unknown lady's dress was like the rustle of a half-remembered lullaby. Twice Lizzie mustered the energy to open her eyes. She saw glimpses of a gloomy hall festooned with spider webs and the sweep of a big, dusty staircase. The lady did not seem to feel her burden. With Lizzie secure in her arms, she ghosted through the house. At last, they came to one of the upper rooms.

'Drude, my dear, I have brought our guest.'

The creak of another door and the glare of another candle.

'Oh, but she is so *thin*, Lethe,' the woman called Drude clucked. 'Bring her straight to the table, the broth is ready.'

No sooner had she been sat down than Lizzie felt the tap of a spoon against her teeth. Rich, meaty stew salted her lips.

'How charming,' Lethe purred. 'See, Drude, how she blinks in the firelight like a newborn pup.'

Lizzie felt a second spoonful of stew wash into her mouth. Heat spread out from her stomach and spilled into her arms and legs. By the time the spoon had scraped the last of the stew from the bowl, she was sitting up and looking at her hosts.

They had called each other 'sister' but Miss Drude and Miss Lethe were not at all alike. Clearly the elder of the two, Drude was dressed in a threadbare nightgown stained with splashes from the broth. Straggles of white hair poked out from beneath her nightcap and brushed against a large, warty nose. In contrast, Miss Lethe had the face of a playful imp. She wore a gown of finest yellow satin and had lacy ribbons tied in her long blonde hair.

'There now,' said Miss Drude, dabbing Lizzie's lips with a handkerchief, 'you must be feeling better.'

'I am, thank you, ma'am.'

'No need for thanks, my pet. But tell us, what has brought you to Havlock Grange on so bleak a night?'

'I've been walking from town to town, trying to find what work I can,' Lizzie explained. 'I came this night to the village not far from here—Little Muchly, I think it is called. An old lady in a cottage by the river told me to go to the big house. I was to tell the ladies there that "Old Sowerberry" had sent me.'

'Dear Old Sowerberry.' Miss Drude showed a set of worn,

black teeth. 'Yes, we have an . . . arrangement with that lady. She sends all needy children to our door.'

'Tell me, my dear,' Miss Lethe said, 'are you quite alone in the world?'

'Yes, ma'am. My mother died giving me life. My father . . .' Lizzie's voice cracked. 'He was killed the month before last at the great battle at Naseby.'

'He was a soldier? For which side?'

'He was a Parliament man.'

Drude nodded sadly. 'Even here, in our lonely house far from the world, we hear tell of this great conflict—this barbaric civil war.'

While Drude had been speaking, Lizzie's gaze wandered around the room. The table at which they sat occupied the centre, its surface cluttered with books, parchment, quills, candles, and a cauldron from which the broth had been served. A large curtain had been used to screen off the far end of the chamber. Within a few paces of Lizzie stood a grand stone fireplace with grotesque faces carved into its columns.

A painting hanging above the fireplace caught Lizzie's eye. The central figure of the picture stared down at the girl, his eyes like two dark gemstones. Aside from the sneer frozen upon his lips, the man in the painting was as beautiful as an angel.

'Our brother,' Lethe sighed. 'Our beautiful, talented brother. How we miss him.'

'Did he die?'

'In a way,' said Drude. 'He lives still, but it is a half-life. He exists only within the Veil.'

These words confused Lizzie. She asked, 'What was his name?'

'Marcus. Marcus Crowden . . . '

The flames of the fire quivered. Lizzie turned and saw the curtain at the end of the chamber flutter outwards.

'Come,' Miss Drude muttered. 'Our sister calls.'

Hands locked onto Lizzie's shoulders. Too shocked to cry out, the girl stumbled forward as the sisters barged her through the room. They reached the curtain and Drude, no longer smiling, grasped the edge and tore it back.

'This is our youngest sister. Say hello, Frija.'

The woman sitting at the spinning wheel lifted her head. She was small—smaller even than little Lethe—and dressed entirely in black. Although a thick veil covered her face, Lizzie felt sure that Frija Crowden was looking directly at her. Frija's fingers played through the spokes of the wheel, turning it slowly, surely.

'I saw your coming, Lizzie Redfern,' she said.

'Who are you?' Lizzie whispered.

'I am the cloud spinner. My eye sees far and my hand speaks truth. See the truth I spin . . . '

Frija's fingers teased a strand from her spinning wheel and cast it loose. The moment it left her hand, the fibre soared across the room and into a dark corner. Like a bright finger, it descended, touching on a large chest or travelling trunk. The lid was thrown back and, as the light strengthened, Lizzie caught sight of the trunk's contents.

Screams caught in her throat.

'Old Sowerberry sends any passing child to Havlock Grange,' Frija murmured. 'They come to seek work, to beg a penny. They are brought in, they are fed . . . and they are never seen again.'

The magically woven strand brightened.

Arm and leg bones poked out of the trunk like the stalks of strange, headless flowers. Little skulls, some with clumps of hair still attached, grinned in the ghostly light. The sight of these remains was frightening enough, but what chilled Lizzie most were the chips and notches scored into the bones. Teeth marks. She looked back at Lethe and Drude and imagined the hungry women sitting at the table, chomping and gulping, sucking and slurping, wiping the juice from their chins. When the bones had been picked clean, they would be thrown into the chest. Such a small grave for so many children.

Lizzie thought about the delicious stew she had just enjoyed and her gaze switched back to the table. Fear sharpened her senses and she noticed things that in the haze of hunger she had missed.

She saw the slick, red gruel dripping down the cauldron's belly. Smelt the faint stench of rotting flesh. Saw the chopping board at the end of the table, its blood-smattered surface littered with chunks of meat and scraps of gore. Six eel-black tongues had been heaped together, ready for dicing. A single jellied eye, shucked from a child's head, sat upon the table and stared up at the ceiling. At one end of the chopping board, fingers and toes had been laid out like a row of little sausages.

Lizzie covered her eyes. She could no longer look at the cannibals' kitchen.

'Such a shame,' Lethe sighed. 'We had intended to keep you alive for a few weeks. Fatten you up; get some flesh on those bones. But I'm afraid Frija has forced our hand. Drude, my love, will you be a dear and fetch the axe?'

'NO!'

Frija's hands left the spinning wheel and shot out towards her sisters. Before either could respond, the spell was cast. Streams of blue light encircled the Crowden sisters, locking their legs together and snapping their arms against their sides. Frija gestured upwards and her sisters were lifted from the ground.

'Treachery!' Drude shrieked.

Lethe smiled her sweet smile. 'My dear Drude, you ought to know by now that Frija cannot be trusted. As soon as she spun her vision of the girl you ought to have bound her hands.'

Frija paid her sisters no heed. She turned to Lizzie. 'Come here, child.'

The girl approached the black-robed figure, her eyes rooted on the thick veil.

'You see the coin resting there below the bobbin? Take it and run.'

The coin glinted in the firelight, bright and golden. Despite all the impossible things Lizzie had seen this night, this seemed the most miraculous. It was a double crown: more money than her father would have earned from a year of soldiering.

She reached for the witch. 'Come with me.'

'I cannot. I . . . I must never be seen. Please, you must hurry.'

Lizzie clasped the coin to her chest. She cast one last, sorrowful look at her saviour and ran from the house.

The witches collapsed to the ground.

'Sentimental idiot!' Drude moaned, picking herself up. 'Now we will have to clear the house of bones, just in case the little wretch tells the constable and—'

'Hush, sister,' Lethe hissed. 'See, she is spinning again.'

Their anger momentarily forgotten, Lethe and Drude gathered around their more gifted sister. Frija's foot rocketed up and down upon the pedal, working the wheel so fast that its whistle could be heard in every corner of the house. Her hands were a blur as she spun the fibre into a pitch-black cloud. Lethe and Drude looked at each other: they had never seen their sister spin a vision of such intensity.

'*He* is coming!' Frija's voice lost its sadness. Now it was cold, hollow. 'Very soon now he will begin his long journey.'

An image formed in the cloud. A boy—tall, thin, brown hair falling across his eyes. Eyes that seemed to fix upon the Crowden sisters. He stretched out his hand towards them, as if casting a spell.

Lethe and Drude fell back.

'He is coming to find us, sisters. The boy conjuror. The Witchfinder.' Frija's eyes dazzled. 'Jacob Harker . . . '

NOW

Chapter 1
The Lost Art of Magic

Jake stepped off the road and into the dark embrace of the trees. Stalks of yellow grass rattled against his shins as he scrambled down a bank of loose earth. He hit the ground, paused for a moment, and breathed in the stillness of the forest. Save for the shimmer of moonlight between the branches, nothing stirred. Not an animal, not an insect, not a bird. He had expected someone—some*thing*—to be waiting for him; a lurking, monstrous presence that would fall upon him as soon as he set foot in its domain. But there was nothing here—just silence, darkness, and the reek of decay.

He sucked down the mouldy forest air and whistled. A second later, he heard footfalls on the bank.

'Over here,' he hissed. 'Follow my voi—'

Something shifted in the darkness. It lashed out and hit Jake like a jolt of electricity, surged inside his head, tumbled and roared in his brain. He could hear nothing, see nothing, beyond that single overwhelming force.

Evil.

In response, a pale blue light appeared between his fingers. Jake managed a weak smile and turned to the others. He took a tattered map from his pocket, ran his finger over the page, and pointed east.

'Two miles till we reach the grounds, then another mile to the Crowden house. Stay close.'

Comforted by the sight of his magic, his father and Rachel Saxby nodded and followed Jake into the shadows.

They had gone a little way, their feet crackling over a carpet of dead leaves, when Jake held up his hand. Rachel and Adam came to a halt.

'Something's not right,' Jake said. 'The colour of the forest—it's different.'

Rachel peered into the gloom. 'What do you mean?'

'Shhh. There's something up ahead.'

The evil that haunted the forest had changed. No longer an invisible force, Jake saw it as a colour running through the trees—a sickly grey smoke, the shade of a rotten egg or maggoty meat. It had a smell, too, that reminded Jake of the day when the sewers of New Town had burst and the filth of a thousand homes had been spewed into the streets. But this was not the only change he noticed. Some distance from where they stood, a lonesome powder-blue light shone between the trunks of the trees. This new colour stood out against the grey evil like a lantern's glow. A familiar fragrance accompanied the colour: citrus and jasmine.

Jake breathed easy. 'It's Pandora.'

At the sound of her name, that handsome, eight-armed woman, who had once mustered an army and saved Adam and Jake from the clutches of the evil coven master Marcus Crowden, emerged into the light. Jake smiled and hurried to greet his friend. It had been only a few weeks since their first meeting in the back office of Crowden's bookshop, and yet it felt as if he had known Pandora for years. She had become a regular visitor to the Harker home, teaching Jake and Rachel the ways of the dark creatures and explaining some of the mysteries of her world. Already it was difficult to think of life without Pandora.

Jake was halfway across the glade when he stopped dead. This instinct for seeing the colour of a soul had come so suddenly and naturally to him that he hadn't questioned it. Now he wondered if it might be something like the feel for evil that he had inherited from the Witchfinder. It was a comforting thought—maybe he was tapping into those old powers again. As soon as this idea occurred to him, however, the magical instinct seemed to fade. Pandora came forward, and the lantern-glow around her grew dimmer until, finally, it was extinguished.

Old doubts began to whisper in Jake's ear. Ever since he had destroyed the Door into the demon realm he had felt the powerful magic of the Witchfinder slipping away from him. He had tried his best to hold on to it, summoning memories of those times when he had sensed the magic at its strongest. Times when he had been angry or despairing, like on the night his mother had been murdered by the witch, Tobias Quilp. Sometimes these memories sparked his powers, more often they failed. His father had reminded Jake that, as a clone of Josiah Hobarron, magic was part of Jake's genes, his DNA. All he had to do was find a way back to that forgotten place inside himself.

Jake tried to push his doubts aside. Tonight was their first real chance to rescue Simon Lydgate. His best friend was counting on him, and so Jake could only pray that the magic would be there when he needed it.

Two of Pandora's arms wound around Jake's waist. A pair of hands gripped his shoulders and another cupped his chin and lifted his face.

'Really wish you wouldn't hug me like that, Pandora,' Jake complained. 'It feels like I'm being frisked by a dozen cops.'

'I hope that ain't prejudice I hear coming from your lips, Master Harker,' Pandora said in her warm, Louisiana drawl. 'Octo-phobia is not cool.'

Yet another hand slapped Jake lightly across the cheek.

'And lookee here, Miss Rachel Saxby, always a pleasure. Please tell me you've been practising with that bow, Rachel honey, we're gonna need all the help we can get tonight.'

Rachel came forward and kissed Pandora.

'Religiously,' she nodded.

'Loving the confidence, girl. Show me.'

In one fluid motion, Rachel swept the bow from her back and reached for an arrow from the quiver. The bow was loaded, the string drawn taut, and the arrow fired with lightning speed and deadly accuracy. It thunked into the skinny trunk of a sapling several hundred metres into the forest.

'Woo-eee,' Pandora breathed.

As Jake watched Rachel trot into the forest and retrieve the arrow, his thoughts returned to that first night back at home after the Door had been destroyed. Despite being exhausted, his father had immediately started to research the Demon Father—that dark, infernal presence that had taken possession of Marcus Crowden. Likewise, Jake had begun practising his magic, trying to hold onto his already fading powers. For her part, Rachel was determined not to be left out. She had no magical ability, but Adam told her that, when the time came, there might well be creatures fighting for the Demon Father that could not defend themselves with magic. He had taken her to his study and, after half an hour of rummaging through his collection of mystic odds and ends, he had found the bow of Nuada.

'Nuada was the one-armed king of the Tuatha Dé Danann,' Adam said, handing Rachel the beautifully-engraved silver bow. 'They were a warrior race that, in the mists of Irish legend, might once have been gods. The sword of Nuada was called Claiomh Solais—the Sword of Light. Once drawn, no enemy could escape its sting.'

Taking the bow, Rachel had run her fingers over its curved sapwood limbs.

'After the Claiomh Solais was destroyed in battle, splinters of the blade were embedded in the heartswood of a bow. This bow.'

'You're kidding,' Rachel laughed.

Adam had puffed out his cheeks. 'I've known stranger things.'

Jake watched now as Rachel slid the arrow back into its quiver. She'd had only a few weeks to practise and yet she held the weapon with authority and poise. He wondered if this was really the result of the magical properties of the bow or of Rachel's own natural marksmanship. He remembered that her father, Dr Saxby, was also a crack shot.

Pandora high-fived Rachel and then turned to Adam. She tried to hide her emotions, but Jake knew her well enough now to read the concern in her face. She hugged her old friend, careful not to brush against his wounded shoulder.

'How are you, sweetness?'

'Good. I'm good, Pandora.'

'You don't look good. You look like an ol' mule rode half to death and then rode the other half. You shouldn't be here.'

'Pandora, please.' Adam inclined his head towards Jake.

'You know something, Adam Harker? For a clever man you do a fine impression of the world's biggest dumb-ass. The boy can see you ain't up to this.'

Jake felt the truth of Pandora's words. Now forced to walk with the aid of a stick, his father looked like a man aged before his time. When Marcus Crowden had cast a hex at Jake, Adam had thrown himself into the path of the dark magic. Now his skin was creased like old paper and his eyes scored with deep lines. Pandora had been treating him with arcane remedies and her potions had succeeded in holding back the worst of the magic. Despite his father growing ever weaker, Jake remained confident that the resourceful Pandora would find a cure.

'I told him to stay at home,' Jake said, flanking Pandora.

'Least someone in your screwy family has some sense, then.'

'Don't talk about me as if I'm not here,' Adam snapped. 'I'm not totally useless, you know. I might even be able to help.'

Pandora rested her forehead against Adam's.

'You ain't useless, friend of mine,' she sighed. 'You just ugly.'

The joke cut through the tension and the four of them burst out laughing.

A deep, rumbling grunt interrupted the hilarity.

'You lot gonna stand there gabbin' all night? My club's itchin' to bust some demon skull.'

Pandora rolled her eyes.

'Ladies and gentlemen, may I introduce Mr Brag Badderson.'

The ground trembled as the creature stomped out of the shadows. Standing at a height of a little under ten feet, Brag Badderson towered over the company. His grey-green skin had the ridged texture of a tree trunk; a natural camouflage which might have accounted for the fact that they hadn't noticed the giant earlier. His huge barrel chest heaved and the nostrils of his tiny, flattened nose sniffed the air. Aside from a pair of raggedy leather shorts, the monster was naked. Moss and lichen had grown in patches on his body and what looked like the remains of a bird's nest clung to his right shoulder.

'I sometimes fall asleep standin' up,' Brag explained, self-consciously brushing away the woven twigs. 'Bloomin' birds think I'm a cliff or summat.'

'What *is* he?' Rachel whispered.

Brag cupped one of his tiny ears.

'Eh? Speak up, girl! Wha's she say, Pand?'

'She was wondering what kind of creature you are, Brag!'

To everyone's surprise, Brag drew himself up to his full height, placed a three-fingered hand on his chest and began to sing in a deep, bass-baritone.

'*They call me Troll—Gnawer of the Moon—Giant of the Gale-blasts—Curse of the rain-hall—Companion of the—*'

'Yes, yes,' Pandora groaned. 'We've heard it all before.'

'Eh? You wanna hear some more?'

'I said—WE'VE HEARD IT ALL BEFORE!'

Brag picked at one of the tusk-like teeth that overhung his bottom lip.

'Some folk got no culture,' he grumbled.

'Brag's a forest troll,' Pandora explained. 'And, as you may have noticed, he's as deaf as a post. He's also hideous, rude, stupid, and has the worst personal hygiene of any creature I've ever encountered, dark or otherwise. But don't let any of that put you off. If it comes to a fight, you could do worse than have Brag Badderson in your corner.'

Jake took in the troll's massive arms and the great stone club that he bounced idly against his shoulder. Pandora was right: this guy was a definite asset to the team!

'Hey!' Brag shouted, shivering a shower of leaves from the trees. 'I may be hideous, rude, deaf and . . . ' He counted the insults off on his fingers. As he had only three on each hand the tally seemed to confuse him.

'And putrid-smelling,' Pandora said.

'Yup, that too,' Brag agreed, 'but I ain't dumb. You said I'd be getting paid for this little gig, Pand, so where's the gold?'

Pandora shot Adam a sheepish look. 'I promised him gold. Thought the big idiot would forget.'

'"*You wanna cross a bridge, you gotta pay the troll,*"' Brag said solemnly. 'That's the Badderson family motto.'

'Badderson, Badderson . . . ' Adam clucked his tongue against the roof of his mouth. 'Of course! Got it!' He took the mobile phone from his pocket and dialled. While he waited for the call to connect, Adam winked at the confused forest troll. 'Ah, hello? Yes, this is Dr Adam Harker speaking . . . Yes, it's been a long time, hasn't it? How are you? The wife? Good, good. And the other wife? Ah, ran away with a Bulgarian ogre—I'm sorry to hear that . . . How many kids now? My, you have been busy, Mr Badderson.'

Brag, who had been cupping his ear and listening carefully, looked thunderstruck.

'Yes, I'm fine, sir,' Adam continued. 'I'm just calling because I have your son here. I was telling him about the old days. You remember the time when I helped to smuggle your family out of Scandinavia during the troll-hunting season . . . ? Indeed, it was *quite* an adventure. Well, I was telling young Brag that I needed a favour, but he seemed quite reluctant to help out, and so I thought . . . Yes, he's here.' Adam held out the phone. 'Daddy wants a word, Brag.'

The troll gulped. He took the phone, which looked like a baby's toy pinched between his formidable fingers.

'Hi, Dad . . . Yeah, but . . . but the family motto . . . The family motto's horse dung? That's not what you say when you've had a few on Sammal's Eve . . . No, please don't put Mum on . . . OK, I will . . . Said I will, didn't I? No, sir. Yes, sir. Yes, tell her I put a fresh pair on this mornin' . . . Yeah, g'night, Dad.' The troll returned the phone and looked down at his feet. 'I'm very sorry, Dr Harker. My dad says I'm to do whatever you tell me and to keep my big, fat, ugly mouth shut.'

Pandora slapped the troll playfully across the knee.

'Well, that's that sorted. Shall we get this show on the road? By the way, Brag, try to keep that great melon of yours below the trees—we're not in the grounds yet, but we don't want to warn them we're coming.'

The reinforced company struck out, moving ever deeper into the forest.

Adam tried to keep his voice low but Jake heard him whisper to Pandora:

'Is the troll all you could muster? I was hoping you could bring at least ten dark creatures with you. Maybe more. Loads of you fought against the Crowden Coven.'

'Times have changed, honey. It ain't just witches we're facing these days. Rumours are spreading like wildfire among the dark creatures: something has been released from the demon realm—'

'But he's not here,' Jake cut in. 'Your contacts, Pandora, they said he's abroad.'

'Boarded a plane this mornin',' Pandora confirmed. 'But when he gets back and finds out what we've done . . . Listen, even *I* thought twice about coming tonight.'

'I guess we should be thankful for small mercies then,' Adam muttered. 'But just what is the Demon Father up to? Weeks have passed since he came through from the demon world, but he still hasn't made a move against us. And all these short trips abroad: the US, Japan, Egypt, Australia, and now Spain. Who's he visiting?'

'Beats me,' Pandora said. 'All we know is that, wherever he goes, his trident mark turns up a day or two later: burned into cornfields, graffiti tagged onto monuments, even scratched into the earth of the Australian outback. Last night, one of my contacts in Tokyo saw it as a red neon light flashing high above the city streets.'

'Whatever he's doing, I'm just glad that this time Pandora found out about his travel plans in advance,' Jake said. 'This is our first real chance . . . '

He reached for Rachel's hand.

'It's now or never. We have to rescue him tonight. Simon's counting on us.'

Adam gave a weary sigh. 'Jake, I know we've had this argument before, but are you sure about this? The Demon Father will have left behind powerful protections to guard the boy. Simon is his son and—'

'I owe him,' Jake said through gritted teeth.

'But you have to consider: he may no longer be the boy you knew. He's half-demon, Jake.'

'He's my friend.' Jake locked eyes with his father. 'My *best* friend.'

Adam nodded. 'Very well, then we better get moving.'

They marched on for another ten minutes or so before

coming to a break in the forest. A fence, four metres high and covered in barbed wire, cut through the trees. The metal sign attached to the chain-link rattled as they approached.

Chapter 2
Blades of Her Ancestors

'There's an old legend about the Crowdens of Havlock Grange,' Adam said, staring up at the sign. 'Marcus was the youngest of the family, and the only boy. He had three older sisters—Miss Drude, Miss Lethe, and Miss Frija. Some say that these Crowden sisters would lure orphan children to the house with promises of food and shelter. They pretended to be kindly spinster women, but after a few weeks of fattening the kids up—'

'They'd eat them,' Rachel said in a hollow voice.

'Bloody witches,' Brag grunted.

'Aren't trolls supposed to eat people, too?' Jake asked.

'Not women and children!' The troll looked offended. 'Only men. Bad men ... mostly. We ain't monsters, you know!'

'Well, we've learned two things about the Demon Father already,' Adam said. 'He knows his history and he has a twisted sense of humour.'

' 'nough gabbin'.'

Brag strode up to the fence and raised his club.

'Let me handle this, troll boy,' said Pandora. 'All mortals present, please stand well back.'

Her hands reached around and disappeared into a fold at the back of her dress. She drew out eight silver daggers from their hiding place and proceeded to juggle them through the air. The thick blades, curved at an angle of about twenty degrees, dazzled in the moonlight. The speed of the daggers made it difficult to see the designs on the hilts, but Jake thought he could make out images of multi-armed men and women dressed in battle regalia.

'These are the weapons of my ancestors,' Pandora called, her voice just audible over the swish of the knives. 'You guys ready for a show?'

Still juggling the daggers high, she ran like the wind towards the security fence. Jake watched the first blade descend towards the wire. The dagger cut through the chain-link and a mini-lightning bolt shot out from the fence. It wrapped itself around Pandora, sparking and fizzing as it locked her in a lethal embrace. A second bolt, and then a third, struck the woman, rooting her to the spot. Before the eyes of her friends, Pandora blazed and burned.

They were powerless to help. To touch her, even to approach, would mean certain death. Rachel screamed and hid her face in the crook of Jake's shoulder. Like a great bear, Brag Badderson dropped onto all fours and, with his back arched, hollered at the fence as if it were a living creature. Aside from drenching the others in phlegm his outburst achieved nothing. Wreathed in jagged blue light, Pandora's body continued to writhe.

Jake thrust out his hand. If he could stop the current, somehow interrupt the flow or, best of all, blow the damn fence to Kingdom Come, maybe there was still a chance to save his friend. He went back to those memories of anger and despair—the sight of his mother's death, the grinning face of Tobias Quilp, the powerlessness he had felt before his connection with the Witchfinder—hoping that they would prompt his magic. With Pandora dying in front of him it was difficult to concentrate. He stared at his cupped palm and willed the blue flame to spark into life.

Nothing.

He screamed inside. He cursed. He screwed his fury into a white-hot spear of energy and visualized it racing along his arm and breaking between his fingers.

Nothing.

He summoned the face, the voice, the presence of Josiah Hobarron in his mind. What he saw was a dim reflection of the Witchfinder, and so he conjured . . .

Nothing.

'Please,' Jake murmured. 'Just this once, *please* . . . '

Pandora shrieked inside her deadly cage of light and energy. Very soon now she would burn up. Her eyes would melt in their sockets, her hair would crackle to a crisp, flesh would roast and peel from her bones. All that would remain was a charred skeleton; a blackened, smoking testament to the failure of Jacob Harker.

Jake couldn't bear it. His eyes misted with tears and he

turned away. He and Rachel stood together, arms wrapped around each other, caught in the flickering light of Pandora's last moments . . .

And then Jake felt a hand on his arm. He glanced up at Adam and, to his surprise, saw that his father was smiling.

'Look closer.'

'But she's dying. Dad, I can't help her.'

'Look,' Adam instructed. 'See.'

Jake wiped away the tears with the back of his hand and forced himself to look back at the fence. To really *look* at the blazing figure of his friend.

'But that's impossible!' he cried, his voice full of wonder and joy. 'That's . . . that's *brilliant*!'

At first, Jake had thought that Pandora's violent thrashing was the result of electricity burning through her body. Now he saw that those whips of blue light had nothing to do with her movements. Pandora's arms moved with a definite purpose. The daggers in her hands slashed through the fence like a hot knife through butter. Thirty seconds later, a heap of shredded metal lay at her feet.

Pandora tossed the daggers high, caught them one-handed, and returned the blades to their hiding place in her dress.

'The Demon Father juiced that baby pretty good,' she panted.

Grinning, she turned to the others and a few stray flashes of electricity crackled between her teeth. Rachel ran to her, hesitated, and when Pandora nodded, threw her arms around her.

'You could've warned us you were going to do that! You scared me half to death.'

'I'm sorry, child, but in case you haven't noticed, I'm not exactly human. Kinda thought the arms gave it away, but there you go. Hey, big man, you OK?'

Brag Badderson sniffed and cleared his throat. 'Course I am. Come on then, you lot. Gab, gab, gab.'

The troll lumbered towards the hole in the fence. Clomping past Pandora, he gave her a hard look.

'Don't you ever do that to me again.'

Jake also tried to feign annoyance, but he couldn't help smiling as he passed his remarkable eight-armed friend.

The forest outside the gate had been creepy enough, but here, in the grounds of Havlock Grange, the atmosphere became ever darker. In some places the trees crowded so close together that Brag had to use his club to beat a path through. Thick branches entangled overhead and blocked out the light of the moon. For the first time, Jake began to hear the rustle of unseen creatures. He took a torch from his pocket, flicked the switch and played the light over the undergrowth.

Like the forest, Jake's thoughts became bleaker. Once again, at the crucial moment, he had been unable to summon his magic. If Pandora had really been in trouble, he could not have helped her. And yet here he was, walking through a hostile forest, his destination the fortress of the most evil being on Earth. His dad's doubts were right: this plan was absolutely insane.

Rachel's hand slipped into Jake's and squeezed. Her smile

knocked all the breath out of his body. Glancing down at his free hand, he saw a pale blue flame skip between his fingers. A second later, it vanished.

'This is crazy, Rachel,' he said. 'We need to get out of here. Now.'

'We can't. Simon——'

'I know, but even if we manage to find Simon, who's to say that he'll still be the person we knew? He's been the Demon Father's prisoner for weeks now. He's probably been tortured, brainwashed. And even then . . . ' Jake could hardly bring himself to say it. 'He's the son of a demon, Rachel.'

'We can't help what our parents are,' Rachel said, her voice like iron. 'I should know. Look, Jake, you can only judge a person by their actions. He saved your life, and now he needs our help.'

Jake pinched the bridge of his nose. 'You're right, I'm sorry.'

'Come on, what's really worrying you?'

'Nothing.'

'You sleep in the next room, Jake; don't think I can't hear you pacing up and down all night. Come on, out with it.'

'It's my magic,' Jake admitted. 'I couldn't help Pandora just now. Rachel, I'm just not strong enough to do this.'

'When you need it, the magic will come. I believe that. Anyway,' Rachel grinned, 'I'm pretty handy with this bow, you know. You get scared, hide behind me.'

'I'll probably take you up on that,' Jake laughed.

Rachel smiled again, and Jake felt a distant memory stir. That smile. That face. A light flickered in some unexplored corridor of his soul, a warm and loving glow just out of reach.

Her face.

Elean—

Jake's thoughts snapped back to the present.

He had sensed something.

They had now entered a clearing at the heart of the forest—a rough circle of barren ground bordered on all sides by ancient trees. Rotten apples lay in piles around the tree roots, as if the evil that infected this place had plucked the fruit from the branches with a withering hand. The moon shone down and bathed the glade in soft, silvery light, making it look like an illustration from a book of fairytales.

Shadows flitted across the clearing. Jake glanced up, expecting to see shreds of cloud passing across the face of the moon. But no, the star-dusted sky was clear and cloudless. A series of crackling, rustling noises came from the far side of the glade, and Jake's gaze shifted back to the trees. He saw the topmost branches waver to-and-fro, as if disturbed by the wind. Then he heard another sound—the flutter of cloth, the flap of a bird's wing, perhaps—descending through the branches.

Jake's hand locked around Rachel's wrist. He called out to the others—

'Stay there. Don't move. Something's coming.'

Adam, Pandora, and Brag stopped and looked back at Jake. With their heads turned away from the forest, they did not see what he saw.

Dark forms moved in the gaps between the trees. Together, the strangers stepped into the light. At their approach, a low moan, like the sough of the wind, called out from the forest. They came forward as one, their faces wrapped in shadow, their eyes shining like pale pebbles in the moonlight.

Frozen to the spot, Jake watched as eight spectral hands extended, crooked fingers unfurling and pointing towards the little group of friends. He saw the flash of white teeth and the dark 'O' of gaping mouths.

They had found the Demon Father's first line of defence.

Chapter 3
Death Scream

Aaaaaaaaaarrrrrrrrrrrggggggggggghhhhhhhhhh!

The monstrous guardians of Havlock Woods came shrieking into the glade.

The first note of their call stabbed at Jake's ears like a white-hot pin. The tone went higher, cut deeper, lancing its way into his mind. It felt as if some mad surgeon had sawn away the top half of his skull, scooped out his brain and filled the space with a hive of angry wasps; insects that whirred around his head and impaled their stingers behind his eyes. Jake fell to his knees. He pressed the heels of his hands against his ears in a desperate attempt to drown out the cries. It was useless. Through mounting agony, he watched the spectral women ghost their way across the glade.

Banshees.

The pages of Jake's dark catalogue—that mental index of myths and monsters that he had been adding to ever since his father introduced him to horror stories—flipped open inside his mind. Though his brain was crippled with pain, Jake forced himself to remember. The banshee: an ancient Gaelic spirit. Some people believed these creatures were the souls of murdered women, others that they were fairies or even forgotten gods. They came in many forms: beautiful young women, frumpy old grannies, sometimes even taking on the shape of hares or weasels. The old tales agreed on one thing only—to hear the wail of the banshee meant certain death.

The eight spirits floated towards the group of friends, their wasted arms outstretched. Jake's hands dropped to his sides. There was no chance of blocking out their song, and so he watched helplessly as the death-singers came forward. He had scoured his dark catalogue for some scrap of information they could use to defend themselves. There was nothing. The banshee had *no* weakness.

The women came closer, and Jake began to see their forms more clearly. They were dressed in ragged grey cloaks with hoods covering their heads. Bone-thin hands reached out from the sleeves and made strange stabbing gestures towards their victims, almost as if they were using their fingers to direct their screams. Although they floated gracefully, their bent backs and rounded shoulders gave them the appearance of raddled old women.

The banshees gathered in a circle around Jake and his friends. The pitch of their wailing increased, and Jake screamed again. With the choir of death now bending down to face its prey, he felt the pressure build inside his head. Any minute now, he was sure that his brain would burst and that his eyes would explode out of their sockets.

Thrum-thrum-thrum—the pound of blood in his ears.

Jake fell onto all fours. His face was lathered in sweat and blue veins stood out in ridges along his arms.

Boom-boom-boom—the blood seeping from his brain.

He glanced at the others. Like him, they were pictures of agony, their faces twisted, their bodies tucked up with pain. Adam was sprawled on the ground and looked as if he was about to pass out. Pandora was still standing, but her eyes were closed and her mouth was a hard, tight line. Rachel had rolled into a ball, knees drawn up to her chin, arms cradled around her head. But where was Brag Badderson?

Jake caught sight of the troll and felt a jolt of surprise.

Brag was standing outside the circle. He looked . . . well, he looked absolutely fine. Unaffected by the banshees' call, the troll was hard at work with his stone club. One of the monsters already lay in a crumbled heap at his feet. Choosing his next target, Brag swung his club high into the air and brought it down with all his might. The banshee collapsed under the weight of the weapon. As she fell, her body seemed to evaporate into nothingness. All that remained was her grey cloak, crumpled upon the ground. The song of her six sisters continued to haunt his ears, but Jake managed a sickly smile.

A moment later, the smile was wiped from his face.

Through the wailing, he heard the horrible snap and crackle of bones knitting themselves back together. The fallen banshees' cloaks twitched. Bony hands slithered from the sleeves and took hold of the collars, lifting them a few metres into the air. Jake's blood ran cold as he watched two heads grow out of the collars. It was the first time he had seen the face of a banshee . . .

These things were neither beautiful young women nor frumpy old grannies.

They were creatures that had crawled straight out of a nightmare.

A few tufts of hair, damp and slimy like pondweed, clung to the first banshee's bald head—a head that was still mending itself after Brag's attack. Parts of the fractured skull came together and pulled the banshee's left eye socket back into place. The eye rolled up from inside the skull and popped into position with a wet *scchhlop*. Both eyes were milky white and didn't have pupils, which suggested that the monster was blind. Its skin was so torn and tatty that Jake could see the blades of its cheekbones poking through the flesh. All this was repulsive enough, but it was the banshee's mouth which really horrified him.

When it reached its full height, the monster worked its jaw from side to side. Then, in one sudden jerk, the jaw dropped down until it settled just below the banshee's chest. From this black hole of despair the screaming started again.

Jake cried out against the renewed chorus. He watched Brag move along the line, smashing the banshees with his club. After each attack, the creatures would pick themselves up from the ground and start rebuilding their shattered bodies. It was hopeless. Eventually, Brag must have thought so too. Leaning on his club, he gave a mournful shrug. He knew as well as Jake that he could sling each of the friends over his shoulder and carry them away from the clearing, but that the banshees would follow. By the time Brag reached the road, they would certainly be dead.

The screaming drained the last of Jake's resistance and he fell onto his side. His gaze swept around the others. Rachel was wrapped in a tight ball; Pandora rocked on her knees; his father lay motionless on the ground. Blood began to ooze from Jake's nose and he coughed red-flecked spittle onto the ground. A fresh wave of despair took hold of him. He had brought them to this. It was all his fault . . .

And then he saw something that gave him a glimmer of hope. There, sitting below the trees at the forest edge, the slimmest of slim chances. He looked up into the mouths of the monsters. At the back of their throats he saw a small, pouting cavity. It was from this *second* mouth that the shrieking came. Whereas the rest of their bodies appeared grey and dead, this organ was a bright, vibrant red. It was *alive*.

Dredging up a final scrap of energy, Jake rolled over and tried to catch Brag's eye. The troll mouthed, 'What can I do?'

Jake licked his lips.

'Ap . . . Ap . . . '

The word was like a knife in his dry throat. He couldn't speak. Instead, he managed to point. Brag frowned, shrugged again, and loped off into the forest. Had the troll understood or had he given up? Maybe he thought the screaming had turned Jake's brain to mush and had decided he couldn't watch any more.

The banshees scented the kill. They bent down to their

prey, mouths drooping, chins scraping the earth.

Aaaaaaaaaarrrrrrrrrrrgggggggggggghhhhhhhhhh!

Blood, thick and warm, trickled from Jake's ears. His vision clouded. He pawed weakly at the ground, trying to reach Rachel or his father, desperate to touch another human hand before the darkness took him. It was no good. They had fallen apart and so they would die alone, victims of the banshees' call . . .

Fwwppp—over the constant pounding of blood, Jake caught the sound of something flying overhead.

The banshee nearest to him stopped mid-shriek. Her eyes widened and her crooked fingers locked around her throat. Her mouth snapped shut and a strange noise rattled between her lips.

'*Crr-akk—kraaa! Kurrr-aaah!*'

Jake grinned through the pain—the troll *had* understood!

Fwwppp—Fwwppp—Fwwppp.

Jake rolled onto his back, just in time to see three rotten apples sail through the air. Each hit their target: those pouting second mouths, the heart of the banshee's wail and the only living part of its body. The apples lodged in the monsters' throats and drowned their song.

There were four spectres still standing, but these had ceased their shrieks and were staring at their sisters. Doubled over, the banshees had their fingers down their throats, trying to pick the apples free. Problem was, their necks were so long they couldn't hope to reach. *Fwwppp*—another apple hit. Jake turned in time to see Brag loading a sixth into a slingshot and taking aim.

The three remaining banshees didn't wait around for the troll to pick them off. Their cloaks swept up around them and they shot into the air, leaving their doomed sisters behind. Like scraps of cloth caught on the wind, they passed over the treetops. Meanwhile, the five banshees left in the glade had fallen to the ground. They spluttered, gagged, and kicked their stick-thin legs. At long last, their milky eyes closed and the monsters lay motionless upon the ground.

Jake staggered to his feet. The clearing whirled around him but a few deep breaths steadied the kaleidoscope. Brag waved his club in the direction of the fleeing spectres.

'That's it!' he roared. 'Get you gone! Bloody banshees!'

He caught sight of Jake, stomped across the glade and swept the boy up into his arms. Crushed in the bear hug, Jake tried not to gag as the smell of troll BO filled his nostrils.

'Clever little blighter!' Brag laughed. 'Apples to the back of the throat! Genius!'

He put Jake down and slapped his back, sending Jake sprawling.

'Oops. Sorry.'

'No worries,' Jake panted. 'You did great, Brag, but what did you use for a slingshot?'

The troll swung a gigantic strip of elastic around one claw.

'Tore it out've me pants.' Brag winked. 'Thank 'eavens me mum told me to put a fresh pair on this morning. I usually go commando.'

'Ri-ight. One thing I don't get, though: how come you weren't affected by the banshees' call?'

'The banshee's what?'

'CALL!'

Brag dug a finger into his ear and pulled out a bucketful of slimy green wax.

'Answer your question?'

Pandora called out—'Something's wrong! Jake, it's your dad.'

Rachel was just getting groggily to her feet. She looked pale but otherwise unhurt. Jake gave her arm a reassuring squeeze as he ran past. Crouched on her knees, Pandora cradled Adam's head in her lap.

'You're bleeding,' she said, as Jake knelt beside her.

He wiped the blood from his nose. 'Doesn't matter. Is he OK?' It was difficult to keep the fear out of his voice.

'He's lost consciousness and his breathing's very shallow.' Pandora stroked Adam's head and loosened his collar. Two other hands used tissues to clean the clotted blood out of his ears. 'He's been so weak, this was just too much for him.'

Jake took his dad's hand. He felt Rachel beside him, her arms around his shoulders.

'It's not your fault,' she whispered.

'I'm going to show you something, Jake,' Pandora said. 'But when your daddy wakes, I don't want you to let on. Thing is, you need to know how sick this good man really is.'

Pandora's movements were so tender that the sight brought fresh tears to Jake's eyes. The so-called 'dark creature' unbuttoned Adam's shirt and stripped it back over his right shoulder. Delicately, she unwound the bandages . . .

His father had assured Jake that the wound Marcus Crowden had inflicted was healing. Both knew that this was not true—that the dark magic was slowly poisoning Adam— but in his worst nightmares Jake had never imagined how bad the situation really was.

The wound had been no worse than a nasty burn the last time Jake had seen it. Now a great gaping hole sat just above the point where Adam's shoulder connected with his arm. It was filled with oozing yellow pus and smelt of sour milk. Jake saw the ball and socket of his father's shoulder bone and thought he was going to pass out. Pandora quickly redressed the wound and buttoned Adam's shirt.

'He made me swear not to tell you, but after tonight I thought you ought to know. The darkness of those creatures— the evil of their song—will have weakened Adam at a time when he hardly has enough strength left to fight Crowden's hex.'

She fixed Jake with a sympathetic stare.

'I'm sorry to tell you this, Jake, but your daddy has only a few weeks left to live.'

Chapter 4
Lair of the Skinwalker

'Brag, will you take my dad back to the car?'

'Course I will, Jake. I'll carry him real gentle. You want me to stay with him?'

Pandora shook her head. 'I've given him a sedative. He'll sleep now until late morning, and I'm sure he'll be safe enough outside the forest. If we're going to continue with tonight's insanity . . . '

Jake and Rachel nodded grimly.

' . . . then we may still have need of that club of yours, Brag Badderson.'

Brag picked Adam lightly from the ground and carried him out of the clearing. Jake thought how small and frail his father looked, cradled in the troll's big arms. Images flitted through his head: his dad waiting for him at the gate after his first day at school; scooping him up and comforting him after a fall; looking for imaginary monsters under his bed before kissing him goodnight. Where was that strong, fearless man now?

In a small voice, he asked, 'Is there really no cure?'

'None that I can find, honey,' Pandora said. 'I've spent weeks looking through occult libraries. I've asked every healer, witch doctor, shaman, and wise woman I could find. All they could tell me was that it's a miracle Adam isn't dead already. He's tougher than a one-eared alley cat, your daddy, but the truth is, he's ailing fast.'

'Why didn't you tell me before?' Jake asked.

'As I said, your dad swore me to secrecy. Told me that he didn't want you distracted from your magical training.'

'That's bull,' Jake snapped. 'I could've helped you talk to those healers, research the hex, anything. Instead you let me think that it wasn't getting any worse; that there was a cure out there.'

'I never made any claims.'

'But you let me think he was OK, Pandora. You know you did.'

Pandora lowered her eyes.

'We've got a few weeks,' Rachel said, taking Jake's hand. 'We'll find something. There's always hope, right?'

Pandora managed to hitch a smile to her lips.

'Sure, sweetness. There's always hope.'

Jake turned away. 'We better get moving.'

They hurried across the glade and plunged back into the forest. Jake released Rachel's hand and ran on ahead. The brittle, yellow grass lashed against his legs and a trace of the banshees' howl throbbed in his ears. He concentrated on these little twists of pain, not wanting to think about what Pandora had told him.

At last, he broke through the undergrowth and stood panting in the moonlight. The grass rustled behind him. A second later, Rachel and Pandora were at his side. Their eyes swept across the long stretch of lawn and up to the old manor house. Hunched at the top of a small slope, Havlock Grange glared back at them, the broken windows that were its eyes seeming to challenge the trespassers.

There was no sign of movement in the house or grounds. Keeping close to the cover of the forest, Jake and his friends made their way towards the Grange. The sky darkened and shadows rolled across the lawn. For a moment, Jake thought that the banshees had returned, but it was only a blanket of heavy-bellied clouds moving in from the north and veiling the moon. The sky grumbled. Splodges of rain smacked against the trees.

The lawn ended at the foot of a wide stone staircase flanked by a pair of weatherworn griffins, their wings draped with moss. The steps led straight to the door of the Grange.

'OK.' Jake licked the rain from his lips. 'We shoot up those stairs as quickly as we can. Once we're inside, we find Simon and then get the hell out. Not much of a plan, I know, but we're operating in the dark here. We know Roland Grype's been left behind with Simon—'

'That man and I are old friends.' Pandora smirked. 'We won't have much trouble with him.'

'Probably not,' Jake agreed, 'but it's unlikely the Demon Father will have left the witch as his only defence. If the banshees were anything to go by, we'll have our work cut out. Now, I just want to say something before we go on. This whole thing was my idea, my stupid plan—if you guys wanna bail . . . '

'Honey, I don't mean to be rude, but sometimes you're as dumb as your daddy. Now let's get that poor boy outta that ugly house.'

There was no more talk. The friends made a break from the forest and swept up the staircase.

The rain strengthened, lashed across the face of the house and drowned out the rush of feet on stone. Jake glanced up and saw the letters carved into the lintel above the great oak door—

HAVLOCK GRANGE
1623

HOSTES MEI TERRITURI FUGIENT

'The Crowden family motto,' Pandora panted. 'My Latin's pretty rusty, but I think it means "Mine enemies will flee in Terror".'

'Not exactly welcoming. Still, I guess it fits in with the architecture.'

Rachel was right. Time had worked its own black magic on the house. Four hundred years of wind and rain had wrenched tiles from the roof and softened the hard edges of the stonework. With its skin of dark, crumbling brick, its broken back and shattered windows, Havlock Grange looked like a crippled giant that had lain down to die upon the hillside.

Pandora pushed against the door. 'Locked. No surprise there.'

'I'll try my magic,' Jake said.

'Or maybe we should just cut to the chase!' a voice roared.

Bare feet boomed up the staircase. Jake turned in time to see one of the stone griffins tremble off its plinth and shatter onto the ground.

Before any of them could stop him, Brag Badderson whirled his club overhead and launched it at the door. The thunder-crack of stone against wood rang in their ears as Brag's club smashed a path into the house. Dust belched into the air, swirled and settled. Tiny splinters of oak, three useless hinges, and a battered lion's head knocker were all that remained of the great door.

'Well,' Jake breathed, 'they definitely know we're here now. We better move quickly.'

He led the way into Havlock Grange.

EVIL.

The force sent Jake reeling back through the doorway. He inadvertently knocked Rachel and Pandora aside, lost his footing, and hit the ground hard. Brag caught Jake's collar between his fingers and lifted him onto his feet. Jake shook his head.

'The demon's not here,' he strode forward, 'but he's left his stink behind.'

The others followed him into the Great Hall.

The room certainly lived up to its name—Jake reckoned you could just about squeeze a Boeing 747 inside, and still have enough room left over to host a medieval banquet. The hall's arched ceiling, ribbed with wooden beams the size of ship masts, reached a height of well over twenty metres. In the middle of the ceiling there was a ragged hole through which the rain poured and the moon lanced down like a giant spotlight. Broken bricks and smashed tiles lay in a heap directly below the hole.

Jake paused. Listened. Apart from the rain that drummed through the ceiling, nothing seemed to stir the stillness. He motioned for the others to follow.

'Rachel, you and Brag search downstairs. Pandora, we'll check upstairs. You've got your phone with you, Rach? Two bleeps and we know you've found Simon. It keeps ringing, you're in trouble. Same goes for us.'

While Brag and Rachel disappeared into one of the downstairs rooms, Jake and Pandora mounted the grand staircase and stepped into a long, gloomy corridor. They lit their torches and began to search the first floor, room by room. Doors opened onto empty bedchambers. Torchlight flashed across dusty drapes, broken furniture, shattered glass.

'We haven't seen that weasel-faced librarian yet,' Pandora said. 'Roland Grype. Maybe he's made a bolt for it and taken Simon with him.'

'I hope not,' Jake muttered, 'or this will all have been for nothing.'

He opened another door, stepped inside, swept his torch around.

'Empty. Pandora, I think we should—'

The door slammed shut.

'JAKE!' Pandora's fists shook the woodwork.

'I'm all right,' Jake shouted, tugging at the door handle. 'Must've been a draught.'

'It's jammed. I'm gonna fetch Brag. Will you be OK for five minutes?'

'Sure.'

Pandora's footsteps echoed away down the corridor.

With nothing to do but wait, Jake decided to explore.

Like the other chambers on this floor, the room was large, damp, and uncarpeted. Three narrow windows, hung with strips of mouldy curtain, overlooked the garden. Jake played the light of his torch over the remains of a huge oak dining table that lay in pieces in the centre of the room. In one corner, he found a cauldron in which a brown-speckled spider had spun a graveyard for flies. The sight made him feel a little sick and he turned his torch on the fireplace. Grotesque faces with chipped noses and toothless mouths stared out from the columns.

'Is—is someone there?'

Jake spun round. His hands trembled and the yellow halo of his torchlight shivered across a faded curtain at the far end of the room.

'Who is it?' the voice pleaded from behind the curtain. 'Is it . . . is it *you*, father?'

Jake had to resist the urge to run across the room and tear back the drape. This could be yet another trap. But surely there was no mistaking that gruff bark of a voice? He approached, hand cupped, magic tingling at the tips of his fingers. He felt grateful that, this time at least, his powers were responding.

A silhouette wavered across the curtain.

'Is it . . . ? NO!' the voice bellowed. 'You won't trick me again . . . ' And now with a crumb of hope—'But is it?'

The shadow of a hand reached out, like a reflection of Jake's.

The boy behind the curtain stepped forward.

'Is it really you?'

Jake grasped the curtain. Blue light danced in his palm.

'My friend . . . '

He tore it back.

' . . . Jake?'

'Simon!'

For a long time, the two friends just stared at each other. Simon was the first to speak—

'I knew you'd come.'

Jake shook his head. 'I'm sorry it's taken so long. I tried . . . I . . . '

Simon's arms locked around him, making it difficult for Jake to breathe.

'We need to get moving,' Jake wheezed. 'Are you strong enough to walk?'

'Sure.'

Jake nodded. He freed himself from Simon's hug and headed for the door.

'I feel as fit as a fiddle. Strong as an ox.'

Jake looked back. It struck him immediately—this

picture wasn't right. Under his ragged clothes, Simon Lydgate seemed to have kept his big, robust frame. Even if the Demon Father had kept him well fed, Jake would have expected the strain of his imprisonment to have had an impact on his friend. Simon's eyes were clear and bright, showing no fear at all. The smile spread evenly across his lips; nothing like the crooked grin of old.

'Then why didn't you try to escape? If you're fit and strong, why didn't you make a run for it? You weren't tied up. You could've smashed a window and climbed out.'

Simon's smile broadened.

'Who are you?'

'I'm Simon Lydgate.' And now the smile became a leer. 'Really, Jake—who else would I be?'

At that moment, the moon found a chink in the clouds. It flashed through the window and across the face of the stranger. Simon Lydgate's green eyes dissolved into smoky red orbs, the colour of coals at the heart of a fire.

Skinwalker.

Jake didn't need to consult his dark catalogue. The name of the creature popped straight into his head. In the legends of the Navajo Indians of south-west America, the skinwalkers or the yee naaldlooshi, were black-hearted witches who sacrificed members of their own family in order to gain mastery of their supernatural powers. The most important of these powers was the ability to take on the form of any person or animal of their choosing. The only way to see beyond the disguise was to catch the scarlet glow of the witch's eyes in the moonlight.

The skinwalker began to close in on Jake.

'I'm your friend,' it purred in its stolen voice. 'Why do you fear me?'

Jake retreated until his back hit the wall.

'I'm Simon. Here, touch me, see that I'm real.'

'I know you're real.'

The witch stopped an arm's length short of Jake. His movements were lithe, almost feline.

'But you're not Simon. You're . . .'

Names. For the Navajo people, names possessed power. If you named the skinwalker to its face, the legends said that the witch would grow sick and die. Jake didn't know the name of this dark witch, but he knew *what* he was . . .

'I name you—*skinwalker*!'

The predator smiled his last smile. Then his lips fell and every scrap of humanity washed out of his face. The red light in his eyes dimmed. He became as cold and as still as a statue.

Muffled voices called out. Rachel—

'Jake, we're here. Are you all right?'

Jake eyed the frozen figure. He sidestepped it and went to the door.

'Is Brag there? Tell him to club away! I want to get out of here.'

'Right-o, stand back!'

The door leapt in its frame.

'Bloody enchanted doors!' Brag bellowed. 'This one's been hexed good and proper!'

An icy hand fell on Jake's shoulder.

'You named me, child. Now you will *see* me.'

'Who's that?' Pandora cried. 'Jake, who's in there with you?'

Jake tried to answer. All that came out of his mouth was wasted breath. What he witnessed in the pale moonlight was so horrible he could not hope to describe it.

The skinwalker's mouth opened wide. In the pink dimness at the very back of its throat, just beyond the tongue and behind a pair of saliva-slick tonsils, Jake saw a single dark eye blink out at him. He shuddered—the Navajo witch was actually living somewhere *inside* this body! *CRACK*— the sound of a jaw dislocating. All around the mouth the lips had stretched taut, like rubber bands that were about to snap.

Two fingers emerged from the throat. Others followed, until a pair of russet-coloured hands had grasped the corners of the mouth. The fingers flexed, tensed, and strengthened their grip. Dry and creaky—the sound of skin stretched to breaking point. Warm and wet—the glug of the skinwalker drawing breath from deep inside this borrowed body.

Rooted to the spot by a fearful fascination, Jake could only watch as the witch *unzipped* his skin suit. With a sudden tug, the mouth ripped apart at the corners. Blood burst from the torn flesh in a fine spray that doused Jake's face. The two tears that had started at the corners of the mouth scissored their way down the neck in rough zigzags. Eventually they met at the chest and came together to form a single and ever-widening gash. The skinwalker's hands slipped along the raggedy lips of flesh. They tightened their grip again, and he peeled away the rest of the body.

Skin rolled down like a sock stripped from a foot. With it came the rags that 'Simon' had been wearing. Both flesh and clothes snagged for a moment around the hips, and the witch had to push and tug them free. Once it reached his legs, the skin suit slipped down easily enough. Finally, it lay upon the floor in a curled, withered pile, like sloughed snakeskin.

Somehow Jake managed to speak.

'Is Simon dead?'

The little witch blinked up at him. Naked from the waist up, he wore a pair of faded blue jeans with a turquoise pendant tied to one of the belt loops.

'Your friend lives,' he said, wiping blood from his dark eyes. 'I can only replicate the form of living creatures.'

'Where is he?'

'Why do you need to know? You will never see him again.'

The Navajo stepped out of the skin pile and strode back to the curtain. He squatted down and picked something from the ground. 'You will die here.'

The door splintered under the continued barrage of Brag's club, but still it held.

'Your friends will not be in time to save you, Jake Harker. The Master himself enchanted that door.'

The skinwalker stepped forward. In his hand he held a short-handled axe decorated along the haft with eagle feathers. He pulled his arm back and launched the tomahawk. The weapon scythed the air and buried itself in the wall a centimetre from Jake's head.

'Summon your magic, boy,' the witch advised, 'or you *will* die.'

The Navajo was strong and quick. Big muscles ran along his arms, across his torso, and down his back. Even without his dark powers, he would have been a formidable opponent.

He made a dash for Jake and, in one smooth motion, wrenched the tomahawk from the wall. The skinwalker's elbow smashed into Jake's jaw and sent him sprawling into the fireplace. Jake cracked his head against the grate. Pain and panic rattled through him. He looked up into a victorious face, slick with blood.

'I cannot believe the Master has gone to so much trouble over such a miserable child.' The skinwalker stood astride Jake, feet planted wide, tomahawk raised. 'He told me that you had bested powerful witches! Told of how you stopped the Demontide and destroyed the Door! What has happened to you, little one?'

Jake held out his hand. The smallest of blue flames crackled in his palm.

'Is that it?' the witch roared. 'Is *that* your power?'

A sneer rumpled the skinwalker's lips. He breathed in and prepared to strike.

Jake turned his face away.

And that was when he saw the ash in the grate. The pages of his dark catalogue whispered to him. In the legends of the Navajo, one of the few ways a skinwalker could be killed was with a bullet dipped in white ash. Jake clung to that fragment of myth. Willed it to be true. He made a grab for the poker that was lying nearby and thrust it into the grate, baptizing its iron head with white ash.

A split second before the tomahawk fell, Jake rolled to

one side. The axe clanged against the fireplace's stone surround. Bent double, arms outstretched, the witch still had hold of the tomahawk. His flank was vulnerable. Jake took his chance and plunged the ash-coated poker between the skinwalker's ribs.

A terrible scream tore its way out of the witch. Shocked, Jake let go of the poker, and the skinwalker tumbled to the ground. With his hand clasped against the weeping wound, he tried to crawl his way over to Jake but the pain was too great. Billows of blood bloomed between his fingers.

His eyes narrowed. His breath shortened. The witch stared at Jake and something like fear tightened his features.

'What are you?' he wheezed. 'My sight darkens, but I see you clearly now. For the first time . . . ' He stabbed a finger at the boy. 'You *burn*, Jacob Harker. Your skin is stone. Your eyes are fire.'

He reached out and his hand trembled.

'Would you forgive me, if I asked? I won't . . . but if I asked, would that be within your power? To forgive a man who murdered his own father for the secrets of the *adish-gash*.' A red trickle ran out from between his lips. His hand clutched at the wound. 'You are no witch, no simple conjuror.'

The skinwalker's head slumped against the floor. With his final breath he repeated the question:

'What. Are. You?'

The enchantment that had been placed upon the door must have been tied to the skinwalker's life-force. At the next blow from Brag's club, it was smashed off its hinges. Rachel and Pandora rushed into the room, followed by an exhausted Brag Badderson. They saw the dead man and the blood spreading out beneath him like a pair of scarlet wings. Jake staggered to his feet.

'Another of the Demon Father's tricks.'

'Bloody . . . ' Brag's brow knitted. 'Er . . . what exactly was he, Jake?'

'A skinwalker.'

'Course. Bloody skinwalkers.'

'You're hurt.'

Rachel brushed back a lock of Jake's hair. Although his forehead hurt like hell from the skinwalker's blow, he almost forgot the pain. At her touch, his heart surged and he felt a flicker of magic spark somewhere deep inside.

You burn . . . What are you?

What had the Navajo witch meant by those words? Perhaps in his final moments he had sensed what Jake really was: a clone of the long-dead Witchfinder. Something unique. Something unnatural.

'Any sign of him?' Pandora asked.

Jake could not look at his friends. He had led them through a night of pain and fear, and what did they have to show for it? Only the scars on their bodies and inside their minds.

'Simon's not here,' he sighed. 'Perhaps he never was. I'm sorry . . . '

The smallest of whimpers sounded from behind the curtain. Daring to hope, Jake dashed across the room and pulled the drape right back. There in the far corner, swaddled in shadows, a shape shivered. The friends moved forward and the boy cried out in terror. Jake motioned for the others to step away while he approached alone, hands held out before him to show that he posed no danger. As he came nearer, he could make out more of the huddled form—its shaven head, its candle-coloured skin, its striking green eyes . . .

'It's all right,' Jake whispered. 'I won't hurt you.'

The boy's chest rose and fell. He was crying.

'The skinwalker kept you close,' Jake said, more to himself than to the boy. 'The closer you were, the stronger his connection to you.'

'Ja-ake?'

Simon's voice rasped like a boot on dry gravel.

Jake knelt beside his friend and took his hand.

'I'm here, Simon. You're safe now.'

'No. Not safe. Nev-er safe.'

Tears rolled down Simon's face and a great shiver ran the length of his body.

'They are coming, Jake. Very soon now. Very soon . . . They bring the darkness with them . . . '

Chapter 5
Face of Flies

The Volkswagen people carrier was where they had left it, parked on the hillside road that overlooked the forest. The sky had cleared and the moonlit road spooled out towards the village of Little Muchly like a silver thread. At the sound of approaching strangers, the old troll standing guard beside the car raised his club.

'Who goes there? Friend or foe? Identify yourself or I'll brash yer brains in!'

'It's us, Dad,' said Brag Badderson, emerging from between the trees. 'And keep your bloomin' voice down— there are banshees in these woods.'

'I ain't frightened of banshees, boy! Any ugly old women start screaming at me and I'll shove my club where the sun don't shine. That'll give 'em summat to shriek about!'

Jake, Rachel, and Pandora followed Brag out of the forest. They shambled over the ground like zombies, exhausted by the trials they had endured. Brag plodded up the bank and onto the road. The boy in his arms didn't murmur as he was laid down on the cold tarmac. Soon after Jake had found him, Simon had fallen into a dead faint and could not be woken.

At a height of just under nine feet, Badderson Senior was a little shorter than his son. He had a bushy grey beard, a bent back, and steady eyes scored with wrinkles. These things aside, father and son looked remarkably similar. Even their stone clubs could be twins.

'Used Dr Harker's phone to call me dad,' Brag explained. 'Thought someone ought to watch over the doc till we got back. Them buttons is designed for human fingers.' He held out the battered mobile. 'I got a bit frustrated with the diallin'. Sorry.'

'Name's Olaf,' Brag's dad put in, nodding at Jake. 'I've knowed your pa a long, long time. Great man.'

'How is he?' Jake asked.

'He looks as rough as my missus in the mornin's, and that's sayin' summat.' Olaf attempted a grin but it fell from his lips. 'He's in a bad way, son, and that's the Odin's honest truth.'

Olaf used the scraggy tip of a fingernail to open the car door. Adam had been laid across the back seat. There was a dark brown crust running from his left ear down the length of his neck. His breathing came in shallow waves, like the hush of a gentle sea. At the sight of his grey-faced father, Jake felt his legs weaken and had to hold on to the car roof for support.

'You have to keep your promise, honey,' Pandora said. 'You mustn't let on that you know.'

'I can't,' Jake whispered.

'You have to. He wanted to keep the grief from you as long as he could. If he starts fretting about *you*, he won't have the energy to fight this thing.'

'Why should he even try? You said yourself, there's no cure.'

'You see that smart, pretty girl over there?' Pandora pointed to where Rachel stood talking to the Baddersons. 'You know, the one you're sweet on? Oh, don't look so shocked, Jake, I've got eyes in my head. Well, it's like she says—there's still hope. Still a reason to fight on. My own daddy once told me: you always gotta fight against the inevitable, girl. Fight it till you can't fight no more. Only then will you find the courage to accept what can't be changed, and the peace that comes with that knowledge.' Pandora smiled sadly. 'You don't understand what I'm saying, do you? You've got such an old soul that sometimes I forget you're really just a kid. But one day you *will* understand.'

She patted his shoulder and called out to Brag, 'Stop your gabbin', troll! Pick that poor boy up and put him in the car. It's time we were on our way.'

Brag did as instructed. Then the trolls bid their farewells.

'Thank you,' Jake said. 'Both of you.'

'It's an honour to help Dr Harker,' Olaf said, his tone solemn. 'My family will always owe him a great debt. The Scandinavian troll purge of ninety-three will live long in infamy, but there were heroes of that time, too.'

Jake suffered another of Brag's bear hugs before the trolls took their leave. While Pandora and Rachel got into the car, Jake looked out across the forest in the direction of Havlock Grange. They had overcome many dangers that night and had faced terrible foes, all to rescue Simon Lydgate, their friend. Now, bloodied, bruised, but victorious, they were going home. Jake should feel elated, or at least content that they had done a good night's work.

'Something's not right,' he muttered, his gaze roving over the desolate forest. 'It was too *easy* . . . '

He had been kicking against the cupboard door for a full five minutes but it still refused to budge. Exhausted, Roland Grype tried another tack. He pointed a finger at the wood-work, mouthed a half-remembered spell, and hoped for the best.

A feeble stream of magic left Grype's finger and limped its way to the door. It collapsed into the wood and, several seconds later, the door creaked open. Grype launched himself into the Great Hall, rolled onto his back and gulped down lungfuls of cool air. Embarrassment overwhelmed the witch and he clenched his fists in frustration. Trapped in a broom cupboard! Yet again, he had made a fool of himself. Mercifully, this time, there was no one around to see.

Having followed his master's instructions, Grype had returned to Havlock Grange to find that Jacob Harker and his friends had smashed their way into the house. He had heard them moving about on the first floor, and had decided to shut himself up in the cupboard under the stairs. If the boy conjuror penetrated the skinwalker's disguise, then Grype would be seen as the only thing that stood between him and Simon Lydgate. Well, he had seen Jacob in action— so forget that!

Hidden in the heat and darkness, Grype's thoughts had flown back to that night a year ago when, in the hollow cavern of Crowden's Sorrow, he had witnessed the boy's power. He remembered the molten magic flying from Jake's fingers, sealing the Door and conquering the Demontide. Soon after, Grype had fled in terror. He had been certain that Marcus Crowden, his master, would perish at the boy's hand. And yet, a little time later, Crowden had found him cowering on the beach. He had forgiven Grype his cowardice and had allowed him to remain part of the Coven.

Throughout that conversation, Crowden had kept his head turned away from Grype, as if he hadn't wanted his face to be seen. Ever since, he had worn a pair of dark glasses. And then there was Crowden's voice—it was colder than before, somehow less human. Grype often thought of that voice that had called out from the demon world, and wondered: was this man that looked so much like Marcus Crowden really his old master?

There were other mysteries, too. What exactly was Simon Lydgate? Grype pictured the boy on the beach that night, standing at Crowden's side, naked and trembling. He hadn't seemed to know where he was—even *who* he was. Why had the Master kept him prisoner here at Havlock Grange for the past few weeks? He must be important, Grype decided, or else Jacob Harker and his friends would not have risked their lives to come looking for him. Grype knew that the boy possessed the ability to change into something monstrous, but although he had been Simon's keeper, casting sleeping spells and feeding him scraps of food, he still did not know the true nature of the beast.

Mysteries, mysteries, and no one to explain them to so lowly a creature as Roland Grype.

Mr Hegarty, Grype's vulture-like familiar, flew in through the open doorway. The demon-bird landed on Grype's shoulder and squawked in his ear.

'They have gone? Good.' Grype stroked Hegarty's beetle-infested plumage. The bird nudged him with its beak. 'Yes, yes, don't fret. I'll make my report.'

The witch gathered up his courage and faced the staircase. His voice quivered like the plucked strings of a harp.

'I summon you, most faithful demon of the Crowden family. Box of endless night, casket of torment, repository of nightmares—I call upon you to lead me to your master.'

Grype's words echoed up the stairs and into the empty corners of Havlock Grange. For a long time nothing happened. The rain eased and the wind fell to whispering around the door. Through the hole in the roof, Grype could see the first watery streaks of dawn lighten the sky.

The air grew suddenly colder. Grype shivered as a blockish shadow passed overhead. The swirling form of Crowden's nightmare box swept into the hall and landed at the top of the stairs. Although he had summoned it, Grype took a step back. He had never been inside the cabinet himself, but he had seen the faces of unfortunate witches as they staggered out of it. He remembered the fearless Mother Inglethorpe—that powerful witch who had been killed by Dr Harker's bullet—and how she had once been forced to endure ten minutes inside the box. Much as he had hated that woman, even Grype shuddered at the thought of her trapped inside the demon.

The door of the nightmare box creaked open.

Screaming voices cut the air. Whether they were the shrieks of souls imprisoned within the cabinet, or the voice of the box itself, Grype did not know. Terror clutched at his heart as the thing floated towards him.

The box stopped a few metres short of Grype. Its doors swung wide and a black cloud rose up from inside. In his panic, Grype staggered back, tripped and landed on the floor with a heavy thump. He watched the cloud twist upwards and spread out across the ceiling of the Great Hall. A harsh buzzing sound droned through the air, and Grype realized that the cloud was not a cloud at all. It was a swarm.

Mr Hegarty fluttered onto Grype's shoulder. Together they watched as a human face grew out of the swarm, each feature made up of thousands of teeming insects. A mouth made of flies called down to the witch:

'My faithful librarian.'

The voice was a little deeper perhaps, and sharpened by the buzz of the insects, but those were the almost musical tones of Marcus Crowden.

'Master.' Grype bowed. 'I hope that your plans are progressing well.'

'Very well indeed. Slowly but surely the threads are coming together. After this visit to Spain, I have only one more journey to make. But come now, give your report.'

Grype cleared his throat.

'Jacob Harker and his friends arrived in Little Muchly earlier this evening, my Master. They entered the forest in the early hours, and soon after encountered the banshees. Once they had defeated the creatures, they smashed their way into the Grange. Jake Harker saw through the disguise of the skinwalker and killed the Navajo witch. He found Simon Lydgate and, with his friends, made his getaway.'

Fly-lips spread into a wide grin. Laughter boomed from the ceiling and a spray of tiny black bodies fell like spittle upon Roland Grype.

'All as I predicted!' the Master crowed. 'I laid my subtle trap and the boy fell right into it.'

Grype nodded. 'I placed the rotten apples around the trees. I arranged the white ash in the fireplace. As you predicted, he saw each of the clues—the hints that would guide him to overcome our "defences".'

'*Tiny* clues,' the Master corrected. 'If they had been too obvious he would have realized that we *wanted* him to rescue the boy. Oh, how the fool has played into our hands! We have seen his strength tested and we know what kind of friends he has at his command. Best of all, we now have our spy in place. After the trouble they went to in order to rescue him, they will never suspect the boy.' The demon laughed again. 'And Simon? He will not even suspect himself! But when the time is right, we will activate him.'

A whirlwind of flies swirled through the hole in the ceiling. The Master's face fractured and broke apart, yet still his voice echoed around the chamber.

'The time is at hand, Mr Grype. Very soon now our enemies will feel the might of demonkind unleashed!'

Chapter 6
Terror in the Tunnel

Too easy. Far too easy.

The thought nagged at Jake, even as the purr of the engine lulled him into troubled dreams . . .

Streetlight glare and the sound of car horns snatched Jake from his slumbers. Resting against his shoulder, Rachel shifted slightly and snuffled her nose. Jake looked onto the back seat. His dad was still unconscious, his crumpled grey skin looking more than ever like worn parchment. Beside him, Simon Lydgate whimpered in his sleep. What nightmares had Simon witnessed during these past weeks? Jake tried not to speculate—if Simon wanted to remember, then they would all find out soon enough. Jake's father would see to that.

A thought struck Jake and he winced—his dad might see to it, *if* he lived long enough.

That had to be Jake's mission now: to find a cure for Crowden's hex. Of course, he had known that Adam was seriously ill, but he had never dreamed that the end could be so near. He had reckoned on his dad having a couple of years, and that in that time Pandora would find a cure. Now he knew the truth. Adam had a few weeks left to live. Jake's mouth set into a hard line. Forget the Demon Father and his mysterious travels overseas; forget magical training and witches and demons. Nothing mattered now except saving his dad.

There is *a cure*, he thought, *and I'm going to find it, whatever the cost.*

The car swept in a wide circle. Jake glanced idly out of the window, blinked twice, and turned to the driver.

'Erm . . . do you mind telling me what the hell's going on?'

Pandora frowned into the rear-view mirror. She had two hands wrapped loosely around the steering wheel and the other six tucked inside her clothes, just in case a passing motorist happened to glance over and see an eight-armed lady driving merrily around town.

'Did you mean to speak to me in that tone, kiddo?' she asked. 'Or are you always as prickly as a porcupine's butt in the mornin's? This was your daddy's idea. Said that if, by some miracle, we managed to save your half-beast buddy, then there was no way you could *ever* go back home. The Demon Father would be on you faster'n flies on fudge.'

'Then where are we heading?'

'A favourite ol' haunt of mine.'

The bright brow of dawn peeped over London rooftops.
Startled by the sudden light, the pigeons in Trafalgar Square
scattered, regrouped in midair, and swooped back down into
the plaza. Commuters emerged blinking from the underground
station like a pack of well-dressed moles. Eager tourists
consulted maps and guides, posed for photos and generally
got in everybody's way. Perched on his column high above
the commotion, Admiral Nelson seemed to follow the path
of Dr Harker's Volkswagen as it reached the south side of
the square.

Pandora turned left onto a broad avenue lined with
important-looking buildings and statues of men on horseback. Jake immediately recognized the road from news
reports: this was Whitehall, the heart of the British government. Some of the most important people in the country
worked behind these grand, imposing walls.

Tucked into a corner of Whitehall was a humble little
side street with a row of dull, dark-brick houses halfway
along. This apparently unremarkable place was Downing
Street, and at Number 10 the British Prime Minister was
still settling into her new job. Cynthia Croft had been in
office only a month. As they passed the gated entrance to
Downing Street, Jake wondered how much the government
and Miss Croft knew about the evil that lurked in this land.
Did the authorities of the world have any idea about demons
and witches?

At the end of Whitehall, Pandora turned onto West-
minster Bridge. They crossed the River Thames and Jake
saw the reflection of the Houses of Parliament rippling in

the murky water. He thought back to that time when he had flown over this river on the back of an enchanted snake.

'You're taking us *there*, aren't you?' he said.

Pandora didn't answer. The car reached the east side of the bridge and, between a clutter of half-finished buildings, Jake glimpsed the glass and steel bulk of Waterloo Station. From there a dozen winding routes led them into the back alleys of the South Bank.

'We're here.'

Pandora pulled over and slipped out of the driver's seat. Jake joined her on the pavement. It was a London street like any other—the bustle of traffic, the sting of fumes, snatches of overheard conversation. The commuters hurrying towards Waterloo gave Jake and Pandora only cursory glances. Certainly no one looked beyond the Volkswagen and down the alley that joined up with the street.

Jake ran fingers through his long hair, breathed deeply, and stepped into the alley. All at once the busy atmosphere of the outside world fell away and a chilling silence wrapped itself around him. He looked up at the sign bolted to the wall:

This was the last place on earth he wanted to be: the little London street that appeared on no maps and that reality seemed to shun. Jake had not been back since the night he had faced Marcus Crowden. The night his father had sustained that dreadful wound. Sensing Pandora at his side, he said, 'Why have you brought us here?'

'It's the safest place for you right now. There are many dark creatures in these parts that are loyal to your father.'

Jake eyed the dripping walls, the filthy windows. The prospect of hiding out in one of these houses wasn't very appealing.

They went back to the car and woke Rachel. Yaga Passage was too narrow for the Volkswagen, and so Jake fed coins into a parking meter and slapped a ticket on the inside of the windscreen. He and Rachel then started to lift the still unconscious Adam out of the back seat.

'We'll leave your dad and Simon here for the time being,' Pandora instructed. 'I've given them both a sedative so they should sleep a while yet.' She checked each of the watches strapped to her eight wrists. 'New York; Tokyo; Rome; Cairo; Lafitte, Louisiana—always gotta know the time back home, my momma hates it if I call in the middle of the night. She starts feeding the swamp hatchlings at around midnight and . . . ' A quick shake of the head. 'Don't ask . . . London! 6:50 a.m. We've got ten minutes before Razor shuts up shop.'

Pandora took off down Yaga Passage.

'Razor?' Rachel raised an eyebrow.

'Guess we'll find out soon enough,' Jake shrugged.

They packed Adam back into the car and hurried after Pandora. As they tore down the alleyway, the sunlight vanished, summer switched to winter, and their skin turned to gooseflesh. A thin layer of ice coated the pavement and clung in patches to the lopsided walls. Halfway down the alley, Jake lost his footing on the ice and tumbled to the ground. Rachel skidded to a stop and helped him up. His thanks were cut short by the sight of the burned-out bookshop opposite.

Crowden's
Emporium of Forgotten & Forbidden Books

The charred sign lay in the filth of the gutter. Jake went to the shattered windows and peered into the blackened heart of the shop. He could see the fireplace where Mr Hegarty had once perched, the empty bookshelves and the torn remains of ancient tomes. After the battle between the dark creatures and the Crowden Coven someone must have come back, looted the place and burned it down. Jake wondered if the curtained doorway in Grype's office still led to the Veil—that realm of nothingness which had once been the Coven Master's prison.

He felt Rachel's hand on his shoulder.

Pandora's voice called out, and they set off again.

At the end of the street they found a small arched passage squeezed between two houses. The tunnelled entrance was low, its ceiling less than a metre and a half off the ground. The cobbled pavement stretched away into utter darkness.

Carved into the stone above the tunnel mouth were the words:

BORDERLAND ROAD
513205

LONDON
TO
GRIMOIRE

'A book of monsters,' Jake murmured.

'What?'

'Grimoire. It's a kind of magic book. They were popular with sorcerers in the Middle Ages—books like *The Secret Grimoire of Turiel* and the *Necronomicon*. Kind of like instruction manuals for summoning monsters, angels, demons . . . ' Jake frowned. 'Why would Pandora want to lead us to a grimoire?'

'Hurry up!' Pandora's voice echoed out of the gloom. 'The doors are closing!'

'Do you think we should . . . ?'

Jake nodded. 'It's Pandora.'

Rachel reached for his hand. With their heads bent to clear the arched ceiling, they stumbled on. As they plunged down the throat of the tunnel, the darkness swallowed them whole. It was even colder here than it had been in Yaga Passage, a deep, grinding chill that gnawed into their bones. The chatter of their feet on the icy cobbles echoed into the fathomless reaches of the tunnel. Several times, Jake thought he caught a glimpse of light up ahead only for it to flicker and vanish, like a candle snuffed out.

'Did you feel that?' Rachel cried. 'Hands!'

Yes, Jake had felt it—phantom fingers against his face. He imagined spider webs the size of punkah fans hanging down from the roof.

Rachel screamed.

Jake's own cry of terror got stuck somewhere in his throat. Without warning, those wispy fingers had solidified into slippery wet tentacles. Jake felt dozens of them lock around his shoulders and lift him from the ground. He tried to cling to Rachel but the unseen tentacles wrenched them apart. Their screams echoed from stone to stone until the tunnel rang.

Lifted high into the air, Jake realized that the low-ceilinged tunnel must have opened out into a vast chamber. Not that he could see this space; everything remained cloaked in darkness. New tentacles reached out and wrapped around his wrists and ankles. He felt himself being passed from feeler to feeler, flipped and somersaulted until he no longer had any sense of up and down. By Rachel's cries he knew that, although they were separated, she was still close by.

A blast of warm air parched Jake's face. His eyes narrowed into slits. Up ahead he could make out a tiny oval of light, like a golden teardrop. The glare almost blinded him, but he managed to take in a few brief glimpses of his surroundings. For the first time he could see the fibrous green tentacles lashed around his wrists and ankles. Passing Jake between them, these strange arms drew him faster and faster towards the oval doorway. Just before he reached the opening, he managed to glance back and see the space through which he had been propelled. Below lay a pit, like a colossal well bored out of the earth. It could not be bottomless because Jake could make out faint white shapes writhing far below. He did not want to think about what these creatures might be. Looking up, he saw an arched ceiling soar overhead, like the roof of the tunnel, only a thousand times larger. Growing between the bricks that made up the ceiling were millions of trailing vines—an upside-down forest of rustling, restless tentacles.

Jake and Rachel were thrust through the oval doorway and into the honeyed world beyond. They tumbled over a hard stone floor and finally came to a stop.

'Are-you-OK?' Jake panted, helping Rachel to her feet.

'Bruised, battered, scared half to death, but I guess I'll live.' Rachel raked fingers through her tousled hair. 'Jake, what is this place?'

For a moment, they stood in awed silence. At their backs was the teardrop doorway; in front of them, an open square the size of a small airfield. It was paved with rough sandstone slabs that blazed in the light of a Mediterranean dawn. Built from the same yellow stone, narrow arcades supported by big Roman columns ran around all four sides of the square. At the centre, water bubbled from the spout of a silver fountain. It's a piazza, Jake thought, typical of the grand squares that he and his father had seen on their trip to Italy last year.

A desert breeze chased around Jake's legs and threw grit into his eyes. Small drifts of sand covered the steps all around the piazza. Jake squinted at the huge red sun beating down from a purple-tinged sky, and thought, *We're not in Kansas any more, Toto.*

'Come on, you two!'

Pandora's command bounced between the crumbling columns. Jake could just make out the eight-armed woman on the far side of the square. He took a deep breath and they set off again.

The sun was relentless. By the time they had reached the fountain, they were forced to rest.

'Let's continue down one of the arcades,' Rachel said. 'Stick to the shade.'

They scooped handfuls of deliciously cool water from the bowl of the fountain, and were about to set off again when Jake paused. He took a step back and stared at the fountain. The design was simple—a silver cup expanded to the size of a bathtub had been perched on a plinth a metre or so off the ground. Water gushed from a spout at the centre and filled the cup to the brim. The sunlight shimmering off the silver blinded Jake while the tinkle of water ran like music in his ears.

'Jake?' Rachel tugged at his sleeve. 'What is it?'

He fell back onto the hard stone floor, water still jewelling his lips.

'Jake? Can you hear me? Are you all right?'

His eyes stayed fixed on the fountain.

The words came to him like the lyrics of a half-remembered song:

'Nightfall's Cup.'

Chapter 7
The Ghost of the Grimoire

Despite the heat, Rachel shivered. Something about those words . . .

'Nightfall's Cup,' she echoed.

Jake got to his feet, dusted his knees. 'Sorry?'

'You said "Nightfall's Cup". What does it mean?'

The ghost of a memory pinched at Jake's face. He looked suddenly much older. And then, just as suddenly, his features cleared.

'Don't know what you're talking about, Rach. Come on, Pandora's waiting.'

Rachel may have had her doubts, but Jake was speaking the truth. The memory of Nightfall's Cup, whatever it was, had been snatched away from him. He gave the fountain one last troubled glance and set off towards the shelter of the arcade arches.

It was cooler out of the sun, but not much. Sweat ran

in tracks down Jake's face and made his hair itch. The only relief came from the breeze that whistled through the teardrop-shaped holes in the wall. They passed a dozen or more, and Jake wondered whether these doorways all led back to London or if they were portals to other cities, maybe even to other *worlds*.

They found Pandora leaning against a column halfway up a flight of sandstone steps. In front of her stood a door studded with vicious iron spikes and set deep into the wall.

'You could've warned us!' Rachel called.

'About what, honey?'

'Oh, I don't know: the crazy tunnel with the groping vine hands maybe?'

'Oh. Yeah. Right. I sometimes forget how easily you humans get spooked. Sorry about that.'

'Pandora, where are we?' Jake asked.

'This is a meeting place.' Pandora tapped the ancient column. 'A borderland staging post between the world of Man and the various worlds of us dark creatures.'

'An in-between place,' Jake said, 'like the Veil.'

'No. The Veil is nothingness—just an empty plain through which the dead travel on their way to whatever lies beyond. This place? I guess you could call it a rest stop. Creatures on their way to Earth—*your* Earth—stay here for a few days before moving on. And *this* is where they stay.' Pandora climbed the steps and rapped six hands against the spiky door. 'The Grimoire Club.'

'That's right,' a voice snarled. 'And you're not getting in, Pandora.'

The door swung open. With a low growl rumbling at the back of his throat, a huge creature emerged from the shadows.

Rachel gasped and took a step closer to Jake.

A pair of yellow eyes fixed on each face. Black lips curled over long canines.

'Who're your friends?' the creature barked.

'None of your business, Razor. Now, run along like a good doggy and tell Murdles I want to see him.'

'What is he?' Rachel whispered to Jake. 'A werewolf?'

'I don't think so. He's something else . . . '

Jake could hear the pages of his dark catalogue whisper to him as he took in the gigantic figure blocking the doorway. The creature that Pandora had called 'Razor' was a two metre tall slab of muscle, dressed in a pair of ragged jeans and nothing else. He had the body of a man, which, although hairy, could not be called animal-like. Razor stood bolt upright, his back straight, legs unbent. His hands ended in fingers, not claws. So far, so human. From the neck up, however, it was a different story.

'I think he's one of the Cynocephali,' Jake said in a hushed tone. 'The dog-headed people. There are stories of their race going back thousands of years. In the Middle Ages, monks used to include them as figures on some of the earliest maps of the world. The Cynocephali were drawn as existing at the very edges of the known world.'

'That's where Man drove us.' Razor tapped one of his long ears. 'No point whispering around me, man-child. Some say we were brothers once, Cynocephali and Humans—that our blood still runs in your veins, as yours runs in ours—but that was a long time ago.' Razor's muzzle curled into a smile. 'Still, it's good to hear of my kind talked about with such knowledge.'

'And respect,' Pandora put in. She gave Jake a sly wink.

'A ferocious and noble race,' Jake nodded.

Razor bowed his head.

'Wait here,' he said, and disappeared behind the huge door.

While they waited, Jake took his first proper look at the Grimoire Club. There wasn't much to see from the outside. The one-storey building appeared to occupy the entire length of the arcade. Unlike the other sides of the square, this area was not interrupted by those teardrop doorways but by a series of wide, arched windows set far back into the wall. Instead of glass, the windows were boxed in with sun-bleached shutters that creaked in the breeze. Jake read the plaque beside the door.

'Sooo.' Rachel bit her lip. 'This is our safe house, is it? Good job, Pandora.'

Pandora looked as if she was preparing a witty comeback when Razor reappeared.

'He'll see you.'

The Cynocephalus ushered Jake and his friends into the club. He locked and barred the door behind them, twisting keys and securing bolts and latches.

'Club closes its doors at 7:20 a.m. sharp,' Razor explained. 'That's Greenwich Mean Time. Mr Murdles originally came from the Old Town and likes to keep London hours.'

THE GRIMOIRE CLUB

Established 1607 (Human Era)
Proprietor—Mr Thaddeus X. Murdles

THE MANAGEMENT TAKES NO RESPONSIBILITY
WHATSOEVER FOR ANY INJURY, MAIMING,
MAULING OR MURDERING THAT OCCURS ON
THESE PREMISES.

A FULL MEMORANDUM OF RULES CAN
BE PROVIDED ON REQUEST, BUT THE
FOLLOWING SHOULD BE NOTED:

1. VAMPIRES: BOTTLED BLOOD IS AVAILABLE IN
THE **TEPES BAR & GRILL** AND FROM THE MINI BAR IN
YOUR ROOM. DRINKING FROM HUMAN MEMBERS OF
STAFF IS DISCOURAGED. THE COST OF RECRUITING
REPLACEMENTS WILL BE CHARGED TO YOUR BILL.

2. WEREWOLVES: PLEASE FEEL FREE TO USE
ANY AND ALL OF THE CLUB'S FACILITIES, BUT YOU
ARE KINDLY REQUESTED **NOT** TO SIT ON THE SOFAS
DURING THE FULL MOON.

3. HUNTERS OF THE ABOVE: THE
GRIMOIRE CLUB IS A NEUTRAL ZONE. PLEASE LEAVE
STAKES, HOLY WATER, SILVER BULLETS ETC. WITH
THE CONCIERGE FOR THE DURATION OF YOUR STAY.

Razor led the way down a long corridor, his bare feet padding through the thick, crimson carpet. The candles burning in sconces on the walls were placed so far apart that Jake and Rachel often had to grope their way forward; a spectacle that provoked a sneering '*Humans!*' from Razor.

'That's right—*humans*,' Rachel called. 'Same species that invented the light bulb. When are you guys gonna catch up, eh?'

'Are you so sure your lot invented the electric light?' Razor grunted. 'I've got an old alchemist friend who says different. Anyway, our clients are romantic souls. They prefer the flicker of candlelight. Plus, some of 'em don't like being looked at too closely, so we keep it nice and dark.'

They had passed several doors, each with shiny brass plates—*Tepes Bar & Grill; Library; Reading Room; Breakfast Room; Games Room.* It was as they reached the last of these that a blood-curdling scream rang out. Quick as a flash, Razor threw open the door. A snarl rippled along his thick black lips.

'IT AIN'T THAT KIND OF GAMES ROOM, MORTIMER!' he bellowed. 'You know the rules! Put the waitress down or I'll come in there and rip *your* throat out, there's a good bloodsucker.'

Before Jake could see inside, Razor slammed the door.

'Surprised he's still up.' The doorman shrugged, and they moved on.

Several corridors later they found themselves outside a door marked **General Manager—No Timewasters.** Razor puffed out his massive chest and knocked.

'Enter!'

'Here's a heads up, Pandora—the boss is in a *bad* mood,' Razor warned.

'What's new?'

'You'll see.'

Razor opened the door into Thaddeus Murdles's office. It was a large room, beautifully decorated with dozens of marble sculptures and bronze figurines standing on column plinths. Scary-looking tribal masks shaped out of dark wood adorned the windowless walls.

Dominating the room was a long marble-topped desk overflowing with papers. Jake noticed that most of these were bills with the words 'FINAL DEMAND' stamped upon them in red letters.

'Come in, Pandora,' a voice fluttered. 'And you, Razor, get out—you know I can't abide the smell of *dog* polluting my inner sanctum.'

'What's it matter to you?' Razor grumbled, loping back through the door. 'You don't even have a nose.'

'I heard that!' the voice shrieked. 'Any more backchat and I'll keep you on a leash! Filthy brute! Please, Pandora, you and your friends take a seat.'

Jake sat down in one of the three luxurious leather armchairs that faced Murdles's desk. Sinking into the creaky leather, he looked around for the manager. Murdles's shrill voice had seemed to come from the other side of the desk, but there was no sign of the man.

'I'm sorry to see you this way, Thaddeus,' Pandora said.

What way? Jake thought.

'Your friends are confused,' came the disembodied voice. 'Give me a moment and I'll be with you.'

The chair behind the desk rolled back on its castors. Unseen feet pressed into the thick carpet and moved over to an antique wardrobe in the corner. The wardrobe door opened and a pale grey suit was plucked from its hanger. Jake watched in amazement as the suit began to fill out.

'Tight fit. I must speak to my tailor.'

It was clearly no ordinary garment: threads began to spool out from the cuffs and collar. They wound their way down and formed the impression of feet and hands. From the collar the threads spiralled round and round, weaving together a neck, a chin, mouth, nose, ears and brow. A few strands were left over to give the woven man a wisp or two of fine, grey hair.

'Mr Murdles is one of the dear departed,' Pandora explained. 'A phantom. A spectre.'

'A ghost,' Jake said. 'And the suit must be made of ectoplasm.'

'Ecto-what?' Rachel asked, eyes wide.

'Plasm. According to psychics and mediums, ectoplasm is the stuff that ghosts are made out of. It takes the form of a thin, grey material, like—well, like that suit.'

A smile creased the manager's clumsy cloth mouth. Murdles part-walked, part-floated back to his seat.

'The boy knows much. Razor told me that he was aware of the Cynocephali. That's *old* knowledge.'

'I picked it up from books,' Jake said.

'Just books? I wonder . . . ' Ectoplasmic fingers tapped

against the arms of Murdles's chair. 'But you are right, this is an ecto-suit. I have worn such garments ever since the day I died—January 8th 1607. A Monday, I remember. Always hated Mondays.'

Jake frowned. 'I don't understand. Why haven't you passed on through the Veil?'

'Only spirits without bodies are sucked through the Veil, young man. The ecto-suit gives me substance, keeps me in the land of the living. But they come at a price. Ah, in the early days, when I first established the Grimoire Club, I could buy dozens of suits at a time, but business has been bad these last hundred years or so. There are other clubs on the borderlands now. And, as you can imagine, the ecto-tailors can charge whatever they want for their wares.'

'You weren't wearing a suit when we came in,' Jake observed.

'They wear out gradually. I may have appeared invisible to you, but there was a little substance left in the old suit. Just enough to open the wardrobe and take out a fresh garment.'

'But you've had a long life, Mr Murdles,' Rachel said. 'Or maybe I should say a long "death". Aren't you ready to— well—move on?'

'Sometimes I think about it, my dear. To pull up the anchor that moors me to this world and set sail for horizons new. But who knows what waits beyond the Veil? And I have done some terrible things in my time.' The cloth eyes crumpled into a haunted expression. 'Terrible . . . But to business.' The ectoplasm rustled as Murdles turned to Pandora. 'A little birdie has told me that you have come to my club seeking sanctuary. I'm afraid that will be impossible.'

'Come on, Thaddeus,' Pandora cajoled. 'How long have we known each other? You owe me.'

Murdles hesitated. 'It's true, you've sent a lot of business my way over the years. The dark creatures respect you . . . But no. From what I hear, you and your friends here have been toying with some very dark powers. If you bring trouble to my door I run the risk of losing my business, and you know what that would mean.' The manager lifted his chin and swept a wispy finger across his throat. 'No more ecto-suits for poor Mr Murdles.'

'But no one need ever know we're here,' Pandora assured him. 'Look, I don't ask for myself, Murdles, it was Adam Harker who thought you would help us.'

'Dr Harker has saved many of my clients, but *I* owe him nothing.'

Pandora tried another tack. 'I have friends on the Ecto-Tailors' Guild, you know. A word from me and your supply of suits might suddenly dry up.'

'Only money talks with those people,' Murdles snapped. 'As long as I pay they'll continue to do business with me.'

Defeated, Pandora dropped back into her chair. While she had been arguing with the manager, Jake had been examining the hundreds of paintings and photographs that adorned the office walls. Housed in expensive frames, there was a golden plaque beneath each. Jake read: *Mullgrew the Magnificent, arch-wizard to the Kings of the Borderlands, 1723; Savage Bones—world heavyweight werewolf boxing champion, 1864; Letty Scrivener, bestselling author of* The Grace of the Seelie Court, *1975.* The pictures had been posed for in the square just outside the Grimoire Club, although it was difficult to make out the square itself. Thousands of dark creatures filled each scene.

Jake stood up.

'I wonder, Mr Murdles, do you know who I am?'

'I neither know nor care.'

'Oh, I think you might. Interesting pictures you have here. These people seemed to have brought in the crowds.'

'That was all a long time ago,' Murdles sniffed. 'Then the Grimoire Club was famous throughout the borderlands. We could draw celebrities here like vampires to a blood bank, and the money they brought in! These days, the well-to-do go to places like the Lizardman Lounge and the Gore Gardens. The sheep follow them there.'

'They'll come back when they know I'm here.'

'Really? And who, may I ask, are you?'

'My name is Jacob Harker. I'm a clone of Josiah Hobarron, the Witchfinder. And I'm one of the last practitioners of pure, powerful Oldcraft.'

Murdles's cloth mouth gaped open.

Jake explained his plan. Murdles would let them stay at the Grimoire Club. They would keep themselves to themselves and not attract any unwanted attention. In return for Murdles's hospitality, on the day they left, Jake would put on a show of his magic in the square.

'Thousands would pay good money to see that!' Murdles crowed. 'The living clone of Josiah Hobarron working his magic outside my door! Mr Harker . . . ' the manager rose and extended his ghostly hand, 'we have a deal!'

Razor and Pandora went back to Yaga Passage to fetch Simon and Adam from the car. Meanwhile, Murdles showed Jake and Rachel to their quarters.

'I'm giving you my own apartment,' he piped. 'No need to thank me.'

Having heard Jake's plan, the ghost had become much more friendly. Now he led them to a red-cushioned door right at the back of the Grimoire Club.

'Will you do the honours, my boy? I have to conserve my strength.'

Jake opened the door and they stepped into a luxurious, ultra-modern apartment. A circular lounge with squashy sofas and a huge flat-screen TV took up most of the living space. To one side of the lounge stood a spiral staircase which disappeared into the ceiling. Unlike the gloomy, candle-lit corridors they had left behind, the apartment was bathed in electric light.

'I may be over four hundred years old but I'm very partial to modern conveniences. The bedrooms.' Murdles swept his hand around the six doors that faced the lounge. 'Please feel free to order as much room service as you like. And now, I will leave you. Sleep well, Mr Harker, Miss Saxby.'

The ghost glided towards the door.

'Ah, one last thing before I go: if you wish to leave the club for any reason, please call for Razor or one of the other doormen to see you out. Walking the corridors unescorted would not be a wise thing to do. There are many dangerous creatures within these walls.'

Jake closed the door behind Murdles and turned to Rachel. She looked both exhausted and bewildered. He went to her, held her close, felt her breath warm against his neck. That determination to concentrate only on his father's cure wavered for a moment.

'Rach, I . . . '

A tap at the door. Murdles's voice came through the woodwork:

'Oh, and Mr Harker? Perhaps tomorrow you could show me some magic? Adieu for now.'

Jake groaned. He didn't think he had the energy to muster even the tiniest magical flame. He'd have to bluff his way out of it. In any case, tomorrow there would be more important matters to attend to: his father's cure and the secrets locked inside Simon Lydgate's head. He turned back to Rachel.

The girl mumbled, sighed. She had fallen asleep in his arms.

Chapter 8
Hypnosis Horror

Fractured images from a fevered dream—

*A silver fountain. The howling mouth of a banshee. A dying Navajo's question—*What are you?

*His father—*You are the Witchfinder . . .

Here is the Orb and here is . . .

A girl with cornflower blue eyes cries for her lost love. A face from long, long ago, hidden in that unexplored corridor of his soul. The face is the same, but the name is different. He yearns for her, and in his yearning the name of the girl comes to him. A name that once gave hope to Josiah Hobarron, his other self—

'Eleanor!'

Jake woke with the silk bed sheets knotted around his body. He tried to hold on to the fragments of the dream but they crumbled in the hard fist of reality. He could remember nothing. Frustrated, he pulled on the dressing gown that had been laid out at the foot of the bed and went to see if anyone else was up.

The lounge was empty. He switched on the TV. One of the twenty-four-hour news channels was showing a press conference from 10 Downing Street. The new Prime Minister was taking questions on the health service. If he had been old enough to vote in the last election, Jake would have cast his vote for Miss Cynthia Croft. She seemed professional, competent, sympathetic. The press pack burst into spontaneous laughter as Chequers, the Downing Street cat, jumped up onto the Prime Minister's podium.

'That you, Jake?'

His father's voice echoed down the spiral staircase. Jake climbed up to a hatchway in the ceiling that led onto a large roof terrace decked out with expensive garden furniture. Blinded by the giant sun of the borderlands, Jake could only just make out the three figures standing at the balcony rail.

'Mornin',' Pandora called, lifting her coffee cup in greeting.

'Good to see you, matey!' Brag Badderson slapped Jake's shoulder in a friendly, bone-shattering sort of way.

The third figure smiled weakly. 'Good morning, son.'

A little colour had crept back into Adam's cheeks but he still looked dreadfully pale.

'You OK, Dad?'

'I'm OK, son.'

The old worried expression crossed Pandora's face. To hide it, she turned to Brag.

'How'd you get here so quick, troll boy?'

'Took the London road through Yaga Passage. Nearly got dropped in the pit twice. Bloody vines!'

'Why *are* you here, Brag?' Jake asked.

'Ain't you pleased to see me?' The troll looked hurt.

'Course I am, it's just—'

'I asked Brag to come,' Adam said. 'I've already spoken to Simon—'

'He's awake?'

'Yes, and he's been asking to see you.'

'Does he remember much?'

Adam shook his head. ''fraid not, but he's anxious to find out what's been happening to him. The Demon Father appears to have placed strong magical blocks in his mind. But it's not just the immediate past Simon's interested in: he finally wants to know what happened to his mother and whether . . . well . . . '

'Whether he killed her,' Jake murmured.

'In his half-demon form, he would have been more than capable. When that side of him is in control, Simon is a danger to himself and others. With that in mind, I've asked Brag to stay with us. His strength could save lives if Simon gets . . . out of hand. I'll do my best to keep the boy calm—I'll teach him ways in which he can control his nature—but we must be always on our guard. Hard as it may be, we must never for one moment forget what Simon is.'

'He's my friend,' Jake bristled. 'He's a good person.'

'Half of him is certainly that.' Adam frowned. 'The other half? Who knows. Now, Brag, Pandora, would you excuse us a moment?'

The troll and the eight-armed woman exchanged glances and moved away.

Jake went to the balcony and took in the view. Surrounding the oasis of the square was a vast, featureless desert: hundreds of miles of yellow sand baking under the merciless red sun. There were no mountains to break up the horizon, no camel tracks to dimple the desert, no sparkle from a distant city. Nothing but sand and sky. Jake saw it as a place of madness, of death.

'This is the borderland,' Adam said. 'They say that under this desert lie forgotten cities. The ancient homes of the old races. Fairies, demons, the Never Seen. Jake, are you all right?'

'Yeah.' Jake grasped the balcony rail. 'It's just the heat.'

Adam led his son to the shade and they sat down, backs against a cool brick wall.

'Pandora told me you fought well.'

'Thanks.'

'That was her compliment, not mine.' A rough edge entered Adam's voice. 'You scraped through the Demon Father's defences with the help of your friends. Whatever he's planning, that kind of weak magic won't be enough to stop him. I've made a decision, Jake.'

Adam turned hard eyes on his son.

'You can't go up against him alone. We need help.'

'What kind of help?'

'The Hobarron Institute.'

'No.'

'Despite what you told him about shutting the place

down, Dr Holmwood has continued developing new weapons. He's asked us to come in for talks at the Tower.'

'Dad, we can't trust him.'

'We've no choice. I'm sorry, son. If you still had that connection to the Witchfinder, then maybe you could face the Demon Father alone, but your magic . . . '

Adam shook his head.

'Don't I get a say?' Jake asked.

'No. Not unless the Oldcraft magic comes back to you. And that's my final word.'

Jake might have argued further, but at that moment a terrible scream rose up out of the hatchway.

'Is he all right? Rachel, what happened?'

Adam hobbled into the room. Bending down, he examined Simon's panic-stricken face.

Jake, Brag, and Pandora crowded into the bedroom. Simon was sitting up in bed, his arms locked around Rachel. Two terrified eyes peeked over her shoulder and stared past Jake, into the lounge.

'I heard *her* voice!' Simon cried. 'She was calling to me. She was *here*.'

'We were sitting, talking,' Rachel said. 'Next minute, he's screaming about his mother.'

'Did *you* hear anyone, Rachel?'

'No. Just Brag and Pandora talking in the lounge.'

'We were watching TV,' Pandora said. 'We heard nothing.'

'She *was* here!' Simon barked.

'OK. Calm down, Simon. Look at me.' Adam took a silver coin from his pocket and started twirling it between his fingers. The light reflected off the coin and danced in Simon's eyes. Adam shooed Rachel off the bed and took her place. 'You're safe, Simon. No one's going to hurt you.'

Jake remembered the time when his father had hypnotized *him*, using the same silver coin. He remembered the peace he had felt, as if all his cares and worries had been lifted from his shoulders. But it had been a false peace, and Jake knew that Simon's doubts and nightmares would soon come back to torment him.

Simon's face became blank, his breathing steadied.

'He's very responsive.' Adam turned to the others. 'I think we should continue the hypnotism now. Go deep and find out what he knows about the Demon Father's plans.'

'It's too soon,' Rachel said, arms folded. 'Can't you leave him alone for a bit?'

'Not if we want to stop the Demon Father. Time is of the essence.'

'Then let's vote,' Jake said. 'All those for continuing the hypnotism now, raise your hands.'

Adam lifted his. Brag's meaty fist soon followed.

'Dr Harker's a great man,' the troll said simply.

After a moment's hesitation, Pandora lifted one of her many hands. 'I don't want to see the boy suffer any more than he has already, but Adam's right—we have to find out what he knows.'

'OK. Those against.'

Jake and Rachel lifted their hands.

'Three to two,' said Adam. 'I'll be as gentle as I can.'

Rachel made a disgusted sound and left the room. Jake wanted to go after her but curiosity pinned him to the spot.

Adam returned to Simon's side. 'Can you still hear me?'

'Yes,' the boy answered in a dull tone.

'I want you to start by telling me about that night in Hobarron's Hollow. The night you saved the Demon Father. What do you remember?'

There was no hesitation. 'I was standing outside the Witchfinder's tomb. The sound of the explosion was still ringing in my ears . . . '

'The Steerpike Bridge massacre,' Jake said, filling in a confused Brag Badderson. 'The Crowden Coven killed seventeen Elders that night.'

'Shhh,' Adam hissed. 'What else, Simon?'

'Pain. Worst pain I ever felt, burning through my body. And then I heard *his* voice. He called to me. Reached out with his shapeless hand. The Demon Father. *My* father.'

'He said that you were his son?'

Simon nodded.

'Then?'

'POWER!' His lips curved into a hideous grin. His barrel chest heaved with excitement. 'I tore the crypt door from its hinges like it was nothing. Threw it aside. I crept into the cavern and waited for my father's call. And then—more pain. Unbearable. My bones screamed, my skin tore apart.'

'You transformed into your demon self.'

'So you say. So you say.'

'What happened when you were taken to Havlock Grange?'

'Darkness. All is darkness.'

'You're sure you can't remember anything? Conversations between the Demon Father and Roland Grype? Anything you might have seen. Think—go back.'

'Darkness. All is darkness.'

Adam sighed and turned to the others. 'I think they kept him drugged with sleeping spells. He probably doesn't know much of what's happened during the past few weeks. I don't think there's any point in pushing him further.'

Simon gripped Adam's shoulder. His smile became ever more wolfish and his eyes blazed.

'*They* are coming, Dr Harker.'

'Who? Quickly, tell me.'

'Dark powers are gathering, drawn together by my father's outstretched hand. They will assemble in the new coliseum. They will receive their mission from their new leader. Then they will fall like fire from the sky. At their touch, fortresses will burn, prison walls will quake and crumble.' Simon's gaze switched to Jake. 'An old enemy will be released.'

Simon fell back onto the bed. His body shook as if he was being electrocuted. Brag leapt forward to restrain the boy. For a moment, Jake thought that Simon would transform into his demon self. Gradually, however, Simon relaxed, his eyelids drooped and his head slumped to one side.

'The Demon Father has commanded it, and his servants will obey,' Simon slurred. '"Kill them all," he has said, "leave none alive to tell the tale . . . " *They will be here soon . . .* '

Chapter 9
Creatures of the Pit

The roof terrace was the ideal place for a barbecue. Sitting under the shade of a wall, Jake watched Brag Badderson throw great slabs of meat onto a huge grill. Thick pork sausages, juicy beef steaks, and gigantic hamburgers spat and sizzled. Jake hadn't eaten for almost twenty-four hours; the smell of the food should be making his mouth water, but what Simon had said during his hypnosis had robbed him of his appetite.

Dark powers were on the move. An old enemy was returning.

After breaking the hypnotic trance, Adam had wasted no time in making contact with Dr Holmwood and the Hobarron Institute. Jake could see the logic of the move, but the memory of the Elders trying to sacrifice Rachel and Eddie Rice was still raw.

'Hey! Anyone up there?'

A head appeared through the terrace hatch.

'Wow, it's hotter'n hell out here.'

Simon climbed up onto the roof. He still looked tired and that haunted expression remained fixed around his eyes. He took a seat in the shade next to Jake, reached over and dragged his friend into a rough hug.

'Thanks, mate.'

'Don't mention it,' Jake grinned.

They drank from a jug of iced lemonade that Jake had brought up from the kitchen and watched Brag flip his burgers. To ease them into more serious subjects, Jake told Simon about the hair-raising journey he and Rachel had taken from Yaga Passage to the borderland. Simon, who had been unconscious when placed into the vine-tentacles by Pandora, showed off his 'mystery bruises'. They laughed at the thought of him sleeping like a baby as he was flung from one dimension into another.

Eventually the laughter dried up and they drifted into a comfortless silence. It was some time before Jake broke through the awkwardness.

'Do you want to talk about what happened, Simon? If you don't I'll understand—'

'No, it's cool.' Simon spoke with that familiar dry bark of words. 'Your dad, he told me what I said under hypnosis: dark powers gathering.' He shrugged. 'Honestly, Jake, I don't know what that means. Dr Harker said he'll help me try to remember . . . Remember these last few weeks. Remember my mother and what happened to her.'

Simon gazed into the rolling desert landscape.

'I'm half-demon. Those were the stories your dad heard from the dark creatures—that a child had been born to a woman and a demon. I need to accept what I am. Face it. To do that, I have to find out what happened to my mother.'

'After you disappeared with the Demon Father, Rachel told us some of the story you told her,' Jake said. 'Your memories of what happened to your mum. Simon, if it isn't too difficult, it might help if we talked about those memories.'

Simon kept his eyes on the glistening horizon. When he spoke, his voice was as dry and as empty as the desert. He told Jake the story of a strange, bleak childhood: how his mother, terrified of her son, had kept him locked in a cellar. Time and again, she had told Simon that he didn't have a soul—that he was evil. Then, one day, she had opened the cellar door and her scream had cut the air like a knife. After that, there were no more memories until he had come to live in New Town.

'I think I'd changed,' Simon said. 'I think I killed her.'

'You can't know that,' Jake protested. 'And anyway, I don't believe you could kill anyone.'

'I can betray people though, can't I? By saving my father, I betrayed *you*. Sidney Tinsmouth knew I would. He told me to fight against my nature, but I was too weak. I'm dangerous, Jake, I shouldn't be here.'

'We want you here. All of us. We risked our lives to save you, Simon. Anyway, my dad can show you ways to control your . . . other self.'

At length, Simon gave a reluctant nod. 'Rachel said she'd

practise the exercises with me. But if I changed—if I ever hurt any of you, I swear—'

'That's why Brag's here,' Jake grinned, trying to lighten the mood. 'You go all fang-boy on us, Brag is allowed to get busy with his club. Isn't that right, Brag?'

The troll looked over, his mouth full of half-cooked burger.

'Huh? Oh, yeah, right. One hairy toe out of line and— *bam*!' His giant fist slammed the wall and the whole roof terrace shook.

Simon blinked. 'OK. That's good. I guess.' He took a long drink of lemonade. 'So, Jake, what's been happening with you?'

'Not much,' Jake shrugged. 'Magic practice, mainly. Course, we've had Rachel staying with us. Her dad calls all the time, but she won't speak to him—can't say I blame her, he did try to use her as a human sacrifice . . . It-it's been really great, having her around.'

'She's an amazing girl,' Simon murmured.

'She is.' Jake swallowed hard. 'Actually, I've been thinking of asking her out. You know, on a date. Just have to work up the courage first, I guess.'

Silence, but for the sizzle of meat and the rattle of sand.

'You *should* ask her out,' Simon said at last. 'She's a great girl.'

And with that, he rose to his feet and disappeared back down the hatchway.

* * *

During the following two weeks, Adam attended several meetings with Dr Gordon Holmwood at the Hobarron Institute. Jake steadfastly refused to accompany his father. He knew that his dad didn't want to deal with Holmwood, but that it made sense from a practical point of view. With their connections and resources, the Elders might be able to make sense of Simon's warning and help to unpick the Demon Father's plans. After a fortnight of sharing information and pooling resources, Jake had to admit that, although much remained hidden, the Institute had at least helped them to track the Demon Father's movements.

The demon had returned from Madrid the day after Simon's rescue. Hours later, a new trident symbol had been found burned into a Spanish hillside. The demon had then remained in England for almost a week before flying to Paris. He had stayed in the French capital for only a few hours before travelling back to Havlock Grange. Seconds after his plane departed, the French authorities had found a strange trident shape scorched into the main runway of the Charles de Gaulle airport. Since then, the Demon Father had not strayed from the Grange. He waited there, like a spider in the centre of its web.

For his part, Jake had spent some of the last two weeks practising his magic; focusing on memories of those times when he had felt the Witchfinder's power. Try as he might, however, his magic remained weak. He didn't have much time to worry about it, though. Every day he would get up before dawn, strike out across the square, and head for the road back to Yaga Passage and London. He had managed to avoid Mr Murdles's requests for a magical display by saying that he wanted the show to be a surprise, both for the assembled crowds and Murdles himself.

'Fair enough,' the ghostly manager had conceded. 'But I expect *great* things, Mr Harker, and so will my guests. Many will have travelled a long way to see you—if you disappoint them . . . Well, we've had bloodshed in the square before.'

Jake put off thinking about the prospect of being pulled limb from limb by hordes of disgruntled monsters. He kept his attention focused solely upon his father's cure. He told Adam that he spent his days practising magic in quiet corners. In fact, he was scouring the many occult libraries that lie hidden in the old city of London. Pandora had already investigated most of them. She provided Jake with a list and, on some occasions, would accompany him to these strange, crumbling buildings tucked away down side alleys or secreted under the earth. Most of the time, however, she was too busy caring for Adam. And so, after two weeks of mouldy books and fantastical librarians, what did Jake have to show for his research?

Nothing. It seemed that Pandora was right—there was *no* cure.

At the end of another exhausting day, a footsore Jake slouched back to the Grimoire Club. Grimy from the dust of old tomes, he wanted a shower, but decided to cheer himself up by dropping in on Simon first. The friends had quickly fallen back into their old routine of jokes and banter. Still, that haunted expression had not left Simon's eyes, and he often woke in the night believing that he had heard his mother's voice. Adam had continued their hypnosis sessions but with no real success. It seemed that Simon's secrets would remain hidden.

Jake knocked on the bedroom door and walked in.

He was about to make some lame joke when he saw Simon and Rachel sitting together cross-legged on the bed. Their eyes were closed and they were holding hands. Their breathing came in steady waves. Although he knew that they were just practising one of the control techniques Simon used to master his 'other self', Jake felt a twist of jealousy.

They came out of the trance together and a smile flashed between them. Then Rachel noticed Jake in the doorway.

'Hey,' she said, getting awkwardly off the bed. 'Any luck today?'

'Nope.' Jake slumped into a chair. 'If you're under a gypsy curse, suffering from lycanthropy, eaten a devil's-head mushroom by moonlight or are being plagued by poltergeists, then come see me, I'll know what to do. But if you've been hexed by a coven master? Sorry, can't help.'

'That's it,' Simon said. 'Tomorrow, we're coming with you. Three heads might be better than one.'

'Mate, are you sure?'

They all knew Simon's fear: that his demon half might suddenly take over. That he would transform in a public place.

'The control techniques are working, I can feel it.' That familiar, crooked smile faltered. 'Anyway, Dr Harker, he's— well, he's—'

'Getting worse,' Jake sighed.

'If there's a cure, we'll find it, Jake. Tomorrow we'll—'

'Why wait for tomorrow?' Rachel interrupted. 'We can start work tonight.'

'Strange as it sounds, occult libraries seem to keep regular hours,' Jake yawned. 'They'll all be closed.'

'The ones in London, yes, but what about the one just along the corridor? The private library of the Grimoire Club?'

'Come on, Rach, don't you think I've thought of that? Murdles won't let humans into the library. Anyway,' Jake gave a wry smile, 'the door's always locked.'

'Can't you use magic to open it?'

'Tried. It must have a spell guarding it.'

'Maybe it's not magically sealed at all,' Simon said. 'Maybe it's just a simple lock. And if that's the case, I could be your man.'

They had all heeded Murdles's warning about wandering the corridors alone at night. Simon had not yet left the apartment, and Jake and Rachel had always been escorted in and out of the club by Razor or one of the other doormen. This was the first time they had ventured into Grimoire alone. Before they left the safety of the apartment, Rachel retrieved the bow and quiver from her room.

Jake eased open the apartment door and peeked into the corridor.

'All clear,' he whispered.

The three friends crept into the hallway. Reaching the library door, Simon dropped to his knees and planted an eye on the keyhole. He took two straightened paperclips from his pocket and started jiggling them inside the lock.

'Simon . . . um . . . how do you know this stuff?'

'Best not to ask, Rach.' Simon winked. 'Wouldn't want you to think any less of me. Ah—got it!'

The lock clicked. Simon pocketed the paperclips, got to his feet and grasped the handle. He was about to turn it when a voice whispered behind their backs:

'Can I help you?'

Jake gasped, Rachel shrieked, Simon barked out a swear word.

They turned to find Mr Murdles floating behind them. The friends stepped aside as Murdles came forward and pushed lightly against the library door.

'I really wouldn't enter the Grimoire Club's library if I were you . . . '

The door swung back to reveal a room the size of a broom cupboard. Two rickety bookshelves had been nailed to the wall and a mangy old mop was propped in one corner.

' . . . it really is such a *dull* room. Now, Mr Harker, I did ask you *not* to wander around my club unescorted.'

'I'm sorry, sir.'

Murdles's face softened. 'Ah well, I cannot stay mad at my boy conjuror. Not when he has promised me such a spectacular show! But tell me, what are you doing here?'

Jake explained that they were hoping to find a book of magical cures. He told Murdles that he was concerned about his father's health and had exhausted most of the occult libraries of London.

'Dr Harker does look rather *deathly*, and I should know,'

the ghost laughed. A look from Jake mopped up the manager's merriment. 'Ahem, yes, well I cannot have my boy conjuror distracted from his magic. If you wish to find a cure you should stop hunting through boring old libraries. You must go and consult the Oracle.'

'The who?'

'The Great Seer of the borderland,' Murdles said. 'The Pythia Priestess. The Oracle of the Pit. If there is a cure for your father, she will tell you how to find it.'

'And how can we find *her*?' Rachel asked.

'I will take you to her. The Oracle is my neighbour.'

Five minutes later, Jake, Rachel, Simon, and Mr Murdles had crossed the moonlit piazza and were standing inside the teardrop doorway—the road back to London. A cold desert wind howled through the tunnel like a mournful spirit.

'Let there be light,' Murdles said.

They lit the oil lanterns they had brought with them from the Grimoire Club. Three steady flames shone out; thumbprints of illumination in the unending darkness. They picked their way across the tunnel floor, a rough terrain of beaten earth pebbled with bricks that had fallen from the roof. High above, the lantern light touched the fingertips of the swaying tentacles.

Murdles led them to the pit that Jake had glimpsed on his first journey through the tunnel. It was circular, like a huge wishing well, with a low stone wall running around the outside. Carved around the wall was the legend:

DESCEND INTO DARKNESS AND YE SHALL FIND ILLUMINATION ·

'I seldom have use for signs and prophecies,' Murdles said, 'and so I leave you here.'

The ghost floated towards the pale-eyed doorway.

'But what do we do?' Jake shouted.

His question boomed around the tunnel and made the tentacles rustle.

'You can read, can't you?' Murdles said irritably.

The ghost drifted away.

Jake turned to Simon and Rachel. 'I don't like this. You guys go back to the club.'

'You don't get rid of us that easy,' Simon grunted. 'Anyway, I owe you a death-defying rescue. You get into trouble, I'll be there.'

'Rachel——' Jake began.

'Come on, boy conjuror,' she said, jumping up onto the wall, 'let's go see the Seer.'

Rachel leaned over the edge of the pit, lantern held at

arm's length. The well plunged down beyond the range of her light. Slick with moss, a narrow staircase descended in a spiral around the inner wall. This was their path to the Oracle.

'There's something down there,' Rachel said.

Jake joined her on the wall. Far below, shapeless forms moved in the shadows.

'I saw them when we first flew over. What do you think they are?'

'A welcoming committee,' said Simon. 'Well, let's not keep them waiting.'

Jake stepped off the lip of stone and into the jaws of the pit. The smell of stagnant water and rotting vegetation rose up and made him splutter. With one hand tracing the damp wall, the other pushing the lantern forward, Jake started the descent. Round and round, he spiralled down, Rachel behind him, Simon bringing up the rear. Each well-worn step crumbled a little beneath his foot and there were places where two or three had collapsed completely. At those points, Jake and his friends were forced to jump across tiny chasms, hoping that the step on the other side would hold.

Halfway down, Simon lost his footing on the wet stone. He slipped and teetered at the edge of the staircase. Rachel heard his cry, spun round and grabbed his hand, pulling him back from the brink. Simon panted his thanks.

It had taken almost twenty minutes, but they were now nearing the end of their journey. The stench of filthy water was stronger here at the base of the abyss. Three metres or so from the bottom, Jake craned his lantern over the staircase.

Thhhsssss—Thhhseeesss—Thhhuuusss

Hooded eyes flashed in the light.

Snakes. Dozens of them. And yet like no serpents Jake had ever seen.

Gigantic in size, they writhed across the dirt floor, their bodies tangled in one great slithering mass. At the sight of the strangers, forty heads lashed towards the stairs. They swayed together, just below the step upon which Jake stood. Forked tongues sizzled and venom dripped from the corners of hungry mouths. What struck Jake as particularly strange was the skin of these reptiles. Instead of scales, they had spongy, pale flesh that appeared transparent in the lantern light. Jake could see the throb of blue veins, the beat of red hearts and the flutter of monstrous lungs. Inside the prison of their long stomachs a hundred spiders and rats slowly decomposed. These sun-starved creatures must have been born in the darkness, Jake thought.

'Maybe we should get out of here,' Simon said.

Jake nodded, and they began to retreat back up the staircase.

Suddenly, one of the smaller snakes separated from the rest and darted up the stairs. It twisted its powerful body this way and that, finding purchase on the wet stones. Jake had no time to react. The serpent was on him in seconds. Its tongue lashed out and venom jetted from its throat. One of the poison sprays hit the lantern and ate right through the glass. Jake dropped the light. Stumbled backwards. The snake lashed out again, fangs bared. Before it could land a strike, Rachel had loaded her bow and loosed an arrow. Piercing the serpent's throat, the arrow pinned the snake to the pit wall.

'Jake!'

Simon's hand shot out, but he was too late.

His face long with horror, Jake slipped off the step and tumbled into the pit.

Chapter 10
The Serpent Inside

Jake hit the ground with a bone-juddering crack. Behind the roar of pain, he could just about hear the frightened cries of his friends.

'Get up! Move!'

'Jake, hurry!'

Arrows *thwwpped* through the air and kicked up the dust all around. Jake rolled over onto his hands and knees and blinked the pit into focus.

An undulating forest of long white bodies reared up before him. A pit of snakes, poised to strike. Why had Murdles led them down here? Had he figured out that Jake had no real magic? Was this his revenge?

Magic. It was worth a try.

Jake held out his hand and concentrated on the flow of power. He thought of his mother, his father, Marcus Crowden, witches, demons . . .

Blue shocks crackled between his fingers. Some of the snakes scuttled back, frightened by the magical energy. An older and perhaps wiser serpent held its ground. It towered over the boy and its cruel, black eyes seemed to mirror Jake's thoughts—*it's weak, it's not enough*. The snake's mouth yawned wide. A hiss fizzled over its forked tongue.

One of Rachel's arrows missed its mark by inches and sailed past the serpent. There was no time for her to reload. Simon cursed and threw his lantern at the snake. Another miss.

The white body arched. The head drew back. Lips curled over a pair of venom-drenched fangs.

The snake launched its strike.

'STOP!'

An invisible force reached out and dashed the snake to the far side of the pit. Its gigantic body twisted through the air and struck the wall so hard that it exploded on impact. Jake saw the snake's huge head disappear in a mist of blood and brains. One eye, still attached to its stalk, ricocheted off the wall and bounced across the ground like a wet marble. It rolled to a stop at Jake's feet.

The other snakes fell back. They slithered to the middle of the pit and disappeared into a large crack in the earth.

It was only now, with the abyss empty, that Jake saw the child.

'Your friends may descend from the Sacred Way,' said the girl, beckoning to the others. 'I bid them—come closer.'

Rachel and Simon joined Jake. Together, they stared at the little figure.

She sat on a high tripod chair that straddled the crack in the earth. In her right hand she held a laurel leaf, in her left, a small bowl filled with silvery water. A red shawl was wrapped loosely around her head and she was dressed in deep scarlet robes. These vivid colours contrasted sharply with her marble-white skin. Jake thought she looked about eight years old, and yet there were aeons of knowledge in those glazed eyes. Her nostrils flared. She breathed deeply and held out her hand.

'Stop there, children,' she commanded. 'If inhaled, the vapours from the pit are apt to drive mortals mad.'

And now Jake saw it—sulphurous smoke rising up out of the crack. It cloaked the little girl in a yellow haze.

'I must apologize for my pets,' she continued. 'I was not expecting guests, and so was taking my rest when you arrived.'

'You're the Oracle of the Pit?' Jake asked.

'I am the Seeing Eye,' she answered in a sing-song voice. 'I am the Prophetess of the borderlands. I am Pythia, I am Delphi, I am Cassandra.'

'Some prophet,' Simon whispered. 'Didn't see us coming, did she?'

'I see *you* very clearly, Simon Lydgate. Better than you see yourself, I'd wager.'

'How'd you know my name?'

'Only from my knowledge of your future. A most interesting future it is, too—many trials and surprises to come.'

'What surprises?'

'Ah, no, no, no. I am not a clear window into future times.

I give my veiled prophecies and you must make of them what you will. One scrap of guiding knowledge for each of you. Who will ask their question first?'

Simon nudged Jake forward.

'Where can I find my father's cure?'

The little girl closed her eyes. She breathed in the toxic fumes that swirled around her. For a long time nothing happened. Then, with sudden and shocking ferocity, her hands gripped the arms of the tripod chair. The laurel leaf she had been holding was crushed; the little earthenware bowl fell to the ground and shattered.

The Oracle's chest rose and fell in violent spasms. She gripped the chair so tightly that her knuckles sharpened into bone-white ridges. Tremors ran along her spine and she gritted her teeth against the pain. Her mouth snapped open and, from deep inside her body, something *hissed*.

Slick with saliva, an emerald green serpent reared up out of the child's throat. The snake turned its head and blinked at Jake. Then, to his disgust, it started to speak.

'Repeat your question,' it lisped, in a voice not unlike the little girl's.

The child's eyes remained closed. Perhaps she was unconscious. Or perhaps she was merely a vessel, Jake thought. Was *this* creature the true Oracle?

'My father's cure,' Jake gulped. 'Where can I find it?'

'*Thhsss.* It is difficult to be sure,' the snake said, writhing in the bowl of the girl's throat. 'You *may* find the cure you seek, but first you must obey the man whose tongue is as forked as my own. At first you will resist, but finally you will see that his plan is the only way to save your father. Obeying the man, you will have to travel far. You will go to the place of the gallows, where at the twilight hour you will face both friends and enemies. If you survive—and that is a big *if*—you must then follow the girl. She will lead you to the preacher . . . Ah, but I have said enough. Listen to the lying doctor and you will have your chance, Jacob Never Born.'

The serpentine prophetess turned to Rachel.

'Missss Ssssaxby. Your question?'

'All I want to know is whether my friends will be safe. If the Demon Father goes to war, will they survive?'

'That future is not set in stone. But let me tell you this— you must learn the grace of forgiveness, child. You must pardon *him* or for ever be haunted by regret. The Dream Men will soon be knocking at every door, you see?'

'And now, Mr Lydgate.'

Simon barked out his question without hesitation—

'I want to know—did I kill my mother?'

'That is a question of the past, not the future. I will tell you this—to find the truth about yourself, you must walk into a trap with your eyes wide open. Violence will be necessary, I'm afraid—the keyholder is a formidable foe—but after some *unpleasantnessss* you will know all. Who you are, what you are, and what horrors still lie in wait for you. That is the end of my prophesying . . . Unless . . . Perhaps the vapours have more to tell.'

The snake's nostrils quivered and it sucked down the smoke. Jake felt a wave of sickness as he watched the little girl's chest heave. How was this creature connected to her?

'*Thhssss.* I do not want to see this! Noooo!'

The snake shivered. In a single smooth motion it slipped back down the child's throat. The little girl blinked, choked, stared at Jake and his friends.

'You brought this here!' she cried. 'This dread omen!'

'What are you talking about?'

'You pretend not to know, and yet *he* told you.' She pointed at Simon. '*Dark powers are gathering. They will be here soon.* Those were his words. He told you, but you did not understand. See, it is written in the vapours.'

As she spoke, the threads of yellow smoke pouring out of the chasm thickened and turned an inky black. They shaped themselves into a familiar symbol:

which held in the air.

'Now they are gathered together in the new coliseum,' the girl murmured. 'Now their covenant will be sealed and they will fall like fire from the sky. Blood and death and destruction. You cannot stop them. It is too late.'

The Oracle looked up at the circle of pale light overhead. 'The universal coven has come.'

A cry, somewhere between a human scream and an animal roar, bellowed around the pit. Jake spun round. He saw Rachel crouched on the steps, Simon's head supported in her arms. The boy shuddered and screamed again, his eyes fixed on the trident.

'We've got to get him out of here!' Rachel cried. 'Simon—he's changing!'

Despite forecasts for a fine summer evening, storm clouds had gathered early over north-west London. Swept in from all directions, they clubbed together to form a colossal black cloud. The odd thing was that this thunderhead just seemed to sit there. There was no rumble, no lightning flash, and not a breath of wind moved in the streets below. The uncarthly stillness soon began to intrigue the residents of Wembley. People peeked from behind their curtains, took pictures with their mobile phones, and stood on their doorsteps exchanging weather-related wisdom.

By late evening, the streets of Wembley were overrun by gawpers. For over five hours the thunderhead had not moved an inch. It was like watching an image paused on a giant TV screen. Nevertheless, at a quarter to midnight the crowd was beginning to tire of the spectacle. A few had started to shuffle off home when a collective gasp of surprise stopped them in their tracks.

A funnel of cloud had detached from the thunderhead

and plunged to earth. Like a dagger, it struck into the very heart of Wembley Stadium—that famous London sports arena.

That new coliseum.

Murmurs rose up from the crowds:

'Never seen anything like it!'

'Get the kids inside, Marge. Call the police!'

'Be serious, Geoff—call the police about a cloud?'

'That ain't no cloud. Look! There are *things* moving inside it. Things flying down into the stadium!'

'I think it's witches.'

'Don't be silly, Danny dear. I've told you before, there are no such things as—'

'Oh my God—look at that!'

Two shorter funnels of smoke branched off from the midpoint of the main shaft. They stretched away from each other, and then, quite suddenly, plunged down to form two sharp points.

'What is it, Stan?'

'Some kind of weird weather phenomenon. A twister, maybe.'

'That ain't no twister, you moron. Marge—get on the phone—999.'

'It's a trident.'

'What did you say, Danny?'

'It's a devil's trident. Witches and devils! Here in Wembley! Cooool!'

High above the gawpers, hidden inside the central shaft of the trident, dark witches soared down into the great stadium. Most flew on the twisting earthen snakes once preferred by the Crowden Coven. Some stood upright on enchanted wooden planks: simple transports that had been used by witches since the Middle Ages. A few who had travelled from the East sat cross-legged on Persian carpets beautifully decorated with stars and crescent moons. The more gifted witches flew unaided. None used broomsticks—that ancient superstition was an invention of storytellers and witchfinders.

The last of them left the funnel and dropped down through the open roof of Wembley Stadium. Then the trident drew itself back up into the thunderhead. Even from inside the arena, the witches could hear the gasps and cries of the crowds outside . . .

The gawpers watched as the thick, black cloud sucked up the trident and then, very slowly, began to descend from the heavens. It fell over the stadium like a dark cowl, masking everything from prying eyes. One or two of the bolder souls who had gathered on Wembley Way, the wide avenue that led up to the stadium, tested their nerve by approaching the wall of fog. Shouts of warning and nervous titters ran around the crowd. One man, braver, or perhaps more drunk than the rest, reached out to touch the undulating darkness.

The cloud lurched forward and swallowed him whole.

'Arthur!' his wife cried.

A bloodcurdling scream answered her. Parents covered their children's ears. Grown men cried out in fear and hid their faces. The screams of the man in the fog were suddenly cut short. Silence. The wind chattered through the streets of Wembley, and all eyes remained fixed on the mist.

'Is he all right?' Arthur's wife asked in a shivery voice. 'Do you think he's . . . ? Oh! There he is! He's coming back out of the fog!'

Something was coming back out of the fog.

Something that had once been a man called Arthur Grant.

Except this man no longer had a face. The figure staggered forward, arms flailing, reaching for the crowd. Its lidless eyes rolled in their sockets and its skeletal jaw snapped up and down. It took a long, rasping breath through skull snub nostrils. When it spoke, strands of torn flesh jiggled around its bony chin.

'Don't go in there,' the skeleton man advised. 'There's something in the mist, and it's hungry.'

Arthur's wife did not scream. She turned and ran. The crowds followed her example and within minutes the streets around Wembley had been emptied . . .

Back inside the stadium, the witches' patience was running thin. All one hundred and thirteen of them were now assembled. They had gathered in the centre of the famous England football pitch, standing on the thick cover that was laid out to protect the turf. To anyone else, being in that darkened stadium surrounded by ninety thousand empty red chairs might seem a little creepy. Not to the witches: they just wanted to know why they had been summoned.

They grumbled and bickered. Their demons squalled and squawked. A tall Egyptian witch in long flowing robes recognized one of the members of the Kansas Coven and went over to greet him.

'Oliver, how are you?'

'Pretty good, Mathias, pretty good. Any idea when this shindig is due to start?'

'Soon, I hope. It was a long flight from Cairo.'

'Tell me about it. My li'l darlin's all tuckered out.'

The Kansas witch stroked the head of the green monkey-demon that clung around his neck. Shaped like the mouth of a giant leech, the circular sucker in the middle of the monkey's face dripped with black pus.

'Say, what do you think of this guy Crowden?' Oliver asked. 'Is he really four hundred years old?'

'I believe so. Word has it that in 1645 he fought the Witchfinder, Josiah Hobarron, and was imprisoned in the Veil. He is a powerful Coven Master.'

'No kiddin'.' Oliver leaned in and whispered: 'Between you and me, he scared the hell out of Simeon, our leader. He's the guy with the bat-faced slug demon, by the way. There's certainly something kinda freaky about Marcus Crowden—did you notice how he keeps his eyes hidden behind those dark glasses. What's that all about?'

'Perhaps it is better not to know.'

'I hear that. So why do you think he's summoned us all to London?'

'It's something big.' Mathias patted the head of his demon—a creature that had the face and body of a black Labrador and the limbs of a gigantic centipede. 'There's not been a universal coven for . . . '

'TIME BEYOND RECKONING!'

Every face looked up at the great lattice arch that soared over Wembley Stadium. There, at its apex, a hundred and thirty-three metres above the ground, stood the Coven Master. He swept two gloved hands through the air and the stadium floodlights sparked into life. The assembled witches blinked in the glare.

'I thank you all for travelling so far, my friends.' The voice boomed, as if amplified through a Tannoy. 'I have had the pleasure of meeting your coven leaders, and I look forward to speaking with you all individually very soon. But now we must act quickly. I cannot maintain this protection for long.' His hands gestured to the cloud that capped the stadium.

A wizened old woman in Romanian peasant dress stepped forward. She held a two-headed frog in her hand. The demon's grasshopper legs arched behind it and rubbed out a brittle chirrup. When she spoke, fear rippled through her voice.

'I am Baba Balescu, Mother of the Bucharest Coven,' she croaked. 'We were honoured to receive you in our territory earlier this year, Master Crowden. We have shown our allegiance by placing your mark on our hillsides. But now we must ask—what is it that you want of us?'

The Master smiled.

'I want to give you power, Baba Balescu. Power beyond your wildest dreams.'

A stir of excited chatter rustled through the universal coven. Simeon, leader of the Kansas Coven, spoke out:

'What is this power?'

The Master beckoned and the nightmare cabinet swirled above the heads of the witches. Its doors swung open and a fiery wind blasted their upturned faces. Those that did not turn away saw a glimpse of distant volcanoes, of rivers running with molten lava and the blackened earth of an infernal landscape.

'I offer you the power of the demon world!' the Master called. 'The full, unfettered majesty of demonic magic at your command! Imagine it—not just one demon to serve you, but thousands!'

'How is this possible?' Baba Balescu cried, a dark joy dancing in her eyes.

'Tell us, Master!' Simeon pleaded. His cry was taken up by the horde.

The figure on the arch held up his hand for silence.

'As some of you may know, last year my coven and I attempted to open a doorway into the demon dimension. We were thwarted by a boy conjuror—the child Jacob Harker.'

'Forgive me, Master,' Simeon interrupted, 'but how could a mere child stand against you?'

'He was helped by a powerful organization. The Elders of Hobarron. It is true that the boy possessed *some* magical skill of his own, but he used the element of surprise to his advantage. Suffice to say that he managed to destroy the Door and prevent the Demontide.'

'Remarkable.'

An elderly man with sun-baked olive skin shuffled through the crowd. This ancient, white-bearded witch leaned heavily upon a staff inscribed with classical Greek letters. A feeble looking cat with a scorpion tail slumped at his feet.

'This child defeated the most powerful coven master in the world. He destroyed the great Door and flung demon-kind back into its prison. And he did all this with the element of surprise?' The old man shook his wrinkled head. 'I think not. There is a rumour running through the world of the dark creatures, Master Crowden. They say that this Jacob Harker is Josiah Hobarron born again. They say he is a practitioner of Oldcraft.'

Most of the witches laughed at this, but not all . . .

'That old superstition?' the Master sneered. 'Surely you do not believe such tales, my dear Adelphos.'

'I believe what my eyes show me,' Adelphos countered. 'I see a man—or something like a man—who was bested in battle by a boy.'

A younger man with the same shade of rich olive skin pressed forward.

'Please, Master Crowden, do not listen to this old fool. He does not speak for the Athens Coven.'

'No, I speak for myself,' Adelphos agreed. 'I believe Jacob Harker is what he claims to be, and that Marcus Crowden is no more. This creature—' a gnarled finger jabbed at the figure on the arch, '—is something *other*. Why else does he hide his eyes?'

'Hold your tongue, Adelphos,' the young man pleaded.

'I will not. I believe . . . ' The witch took a moment to gather his courage. 'Hear me, brethren witches, I believe this boy conjuror works his magic *without* demons!'

'Blasphemy!'

'I believe he is an agent of Oldcraft!'

'Heresy!'

'I believe this with all my soul. I believe it so much that I cast away my own demon!'

The old man stepped away from his cat. He held out his hand and muttered a few words. Bolts of fire crackled from his fingertips and shot out towards the demon. Before the magic could hit, the nightmare box made its move. With its doors still wide open, it plummeted down into the bowl of the stadium. Adelphos Mitro looked up into the descending jaws and tried to cry out. The cabinet slammed to earth and swallowed both the witch and his scream.

The box shuddered, as if digesting tough old bones. Then it flipped upright, its door snapped shut, and it soared back into the air.

'Is there anyone else who wishes to question me about Oldcraft . . . ?' the Master asked. 'I thought not.'

With its witch now dead, the scorpion-tailed cat burst into flames and returned to the demon world.

The young Greek witch threw himself onto the ground beneath the arch.

'Please forgive us, Master. None of the Athens Coven would ever doubt your word.'

'Get up out of the dirt,' the Master called, 'and listen to me, all of you. The Door which was destroyed cannot be reformed. That weak point between our world and the demon realm has been sealed off for ever. But hear this—it is within our power to create *a second Door*.'

Awed silence.

'That is why I have travelled the world to meet you. That is why I brought you here. To create this Door will require dark magic beyond any that can be summoned by one coven alone. And so we must pool our powers into a single spell—the creation of a Demon Doorway!'

Excited chatter followed this pronouncement.

'Is it possible?'

'Imagine what we could achieve with legions of demons at our command!'

'Nothing could stand against us! No government, no army!'

'The world would be ours to rule!'

'We would be living gods!'

'ENOUGH!' the Master bellowed. Then, in a softer tone: 'Be still, my brothers and sisters. Before we can even think about summoning the Door, there is something we must do.'

The figure stepped off the arch and flew down into the stadium. Witches drew apart as the Master walked into the centre of the universal coven. They saw themselves reflected in his dark glasses, and some of them wondered about what old Adelphos had said—*something other . . .*

The handsome face looked at each coven in turn.

'Only one thing stands between us and true, demonic power. An old foe must now be vanquished. The time has come to destroy the Hobarron Elders once and for all.'

A roar of approval rang around the stadium.

'Are you ready to fight, my witches?'

'Yes!'

'Are you ready for slaughter? For mayhem? For carnage?'

'YES!'

'Then follow me!'

The Master rose into the air. His new disciples joined him, riding into the thunderhead and black reaches beyond.

'KILL THEM ALL!' the Master commanded. 'LEAVE NONE ALIVE TO TELL THE TALE!'

Chapter 11
Fire from the Sky

His patrol complete, Brett Enfield returned to the security hut at the gate of Hobarron Tower. Before entering, he flashed his torch along the road that led back to New Town. Something small, a field mouse perhaps, darted off the tarmac and into the cornfields. Brett patted the Doberman at his side.

'Heel, Cerb.'

Cerberus grumbled.

'I know, I'm hungry, too,' Brett sympathized. 'Let's get some chow.'

He unhooked Cerberus's leash and the dog bounded through the hut's open door. Snuffling noises came from inside: the sound of an impatient animal seeking his supper. With thoughts of a hot meat pie filling his head, Brett was about to join his canine partner when something caught his eye.

Shapes moving through the sky.

Flying figures silhouetted against the face of the moon.

Cerberus had forgotten his dinner. He slipped out of the hut and nudged his master's leg. Brett looked down into a pair of moist brown eyes. It was the whimper at the back of the dog's throat that frightened him more than anything else. Brett had never seen Cerberus scared before.

Sirens cut the air. Amber alert lights flashed around the perimeter fence and swept across the face of Hobarron Tower.

Before Brett could catch his breath, a young Japanese girl dressed in jeans and a denim jacket landed in front of him. In other circumstances, Brett would have appreciated her beautiful, flawless skin and the lustrous black hair that fell down her back. Instead, all he could do was stare at the horrible scarred flesh of her throat. His thoughts flew back to all those checks he had performed since coming to work at the Institute. Dr Holmwood had always instructed him to pay careful attention to visitors' necks.

The girl began to murmur under her breath. She held out her hand as if in greeting. Cerberus growled.

'Bad dog,' the girl said. 'You will play with my pet now. Come, Mr Sickert.'

Eyes burned red in the hedgerow. Brett watched, dumbstruck, as a creature the shape of a rabbit but the size of a fox padded out onto the road. A bloody stump occupied the place where the rabbit's right ear should be. Torn and ragged, much of the left ear also appeared to have been ripped from its head. Anyone might think that the poor animal had been attacked, but that was not the case. The remnants of an ear rolled around inside the rabbit's mouth: the thing was eating itself alive.

Those red eyes fixed on Cerberus. Mr Sickert spat the flesh from his mouth and licked his blood-splattered lips with a thin, lizard-like tongue. Then, using his powerful hind legs, the thing launched itself at the dog. With one lethal bite it tore the throat out of the Doberman. Cerberus dropped twitching to the ground. A gush of hot blood pumped out of the dog's throat and Mr Sickert planted his lips over the wound and drank deeply.

'What a clever bunny,' the girl grinned.

Brett fumbled for the weapon on his belt. His sweating hands made his movements clumsy.

The girl made a gun of her fingers and pointed at the guard.

'No . . . ' Brett pleaded.

'Bang!'

The hex struck Brett and spun him round. He staggered away from the gate, hand clasped over the wound at his stomach. He felt the spill of blood beat against his palm and froth through his fingers. He managed eight short steps before his legs gave way and he hit the road.

Through dimming eyes, Brett Enfield—security guard and friend of Jacob Harker—watched the army of witches descend. Bolts of magic flew from a hundred hands and shattered the glass face of the tower. Chunks of masonry rained down from the roof. The ground beneath Brett trembled and he saw gigantic cracks snake along the tower walls. People appeared at the broken windows, framed by fire, waving and screaming. Their cries for help were answered with a barrage of dark magic.

Brett's blood eased to a trickle. Though he knew that the night was warm, he shivered. He no longer counted the time in minutes and seconds, but by the slow, dull thud of his heart. At last, Brett closed his eyes against death and destruction, witches and demons. His thoughts turned to his wife and his little boy. Their kind, loving faces stayed with him as he journeyed into the darkness.

'Rachel, get away from him.'

A faint blue flame ignited in Jake's hand.

'He won't hurt me,' Rachel said. 'He could never—'

Another scream from Simon cut her short. He was changing. With his gaze still rooted on the smoky trident, Simon's pupils sharpened into slits.

'The symbol—we need to get rid of it,' Jake said.

He turned to the Oracle.

The tripod chair was empty. The serpent and the child had vanished. Jake tore the shirt from his back and ran across the pit. Standing astride the crevice, he wafted his shirt through the smoke, trying desperately to disperse the trident.

Meanwhile, Simon's transformation quickened. His back hunched and his shoulders arched over his head. His bones crackled and reconfigured into new positions. Skin stretched, toes lengthened, fingernails thickened and sharpened into claws. Rachel held the changing face in her hands.

'I'm here, Simon. Breathe.'

Simon's nose wrinkled. With a warm, wet crack the bone snapped. Nose and mouth pushed out from his face to form a wolfish muzzle. The scar that ran down his upper lip split apart and pulled back over a set of ragged and still-growing teeth. Tears streamed from the boy's ferocious green eyes.

'G-go! Get out!'

'But you'll be all right,' Rachel gasped. 'You won't hurt me. You could never...'

Simon's T-shirt tore along the seams. His muscles strained and his spine rippled as dark hair sprouted from his skin. A cry, dripping with both horror and hunger, tore its way out of his throat: '*Rrrruuuunnnn!*'

But Rachel did not have time to run. The transformation had gone too far. Unable to control himself, Simon lashed out. His clawed hand struck Rachel's face and sent her flying across the pit. Jake turned in time to see a fine spray of blood shoot into the air. Helpless, he watched as Rachel's head smacked against the hard stone wall of the well and her body crumpled to the ground.

An inhuman face turned to Jake. Something like a smile played around the beast's jaws. Then its eyes switched back to Rachel, unconscious on the ground. An easy kill. The creature tensed and sprang from the steps.

Jake felt the magic flare in his heart and rage through his body. No need to search among dead memories and emotions—he didn't have to think about what he was doing. He held out his hand . . .

The creature was still in midair when the stream of blue

light lanced against its flank. It yelped and tumbled side-ways, missing Rachel by inches. Jake felt the vibrations as the half-demon hit the ground. Magical energy fizzled and died in his fist. He rushed to Rachel's side. His heart sang—she was breathing. Brushing the hair back from her face, he saw three shallow cuts made by the creature's claws. A sob rattled in Jake's chest as he kissed the unscarred side of Rachel's face. Then he looked over to where the beast lay sprawled unconscious, and his eyes narrowed.

Jake stood up. Blue light—darker this time—crackled once more in his hand . . .

'JAKE! Are you down there?'

The magic vanished. Jake blinked, as if coming out of a dream.

'Brag? Is that you?'

The troll's head craned over the pit.

'Your dad sent me to find you!' Brag shouted. 'Something's happened. Something bad.'

By the time they had lifted him out of the pit, Simon had changed back to his human form. Jake's magical blast had burned the flesh around his ribs, but he was otherwise unharmed. Both he and Rachel were still unconscious and so had to be carried back to the Grimoire Club. With Simon slung over his shoulder, Brag held the door open for Jake.

The club seemed unnaturally quiet. Usually there was laughter, the babble of conversation, even the odd scream echoing down the corridors.

'Where is everyone?'

'In the bar watching the TV,' Brag grunted, kicking the door shut.

'*All* of them? What's going on?'

'You'll see for yourself soon enough.'

With Rachel in his arms, Jake hurried along the hall. Her soft breath sighed against his neck and he felt the prickle of tears. If he had lost her . . .

'Found 'em!' Brag bellowed.

Pandora opened the apartment door. Her gaze passed from Simon to Jake before coming to rest on Rachel's wounded face. Concern flashed in those intelligent eyes.

'He changed?'

Jake nodded, and Pandora lifted Rachel out of his arms.

'We'll have to talk about this later,' she said. 'Your father's waiting.'

Jake found his dad hobbling back and forth across the lounge. Adam's eyes darted between the television and the phone. He gnawed at a hangnail and ran fingers through his thin grey hair. Jake's breath caught in his chest—was this old man really his father?

Adam caught sight of Jake and a mixture of relief and anger muddled his features. Brag and Pandora carried Simon and Rachel into the lounge and laid them on the sofa.

'What's happened? Where have you been?' Adam demanded. He shuffled over to his son and caught Jake in a rough hug. 'Are you all right?'

Jake explained what had happened in a few short sentences. The only thing he kept back was his reason for visiting the Oracle. If he spoke about the cure then he would have to break his promise to Pandora.

'Prophecies,' Adam muttered. 'Tonight they're coming true. Remember what Simon told us during his hypnosis? "Dark powers are gathering, drawn together by the Demon Father." Now we know the meaning of those words. He has assembled a universal coven.'

'A what?'

'A brotherhood of witches drawn from across the globe. I believe that's what the symbol meant. After he had visited them, the coven would display his trident as a mark of allegiance. Tonight this universal coven had their first meeting.'

Adam gestured towards the TV. It showed a grainy picture of a huge cloud gathered over Wembley Stadium.

'That was where they received their first orders.'

Jake's mouth ran dry.

'What orders?'

Adam switched to another news channel.

'Orders to kill.'

Flashing blue lights. Ambulance sirens. A reporter standing in front of a police cordon, her voice jittery with excitement and horror. Paramedics raced through mountains of rubble, the dead and dying in their arms. Great plumes of fire billowed against the night sky. And there, in the background of the shot, an inferno raging in the shattered heart of Hobarron Tower. It was like a vision of hell.

Rachel stirred. She glanced between frightened faces before focusing on the TV.

'My dad . . .'

The reporter handed back to the studio. The anchorman shuffled his papers.

'Horrific scenes of what is believed to have been a terrorist assault on the headquarters of the Hobarron Institute. Staggering news is reaching us that another site has also been attacked. The birthplace of Dr Gordon Holmwood has been devastated by a separate but equally lethal onslaught. The little village of Hobarron's Hollow . . . '

Pictures flashed onscreen: burning cottages, the old church on the hillside smashed to rubble, Holmwood Manor ablaze.

Jake went to the phone.

'Eddie,' he croaked.

Adam took the receiver from his hand.

'I can't get through to anyone. Not Dr Holmwood nor Malcolm Saxby.' His gaze flitted to a distraught Rachel. 'Mildred Rice isn't picking up either. None of the Elders are.'

The anchorman was back onscreen.

'We pass now to Downing Street where the Prime Minister is due to make a statement.'

The picture flipped to show that famous front door. A podium had been set up outside Number 10 and the Prime Minister had taken her place behind it. She looked tired but very serious. Miss Cynthia Croft stared directly into the camera while flash bulbs went off all around her. Perhaps frightened by the late-night hubbub, Miss Croft's cat, Chequers, mewled at her feet.

'Good evening, ladies and gentlemen,' she began. 'I want to begin by telling you that this outrage perpetrated against the Hobarron Institute and the people of Hobarron's Hollow will *not* stand.'

A low growl rumbled in Simon's throat. Without a second's hesitation, Rachel went to him and cradled his head in her lap. The eyes of the others never left the TV screen.

'As yet, we have no intelligence about who might have committed these hideous crimes, but rest assured, people of Britain, we *will* find them.' Cynthia Croft's tone hardened. 'We will hunt them down. We will punish them. To that, I have sworn.'

A reporter called out from the crowd:

'Prime Minister, there has been talk of *creatures* falling from the sky. Eyewitnesses have reported seeing, well, witches. Witches and demons.'

Nervous laughter from the press, followed by a long pause.

Miss Croft did not smile.

'We live in a grown-up world, ladies and gentlemen. A grown-up world with grown-up terrors. Fictitious monsters need not concern us.'

Adam switched off the TV. As soon as the screen blipped to black, the phone rang.

'Adam Harker speaking . . . Yes. Yes, I understand. Of course, we will be there as soon as possible. Goodnight.'

Adam replaced the receiver. He shook his head and glanced back at the others.

'We've been summoned home.'

Chapter 12
Evil Unleashed

The sun's first rays had just yawned over the horizon when Dr Harker's Volkswagen left the outskirts of New Town. The car trundled along the road and kicked up the soft ash that had settled on the tarmac. Blown out half a mile from Hobarron Tower, pebbles of glass crunched under the car's tyres. Jake stared ahead, unable to believe what his eyes showed him. The once majestic tower was gone. In its place, a confusion of jagged glass and twisted metal stabbed at the bleeding sky.

Jake reached onto the back seat and shook the sleeping girl. Rachel blinked swollen eyes.

'We're here.'

There were holes in the security fence large enough to drive a bus through. The cameras had been smashed to smithereens and the cabin at the gate was now a burned out shell.

Evil Unleashed

'My God,' Rachel whispered.

A man in military uniform waved them to the gate. Adam wound down his window and handed over three passports.

'Dr Adam Harker, Jacob Harker, and Miss Rachel Saxby. We're expected.'

The soldier scrutinized their faces and checked the names against the paperwork on his clipboard.

'Please drive on through to the plaza, Dr Harker,' he said, handing back the ID documents.

'Just a minute.' Jake couldn't take his eyes off the black-walled security hut. 'Brett Enfield—he was a friend of mine. Was he hurt?'

The soldier ran his finger down a long list. He found the name and tapped the clipboard.

'Brett Patrick Enfield. I'm sorry, your friend died in the assault. He fell right where I'm standing.'

All those silly jokes and games he and Brett had enjoyed over the years came back to Jake. The open, honest-faced guard had been a fixture of his childhood. A good man. In his mind, Jake saw him again, slumped in his seat in the cabin, head in a newspaper.

Afternoon, fella! How was school?

Steam from burst water pipes covered the plaza in a white fog. Somewhere inside the fog, lights strobed on and off—blue-black, blue-black, blue-black—a shivery, nightmarish flicker. Adam parked and they got out of the car. Colossal shadows cast by slabs of masonry and melted girders loomed through the mist. Giant cracks splintered the ground.

Something caught Jake's eye and he raced across the

139

plaza. Adam and Rachel followed. They found him standing over crumbs of white stone, some so tiny they were little bigger than baby teeth. He picked up one of the larger pieces and showed it to them—

'Olivia Brown's memorial,' he said. 'They destroyed it.'

A voice called out:

'A little girl who was murdered by a witch and a demon. I wonder how many more must die?'

Dr Gordon Holmwood emerged from the mist.

The leader of the Hobarron Elders was very much as Jake remembered him. In fact, despite his spindly legs and rotting yellow teeth, Dr Holmwood didn't look much older than Adam Harker, a man almost half his age. The doctor held a cigarette between his nicotine-stained fingers. He drew on it with all the hunger of a drowning man sucking down his last lungful of air.

The small, dark-haired boy standing next to Holmwood took one look at Jake and rushed over. Rachel and the Harkers took turns in hugging the kid.

'It's good to see you, Eddie,' Adam said, ruffling his long locks. 'Growing your hair like Jake, eh?'

The boy blushed.

'Is your mum OK?'

'We hid in the cellar,' Eddie nodded. 'I remembered

reading something in one of my old horror comics—*Crypt of Fear*, I think it was—that if there's an earthquake you should shelter under an arch or in a doorway. The cellar at the Manor has an arched roof so . . . '

'Horror comics save the day again,' Jake smiled.

Eddie's own smile was short-lived. 'Lots of Hollow people didn't make it. There were bodies in the streets. People I'd known since I was little.'

Adam glanced at Holmwood. 'My sister?'

'Joanna survived.'

Jake hugged Eddie close.

Meanwhile, Rachel was staring at the man on Dr Holmwood's right. Malcolm Saxby came forward and held out his arms to his daughter.

'I'm glad you're alive,' Rachel said, trying to hide the throb of emotion in her voice. 'But nothing's changed. You understand? You are *not* my father.'

Dr Saxby winced, lowered his hands, and slunk off into the mist.

'Rachel, why don't you and Eddie get some breakfast,' Dr Holmwood said. 'There's a canteen set up by the gate. The Harkers and I need to talk.'

'Rachel stays,' Jake insisted.

'It's all right,' Rachel said. 'I could do with a breath of fresh air. Come on, Edster.'

They walked away, arm in arm.

Knees cracking, Holmwood sat down heavily on a chunk of cement. Under the shadow of his shattered dream, the doctor sighed.

'Perhaps I should have listened to you, Jake. When you spoke with the Witchfinder's voice, perhaps I should have taken heed. Closed down the Institute, disbanded the Elders. If I had, maybe this would never have happened.'

'You were ancient enemies,' Jake said. 'I think the Demon Father would have come after the Elders, Institute or not.'

'It's very kind of you to ease an old man's conscience.'

'It's not kindness. You'll always have your share of blame, Dr Holmwood.'

'You're wise beyond your years, Jake. I always said so.' The doctor drew deeply on his cigarette. 'The truth is, I kept the Institute running because I thought we could continue the fight against demonkind. I was wrong. The power of this place was always in the connections I made with governments and the wealthy people who funded us. But ever since that woman was elected—'

'Cynthia Croft?' Adam asked. 'The new PM?'

'I've had private meetings with her. She's a practical woman—studied chemistry at university—the sort who will only believe in something if it can be quantified, measured, analysed. She doesn't credit all this "demon nonsense". Her words. Since that meeting, our connections in the police and military have dried up. Our supporters have fallen away. Even before this attack, the Hobarron Institute was a spent force.'

'But you still had the defences,' Adam said. 'The tower, the Hollow, both were protected by magical charms. How did the Demon Father get through?'

'He had over a hundred witches in his army!' Holmwood

laughed bitterly. 'A universal coven. He smashed through our defences within seconds. And now . . . '

The doctor watched Jake through hooded eyes.

'Now he has even greater numbers at his command.'

'Oh God.' Adam stood up. What little colour he had drained from his face. 'It never occurred to me . . . But if that's true then we're finished!'

'What is it?' Jake asked. His dad's panic was infectious.

'Your father told me what the Lydgate boy said under hypnosis.' Holmwood flicked the stub of his cigarette into the mist. '*They will fall like fire from the sky. At their touch, fortresses will burn, prison walls will quake and crumble.* This tower was that fortress. These were those prison walls.'

The Institute vaults. Now Jake remembered. The tragic sorcerer Sidney Tinsmouth had told him that the Elders kept dark witches imprisoned beneath the tower.

'An old enemy will be released,' Jake said, reciting the last few words from Simon's trance. 'Don't tell me . . . No!'

'I'm afraid so.' Holmwood bowed his head. 'Among the hundreds of witches the universal coven set free was a man we had scheduled for execution. Unfortunately, they took him before that sentence could be carried out. And now the Third in Command of the Crowden Coven is at large once more.'

'No!' Jake repeated. 'NO!'

Fury burned through his body. He saw his mother dangling over the canal. Saw her silent scream. Saw her die all over again.

Holmwood's words came to him as if from far away—

'Tobias Quilp walks free.'

Bad dreams roused the witch from his slumbers. He cried out and his body shivered so much that the four-poster bed quaked beneath him. He clasped his head in his hands and buried his face in the pillow.

'No more!' he pleaded, his cut-glass accent ragged at its edges. 'Please, just kill me. Let me die.'

Slowly, the horror of the past eight months began to ebb away. The witch drew his knees up to his chin and stared at his reflection in the dusty old mirror on the other side of the room. The man he saw looked nothing like the Tobias Quilp of old. True, his skin was still deathly pale and a tiny spark of cruelty continued to glint in those china blue eyes, but where was his confidence? His swagger? Where was that cold, remorseless intelligence?

'I am broken,' he whimpered.

'Then *I* shall mend you.'

His old master's voice. Deeper, perhaps, but as musical as ever.

Marcus Crowden stepped out of the shadows. Quilp could not hide his surprise. Where was the dirty rag that always covered Crowden's face? And why were his eyes hidden behind a pair of dark glasses? These questions fell away the moment Quilp spied the wooden box in his master's hands.

The lid rattled.

Quilp licked his lips. He held out his hands, like a child about to receive a Christmas present. Tears ran down his cheeks. Then, at the last moment, he snatched his hands away and pinned them under his arms. He looked suspiciously around the bedchamber.

'It is a trick!' he cried. 'A new torment designed by the Elders! You are *not* my master!'

'Mr Quilp, you will listen to me—'

'No. I have told you before—I will not betray Marcus Crowden or my coven. You may torture me as much as you please.'

'I have not come to torture you.'

'Have you not?' Quilp laughed. 'Then you are done with *this*—and *this*—and *this*?'

The witch thrust out his hands. Deep, ugly scars crisscrossed his palms, as if made by the tip of a knife or the sharp belly of a razor. He ripped open the buttons of his shirt. From chest to stomach, his flesh was a yellow and purple mass of acid-scorched skin.

'Pull yourself together, you pathetic creature,' the Coven Master sneered. 'Such torture is nothing compared to my own dark imaginings. Now take the box.'

Daring to hope, Quilp stretched out his hands. He snatched the box and laid it in his lap.

'Open it.'

His fingers quivered. He tore away the chains and flipped the lid.

'Is it you, my pet?' Quilp murmured.

Dull yellow eyes gleamed in the light. The thing inside the box snuffled, chuntered, howled. It reached out and gripped the sides of its prison. Slowly, painfully, the demon crawled out of the chest and into Quilp's lap. Overjoyed, the witch rocked the demon in his arms like a baby.

'My own dear Pinch, you've come back to me.'

'I brought him back,' the stranger said. 'I saved you both.'

'Who are you?' Quilp whispered. 'You are *not* my master.'

The beautiful face smiled. 'You are more perceptive than the others, Mr Quilp. I will tell you the truth, but it is to go no further, you understand? Your master, Marcus Crowden, had his chance to break through the Door and release demon-kind. He had the Demontide in his hand, and do you know what he did?'

Quilp shook his head. He could feel Pinch clinging to him—was the demon afraid?

'He let a boy defeat him. A child. I watched all this as it unfolded and I decreed that such failure should not go unpunished. And so I came into this hostile world. I poured my spirit into the body of Marcus Crowden, destroying his soul in the process. And now, with human form, I can achieve what he only dreamed of. I can bring about the Demontide.'

'But who are you?'

The Master pinched the bridge of his dark glasses between his fingers . . .

'This is who I am.'

. . . and slid them from his face.

A pair of blood-soaked eyes, without white or iris or pupil, stared back at Quilp.

'Demon Father,' the witch breathed.

'It is our time now, Mr Quilp,' the Demon Father nodded. 'The Age of Man is passing. Soon it will be a memory;

a story told only around the campfires of the dark creatures. The Age of Demon and Witch is at hand. I have chosen you, faithful Tobias, to stand by my side as we enter this new dawn. Will you serve me as my most trusted adviser?'

'Of course, but what of Esther?'

'Esther?'

'The Second in Command of the Crowden Coven. Esther Inglethorpe. She should be your first choice.'

'Ah yes, I had forgotten about Mother Inglethorpe.' The demon slipped the glasses back onto his nose. 'I am sorry to have to tell you this, Tobias, but your lover and mentor is dead. Killed during the battle to open the Door.'

Quilp had endured such pain these last few months that he did not believe he could feel any more. He was wrong. The news that Esther had been murdered cut him to the heart. He felt the first stirrings of dark magic at his fingertips.

'Who killed her?'

'Dr Adam Harker fired the bullet, but the one truly responsible? His son, Jacob. You remember him, don't you? The child you failed to kill. The boy who defeated your master and wiped your coven from the face of the earth. The real killer of your beloved Esther. Maybe it is time, Mr Quilp, that you settled that score.'

Chapter 13
The Man with the Forked Tongue

Jake smashed his fist against a huge slab of masonry. Examining his bloodied knuckles, he muttered, 'I'm going to kill him.'

Adam put an arm around Jake's shoulder.

'It's natural to feel that way,' he said. 'But that's not you talking. You could never hurt anyone.'

'*You* were going to let me kill the Demon Father,' Jake snapped. 'The night I destroyed the Door, you let me take the gun.'

Scars of colour whipped into Adam's grey cheeks.

'That was different. That thing wasn't human.'

'Tobias Quilp isn't *human*. Not after what he did to Mum. I'm going to find him and I'm going to kill him, and there's nothing you can do to stop me.'

Adam was about to argue further when Dr Holmwood cut in—

'Even if you do find him, Jacob, you won't be able to kill him. I've heard on the grapevine that your powers have faded. How can you hope to stand against Tobias Quilp when he has all the might of the Demon Father to protect him?'

'My powers come back when I need them . . . Sometimes. Anyway, I don't care.'

'Do not be foolish,' Holmwood said with a touch of his old authority. 'Do you think your "original" would throw away his life so easily? No. The Witchfinder was clever, calculating. Josiah Hobarron would have a plan.'

The doctor rose to his feet.

'Gentlemen, if you will follow me.'

Holmwood led the way into the mist. They crossed the plaza and made for the entrance to the tower, now blocked by a mountain of masonry.

'What's going on, Gordon?'

Holmwood didn't answer. He took a small torch from his pocket and clamped it between his teeth. Then the doctor started to shuffle through a tiny gap in the blocks of fallen stone. Jake followed, trying not to think about the tonnes of concrete, iron, and glass balanced precariously overhead. He stumbled through into what had once been the tower's reception area and his hand flew to his mouth. Everywhere he turned—blood. Blood on the walls, on the stairs, dappling the ceiling and lying in great pools on the floor.

'They were here,' Holmwood said, gesturing towards the caved-in doorway. 'Hundreds of them. Friends and colleagues

I'd known for years. We moved their bodies at first light.'

'But you—' Jake caught his breath. 'You would have been their main target. How did you survive?'

'I'll show you.'

While Holmwood headed for the stairs, Jake looked back through the gap. There was no sign of his father.

'Dad?'

Adam's haggard face appeared on the other side of the rubble.

'I can't get through, Jake. I don't have the strength.'

That was the first time Adam had admitted his frailty. Jake winced at his father's words.

'It's OK. We won't be long, Dr Holmwood just—'

Adam leaned into the gap. What he said next came in an urgent whisper:

'Don't believe everything he tells you, son. He speaks with a forked tongue.'

Jake shivered despite himself. He remembered the words of the Oracle: *You may find the cure you seek, but first you must obey the man with the forked tongue . . .*

'Keep your wits about you,' Adam called.

Jake could only nod. He followed Dr Holmwood to the stairs and they began their descent into the bowels of the tower. From some distant part of the building came the crash of tumbling walls.

'Is it safe here?' Jake asked.

'I should hardly think so.' Holmwood took another cigarette from his pocket and lit up. 'Nothing is safe any more.'

They reached the basement. A long grey corridor stretched

away into darkness. At the end of the hall, Holmwood flashed his torch against a large steel door:

HOBARRON WEAPON
NO UNAUTHORIZED PERSONNEL

He swiped a keycard across a panel on the wall and the door swung back.

'Welcome, Jacob, to the room in which you were born.'

Jake stepped inside the musty laboratory. Head reeling, he walked around in a daze. He reached out to touch one of the high-tech pieces of machinery only to flinch away at the last moment, as if shocked. This was where the great experiment of Claire and Adam Harker had been conceived. Within these four walls, Jake had been assembled from the genetic material of Josiah Hobarron, a dead man.

'I wasn't born here,' Jake said. 'This was where I was *made*.'

'You could look at it that way, I suppose,' Holmwood mused. 'But I didn't bring you here to talk about the past. You wanted to know how Dr Saxby and I survived? We locked ourselves inside this laboratory. It once housed our most precious secret—our grand Hobarron Weapon—and so it was built to withstand hurricanes and earthquakes. Not only that, but powerful magical charms protected these walls. When the universal coven descended, *this* was the only safe place in which to shelter.'

'What about the others? You left them to die.'

'I couldn't save them,' Holmwood snapped. Then, in a quieter voice, 'There was no time . . . I heard their screams, Jake. I heard . . . '

The old doctor sat down on the corner of a dustsheet-covered desk.

'Whatever you think of me, you must listen to what I have to say.' Lemon-coloured lips dragged at the cigarette. 'The Elders of Hobarron have existed for over three hundred years, but I tell you now, we have *never* faced an enemy like this. The most evil being in creation—the father of all demons—now exists in the body of a powerful sorcerer. Unless he is stopped, he *will* use the combined magic of this universal coven to open a second Door into the demon dimension. There is only one person now who can stand against him—you.'

'But you said yourself, my powers are weak.'

'You will find them again.'

'I can't. I've tried.'

'You haven't been looking in the right place.'

Holmwood opened a drawer in the desk. He reached inside and withdrew a glass ball that shimmered green in the torchlight. At the sight of the orb, voices rang in Jake's head: a cacophony of cries, both hideous and beautiful.

'You've seen something like this before.'

'My mum. She used a ball like that to ward off Tobias Quilp.'

'No. Go further back. Tell me what this is.'

Jake screwed up his eyes. Tried to remember. And then it hit him—he had seen the orb in his dreams of the Witchfinder . . .

'Josiah Hobarron's witch ball.'

'Exactly!' Holmwood gave a serpentine grin. 'In some of the old stories and legends of the Witchfinder *this* was the source of Josiah's powers. Other tales tell of different objects—chalices and swords—but most agree that the witch ball at least inspired his magic. It gave fuel to the fire of his sorcery.'

'But Quilp said that the witch ball had been lost many years ago,' Jake argued.

'So it was. This is just a replica. We had many such orbs made for defence purposes. Your mother used hers on the night she was killed. The real witch ball hasn't been seen since Josiah Hobarron's death.'

'He lost it,' Jake said slowly. 'When the freezing spell he used on the Door backfired he tried to make it out of the cave. That was when he lost the witch ball. I saw it in my dreams—it rolled away into the shadows of Crowden's Sorrow.'

Holmwood leapt to his feet. 'Excellent. Then my plan will work.'

'What plan?'

'You know a lot about myths and legends, don't you, Jake? Then tell me—have you ever heard of the Khepra Beetle?'

'That's enough!'

Adam staggered into the laboratory. His face contorted

with fury, he pointed a shaking finger at his old boss.

'You will *not* use my son in this way, do you understand?'

'It's for the greater good, Adam.'

'That old excuse again! No, Gordon, I won't allow it. Come on, Jake, we're leaving.'

'But, Dad, listen—this might be the only way to stop the Demon Father and get to Quilp.'

'You don't know what you're talking about. Now, move!'

Jake stormed out of the room. Holmwood brushed past Adam, who shuffled along as best he could. Jake had reached the reception area when Holmwood caught up with him.

'Listen to me,' the doctor panted. 'Your father doesn't see the big picture. His love for you blinds his rational mind. If we are to have a chance against the Demon Father you *must* take the Scarab Path. You want to avenge yourself on Quilp? You want to find that powerful Oldcraft magic so that you can destroy him?'

'More than anything, but my dad . . .'

Adam's shadow loomed in the stairwell.

'Jake?' he called. 'Are you there?'

'Listen to that voice.' Holmwood grasped Jake's shirt and pulled him close. 'That is the voice of a dying man. How much longer has he got, eh? I know you've been searching for a cure. Well, hear this—the witch ball *is that cure*. You could use the phenomenal magic contained in the orb to make your father well again! You could use its power to torture Quilp in a thousand different ways! All you ever wanted can be yours, but only if you take the Scarab Path. I'll be waiting for your call.' Holmwood glanced over his shoulder.

Frail and grey, Adam staggered up the last few steps. 'Better not leave it too late, Jacob.'

'What is the Khepra Beetle?' Jake demanded. 'What's the Scarab Path?'

Adam banged down his fist on the desk.

'Suicide. That's what it is.'

By the time they had returned from the Institute it was early afternoon and the monstrous guests of the Grimoire Club were stirring. Razor, the Cynocephalus doorman, had hurried them down the corridor and into the safety of their apartment. After saying goodbye to Eddie Rice, neither Rachel nor the Harkers had spoken a word on the way home. Still wrapped up in their own thoughts, they had entered the lounge.

Simon, who had been sitting on the sofa nursing his scorched ribs, shot to his feet. He and Jake exchanged glances. It seemed to take a lot of effort for Simon to look at Rachel, and he soon lowered his gaze again.

'Hello,' he murmured. 'I-I just wanted to say: last night, I . . .'

Jake hadn't wanted to hear it. He had followed his father into the study and slammed the door behind them. That was when the argument started.

'That's not an answer!' Jake exploded. 'Dr Holmwood said that only Josiah's witch ball can defeat the Demon Father. To get it we need to use the Khepra Beetle.'

'Holmwood's wrong. In any case, the beetle is highly

dangerous. I know of only one case in which it's been used successfully. And even then, the man who took the Scarab Path came back changed. Horribly changed.'

'What do you mean?'

Adam dropped into the chair behind the desk.

'Jake, the Khepra Beetle is old, old magic. Powerful beyond anything known to Man. It goes back to ancient times—before the Romans and the Greeks, perhaps even before the Egyptians themselves.'

'Khepra,' Jake mused. 'I thought I'd heard that name before. Wasn't he a god or something?'

'An Egyptian sun god,' Adam confirmed. 'He was a deity of resurrection and renewal. As the bringer of the new day, he has seen every dawn since the birth of the world. It is said that Khepra controls the very corridors of Time.'

Dimly, Jake began to see the shape of Dr Holmwood's plan. He leaned over the desk and locked eyes with his father.

'It's worth a try.'

'You don't understand. This thing . . . Some legends say that only the Never Seen have the skill to use it properly; that in truth it comes from their celestial halls, and was crafted long before the time of the ancient Egyptians. Perhaps before Time itself had fully unfurled throughout the galaxy . . . Jake?'

At his father's words, a sudden darkness had clouded Jake's mind. He thought he was going to faint, but managed to stumble to a chair. He heard Adam moving about and felt a glass of water press against his lips.

'Drink.'

Jake took several choking gulps.

'I'm all right,' he spluttered. 'It's just the heat.'

Adam fell back into his chair.

'The beetle is not an option, Jake. End of story.'

'If it helps me get the witch ball—'

'I said "no".'

'So I'm just supposed to sit back and let Quilp go free? That *thing* murdered my mum—*your wife*!'

'And you want to kill him, do you? You think that will make you feel better?'

'When he was in the cells, when he was being tortured by the Elders, I didn't have to think about him,' Jake said quietly. 'He was paying for his crime, getting what he deserved. Justice.'

'Torture isn't justice, Jake; you know that.'

The truth of his father's words stung Jake. 'I'm going after him whether you like it or not,' he said. 'And I'm going to make him suffer, just like Mum suffered.'

Adam sighed and shook his head. 'When you grow up, you'll understand that revenge is *never* the answer. It just brings more pain, more heartache.'

'When I grow up? I'm sixteen years old!'

'Yes. Just a child.'

'I've saved the world! I stood against Marcus Crowden and I beat him. Could a child have done that?'

Adam didn't answer.

'So what *are* we going to do, eh?' Jake continued. 'Wait around for the Demon Father to pick us off, one by one?

Wait until he has opened another Door and demonkind has enslaved the planet?'

'I'm working on it,' Adam murmured. 'I just need more time.'

'You haven't got any more time, Dad,' Jake blurted out. 'You're dying!'

Long seconds of painful silence followed.

'Who told you?' Adam rasped.

'Isn't it obvious?' Jake said, not wanting to betray Pandora's trust. 'Tell me honestly——how much longer have you got?'

'A few weeks. Maybe less.' The answer came without hesitation. 'And I don't want to spend the time I have left mourning my son.'

'The witch ball could save you. I could bring it back. I could——'

'You just told me you're not a child.' Adam held his son's gaze. 'But children never want to let go. They hold on with all their might to the things they love and refuse to face what can't be changed. If you want be a man, Jake, if you truly want to grow up, you need to understand that sometimes the bravest thing you can do is to say goodbye.'

'No.' Jake fought back the tears. 'No, I won't ever say goodbye to you, Dad. Not ever.'

Chapter 14
The Scarab Path

His father's plea for him not to meddle with the Khepra Beetle had shaken Jake's determination. Before he decided what he was going to do, he wanted to talk it over with a friend. There was no sign of Pandora in the apartment and so, reluctantly, he went in search of Rachel. Usually she would be the first person he would go to but, after her encounter with Dr Saxby that morning, Jake had figured that she needed some time alone. Well, he wouldn't intrude for too long.

He was at her bedroom door when the voices brought him up short.

'I heard her again last night. My mother. She spoke to me in my sleep, she said that I would be punished. Why would she want to punish her own son, unless I *had* killed her?'

It was Simon, talking like a lost child.

'They were just dreams. They can't hurt you, Simon.'

'I killed her, Rachel. I know it. And last night I almost killed you.'

'It was just a scratch. Nothing.'

'If Jake hadn't been there . . . '

'You wouldn't have hurt me. Not seriously. You couldn't.'

'Couldn't I? The human half of me is weak, but the demon half is strong. Master Crowden was right: he called me "evil incarnate".'

'Simon, listen to me—this whole thing—the story about your mother's death, your childhood, your demon half: none of it makes sense.'

'What do you mean?'

'Your past, it's like a story. A fairytale. It isn't true.'

'But you've seen what I am. The monster.'

'But I don't *believe* in that monster. Something about it isn't real. Look, I don't really know how to explain what I mean, but I know this—you're a good person, Simon.'

'No. There's no good in me. Just violence and hate.'

'I don't believe that. I know you. I . . . '

Jake pushed against the door. It swung silently open. Two figures were sitting on the bed, hands touching, eyes locked.

'I love you.'

Their lips met, and Jake felt the world darken around him. The sting of his best friend's betrayal poisoned his thoughts. He began to see the history of the past few weeks in a twisted new light: all that time Rachel and Simon had spent alone together, practising 'control techniques'; all those little chats Jake had shared with his best friend, in which the back-stabber had played the part of older brother dispensing wisdom. Jake remembered that conversation on the roof ter-race, the day after Simon's rescue:

'*I've been thinking of asking her out. You know—on a date.*'

'*You should . . . She's a great girl.*'

Now the betrayer, the Judas, opened his eyes and saw Jake watching them.

A dark blue light tingled at the tips of Jake's fingers. It was all he could do not to hurl the hex. Rachel followed Simon's gaze—

'Oh, no. Jake, please wait. Listen—'

But Jake didn't want to listen.

He ran.

Ran along the empty corridor of the Grimoire Club. Burst through the open door and into blazing sunlight. Tore across the desert-dusted square and into the coolness beneath the columns.

He had not heard any following footsteps, but as he reached the teardrop doorway a hand grasped his shoulder.

Magic crackled in his fist. He spun round.

Simon looked at the flaming hex and stepped back, arms spread wide.

'If it will make you feel better.'

Jake stared through a haze of tears. The flame roared. Why not do it? Why not share with his 'friend' a little of the hurt *he* felt? Jake thrust out his hand . . .

And then he caught sight of the fountain that stood in the square. The fountain shaped like a silver chalice, dazzling in the sunlight. The sound of water whispered in his ear and the hex vanished from Jake's fingers.

'You love her?'

'I didn't know how to tell you.'

'And she feels the same way.' Jake's voice cracked as the kiss replayed in his mind. 'Yeah, right, course she does.'

Simon reached for him, but Jake stepped back.

'Mate, honestly, I didn't mean to hurt you. You've been like a brother to me, I just—'

'Doesn't matter about me. But if you ever hurt her, *monster*—' Jake's lip curled over the word, 'I'll come back and I'll hunt you down. Do you understand? I won't show you any mercy.'

'You won't need to.' Simon bowed his head. 'If I ever hurt her, I would kill myself in the next breath.'

Jake gave a curt nod and turned back to the doorway.

'Please, Jake, can't we talk? You're breaking my heart. Can't we just—'

'No. Goodbye, Simon.'

With that, Jake threw himself into the darkness.

'He's just left the Grimoire. He's coming to you, I know it. Please, Gordon, *don't* put him on the Scarab Path. He's hurt, confused, angry; he doesn't know what he's doing. For the sake of all those years we worked together, I'm asking you— *begging* you—don't do this. He's my boy. My son.'

'He is *not* your son, Adam. He is, and always has been, the property of the Hobarron Institute.' Dr Holmwood breathed cigarette smoke down the phone. 'It was my money that gave you the resources to create him, and now I'm cashing in my investment.'

A pause, filled only with the crackle of static.

'What are you saying?' Adam murmured. 'He's just a boy. A human being.'

'He is an experiment, and a very successful one. "Jacob Harker" is just a label. This child is the "Hobarron Weapon", and it is time that weapon was used again. Last night I waded through the blood of my friends and colleagues, Adam. I saw with my own eyes the power of this Demon Father. Whatever the cost, he *must* be stopped.'

'Gordon, no—!'

Dr Holmwood put down the receiver and reached into his desk drawer. He took the amulet from its hiding place.

'Hello, my little friend,' he whispered. 'Are you ready to work your wonders?'

The heavy metal door slammed shut behind Jake. He found himself blinking in the halogen glare of a state-of-the-art laboratory. Before his eyes fully adjusted to the light, he saw the lean shadow of Dr Holmwood bearing down on him.

'Welcome, Jacob. I'm so glad you've come.'

Jake managed a tight smile. He was already questioning the wisdom of coming back to the Hobarron Institute. After fleeing from his father and his 'friends', Jake had wasted no time in calling Dr Holmwood. A long black limousine (not unlike a hearse, Jake had thought grimly) had been sent to collect him. Now here he was, standing in one of the few unscathed buildings at the edges of the Institute's property, ready to trust a man who only a few weeks ago had wanted to use him as a human sacrifice. Jake reckoned he must be losing his mind, but he supposed that this was the nature of war: to destroy enemies like Tobias Quilp you sometimes had to make difficult alliances. Deals with the devil, you might say.

Jake took a quick glance around. A bank of whirring computers occupied one wall while, at the far end of the room, a sterile area like a surgical theatre had been set up.

'After your visit this morning, I was called to Downing Street,' Dr Holmwood said, leading the way across the lab. 'The new Prime Minister has cut all remaining ties with the Elders and has advised her fellow world leaders to do the same.'

'But she must know that demons destroyed the tower.'

'Cynthia Croft flatly refuses to believe in such things.'

They reached the surgery area. Holmwood banged his fists against a metal operating table.

'With a stroke of her pen, she has taken away the Institute's power and influence. Now our only hope rests with you, Jake. Are you prepared to journey on the Scarab Path?'

'If it leads me to the witch ball, yes.'

'Good.'

Holmwood reached out a closed fist to Jake. Slowly, reverently, he opened his hand.

'This is the Khepra Beetle,' he said, a touch of awe in his voice. 'The key to the Scarab Path.'

Jake wasn't sure what he had expected, but the amulet in Holmwood's palm was something of a disappointment. The highly-polished blue and black stone was roughly the size of a matchbox. On closer examination, Jake saw that it had been crudely painted to resemble a dung beetle.

'Not much to look at, is it?' Holmwood echoed Jake's thoughts. 'Just a piece of soapstone with a few hieroglyphs daubed on the back. But do not be fooled. This seemingly innocuous talisman contains magic of phenomenal power.'

'My dad said it was named after an Egyptian god.'

'Some stories say that this little stone contains the very soul of the old sun god himself,' Holmwood nodded. 'But in truth, no one really knows what the beetle is or where it came from. All that is certain is that it is both wonderful and dangerous.'

'My dad said he knew a man who'd used it. That he'd come back "changed".'

'Fletcher Clerval.' Holmwood grimaced. 'An old friend of Adam's. Fletcher had some minor magical gifts which he thought might be enough to sustain him on the Scarab Path. He survived the experience, but only just. His is a sad tale.'

In other circumstances, Jake would have insisted on hearing the story, but his furious desire to get his hands on the witch ball made him impatient.

'Save it for another day. I want to know how this thing can help me find Josiah's witch ball.'

Holmwood looked relieved. 'Then lie down.'

There was a moment's hesitation—a second during which, once again, Jake questioned the wisdom of trusting Holmwood. But what did he have to lose? His best friend had betrayed him; the girl he cared for wasn't interested in him; his father was dying before his eyes; and Quilp and the Demon Father were free to work their evil. He had to do this.

He jumped up onto the table.

Before he had a chance to react, metal clamps locked around his wrists and ankles.

'What's going on?'

'Stay calm, the restraints are for your own protection. We don't want you wriggling off the table when the pain begins, do we?'

Holmwood placed the amulet on Jake's chest.

'What pain?'

'Travelling on the Scarab Path is a somewhat *rigorous* business. Even if it is done correctly, the physical trials can be extreme, and the human body is so very fragile. Now, you must listen carefully to what I am about to say . . . '

Holmwood touched the amulet with his forefinger.

'You must prepare your mind.'

He tapped the talisman again . . .

'You must concentrate.'

. . . and again.

'It is such a dangerous form of magic.'

Tap

'Time travel.'

The amulet flinched.

Twitched.

Shivered.

With a sound like the snap of little bones, a series of egg-shell cracks appeared across the back of the painted beetle. Fragments of delicate stone fell away as, piece by piece, the thing beneath the shell revealed itself. Jake caught glimpses of the creature's hard black body shining dully in the light. Six tiny legs broke free of the soapstone casing and tickled Jake's chest. The last crumb of stone fell away and a small, hideous head, horned with a pair of quivering antennae, emerged. The beetle turned its empty eyes on Jake.

'Quickly now,' Holmwood hissed. 'Focus your mind on the witch ball.'

With his mouth clamped shut, Jake could not speak. He felt the beetle climb along his neck, scurry over his chin and brush across his lips. A moan of disgust purred at the back of his throat.

'Visualize the ball falling from Josiah's neck,' Holmwood continued. 'See it hitting the floor and rolling into the shadows. Picture when and where it was lost: the thirteenth of June 1645; the town of Hobarron's Hollow, then called St Meredith-by-the-Sea; the cavern that came to be known as Crowden's Sorrow. Picture yourself in the cave moments after the ball vanished. You will find it waiting for you there, in the darkness.'

The insect used its front legs to clean its mandibles— those pincer-like jaws that sat at the front of its head. Then, to Jake's utter horror, it started to force its way into his left nostril.

'What's happening to me?' he screamed.

The beetle squeezed along his nasal cavity. With a strange popping sound that echoed inside the chamber of his head, Jake felt it move into the space behind his eyes. Little legs danced across his optic nerves. He heard the thrum of the insect's movements and screamed again.

'The beetle is burrowing into your head,' Holmwood said in a matter-of-fact tone. 'Soon it will find a seat for itself between the right and left hemispheres of your brain. Its pincers will dig into your brain tissue and it will feed upon the emotional energy that is flooding through your mind. All your thoughts must be focused on the witch ball. The beetle's magic will take you to it.'

It was almost as if the beetle was following Holmwood's instructions. Jake sensed it using the optic stalk as a kind of bridge to his brain.

'I can't!' Jake shrieked. 'I can't think . . . It hurts!'

'Focus!' Holmwood insisted. 'If the beetle picks up on fragmented thoughts then it will transport your body in a *fragmented* way. Parts of you will be taken to one place and time, other parts will end up elsewhere. You could be torn to pieces!'

'Is that what happened to Fletcher Clerval?' Jake cried. 'He came back *changed*.'

'No questions. Concentrate on the witch ball.'

It was too late to argue. Jake had to follow Holmwood's instructions. He could feel the Khepra Beetle creeping around his skull. It reached the spinal link at the back of his brain and burrowed its way up to his visual cortex—that place in the brain where all sight-memory is stored. The hard black body pressed into the warm, wet tissue.

Pincers hooked into Jake's brain.

The Khepra Beetle started to feed.

Pain seared through Jake's body. His fists clenched, his

teeth snapped together, and the heels of his feet rattled against the metal table. A voice called out to him, but next to the roar of agony it was no more than a whisper—

'The witch ball . . .'

At those words, the image of the green glass ball flashed into Jake's mind. Responding, an orb of magic sparked in his hand. The ferocity of the spell seared through the metal clamps. Deep inside, Jake could hear the beetle chirrup with excitement. Another stab of pain, this time outside his head.

Holmwood cried out, 'You *must* focus your thoughts or you will be ripped apart!'

'*Aaarrrrghhhh!*'

Agony lanced into Jake's right shoulder. It felt as if his arm was being wrenched out of its socket. He could not ignore the pain, and that made it difficult to narrow his thoughts onto the witch ball. Every time he tried to summon an image of the orb other pictures would flash into his mind—his father, sick and dying; Quilp working the hex that had killed his mum; Pandora and Brag fighting at his side; the demon Door with its glowing symbols; the silver fountain in the middle of the square; Razor, dog-headed doorman of the Grimoire Club; the triumphant face of Marcus Crowden, or was it the Demon Father? Simon and Rachel, wrapped in each other's arms . . .

And then another image flashed into his mind. Not the witch ball, but a face. *Her* face: cornflower blue eyes, golden hair . . .

Blue light roared around Jake's body. The magic spread out and enveloped him in a crackling blanket.

'Can you hear me?' Holmwood shouted, his back pressed against the wall. 'Keep focusing. When you've got your hands on the witch ball the beetle should recognize that you're ready to come home. All you have to do is think of *this* time, *this* place, do you understand? As long as it doesn't sense that you're in mortal danger, the beetle will remain inside your head. It's your only way back . . . '

The bellow of magic drowned out the doctor's words.

The Khepra Beetle locked on to the single strongest image in Jake's mind. The mysterious girl with the blue eyes. It sent out its temporal feelers and tried to locate her in the great expanse of time and space. Then, using Jake's own well of hidden magic, it opened a portal into history.

The Scarab Path.

The invisible gateway crackled above Jake's body. Through it, he caught a glimpse of a town square hemmed in by old-fashioned, timber-framed buildings. Horses rubbed shoulders beside what looked like a tavern. Crows pecked at the hard earth while a pack of dogs raced across the marketplace.

The Khepra Beetle clicked happily, and Jake disappeared into thin air.

Chapter 15
The Burning Boy

'Jake was right all along!' Adam spat out the words. 'He warned me not to get involved with the Institute again, but I didn't listen, and now he's paid the price for my mistake. So tell me honestly, Gordon, did he survive the Scarab Path?'

Dr Holmwood took a pack of cigarettes from his jacket pocket and lit up.

'I believe so. It was a wondrous sight.'

Adam's face twitched with anger.

'I don't understand,' Rachel said, 'what's happened to Jake?'

They were all crowded into the study at the Grimoire Club. Brag Badderson lurked by the door, his head bowed so that he could clear the ceiling. Rachel and Simon sat together in one corner while Pandora stood behind Adam, a look of fury on her beautiful face. Holmwood had arrived a few minutes ago to a decidedly frosty reception.

'Do you want to explain or shall I?' Adam didn't wait for an answer. 'Our good friend Dr Holmwood here has come to tell us that he has killed my son.'

Simon's head snapped in Holmwood's direction and a deep growl rolled through his lips.

'Keep your temper, Mr Lydgate,' Holmwood instructed. 'I haven't killed anyone. I've just sent Jake on a little trip.'

'He's as good as dead,' Adam said. 'You see, Dr Holmwood has sent Jake in search of Josiah Hobarron's witch ball. To be sure of finding it, Jake has travelled back to the year 1645.'

'What?'

'Don't fret, Miss Saxby. As soon as Jake finds the witch ball he'll return, safe and sound.'

'*If* he finds the witch ball,' Adam corrected. 'The Khepra Beetle will only return him once he has achieved whatever mission was in his mind when he was transported.'

'I don't understand any of this,' Simon said. 'Why has Jake gone looking for this thing?'

'Because it contains magic powerful enough to destroy the Demon Father,' Holmwood said. 'Without such sorcery we cannot hope to stand against him.'

'I told Jake it was too dangerous.' Adam collapsed into his chair. 'He wouldn't listen. He was too upset.'

Simon and Rachel exchanged guilty glances.

'Once he finds the witch ball, all will be well.' Holmwood sucked his cigarette down to the stub. 'I'm sure that he is hunting through the cavern as we speak.'

'Well, there's only one way to find out.'

Adam shot to his feet and started rummaging through the bookshelves behind the desk. Over the last two weeks, he had arranged for his library of occult books to be transferred from the Harker house in New Town to the Grimoire Club. After ten minutes of searching, Adam let out a relieved sigh and pulled an immense leather-bound volume from the shelves. Thousands of pages thick, it landed on the desk with a heavy thump. Holmwood stared at the golden symbol on the cover—a dragon swallowing its tail—and his eyes widened with surprise.

'It can't be!'

'It is.' Adam couldn't hide the delight in his voice. 'The *Codex Tempus*. The *Book of Time*.'

'But a genuine codex would be worth millions!'

'Not if you know the right people.' Adam nodded towards Pandora.

'What's a Todex Cempus?' Brag said, brow knitted.

'*Codex Tempus*,' Holmwood corrected.

'I was asking Dr Harker, not you, old man.'

Adam managed a wry smile. 'The *Codex* is a living history of temporal wanderers.' The troll's frown deepened. 'Time travellers, Brag. Anyone who has, or is, existing outside their own time-frame will have their adventures recorded within these pages.'

'But that book was written *before* Jake went back in time,' Simon objected. 'How can it tell his story?'

'I told you—it's a *living history*. The *Codex Tempus* was created by a monk, Brother William the Recluse, in the thirteenth century. He was one of the Benedictine brotherhood, the so-called black monks. These brothers were a strict order:

they fasted, wore shirts made of coarse material, and very often spent years in solitary confinement. The story goes that, after decades of isolation, William went stark staring mad. He told his brothers that a demon had come to him in a vision. This creature had offered William the power to see all of Time and Space.'

'What was the catch?' Simon asked.

'No catch. No price. No favour. The power was his, free of charge.'

'Why would a demon be that generous?'

'Because it wanted to destroy the monk's mind. And once William accepted the gift, his fate was sealed. The demon opened William's eyes to the endless and unloving march of Time, and his fragile human mind broke under the weight of it. Believing that he was possessed, the other monks dragged William to Prior Tybalt, the head of their monastery. Once in Tybalt's presence, William started babbling about the secrets of ancient civilizations and the technological wonders that were to come. The Prior saw terror in the eyes of his monks. If such blasphemous talk went unchecked it would set a bad example to the brethren. And so he decided on the ultimate punishment: Brother William would be walled up alive.'

A gasp from Rachel did not interrupt Adam's flow.

'The monks threw William into a tiny cavity in the monastery's outer wall and, brick by brick, sealed him inside. His screams could be heard for days afterwards. When they finally stopped, the monks reported a strange scratching sound coming from behind the wall. Some of them later confessed that William had begged for a book of blank vellum pages, a bottle of ink, and a quill to be buried with him, and that they had agreed to this last request.

'Centuries passed. In the reign of Henry VIII, the monastery was dissolved and the walls were knocked down. Behind one such wall, the king's commissioners made a grisly discovery: the skeleton of a man dressed in a tattered black habit. Lying at his feet was a great book, its pages filled with strange predictions.' Adam laid a hand on the cracked leather cover. 'This is the tome of William Reclusus. His *Book of Time*. His *Codex Tempus*. And the strangest part of the story is, he is *still* writing it.'

'But he's been dead for centuries!'

'William lives within these pages. I believe that, through the horror of his death, his conscious mind became imprinted in the book. He still sees all of Time and those that wander in it. He tells their stories here.'

Adam flipped to the back of the *Codex*. Simon and Rachel joined Dr Holmwood and Pandora at the desk. They watched Adam's finger move down an index of names.

'He's here!' Adam's finger trembled as it traced:

'HARKER, Jacob Josiah—travelled to 26th August, Anno Domini 1645—arrived in the town of Cravenmouth, Englande. Entry at page 1153.'

'That's not right!' Holmwood blurted. 'The date, the place. He's supposed to be in Hobarron's Hollow!'

'I told you,' Adam snarled. 'Time travel is dangerous, unpredictable magic. I just hope Jake's OK, for your sake.'

Adam turned to Jake's entry in the *Codex*. The page was blank.

'Does that mean he didn't make it?' Rachel asked in a panicked voice. 'I don't under—'

The sound of a phantom quill scratching against parchment rustled in the air. Letters, small and neat, started to appear on the page:

'This is the storie of a traveller in TIME.

In the yeare of our Lord 1645, Jacob Josiah Harker, as he was known to mortal men, did arrive in a place called Cravenmouth, a most godly towne on the east coast of Englande . . . '

The laboratory disappeared and Jake found himself in a realm of utter darkness. With no ground beneath him, he floated through the freezing void. His skin prickled into gooseflesh and ice crystals crackled in his hair. He lifted his hands to his eyes—not even a smudge of flesh to texture the nightscape. He tried to call out. The sound left his lips and vanished, as if an unseen hand had reached out and snatched it away.

Time slipped by. Would he remain here for ever? Jake wondered. Was that the price of his muddled thoughts?

Pain returned, bright and brilliant. As the magical blue flame reignited around his body, Jake saw a tear open up in the curtain of darkness. Wind blasted his face. Light flooded his eyes. Jake stumbled forward and the opening sealed up behind him.

The Burning Boy

He saw colours, shapes, shadows: sunlight on dusty ground; horses' hooves pawing at the earth; the panicked flight of a bird. Commotion everywhere: running feet, barking dogs, shouts and curses, oaths and prayers. Through the haze of magical fire that engulfed him, Jake saw that he was standing in the town square that he had glimpsed through the portal.

The people fled. They tore into the side streets that ran away from the heart of the square like narrow arteries. Gripped by his own sense of panic, Jake's gaze swept around a circle of white-washed, timber-framed buildings. Tall and short, lean and dumpy, they seemed to have been stacked together like a ring of irregular dominos. A brick-built structure raised on four huge pillars dominated one whole side of the square. **SHIRE HALL** had been carved in big letters in the stone lintel above the door. The grand arched windows and the wide flight of steps that led up to the door marked the hall as a place of importance.

Rubbing shoulders with the hall was an altogether different building—a crooked, tottering pile, three-storeys high and caked in soot and grime. At every window astonished faces pressed against the glass, their eyes fixed on Jake. Above the door, a badly-painted sign creaked in the breeze: *THE GREEN MAN TAVERN.*

Literally a stone's throw from the tavern stood the town pillory. A boy about the same age as Jake had been locked into the wooden T, leaves of rotten cabbage tangled in his long hair. Terrified, the boy turned his head away from Jake and whimpered.

Jake's gaze switched to the small group of men and women who had remained in the square. A dozen or so in number, they had gathered around the door of a rickety wooden hut. Another sign: *Martin MONKS, sergeant-at-mace—Traders' goods to be Weighed Here on Market Daye*. Jake heard their frightened talk over the roar of the flames.

'What is it?' a woman cried. 'What horror has gathered here?'

She took another look at Jake and hid her grimy face in the folds of a bloodstained apron. A grizzled man with white dust in his hair grasped the collar of the boy standing next to him.

'It's a sign, Caleb, my son! An omen of the Last Days. An angel draped in vestments of fire has come to the town of Cravenmouth to proclaim to all: repent, ye wicked sinners, repent!'

The boy wiped hands down his flour-dusted shirt. Bakers, Jake thought, and that woman must be some kind of butcher.

'An angel perhaps, father,' the boy said. 'But might it not be a witch come amongst us?'

'Angel or witch, the message of the creature stands. He brings Armageddon in his wake. See, he burns ever brighter!'

Pain seared through Jake and the magical fire swelled around him. In an attempt to rid himself of it, he drew the magic inwards, focused it into his hands, and released it. Balls of light shot across the square. One crashed through the arched window of the Shire Hall; a second hit the roof of the barber's shop and began to smoulder in the thatch; the third bowled towards the little group of onlookers. A collective scream rose up and they scattered like ninepins. A second later, the fireball smashed into the wooden hut, reducing it to charred kindling.

Jake threw back his head, opened his mouth, and bellowed. He felt the last lash of magic strike out from that hidden place deep inside. It spouted from his throat in a column of liquid fire that soared overhead, breaking apart the low-hanging clouds and piercing a path into the sky. A whirlwind erupted from the column and skirled around the square. It caught at the embers in the thatched roof of the barber's shop and whipped them into flames. It shrieked through the window of the Shire Hall and set the fire dancing within.

At last, Jake felt the magic splutter out like an exhausted candle. His mouth snapped shut and the column collapsed. The infernos on the roof of the barber shop and inside the Shire Hall disappeared. Falling to his knees, Jake heard the Khepra Beetle click contentedly inside his head.

Slowly, the people of Cravenmouth returned to the square. At the front of the crowd were the father and son bakers, the woman with the bloody apron, and a well-dressed man in his thirties with sharp green eyes and an air of authority.

'Is it safe?' the woman asked. 'No, don't go near!'

'Hush, Mary Dower. There is no more fire, no more hellwind. The witch has spent all its dark magic.'

'Do not be so sure, Caleb, such things have wiles.'

'It has taken on the guise of a boy!' the elder baker cried. 'See what fair skin he has, what strange clothes.'

The well-dressed man, clad in immaculate black doublet and breeches, came forward. His intelligent green eyes examined Jake before flitting back to the crowd.

'Keep your distance, good people,' he said, his voice calm. 'Witch or no, let the sergeant-at-mace and the constable go to their work. Gentlemen, see now to your charge.'

Jake looked up at the crowd that closed in around him. Fear and excitement mingled in their faces, and something else, too. Hatred. The immediate and uncomplicated loathing for something mysterious and unknown. Only the well-dressed man had any kindness in his eyes. Jake held out his hand—a gesture of reassurance.

'He's ready to strike again!' Mary Dower shrieked. 'Stay well back, friends! He will blast us all with his unholy fire!'

Jake's words came in dry splutters:

'No . . . I . . . w-won't hurt you . . . Please . . . '

'The witch lies! Quickly, Mr Monks, silence its tongue!'

His fellow townsmen bundled the sergeant to the front of the crowd. Full of nervous bluster, Martin Monks slapped away the urging hands. He was a plump man of about forty years of age, his fleshy, clean-shaven face framed by shoulder-length white hair. Monks's hand went to the brace of weapons belted around his stomach. He selected a rusty wheel-lock pistol.

'NO!' Jake shouted. 'Wait . . . '

Mr Monks did not wait. He loaded powder charge and ball, took an uncertain step forward and raised the pistol. With one piggy eye screwed shut, he sighted his target down the barrel.

Sensing the impending death of its host, the Khepra Beetle loosened its grip on Jake's brain.

'NO!'—not Jake's voice this time. The well-dressed man's. But he was too late.

Sergeant Monks pulled the trigger and the thunder-crack of the pistol echoed around the square.

Chapter 16
Trapped in Time

Martin Monks, sergeant-at-mace, fired the pistol . . .

The phantom quill scratched to a stop. Ink spluttered across the page.

All eyes turned to Adam Harker.

'What's happened?' Rachel asked in a stricken voice. 'Why's it stopped?'

Adam tore through the next twenty or so pages of the *Codex Tempus*. They were all blank. He turned back to that last sentence.

'Does it mean . . . ?' Simon had to squeeze the words from a reluctant tongue. 'Is Jake dead?'

Guilt clutched at Simon's heart. *His* actions had set Jake on this deadly road into the past. He should have handled the situation better; explained to Jake that he had never meant to fall in love with Rachel.

'The *Codex* contains many ongoing stories, but it has only

one author,' Adam said. 'It's possible that the consciousness of William Reclusus has moved on to a different tale. If . . . if there is more of Jake's story to tell, then he will return.'

'But when?' Rachel asked.

'Minutes, hours, days. There's just no telling, I'm afraid.'

Rachel buried her face against Simon's chest. For a long time, the people in the study stayed where they were, frozen like figures in a game of musical statues. Adam stared at the empty pages of the *Codex*. Dr Holmwood made a steeple of his fingers and clicked his yellow tongue against the roof of his mouth. Pandora stood at the door whispering to Brag, filling in those parts of the story the troll had not understood.

Meanwhile, guilt continued to gnaw at Simon. He should have chased after Jake, caught him in Yaga Passage and *made* him listen. Hell, knowing the pain his friend was in, Simon should have foreseen that he was about to do something stupid. He was stronger than Jake: he could have wrestled him to the ground and dragged him back to his father. Jake would have fought him all the way, and might never have forgiven him, but at least he would now be safe. Yet again, Simon felt that he had betrayed his best friend.

From the bleakest shadows in Simon's mind, a shapeless hand reached out . . .

Betray . . .

He looked around the study. No one else seemed to have heard the voice. Probably just his imagination. He had almost convinced himself of this when the voice called out again:

Hear me, my son. The time has come. This is the knowledge you have waited for. Now, remember the lesson I taught you . . .

Simon blinked. The room seemed to darken around him. Shadows stole along the walls and the hard edges of the study softened, blurred, and faded. Simon was about to say something when his mouth clamped shut and his throat tightened. The weight of Rachel's head against his chest disappeared. The walls of the study disintegrated into wisps of smoke that billowed and swirled before reforming into a new configuration.

The bedchamber at Havlock Grange. The room that had been his prison for over a month. Simon found himself huddled in his corner behind the curtain, watching the shifting glow of candlelight play across the drape. Footsteps creaked on the rotten floorboards. They came closer, closer. Like a terrified child, Simon watched through his fingers as a gloved hand pulled back the curtain.

'My dear boy, it is time we talked.'

The Demon Father—*his* father—crouched down and Simon saw himself reflected in the creature's dark glasses.

'They will be coming for you soon, my son. Jacob Harker and his friends will battle their way through many dangers to rescue you. And rescue you they shall.' The flash of a victorious smile. 'I have seen to it that their triumph is assured.'

'Why?' Simon's voice, broken and timid.

'Because I want to see the boy conjuror tested. I must know his strengths and weaknesses before the final battle. And there is another reason . . . '

Simon flinched as the gloved hand stroked his cheek.

'I need to have my spy in place. In every war there is a crucial moment, a turning point at which the fate of the conflict may be decided. Often this time comes long before the first bullet is fired. You are to keep your eyes and ears open, my son. When the time is right your unconscious mind will know it. And then . . . '

The Demon Father removed his glasses. Simon scuttled back against the wall, tried to turn away, but could not help staring into the blood-heavy eyes of the monster.

'Then you will answer my call. You will give me the knowledge I seek. You will betray your friends.'

The walls of the prison bedchamber melted away and were replaced by the hard reality of the study.

No longer master of his will, Simon felt himself turning away from Rachel and heading for the door.

'Simon? Are you OK?' Rachel called after him.

'Sure. Need some air.'

'Do you want me to come with——?'

'No. Need some time alone.'

Still deep in conversation, Brag and Pandora parted to let him through. Simon closed the study door behind him and crossed the lounge with swift, robotic steps. He picked up the cordless phone. Little gears were turning in his mind, working the mechanism of a hidden memory. The digits flashed into his head and he dialled. After the third ring, the call was answered.

That soft, menacing, musical voice——

'Dutiful son, what have you learned?'

Simon hesitated. He felt the weight of words crowd into his mouth. It was all he could do to hold them back for a few precious seconds. He spied Adam's long-bladed scissors resting on the phone table—the ones the doctor used to cut articles out of psychology journals. Simon's hand was like a dead weight but he managed to fumble and grab hold of the scissors. He would have to be quick. As soon as he opened his mouth the words would come tumbling out in a treacherous flood.

'Speak, my son,' the voice hissed. 'Tell me what you know.'

He tried to drop the phone but it was as if the receiver was glued to his ear. He lifted the scissors to his mouth, felt the cool touch of steel against his lips. There would be pain soon. Horrible, burning, screaming pain. Blood would gush down his throat and he would spit the severed flesh from his mouth. He would never speak again, except in slow, slurping mumbles. It was a sacrifice he was willing to make, if it kept Jake and his friends safe.

'What are you doing, boy? Nothing silly, I trust. You cannot fight me.'

Simon shuddered. It was now or never. He put his thumb and finger into the eyes of the scissors and opened his mouth wide. He stuck out his tongue and slipped it between the shining blades. The wet, pink tip glistened in the light. Simon closed his eyes. Tensed his fingers. One quick, brutal snap, and it would be over. Just a little courage and . . .

'SPEAK!'

At the command, the scissors fell from Simon's hands and clattered to the floor. He felt the blades sting the side of his tongue, but the graze was superficial. It didn't even bleed. Words bustled behind Simon's lips and, like a desperate sinner confessing to a priest, he blurted out the secrets he knew.

He told the Demon Father how Jake had travelled back to 1645 in order to retrieve Josiah Hobarron's witch ball. With the magic contained in the ball, Jake hoped to cure Adam Harker and destroy Tobias Quilp and the Demon Father. But something had gone wrong, and Jake had overshot the time-frame by several months. He had arrived on 26th August 1645 in a town called Cravenmouth. Believing him to be a witch, the local sergeant may already have killed the boy.

A long pause greeted the end of the story.

'You have done well,' the sweet voice said at last. 'Soon we shall see each other again, my child. Farewell.'

Simon heard a click and then the drone of an empty line. He looked down at the scissors and wished with all his heart that he had managed to cut out his tongue.

'*Eleanor!*'

Jake gasped and surfaced out of the dream. A dream about an unknown girl that fractured around him and was quickly forgotten.

Feeble rays of sunlight touched Jake's face. He moaned softly and raised himself onto one arm. He was lying on a rough flagstone floor dusted with straw and peppered with rat droppings. There was no blanket beneath him and the straw did little to keep out the bone-aching chill of the stone. He had been stripped of his clothes and dressed in a long coarse shirt that smelt of the sewer.

A sharp pain throbbed in his jaw. His fingers traced the tender flesh that had erupted along the right side of his face, temple to jawbone. Hot to the touch, his skin was as taut as a drumhead. Gingerly, he touched the inside of his mouth with his tongue and probed the back teeth behind the worst of the swelling. The testing tip was too much for one molar and it popped straight out of the gum. Jake spat the tooth and a mouthful of blood onto the floor. Then, groaning, he leaned back and took in his surroundings.

The room was a freezing stone box with dripping, moss-coated walls. Within easy reach stood a squalid wooden bucket over which a cloud of flies and bluebottles droned. A narrow window and a door studded with iron nails completed the picture. Jake tried to think back. Where was he? How had he got here?

As if to remind him, the scarab clicked its legs. When it had sensed Jake's impending death, the Khepra Beetle had relaxed its grip, ready to leave its doomed host. The sergeant's gun *had* been fired; Jake remembered hearing the whip-crack report of the pistol. So why wasn't he now missing the best part of his head?

Jake's hand returned to his face. His fingers roamed along his jaw and to the back of his head. He explored each inch of skin, praying that he wouldn't find any serious damage. His prayers were not answered. Reaching the side of his head, Jake discovered that his right ear was gone—blown clean away by the shot. In its place was a small circular hole plugged with dry blood. And now Jake realized that the dull sensation at the side of his face was not just the result of swelling. He was partially deaf.

He tried his best not to panic. Magic, he thought. The

power of the Witchfinder would heal him. Afterwards he would use the raw Oldcraft to free himself from the cell. He held out his hand, his gaze concentrated on the bowl of his palm. As usual, he delved into those memories of pain and despair that had ignited the magic before. They came to him as clearly as ever, the first among them being his mother's murder at the hands of Tobias Quilp. That memory in particular nearly always provoked a magical response.

Not this time. Deep inside, where he had felt the glimmer of Oldcraft before, there was a dry emptiness. He swore and focused again on his mother's death . . . Nothing. It was as if the whirlwind of power that had come to him through the Scarab Path had exhausted the last of his magic. Not wanting to believe that this was true, Jake crawled across the cell and pressed his hands against the locked door.

Open, open, open, OPEN!

Not a flicker. Not a spark.

He soon gave up on magic and pushed and hammered, dug his nails into the jamb and tried to prise the door open. It didn't budge an inch.

Pain, fear, and confusion overwhelmed Jake. He returned to the back of the cell and slid down the wet, weeping wall. He clasped his hands around his knees and rocked back and forth. Separated by vast tracts of time from his father and his friends, he knew that he would die here. To the people of this town he was a dark sorcerer—an enemy to be thrown into a cell and left to rot. He would die as surely as his father would die centuries from now, both of them cursed by magic to leave this life before their time.

Jake looked around his little prison and felt despair clutch him in a cold embrace.

Time passed, each hour marked by the shaft of sunlight that crept across the floor. Occasionally, Jake would hear a hopeless scream or lunatic shriek echo out from some distant part of the prison. Despite these hellish cries, he felt despair begin to loosen its grip on his heart. He took strange comfort from the fact that the Khepra Beetle was still lodged inside his brain. The creature was obviously concerned with its own preservation and therefore sensed any threat to its host. As long as the beetle's pincers remained tucked into his grey matter, he had a fighting chance. All he had to do now was find a way out of this prison.

Jake staggered to his feet. He had already tried the door and so he looked to the window. The barred opening stood at the end of a narrow channel that sloped down into the cell. This channel met the wall at a point just level with Jake's shoulders. He managed to scramble up the wall and onto the slope, but holding his position was tricky. Twice he tumbled back, falling a metre and a half onto the hard stone floor. At the third attempt, he managed to brace his back and feet against the walls of the passage. Breathing hard, he whipped around so that his head was facing the window and his stomach was flat against the slope. Then, using his fingers and toes to find purchase, he inched his way along the channel. At last, he reached the bars and hauled himself up to the window.

The view made his heart sink.

Far below, he could see the huge green mound upon which his prison stood. To left and right, towers and battlements, barbican and bailey. From what he could make out, he was being held inside the keep of a great castle protected by a mighty wall and drawbridge. There was no escaping such a place.

Less than half a mile beyond the castle's dried-up moat, Jake could see the town of Cravenmouth. The large community was encircled by an ancient wall dominated by two gatehouses stationed at either end of the town. In the fields outside, hundreds of men, women, and children were at work, picking at the ground, bundling sheaves of corn, guiding the ploughshare over rutted earth.

Most of the labourers seemed to be in the fields, but a few were at work around the wall. Using primitive wooden cranes, they moved blocks of stone into position. Cannons and mounted guns stood on the turrets of the gatehouses, their barrels pointing down the road that led from the forest to the town. Jake suddenly remembered that he had arrived in an England in the throes of civil war. The forces of the King and Parliament were fighting for the right to rule. Like every other town in the country, Cravenmouth feared bloodshed and so was rebuilding its fortifications.

Footsteps. The jangle of keys. The grind of a lock.

Jake slid back down the channel and tumbled to the floor. A moment later, the cell door was flung open. They came at him in a rush—Sergeant Monks and three other men, their faces hard but their eyes betraying their fear. Before Jake could think about reacting, they had fallen on him. Monks pressed his boot into Jake's throat while the others busied themselves with ropes and shackles. His gaolers were artists in their trade, and within seconds he found himself chained to the wall of his prison.

Monks straightened up and wiped the sweat from his brow.

'Comfortable, I trust?'

Jake held out his hand. 'Please, I need to explai—'

'None of that!' Monks screeched, jumping back. 'Not unless you want that damned witch hand cut clean off.'

'But I'm not a witch.'

'Hear that, lads? Not a witch, says he! Well, you mayn't look like an evil old crone, but young men such as yourself are tried as witches every day in this godly realm.'

The other men laughed and spat on the ground, first to their left then their right.

'But I can explain if you'll just listen,' Jake pleaded.

'Oh, you've a smooth tongue, no doubt. Smooth as your master's, I'll be bound.'

'My master?'

'The arch fiend, Satan himself! That's who you serve with your black imps. No doubt you've been consorting with them already, inside the very walls of Rake Castle.' Monks's piggy eyes flickered around the walls, as if he suspected that Jake's demons might still be lurking somewhere in the brick-work. 'Well, you'll play with them no more now that you're fettered. We should've bound you hours since, I suppose, but my nerves were sore tested by your coming amongst us. And then what with the vicar lecturing me—'

'The vicar?' Jake thought back. 'The well-dressed man with green eyes.'

'That's him,' Monks confirmed. 'Mr Leonard Lanyon. You owe him your life. I was ready to shoot you down, but he knocked the pistol out of my hand. Only managed to graze the side of your head.'

'Graze? You blew my ear off!'

'You're still pretty enough, with your soft, clean skin.'

Jake's mind buzzed: this Leonard Lanyon had shown him mercy—perhaps he might be willing to help.

'I'd like to thank Mr Lanyon. Will you ask him if he'll see me?'

'I ain't your messenger boy!' Monks hawked phlegm into his throat and lobbed it into Jake's face. 'You may well be thankful to Mr Lanyon now, but I'd wager that by the end of the week you're cursing his name and wishing for the easy death my bullet might've granted.'

'What d'you mean?'

'Hear that, lads? He doesn't know!'

Another bout of laughing and spitting.

'Well, I did hear that witches had the All Seeing Eye,' Monks said, choking back his mirth. 'Don't you know what's a-coming, boy? Don't you know *who* is on his way this very hour, this very minute, to the fair town of Cravenmouth?'

Jake could only shake his head. Monks dared a step closer to his prisoner. He squatted down and levelled his eyes with Jake's.

'The vicar won't be able to save you this time. All that fine talk of execution without a trial being murder! Well, now

Mr Lanyon will have his trial. Oh yes, *he* has been sent for, you see? All the town burgesses agreed and Richard Rake, Earl of Cravenmouth, put his seal on the letter. Now he is coming, and his tread upon the road is the certain sound of doom.'

Jake's tongue felt like a strap of dry leather in his mouth. 'Who's coming?'

Monks ushered the other men out of the cell. Then turned and leered at Jake.

'Matthew Hopkins is the name.'

Jake's eyes widened. His skin puckered and his blood ran cold.

'Say your prayers, boy, for the Witchfinder General has you in his sights.'

Chapter 17
Demonic Deception

Looking out from the rooftop balcony of the Grimoire Club, Rachel watched the blood-red sun slip behind the sand dunes. On cue, the twin moons of the borderlands appeared in the violet sky. When she had first arrived here, Rachel had been uneasy with the strangeness of this place. Everything had combined to unsettle her: foreign skies and unending deserts, ghostly managers and dog-headed doormen, monsters around every corner. Only Jake and Simon had steadied her. They had been her anchors to the real world, but now one of those anchors had gone and she felt herself drifting.

She hadn't meant to hurt Jake, but ever since meeting him in Hobarron's Hollow she had been drawn to Simon's soulful, wild spirit. It had been agony to be separated from him these past weeks, imagining what horrors he might be living through. To have Simon back in her life had been so wonderful that she hadn't stopped to think about Jake. Although she'd known that he had feelings for her, she had not realized how much he cared until she saw him standing in the doorway, watching her and Simon. Such hurt in those eyes, such pain. Now Jake might well be dead, and Rachel couldn't help thinking that it was all her fault.

'Rachel, are you there?'

Adam Harker hauled himself up the stairs and onto the terrace. The poor man seemed to be growing weaker by the hour. Rachel rushed to meet him.

'Is it Jake?' she asked, half-hopeful, half-fearful. 'Has the story started again?'

Adam reached for the support of the balcony rail.

'The *Codex* has started writing again.' He took a deep, ragged breath. 'Jake's alive.'

Rachel gasped and her tears flowed freely.

'But he may not live much longer,' Adam continued. 'He'll soon be at the mercy of one of the most dangerous men that ever lived. A psychopathic killer who murdered hundreds of innocent people . . . '

Adam told Rachel that Jake was now being held prisoner on the charge of witchcraft. Despite the objections of Mr Leonard Lanyon, the vicar of Cravenmouth, the town elders had decided to call in a specialist to investigate the case: Matthew Hopkins, the infamous Witchfinder General. Richard Rake, Earl of Cravenmouth, had agreed to dispatch his servant in search of the Witchfinder.

'But if all this happened in the past surely we can research how it turned out,' Rachel said. 'If Hopkins went to Cravenmouth and tried Jake wouldn't there be a record of the outcome?'

Adam shook his head. 'Time is in flux. History as we know it is changing *now*. It's difficult to explain, but it's as if the events in 1645 are moving along at almost the same pace as time here is moving. We won't know what happens to Jake until it happens—effectively, until we read about it in the *Codex Tempus*. When things are finally settled, the history books will reform around those events.'

'What do you mean, "when things are finally settled"?'

Adam closed his eyes. 'Either when Jake retrieves the witch ball and returns to us or . . . ' his voice trembled, 'or when he dies on the Witchfinder's scaffold.'

A short silence followed, textured by the moan of a distant sandstorm.

'There's another reason I came to find you, Rachel. I need to ask your forgiveness.'

Rachel was surprised. 'You took me in, Adam, gave me a home—why would I ever need to forgive you?'

'Because I did as Simon asked.' Adam reached into his pocket and withdrew an envelope. Rachel saw her name written in Simon's rough hand. 'Because I waited an hour before I gave you this.'

She tore open the letter.

My love. My world—

You wouldn't believe me when I told you that there was evil in my soul. Well, now I've proved it to you, and to myself.

I've betrayed you, Rachel. Betrayed Jake and Dr Harker and Pandora and all those who showed me kindness. Betrayed

*my conscience and my humanity. I have told the Demon
Father about Jake and the Scarab Path. I don't know what consequences my actions will have, but if I stay here I dread to
think what could happen.*

*I'm going far away, Rachel. I'm going to find out who I
am. What I am. Something tells me that it will be a dangerous
road, and I'm not sure that I'll ever see you again. But I know
you'll be with me in spirit . . . walking beside me to the end of
the road.*

My love, for ever
Simon

Rachel looked up from the tear-stained letter.

'They're gone,' she said. 'Both of them. Gone . . .'

While kettles sang and demons squabbled, the witches stoked
their camp fires and complained about another bad night's
sleep. Most could not understand why they had to camp
outside when the manor house stood empty. True, it looked
like a draughty old ruin, but a room in Havlock Grange was
surely better than roughing it out in the open. Despite their
pleas, Master Crowden had forbidden anyone except himself,
Mr Quilp, and Mr Grype from entering the house. No one in
their right mind would contradict the Master, not after what
had happened at the stadium.

With mugs of hot tea to lift their spirits, the witches soon
forgot their complaints. They gathered together and began
reliving their great victory.

Tobias Quilp and Mr Pinch walked through the lines of

tents and listened in to the chatter. At the eastern edge of the camp, where the lawn met the forest, a South African witch held his coven spellbound. Tall and bearded, the man was dressed in flowing robes and had a brimless hat perched on his head. He told the tale of how, in an onslaught of claws and teeth, his crocodile-headed demon had slaughtered five Institute employees in as many minutes. The other witches laughed and banged their staffs in approval.

Spying Quilp, the storyteller beckoned to him.

'Come, brother, sit with us.'

Quilp's gaze passed around the South African coven. Wide, excited eyes looked up at him.

'Thank you, no,' he said, and started to move on.

The storyteller's face darkened. 'Too grand to share our fire, Mr Quilp? As I remember, it was *our* coven that released you from your captivity. Were it not for us you would still be the plaything of the Elders.'

Quilp and Pinch spun round. The men and women clustered around the fire drew back, as did their demons.

'Peace, brother.' A younger witch sporting large hoop earrings bowed before Quilp. 'Jacques meant no insult. We have all heard of the great magic you wield through your demon. In any case, we are all one coven now, are we not?'

Quilp tapped the side of his leg and Pinch came to heel. He nodded stiffly and walked away.

Marching between the tents, Quilp took in only snapshots of what he saw. Over two hundred witches had made their temporary home in the grounds. Their laughter, curses, and conversation filled the air, and from every corner came the chatter, chunter, whinnies, and whines of demons. Demons that walked and waddled, crept and capered, scuttled and skulked. Demons that resembled animals and insects, birds and fish; even some, like Mr Pinch, that looked vaguely human. More demons and witches than Quilp had ever seen, and yet the spectacle was of only passing interest.

His thoughts kept returning to Jacob Harker. While the other witches revelled in the destruction of the Hobarron Elders, Quilp could think only of avenging the death of his beloved Esther. His plan was simple: first, he would kill the boy, slowly, horribly, then he would go after Dr Harker. As soon as the Demon Father allowed it, Quilp would take his revenge.

He left the grounds and entered the Great Hall. He had barely stepped over the threshold when a voice called down to him: 'Tobias, he wants to see you.'

Quilp looked up to the head of the stairs. Roland Grype was staggering under a mountain of old books, his vulture-demon perched on the topmost volume. Quilp bounded up the staircase and followed Grype into the shadowy reaches of the house.

'What's all that for?' he said, eyeing the pile of tomes.

'Last night, the Master entrusted me to carry out a little task.' Weakening under his burden, Grype nevertheless managed to puff out his chest. 'I was to go to the occult libraries of London and seek out certain books.'

They came to a door at the end of a dismal corridor. Quilp knocked and the door swung open.

The chamber beyond was cold and dark. As Quilp's eyes

adjusted to the gloom, he saw the figure of his master sitting on an ornate wooden throne that stood in the centre of the room. Carved into the arms and legs of the throne were a dozen miniature human faces, frozen in the act of screaming. They appeared so lifelike that, for a moment, Quilp believed he could hear their cries rustling in his ear . . .

'Come forward, gentlemen.'

Quilp's gaze switched to his master. A candle standing on a little table beside the throne bathed the Demon Father's angelic features in a soft, flickering glow. When Quilp looked back, the faces in the chair seemed to have vanished. Perhaps it had been a trick of the light.

'I see you have accomplished your mission, Mr Grype,' the demon beckoned. 'Bring me the books.'

The witches waited while their master sorted through the tomes. Eventually, he came to a slim volume embossed with gold lettering. Before the book was flipped open, Quilp caught sight of the title—*The Iconography of the Old Ones*. The Demon Father rummaged through the book, ancient paper crumbling at his careless touch. He stabbed a finger against one of the pages.

'As I thought! Well, well, this changes everything.'

Quilp found himself reflected in the dark moons of the demon's glasses. Then the creature's gaze turned to Grype.

'I have another task for you, my faithful librarian. I want you to assemble the universal coven in the Great Hall. Be quick.'

Grype bowed and bustled away. When the door slammed shut, the Demon Father called Quilp to his side. The witch shuddered. He had faced many horrors in his fifty years, but only this unholy creature possessed the ability to truly frighten him. The demon tapped the book.

'Tell me, what do you make of this?'

The page that lay open was a mess of squiggles and hiero-glyphs, but the picture at the centre was clear enough. The green glass ball had been drawn with such skill and artistry that it seemed to glimmer with a light of its own.

'Josiah Hobarron's witch ball,' Quilp said in a hushed voice.

'Mortals!' the Demon Father sneered. 'You have such limited vision. But tell me, why do you call it "witch ball"?'

'That's how it's always been known. The legends of Josiah Hobarron claim that his magic was contained within, or inspired by, the orb. Is it important?'

'It is momentous.' The demon closed the book thought-fully. 'Only a few beings that exist on this Earth would rec-ognize the true nature of the orb. It is fortunate for us that *I* am one of them, although I have not seen its like for untold millennia.'

Intrigued, Quilp leaned forward. 'What is it?'

'It is a Signum.'

Quilp searched through his knowledge of arcane myth and lore. He found no trace of the word.

'This is a troubling development, Mr Quilp, but now that I know of the Signum's existence the true nature of our enemy is clear.' The demon's lips set into a thin line. 'Such opposition cannot be underestimated, even in these idle days . . . Still, our spy in the Harker camp has made contact and the information he has provided may yet help us to destroy all those who stand in our way.'

The Demon Father went on to explain how the messages of treachery hypnotically implanted inside Simon Lydgate had been 'activated'. Through Simon, they now knew that Jacob Harker had travelled back in time to retrieve the witch ball.

'Our first priority must be to get Simon away from Dr Harker,' Quilp said. 'The spy has served us well, but he may know things that could cause us difficulties.'

'Do not distress yourself,' the demon said. 'Simon has already left his friends. In due course he will be picked up by an old acquaintance of mine and cared for until I have the opportunity to reclaim him. In the meantime, something must be done about Jacob Harker.'

Quilp's heart quickened. He sensed that his moment was at hand.

'I have kept you on a short leash, Tobias; it is time now to set you free. At all costs, you must prevent Jacob Harker from finding the witch ball.'

'But how?'

'You must join him in 1645.'

'Time travel is powerful magic,' Quilp said. 'Far beyond the abilities of any normal witch.'

The Demon Father rose from his throne. 'Follow me.'

Witch and master left the chamber and strode through the old house.

'There are only three methods of time travel,' the demon instructed. 'The first was used by Jacob Harker—temporal transport by way of the Scarab Path. The second is a direct appeal to the Unseelie Court, that haven of dark fairies that exists somewhere beyond the borderlands. Meddling with such creatures always comes at a cost.'

'And the third method?'

They had reached the staircase. Crowded into the Great Hall below, the assembled witches murmured between themselves.

'A universal coven.' The Demon Father smiled. 'Their combined magic will be just about sufficient to open a time portal. I shall direct the spell from here. By my will you should arrive at the correct moment in history.'

'But the consequences! The—the raw power could destroy—'

'Hush!' the demon snarled. '*You* will be safe enough. I have provided you with a vessel of sufficient strength to withstand the tempest of inter-dimensional travel.'

He pointed to where the nightmare box stood in the centre of the hall. As if in response, the jaws of the cabinet yawned open.

'No! Please, Master.'

'Think, Quilp! With the Signum, Jacob Harker will increase his magic tenfold. He will return here and lay waste to every demon and witch in existence. And even if the Demontide were to break before he came back, the witch ball could still be used to slaughter thousands of my kind.'

'But if we do this then there is no chance of creating another Door,' Quilp whispered. He gave the assembled crowd a sideways glance. 'The universal coven will be finished.'

'With the power of the witch ball we no longer need the coven to conjure a second Door. Go back, Mr Quilp. Retrieve it for me. Then you may take your revenge on Jacob Harker. Are you still my faithful servant?'

Quilp gave a sharp nod.

'Good. Now, when you arrive in 1645 you will find that this house is occupied by three witches. The sisters of Marcus Crowden. Convince them that you are working on behalf of your old master and they will help you. Once you have the witch ball, step back inside the cabinet and you will return to me. Now, go.'

Quilp took Mr Pinch's clawed hand and witch and demon descended the stairs. They reached the crowd and questions rang out from all sides. Most were excited queries about whether the time had come to summon the second Door. A few were more cautious—why had Master Crowden gathered them here?

Quilp moved silently through the throng until he reached the centre of the hall. Situated just below the hole in the roof, the nightmare cabinet waited for him. Pinch danced merrily into the box but Quilp hesitated. He glanced at Grype who stood nearby, wringing his sweaty hands. There was no love lost between the witches, but Quilp felt a strange jolt of pity for the librarian. They were all that remained of the true Crowden Coven.

'Get out of here,' he whispered.

Grype came forward, his vulture-demon squawking on his shoulder.

'I'm sorry?'

'Leave this place, if you value your life.'

With that, Quilp stepped into the box. He saw no hellish landscapes, no nightmare visions—the cabinet was a well of emptiness. Looking back into the Great Hall, he watched Grype squeeze between the witches and make for the door. The universal coven was too preoccupied to notice his going. Every eye was fixed on the figure at the top of the stairs.

'Brothers and sisters, HEAR ME!' the demon called. 'The time has come to pool our magic and to summon the great Door. Are you ready?'

A chorus of cheers.

'Then join hands and we will begin.'

Breathless whispers; the rustle of hands.

'You must focus your attention on the cabinet. Your powers will be channelled through the box and through Mr Quilp. The Door will then be constructed directly above them. When I give the word, you will release the full extent of your magic. Rejoice, my faithful witches, for the Demontide is at hand!'

Two hundred and forty-three faces turned obediently to Quilp. Nervous smiles and excited twitters passed between the crowd while their demons lay quietly at their feet. Quilp studied those monstrous faces and seemed to read the same dark message in each. The demons knew very well what was about to happen. For the sake of the greater mission, they were willing to sacrifice their masters. Quilp stole a glance at his own demon. Mr Pinch's yellow eyes danced excitedly in his head, and Quilp wondered how far the demon's loyalty to him extended.

No time for such questions and doubts.

It was beginning . . .

Slowly, the nightmare box started to revolve. Quilp watched a circle of faces pass by. They were whispering, intoning spells, reaching deep to summon their magic. Again, he felt a stab of remorse: these were brother witches—he should call out, warn them of what was to come. But guilt was an alien emotion to Tobias Quilp and was easily swamped by his need to revenge himself on Jacob Harker.

Behind the universal coven, the Demon Father raised his hands.

'Release your magic, brethren! Let it flow!'

The witches' arms shot out from their sides and pointed towards the cabinet. The demons flinched, as if in pain. A strange gurgling sound rattled at the back of the witches' throats. Their eyes snapped open and agonized screams cut the air. Jagged forks of blood-red magic exploded from their mouths. As the box rotated, Quilp saw flashes of the Demon Father reaching out and directing the lightning streams to a point just above the nightmare cabinet.

'More, my brothers and sisters! Give me your power!'

Raw, brutal magic burned the witches' lips to pouting cinders. One of the Japanese coven shrieked with pain and her eyes exploded out of her head. Twin columns of magic streaked out of the empty sockets and joined the crackling mass that had gathered above the cabinet. Seconds later, the entire gathering had lost their eyes. Faces burst into flame and skin folded down like melting candle wax. Under the liquid heat of magic, clothes and hair ignited. Soon all two hundred and forty-three witches were aflame, burning like Guy Fawkes effigies.

The demons added their own horrific cries to the chaos. They too were on fire, returning now to the desolation of the demon dimension. Heaps of charred corpses tumbled to the ground and black ash floated into the air. As the last of the witches fell, Quilp saw the Demon Father smile and make a plunging gesture with his hands.

'Safe journey, Mr Quilp!' he called.

The door of the nightmare cabinet slammed shut.

In the darkness, Quilp reached for Mr Pinch's hand.

'It's all right, my pet,' he whispered. 'We're on our way.'

Chapter 18
The Nightmare Begins

They came at night, under the door, spreading across the floor like a black carpet. Cockroaches. Thousands of them. The *tick-tick-tick* of their legs made every inch of Jake's skin crawl. He did his best to shoo them away but the roaches were never gone for long. They would regroup in the corners of the cell and march out again, making for the boy and his thin straw bed. The only part of Jake that seemed to welcome the cockroaches was the scarab tucked away inside his skull. Whenever the beetle heard the insectile clicking it would chirrup happily in response.

Only one thing succeeded in scattering the roaches, and that was the rats. Chased along the prison corridors by the gaolers, the half-starved rodents would scamper under the cell door and find a feast waiting for them. At first, Jake had felt grateful—the rats' midnight supper saved him from a night of creeping, crawling torture. But when they had exterminated all the roaches, the rats had turned their attention to him. On his second night in the keep, Jake had woken to the tickle of whiskers and the sudden, sharp bite of wicked teeth.

Much to the annoyance of Sergeant Martin Monks, by the end of the week the Witchfinder General had still not arrived. The delay was a blessing. It meant that Jake still had a chance to speak to the one person in Cravenmouth who had shown him mercy: Leonard Lanyon, the man who had saved him from Monks's bullet. Every day, Jake begged Monks to deliver a message to Lanyon, asking the vicar to visit him. Every day, Monks reported back that 'Mr Lanyon begs the pardon of Mr Harker, but as a good Christian he cannot converse with such a damnable witch.' Jake doubted that Monks had *ever* spoken to Lanyon on his behalf and, as time passed, he saw his chance slipping away.

Day by day, hour by hour, Jake weakened. He was fed just once a day. In the mornings, Monks would open the cell door and throw a wooden bowl in his general direction. At first, Jake had been unable to eat the thin stew of roots, beets, oats, rat bones, and old apple cores. Three days into his imprisonment, the gnaw of his stomach had forced him to lift the bowl to his lips and choke back the food. A rancid slop peppered with maggot eggs, it flushed straight through his stomach and made him sick.

On the fifth day, he felt feverish. On the sixth, delirium set in and he could no longer tell the difference between the real world and his nightmares.

Lost in dreams, Jake witnessed the victory of the Demon

Father. The Door had been summoned and the Demontide had engulfed the world. Buildings burned, rivers ran red, and the sound of monsters hatching their young filled the air. Demons ran like feral dogs through the empty streets and fed on the corpses of men, women, and children. Only a scattering of humankind remained. Playthings of the demons, these unlucky few turned their faces to the burning sky and cursed the name of Jacob Harker.

Jake moved on through the dream. He saw his father racked with pain as Crowden's hex ate its way through his organs. He saw powerful demons pursue Pandora into Yaga Passage, fall upon her, and wrench her eight arms from their sockets. She writhed on the ground and spat Jake's name into the dirt.

To the north of the lifeless city, the Demon Father had established an arena of blood for his hideous children. Jake watched, helpless, as Rachel was led out into the centre of the new coliseum, lashed to a post and left there. A restless hush settled over the demonic crowd. Then a cage was pushed into the arena and the horde shrieked its approval. The half-demon creature, Simon Lydgate, was released from his shackles. His yellow eyes found Rachel and he launched himself at the girl, his massive claws shredding and tearing . . .

On the ninth day, Jake's fever broke.

The nightmares fell away and he felt the hard, cold reality of the prison cell around him. As his senses returned, Jake heard the lonesome beat of a drum drifting over the fields of Cravenmouth. He grasped the brickwork and staggered to his feet. He had already lost a lot of weight and his legs trembled beneath him. Although chained, he could still just about climb up to the window and look out.

It was still dark outside, but the peasants were already leaving their ramshackle homes and heading into the fields. A cock crowed and dawn shouldered its way over the forest. Alerted by the drummer boy, the peasants stopped in their tracks and turned to the forest road.

A man on horseback was moving sluggishly towards the town. A small figure robed in black, his tired head rolled with the motions of the horse. Two large saddlebags hung either side of his mount and a long staff had been tied to the horse's flank.

The drummer marched out from the gatehouse to meet the man. Reaching him, he lifted a drumstick to his brow in salute. Then he executed a stiff about-face and escorted the stranger into Cravenmouth. All the while, the boy drummed out the same dull beat—*thum . . . thum . . . thum*—a sound that echoed across the still-waking town and turned Jake's heart to lead.

The cell door swung open.

'What have we here?' Monks bellowed, a grin plastered across his fat face. 'Looking out for the omen of your doom, witch? Well, it has come, as sure as death.'

The other gaolers entered the chamber and grappled the prisoner down from the window. Jake cried out as he was hurled against the stone floor. Meanwhile, Monks lifted his musket overhead.

'Ready to meet your maker, boy?'

The sergeant slammed the rifle butt into Jake's face,

crushing his nose and splitting his mouth apart. Jake felt a brief moment of pain before the darkness claimed him.

When he eventually came round, Jake's hand went straight to his face. The swelling from Monks's previous attack had only just gone down; now the skin was taut again, the muscle beneath blooming. His index finger shivered as he traced the zigzag of his broken nose.

Dragged from his cell, Jake had been taken to a large, stone-flagged room roughly the size of a football pitch. It might have been a banqueting hall once upon a time, but all the furniture had now been removed and the only decoration was a mouldy tapestry showing Norman knights fighting against Saxon soldiers. Judging by the huge grey stones from which the room had been constructed, Jake guessed that he was still within the castle walls.

Something caught his eye: a boy, roughly his own age, sitting in a chair at the far end of the room. Frightened eyes stared out from beneath straggles of filthy hair. His face was covered in bruises and his mouth was torn and bleeding. Although not skeletally thin, his cheeks stood out like blades in his face. The kid had the look of something hunted. Jake turned his head slightly and the boy mimicked the movement.

Shaken, Jake turned away from the great wide window and the horror of his own reflection.

Voices. Shadows on the floor. Jake realized that he was not alone.

'I must stress my objection once again, my lord. We

should not place our trust in that . . . *gentleman*.'

Jake looked up. The first person he saw was Martin Monks, his musket slung over his back and a great hoop of keys twirling around his fat finger. Next to the sergeant stood a middle-aged man with a short, pointed beard and light blond hair that hung down to his shoulders in ringlets. From the finery of his dress, Jake guessed that this was Richard Rake, Earl of Cravenmouth. Jake recognized the third man at once. Immaculately dressed in a costume of black, Mr Leonard Lanyon gazed down at Jake.

'I have heard many reports of the Witchfinder General,' Lanyon continued. 'It is said in some parts that his desire to seek out witches knows no limit. That he may even manufacture evidence when no real proof is to be found.'

'Yes, yes, vicar,' the Earl waved an airy hand. 'You said all this at the meeting of the town burgesses, but the decision went against you. Mr Hopkins has already settled into The Green Man and we have agreed to pay his expenses and a fee of twenty shillings—'

Monks gaped. 'That's a month's wage!'

'We cannot very well send him away now,' said the Earl, ignoring Monks's outburst.

'But this boy is in no fit state to be interrogated,' Lanyon objected. 'Look at him! He can barely sit up unaided. I'd like to know what kind of treatment he has had at your hands, Mr Monks. You deprived him of an ear, sir, was that not enough?'

'He has been violent, vicar!' Monks complained. 'Me and my boys have had to restrain him many times this past week.'

'Indeed? I should like to know how a half-starved wretch

could cause problems for three burly men.'

'But-but, he's a witch!'

'You've already made up your mind then, Sergeant? Then what is the use of this Witchfinder come from Manningtree?'

'How can anyone doubt what he is, sir? Did you not see how he came among us that day? How he appeared out of nowhere wreathed in magical flame?'

During the to and fro of the conversation, Jake had tried to find a point at which he could speak. He wanted to tell them that the whole thing had been a mistake. He wasn't a witch and he hadn't meant to frighten the townspeople. Several times the words formed in his head only to die on his swollen lips. How could he even begin to explain who he was and why he had come to Cravenmouth?

Is the sergeant right, boy? Are you truly a witch?

Jake wetted his lips, ready to answer the vicar's question. And then he realized that Lanyon had *not* spoken out loud. His voice had come to Jake like an unbidden thought.

How are you doing this? Jake answered inside his mind.

I am not the one who needs to answer questions. Quickly now, there isn't much time: do you mean us harm?

No, Jake insisted. *I swear. Please, can you help me?*

I'll do what I can, but you must understand that, if it is proved that you have used magic, I cannot aid you. In these desperate times all *magic is seen as evil. Even ministers such as I have been accused of witchcraft, and as much as I may wish to help, I will not endanger my life to do so. I will not be another victim of this cruel man, this self-appointed—*

'Witchfinder General!'

The guard's voice echoed up the stairs. At his call, the mental link between Jake and Leonard Lanyon was broken. While Monks and the Earl turned to the arched doorway that led to the stairs, Lanyon locked eyes with Jake and pressed his finger to his lips.

'Take heart,' he whispered. 'I will aid you if I can. In the meantime, whatever is done to you, you must *not* confess.'

Footsteps on the stairs. A shadow sweeping across the wall. Under the darkness of the doorway, a figure paused, his tall staff clutched in a bony fist. A pair of watery blue eyes shaded under a wide-brimmed hat passed from face to face.

'God be with you, gentlemen,' said the stranger. 'I have come in answer to your call. Now, show me to the witch.'

Chapter 19
The Subtle Art of Torture

The Witchfinder General stepped into the light.

Although his body was painfully thin, Matthew Hopkins was nothing like the wizened scarecrow Jake had seen depicted in old horror movies. This man was in his early to mid-twenties, he was of average height and slight build. His face was pinched, his features unremarkable. Ash-blond hair and a neatly cut beard curled down over the broad linen collar of his shirt. He wore a high-crowned hat, buckled boots with spurs, and a three-quarter-length cloak. Jake thought that he looked like the most ordinary little man he had ever seen.

'My apologies,' the Witchfinder said, 'I have not introduced myself. I am Matthew Hopkins.'

Perhaps it was the fact that he was now deaf in one ear, but Hopkins's voice was so low and rasping that Jake could barely hear it. The Witchfinder's weak blue eyes moved between Sergeant Monks, Mr Lanyon, and Earl Richard. At last, they came to rest on Jake.

Hopkins's eyes widened. His mouth dropped open in surprise and his hand clutched at his staff. A moment later, he had rearranged his face into an expression of grave sincerity and was bowing before the Earl.

'My lord, since I received your summons the weather has been fair and the roads and bridges sound. God indeed wished me to come here.'

'You are most welcome, Master Witchfinder,' the Earl said. 'I'd wager we have here a case unlike any you have yet investigated.'

'That is quite likely, my lord,' Mr Lanyon cut in. 'For I have heard that Master Hopkins has been hunting witches only a short time.'

Hopkins's eyes flashed with anger, but again he managed to mask his emotions.

'Quite true, Mr . . . ?'

'Leonard Lanyon. I am the rector of the Holy Trinity church here in Cravenmouth.'

Hopkins bowed deeply. 'My campaign to free this land from devilry is indeed still in its infancy, sir. Earlier this year, in my home town of Manningtree, I experienced at first hand the evil of witchcraft. While investigating a coven, I was set upon by a demon that came to my bedchamber in the shape of a great bear. It had been sent by those fiendish witches that I had made it my business to hunt down. That very night I heard the call of my Lord and Saviour: *You must seek out all such sorcerers and devils*, He said. *Find them and destroy them.* You no doubt recall what the Bible tells us, Mr Lanyon? The Book of Exodus, chapter twenty-two, verse eighteen—"Thou shalt not suffer a witch to live."'

'I remember another commandment from Exodus,' Lanyon said. '"Thou shalt *not* kill." Life is precious, Master Hopkins, and there is need of great inquisition before it is taken away. And remember also the Law of the Land which prevents witchfinders from torturing a confession from their prisoners. I will be watching closely, sir.'

With that, the vicar turned on his heel and left the chamber. Hopkins watched him go, his face unreadable.

'Well, I too must away,' said the Earl, fussing with his calf-skin gloves. 'I trust that you have read carefully the letter we sent setting out the story of how the suspect arrived here?'

'I have. But the evidence of eyewitnesses can be proved false, my lord. I cannot be sure of the prisoner's guilt until I have gathered evidence from his own lips. I propose the usual methods to get the truth out of him.'

'Which are?'

'Watching and Walking, for a start. We may also have use of the bodkin. All effective techniques for seeking out witch-craft, I assure you. Regrettably my usual associates, Mr John Stearne and Mother Briggs, are not with me, and so I will need at least one person to act as my assistant. Perhaps this fine gentleman?'

Sergeant Monks flushed red. 'It would be my honour, sir.'

'Excellent. Now, I should like a moment alone with the prisoner.'

'Is that wise?' the Earl said, eyeing Jake as if he might

escape his bonds and strike them dead at any minute. 'What if his demons appear?'

'Have no fear, my lord. It is well known that, once a sorcerer is caught and properly examined according to God's Law, then his magic will no longer avail him.'

'Then God be with you in your task, sir. Come, Sergeant.'

Monks followed the Earl out of the banqueting chamber, leaving the Witchfinder alone with Jake.

Matthew Hopkins moved slowly across the room. By the way he walked, legs bowed, footsteps faltering, Jake saw that the tall staff he carried was not just used for effect. A dry cough rattled at the back of Hopkins's throat and his eyes crinkled with pain. Taking a brown-spotted handkerchief from his pocket, he wiped his lips. The legendary Witchfinder General stood in front of Jake, a dark, spidery figure silhouetted against the sunlit window.

'I have to talk to you,' Jake blurted out. 'I have to explain—'

'Explain what, old friend?' Hopkins asked in his reedy voice.

'W-what?'

'What do you wish to explain, Brother Witchfinder?'

'I don't understand. Who do you think I am?'

'Let us not play games, sir. They have treated you quite roughly, but I have sharp eyes and a thousand bruises could not deceive me. I'd heard tell that you had died a few months ago. Perished in a little village on the coast, so the story went, the victim of a foul witch master. Instead I find you here, looking younger and healthier than ever. It is good to see you, Josiah.'

In a flash, Jake understood. Hopkins believed that *he* was Josiah Hobarron. Jake remembered Sidney Tinsmouth telling him that Hopkins had known Josiah. Not only that, but that Josiah had often thwarted the Witchfinder General's work. As if echoing these thoughts, Hopkins's lip curled over his stunted grey teeth and he whispered, 'I have always suspected you of being in league with demonic forces, Josiah Hobarron. The way you turned the minds of magistrates against me! The passion with which you saved all those wretched women from the gallows! Well, no more. Now I have your life in my hands, sir. Now you will pay a hundredfold for your insolence.'

'But I'm not Josiah Hobarron! I'm—'

'A dead man,' Hopkins said quietly. 'But before you die, you will suffer. By God, you *will*.'

'Just wait and listen!' Jake cried. 'You have to believe me, I'm *not* Josiah Hobarron.'

'Stopper his mouth, Mr Monks.'

Summoned by the Witchfinder's call, the sergeant had returned. He crossed the chamber and slapped a hand over Jake's mouth. With his other hand, he tore a filthy neckerchief from his throat and, quick as a flash, lodged it between the prisoner's teeth.

'Much better,' Hopkins approved. 'Now we can begin. Mr Monks, I am about to teach you the secrets of my trade. Please attend carefully.'

'Yes, sir.'

Monks made a clumsy little bow that, in other circumstances, Jake would have found funny.

'To prove the existence of a witch there is a hierarchy of evidence. In descending order we have: confessions, eyewitness reports of demonic familiars and, lastly, the witch's mark. We begin, as always, on the lowest rung of this evidential ladder. I have left an old saddlebag on the stairs—will you retrieve it for me?'

'Yes, sir. Anything else?'

'A table, about yay big.'

Hopkins tapped a finger against his hip and held out his arms at full stretch. While Monks bustled away, Hopkins put his lips to Jake's good ear.

'Let us start gently, Josiah. Ease you into the agony.'

Monks returned, bag in hand, his fleshy face flushed with excitement. Another of the guards carried in a heavy wooden table and set it down in front of Jake's chair.

'Who is your friend, Sergeant?'

'Walter Utterson.'

'If Mr Utterson will stay with us and act as witness . . . ' Hopkins said, dropping to one knee and rummaging through the bag, ' . . . we can begin.'

The Witchfinder brought out a huge pair of rusty scissors and a knife with a curved blade. He snipped the scissors through the air, an inch from Jake's busted nose.

'Strip him of his clothes and tie him face down to the table,' Hopkins instructed.

Jake tried to fight against the hands that bundled him from the chair. He was so weak that it was like a puppy fighting against tigers. Monks and Utterson dragged the coarse prison clothes from his body and slammed him naked across the table. He felt the burn of ropes being tied across his back, locking him into position.

'Good, good,' Hopkins cooed. 'Now we must shave the boy.'

'Shave him?' Monks frowned.

'We must examine every inch of his body if we are to find his witch marks.'

'Sorry, sir, but what are "witch marks" exactly?'

'I have not said? Forgive me. I sometimes forget that not everyone has studied the demonological texts as closely as I. Well, in short, to sustain his demon familiar a witch must suckle the creature. Every witch will have a place on his body where his demon draws blood, and this place will be insensible to pain. Cunning witches often hide the mark beneath their hair, and so . . . '

Hopkins flourished the scissors.

Monks and Utterson held Jake steady while the Witchfinder went to work. Within a few minutes, Jake's long hair had been hacked into stubby tufts, but Hopkins was not finished yet. He ordered soap and water to mix a lather, which he spread across Jake's scalp. With the curved knife, he removed the last few clumps of hair.

'And so the real work begins, gentlemen. Witch marks are not always obvious to the naked eye. We must sometimes seek them out with the bodkin.'

Hopkins delved into his bag and brought out three shining implements with carved wooden handles. At the end of each was a thin needle, about seven centimetres long, its tip pointed.

'One for you and one for you.' Hopkins handed the guards their bodkins. 'Our task now is to test the suspect's skin. If you believe you have discovered a witch mark, you must plunge the needle into the flesh. If it is a true mark, Mr Hobarron here will feel no pain and he will not bleed. Now, it is possible that people like your vicar, Mr Lanyon, would call this torture, but remember that we are trying to save this man's immortal soul. Is that not worth a little pain?'

'Yes, sir,' the guards responded.

'Excellent. Now watch how it is done.'

Like a diviner searching for an underground spring, Hopkins teased the bodkin along Jake's spine. Its cold tip pressed against the flesh just behind his left lung.

'Perhaps here . . . '

The needle punctured his back, and Jake screamed. He felt the shaft twist inside his body and then pop back out again. Blood pulsed from the wound and ran in hot trickles down his side.

'Alas, I was mistaken,' Hopkins sighed. 'Your turn, Mr Monks.'

For over half an hour they used Jake's body as a pincushion. At first, the Witchfinder's assistants were hesitant, even delicate, testing at random points for those areas that did not result in a scream. But as the minutes wore on, and Jake's cries continued to rumble in his chest, their examination became impatient and brutal. They pierced and pried and probed; they jabbed and stabbed and hacked.

'What about here, Master Hopkins?' Monks asked the question like a school swot desperate to please his teacher. 'We'd never see the mark underneath all this dried blood.'

Monks tapped the bodkin against the closed hole that had been Jake's right ear. Sensing the needle point, the raw, exposed nerves sent tendrils of agony lashing into Jake's brain.

'An excellent idea, Mr Monks,' Hopkins crowed. 'We will make a witchfinder of you yet. Yes, I think you should probe a little deeper there.'

'N'aw!' Jake screamed through the gag. 'P'ease. Down't!'

Hopkins smiled and nodded at Monks. From some place deep inside the blasted organ of his ear, Jake could hear a rustle as Monks positioned the needle point.

'Confess,' Hopkins whispered, 'and your torment will be at an end.'

Jake closed his eyes. His thoughts turned away from the torture chamber and he reached back inside his mind. It did not take long to find what he was looking for. The Khepra Beetle was still lodged happily between the hemispheres of his brain. If he was about to die, the scarab would have shifted by now. *It* knew that Hopkins was bluffing. Jake refocused on the Witchfinder.

'G-go to he-ell.'

Chapter 20
walked, watched, Swum

'Bring him to the stool.'

The gag was removed, the ropes slackened, and Jake was dragged to his feet. He felt blood ooze from the dozens of wounds made by the bodkins.

'Before we proceed . . . ' Hopkins rummaged inside his saddlebag and brought out a quill, a bottle of ink, and a large book, ' . . . I must make a note in my ledger of our discoveries thus far.' He rested the ledger on the bloodstained torture table, dipped his quill and started to write: ' "Examination for witch marks on the person of Master Josiah Hobarron. Found: two points just below the right and left shoulder blades. Both with hardened skin. Both insensible to pain." '

'THAT'S A LIE!'

Ignoring Jake's outburst, Hopkins put his ledger aside.

'Good. Now, gentlemen, place the prisoner on the stool exactly as I instruct.'

Lifted by the arms, Jake was made to kneel on the seat of a high wooden stool. His legs were tucked beneath him and crossed at the ankles. His feet were tied together and his hands secured behind his back with heavy manacles. He knelt there like a penitent priest.

'What now?' Monks asked.

'Now, gentlemen, we watch.'

'Watch? For what?'

'For his demons. They will visit him soon enough.'

'But the witch marks,' Utterson said. 'Surely that's all the evidence we need.'

'I am building a case, brick by brick.' The Witchfinder walked to within an arm's length of his prisoner. His watery blue eyes held Jake's. 'The mark, the magic, they are pieces that will make up the whole. The demons come next, and then the confession.'

Jake knew the history of witch trials well enough to know that this was utter garbage. Some witches had been hanged on the evidence of the witch mark alone. In fact, with the statements of the townspeople who had seen his arrival, Hopkins had more than enough proof already. So why was he playing this game? The answer was obvious. He wanted 'Josiah Hobarron' to suffer. Hobarron had thwarted Hopkins's work as a witchfinder, and now it was payback time.

Six days of starvation. Six days of torture. Six days in which Jake's young body had been transformed into the horrific vision that confronted him every time he glanced at his reflection in the window of the banqueting hall. Dull eyes stared out from hollow sockets. Skin stretched taut over his bald head. The puncture wounds made by the bodkins gaped when he breathed and thick green strands of infection bled out.

He had not moved from the stool. The idea behind 'watching' was that, if a suspected witch was observed constantly for a space of several days, then his demon must eventually come to him to be suckled. It was important that the witch should be kept awake during this time. If Monks or Utterson saw Jake flagging they were encouraged to throw icy water over him.

The sun rose and fell, rose and fell. On the sixth day, they began to 'walk' their prisoner. Jake screamed as he was lifted from the stool. Pockets of blood had collected in his legs and now they struggled to flow through cramped veins and arteries.

'Run him up and down the room,' Hopkins instructed. 'He must be alert or his demon will not come to him.'

Monks and Utterson held Jake under the arms and raced from wall to wall. Worn down from constant kneeling, the paper-thin skin of his knees broke apart. Back and forth they dragged him until his screams became too much, and even Mr Monks had to stop.

'He can't take much more, sir,' Monks panted. 'He's half-dead and I fear we'll run him the other half if we keep this up.'

'Very well,' Hopkins nodded. 'Set him down on the floor.'

walked, watched, swam

Jake fell into a bony heap and the gag was removed.

'Water,' he wheezed. 'Please.'

Another nod from Hopkins. Monks dipped a flagon into the barrel of water that stood by the door. Hopkins had had the barrel brought up from the yard, hoping that the sight of water would add to Jake's torment. Monks stooped down and pressed the cup to Jake's broken lips.

'Enough,' Hopkins said.

'Some more,' Jake pleaded. 'Just a little . . .'

The Witchfinder dashed the flagon from Monks's hand.

'Put him back on the stool.'

'No!' Jake struggled against Monks. 'You can't!'

The sergeant was about to strike Jake when a voice boomed through the chamber.

'In God's name, let him be!'

Monks jolted back as if he had been stung. Free at last, Jake slumped against the wall and took a deep, shivery breath. He was so weak that it was difficult to focus, but at last the chamber and the people within steadied. Monks, Utterson, and Hopkins bowed before Richard Rake, Earl of Cravenmouth. To one side of the Earl stood Leonard Lanyon, his horrified gaze moving over Jake's tortured body.

'What is the meaning of this?' Lanyon asked, his voice trembling with rage.

Hopkins looked puzzled. 'The meaning of what, sir?'

'The meaning of this TORTURE CHAMBER?'

Earl Richard laid a jewel-encrusted hand on Lanyon's shoulder.

'Peace, Mr Lanyon,' he said. 'Mr Hopkins knows his

business better than we do. I'm sure he has an explanation for the prisoner's condition.'

'I hope he can also explain why I have been denied access to Master Hobarron,' Lanyon seethed. He glanced at Jake, his face full of regret. 'Every day I have come to the castle to minister to the prisoner's needs. Every day I have been turned away.'

'Quite so,' Hopkins interrupted. 'If you will forgive me saying so, sir, you have too soft a heart to battle against the forces of darkness. As soon as I arrived, I saw your sympathy for the witch and, knowing such creatures as these, I felt sure he would take advantage of your kindness. I had to keep you away, lest he work his evil will upon you.'

'That seems reasonable,' the Earl said. 'But the prisoner has obviously been ill-treated, Master Hopkins.'

'My Watchers and I have done no more than examine and observe. I would swear that on my Bible.'

'And what are your conclusions? Is he a witch?'

'Alas, although I have gathered much evidence as to Mr Hobarron's guilt, he has not confessed. There is one last weapon in the witchfinder's arsenal, gentlemen. I must be allowed to swim the prisoner.'

Lanyon looked horrified. 'You must *not* agree to that, sir! The swimming of witches is the worst form of barbarism.'

'I disagree,' Hopkins said. 'The late King James approved of the swimming test as a true way to discover witches. Although the king's ungodly son has now been chased from his throne, his father's opinion on witches is still most wise. I am only advising we use such a method because I want to be

absolutely sure of Master Hobarron's guilt . . . ' Hopkins shot
Jake a sly smile, 'before we hang him.'

'Sire, I beg you—'

Earl Richard held up his hand. 'I am minded to approve
Master Hopkins's request. Let the witch be swum.'

'Thank you, my lord.' Hopkins bowed. Then he turned
to the vicar and his face darkened. 'Mr Lanyon's objections
can go on record in my little ledger. I have other such statements there from men of the cloth. Of course, a good many
of them were later discovered to be witches themselves, and
hanged for their trouble.'

You told me not to confess, Jake projected the thought
towards Lanyon. *You said you'd help me. You have to do
something!*

Lanyon looked from Jake to the smiling face of the
Witchfinder General.

I'm sorry. Jake could hear the quiver of fear in Lanyon's
thoughts. *God forgive me, but I* cannot *help you.*

The sky was dull, the sun masked behind grey clouds.
Nevertheless, the light hurt Jake's eyes as he was half-led,
half-carried through the castle's outer gate. The company,
made up of the Witchfinder and his assistants, the Earl, Mr
Lanyon, and Jake, passed under the jaws of the portcullis and
onto the drawbridge.

'A pity that the moat is dry,' Hopkins observed. 'It would
have served us well.'

'The river isn't far,' Monks said.

Jake managed to lift his head and follow the direction of the sergeant's fat finger. In the near distance, he saw a shimmering blue thread snake its way out of the forest and roll down through the fields. Partway along the river's course stood a millhouse, its great wheel churning the waters.

It took the company ten minutes or so to cross the fields and reach the river. En route, they picked up a procession of gleaners, yeomen, and plough-hands, all eager to witness the spectacle of the swimming test.

The Witchfinder came to a halt on the bank of the mill-pond. This deep pool stood before the rush of the wheel, its underwater forest of reeds swaying in the swell. Hands released Jake and he fell to the ground. Above the roar and clatter of the millwheel he heard the talk of the crowd.

'Is he really a witch, Ma? He don't look bad.'

'Witches are cunning, Michael. Sometimes they can deceive us with pleasing forms.'

'Pleasing forms! Look at the poor creature, Mary Goodwife. He's nowt but bones and bruised flesh. What have those devils at the keep been doing to him?'

Hopkins turned to the crowd and made a deep bow.

'Good people, as some of you may know, the swimming test is one of the surest methods to discover a witch. Some may call it superstition, but I say there is much wisdom in the old ways.'

'Hear, hear!'

'Well said, Master Witchfinder!'

Hopkins bowed again. 'Now, I call upon you to bear witness. If the suspect sinks to the bottom of the pool then he is as innocent as a newborn babe. But if he floats we will know that he has embraced witchcraft and has renounced his baptism. In this case, the pure, godly element of water will reject him.'

Hopkins gave Monks a nod and both men knelt beside Jake. Mr Lanyon and the Earl were standing with the crowd and could not hear what passed between Jake and the Witchfinder.

'You want me to say that I'm a witch?' Jake's voice cracked under the weight of his despair. Mr Lanyon had been his only hope, but the vicar would not risk his neck for a stranger. Now, as he stared into the frothing, churning waters, a final burst of resilience flared in Jake's heart. 'I wouldn't give you the satisfaction, you pathetic lunatic. I'd rather drown.'

'Oh, you won't drown,' Hopkins whispered, stealing a glance at the crowd. 'No one that *I* accuse of witchcraft ever does . . . Mr Monks, you will bind him exactly as I taught you.'

Monks took a ball of twine from his pocket and cut two short lengths. While Hopkins held the exhausted prisoner, Monks tied Jake's opposing thumbs and big toes together. In this hunched position, Jake was rolled onto his side and a thicker, longer rope was secured around his waist.

'All ready, sir.'

'Then cast him into the river!'

Between them, Monks and Utterson carried Jake down the bank. When they reached the riverside, Jake looked back and saw that the crowd had ceased its chatter. Among the faces, only Mr Lanyon looked away, his expression one of utter shame. Monks nodded at Utterson, and together they pitched Jake into the river.

The icy water robbed Jake of his voice. He tried to swim, to kick his arms and legs, but the twine held fast. Locked in that huddled ball, he started to sink. The whitewashed walls of the millhouse, the dark, dripping paddles of the wheel, the people on the bank and the pale sun overhead: all of it shimmered and grew dimmer.

Once, long ago it seemed, Jake had used magic to save himself from drowning. Now he did not even try to summon his powers. Bubbles erupted from his nose and he took in a bellyful of water. He tried to cough it up but more water flooded down his throat. He could feel the thinly scabbed wounds on his back reopen and blood bloomed around him. He sank, down, down, down into the misty red river.

Then the rope around his middle pulled taut. A small tug, and Jake felt himself turning in the swell. The current cradled him as he was rolled back through the reeds and towards the sunlit world beyond. He broke the surface and coughed up pints of river water. Through the swish of his blocked ear he heard the cries of the crowd:

'See, he floats!'

'Just like the Witchfinder said—the water will not take him!'

Another tug of the rope, done so gently that no one on the bank noticed. No one except Mr Lanyon, who glared at Sergeant Monks. For a moment, Lanyon looked as if he was about to say something, then he glanced at the Witchfinder and the words died on his lips. Shivering, the vicar turned and walked away.

The rope seized Jake's stomach and he was pulled to the bank.

A voice called out—

'Witch!'

The word was taken up and passed around.

'Witch!'

'Witch!'

'WITCH!'

By the time Jake reached the bank the cries had become a chorus.

'WITCH!' 'WITCH!' 'WITCH!'

And then—

'Hang him!'

'String him up!'

'Build the gallows high!'

'In the name of God, rid us of this EVIL!'

Jake was dragged up the bank and thrown at the feet of the Witchfinder General. His eyes came to rest on that quietly savage face. Matthew Hopkins smiled triumphantly and mouthed the words:

'Death to the witch . . .'

Chapter 21
The Devil's Disciple

The cart rumbled down the rutted road. Every jolt twisted Jake's tired muscles and rattled his aching bones. He was standing in the bed of the cart, hands tied in front of him. At each corner sat a guard holding the end of a thick chain which ran back to the manacle locked around Jake's throat. When the cart lurched, the chains pulled tight and the iron collar cut into his flesh, causing blood to trickle down his crisp linen shirt and his fine black breeches. Seeing the finery of his dress a few of the poorer peasants lining the road took up the now familiar chant of 'WITCH!' and spat at the prisoner.

Jake had to hand it to Matthew Hopkins: the Witchfinder General could manipulate earls and paupers alike. After the swimming test, he had petitioned Richard Rake to hold Jake's trial as soon as possible. Jake had still been lying on the bank, recovering from the ordeal, when he overheard the conversation. At first the Earl had been reluctant. Any case of witchcraft ought to be tried by the judges at the next Assize court, he said. Hopkins immediately objected—the next Assizes would not take place until March the following year . . .

'The witch's evil is infecting this godly town.' Hopkins placed an imploring hand on the Earl's arm. 'Every day there are stories of ill omens. Only this morning I heard tell of a demonic hooded woman seen in the woods just outside Cravenmouth. For the sake of your people, you must act now, my lord!'

'I *am* an Assize judge . . . ' the Earl considered. 'All right, Master Hopkins, you've convinced me. In three days hence we will hold the trial in the Shire Hall.'

The mutterings of the crowd by the river had not been missed by Matthew Hopkins. As soon as they returned to the keep he had instructed that Jake must be fed and washed, that his wounds be tended by the barber surgeon and that new clothes be brought up from the town. And so, three days after his torture had ended, Jake now presented a less wretched figure to the crowd. Any sympathy the poor might have had for him vanished as soon as they saw those expensive clothes.

A piece of rotten fruit smacked against Jake's face.

'Can't we let him sit, Mr Monks?' one of the younger guards asked. 'He's an easy target standing up like that.'

'What say you, witch?' Monks smiled. 'Care to drop ye down?'

Jake looked over his shoulder at the narrow wooden box

behind him. Sergeant Monks rapped the coffin lid.

'No thanks,' Jake said. 'In fact, I don't plan to go anywhere near that thing.'

'Really? Think you'll get off, do you?'

Jake reached into his mind and felt the presence of the Khepra Beetle.

'Stranger things have happened,' he said.

'Oh yeah? Like what?'

'Oh, I don't know,' Jake mused. 'Like the offspring of a warthog and a dairy cow being selected for the position of town sergeant?'

Monks glared and the other guards burst out laughing.

The cart reached the south gate of Cravenmouth and passed under the wall. Eager to catch a glimpse of the witch, the watchmen craned their heads over the battlements. The prison wagon blinked out of the summer sunshine and entered the winding streets of the town. The driver slowed his ancient pony to a trot. It was too narrow here for the crowds to gather, though a few barefoot children raced ahead of the cart, tapping sticks at doors to announce the witch's passing. Faces appeared at the windows of the crooked houses. One evil-looking old woman, probably too weak to join the party, shrieked and emptied her chamber pot over the sill.

'God's curse on all witches!'

The foul shower missed Jake and hit Sergeant Monks square on the head. Monks roared and wiped the greenish brown water from his face.

'You'll answer for that, Abigail Sneap!' he cried. 'I'll see your bony old backside in the stocks!'

Mother Sneap shrieked again and disappeared back into her room.

'Nicely tanned, Mr Monks,' Jake grinned, 'it's a good look for you.'

Again, the guards had to stifle their sniggers.

After ten minutes of rattling through shadowy streets, the cart entered the square.

'He's here! The witch has come!'

A rumble of turning feet. Voices rose up and shook the air.

Jake's mouth dropped open in surprise. Hundreds, perhaps thousands, of people were squeezed into the square. A sea of staring, blinking, gaping, gawping faces. The driver snatched the reins and shot up from his box.

'Make way! In the name of the Law, make way!' He eyed the rotten fruit cradled in the arms of a gang of rough-looking men at the front of the crowd. 'And don't you be throwing any foulness this way. Like as not, you'll see the witch suffer enough before the day is out. Now, make a path!'

He cracked his whip and the people parted.

From his position on the bed of the cart, Jake could see the entire square. People were hanging out of the windows of the shops, some of them waving at Jake as if he were a celebrity. There were kids perched precariously in trees, men and women standing on buckets and barrels. Halfway into the square, an enterprising carpenter had erected a large platform and was charging people a penny to climb the rickety scaffold so that they might 'have a fine view of the witch's last moments!'.

Bakers with trays of buns, pies, and puddings moved through the throng. There were saddlers and ironmongers, pedlars and ballad-sellers. Wandering barber surgeons offered to trim a straggly beard or pull a bad tooth. A few traders had even set up stalls. Standing beside a travelling apothecary, and trying to out-bellow him, was a chapman selling pamphlets:

'Today we witness the godly work of Master Matthew 'opkins!' the man cried. 'But in *these* pages you will read of how the Witchfinder General began his Divine Crusade against all black-souled witches! Read of 'opkins's first witch-hunt in his hometown of Mistley! Marvel at how he fought off the demon bear sent to kill him! Weep over the murder by witchcraft of his beloved pet greyhound!'

As the cart moved on, Jake saw fiddlers and drummers, tumblers and acrobats. Outside the door of The Green Man tavern a troupe of actors had just started a theatrical performance. A man with ruddy cheeks and a booming voice stepped forward and addressed his distracted audience.

'Good people, please attend! For your delight and moral education we poor players will now act out A Most Gruesome Tragedy entitled "The Lament of the Pendle Witches".'

The audience applauded and the play began.

'Any other day I'd arrest that lot,' Monks grumbled. 'Plays being outlawed an' all. Still, I wonder if one day they might act out the story of the Cravenmouth Witch.' He shot Jake an evil glance. 'I know how *that* play will end!'

He pointed at the structure taking shape in front of the Shire Hall.

The half-built gallows cast a thin shadow over the square.

'English justice,' Jake said, forcing a smile. 'None better.'

Despite his bravado, Jake had to turn away from the inverted wooden L of the gallows. He closed his eyes, but nothing could drown out the *tap-tap-tap* of the carpenter's hammer. Inside, he felt the beetle stir and its pincers slacken their grip on his brain.

When he opened his eyes again, they had reached the steps of the Shire Hall. Monks got down and waddled to the back of the cart. He cut the rope around Jake's feet and the guards helped to lift the prisoner to the ground. As Jake was led to the stairs, the crowd surged forward.

Monks gave a signal and twenty or more brawny watchmen appeared from behind the pillars of the hall. Armed with muskets, pikes, and halberds, the men lined up in front of the crowd.

'The Hall is full!' Monks shouted. 'Once the jurors have reached a verdict the town crier will step out and announce it.' He glanced at the gallows and gave a knowing smile. 'Then what may be done may be done.'

'Fair enough!' a voice cried out. 'We don't need to hear the blather as long as we sees the hanging!'

Laughter greeted this remark and rumbled its way back into the square as the joke was repeated. Then the blare of a trumpet sounded and cut the merriment dead. Jake looked over the heads of the crowd. A beautiful closed carriage pulled by a pair of snow-white horses was making its way towards the Hall. The driver and the footmen were liveried in clothes so fine that they drew gasps from the people.

Monks ordered the prison wagon away and, seconds later, the carriage drew up in its place.

A servant opened the door and Richard Rake stepped out, followed by Leonard Lanyon and Matthew Hopkins. Some of the crowd gave awkward little bows while others applauded their betters. The Earl mounted the stairs. At the Hall door, he turned and held up his hand for silence.

'Good people of Cravenmouth, it is customary before a trial such as this for a minister to say a prayer. I therefore invite Mr Lanyon to address you.'

Lanyon hurried past Jake without a word.

'M-my flock,' Lanyon flustered. 'I . . . I . . . '

Silence in the square. Neighbour glanced at neighbour and shrugged. Jake could see the struggle in Lanyon's eyes.

'I pray that Earl Richard and his magistrates will remember that the sword of justice must be tempered with mercy. I pray that we may all understand that life is precious and . . . '

Lanyon's gaze rested on Matthew Hopkins. The Witchfinder shook his head and smiled.

'That is all,' the vicar sighed. And then, in a softer tone that Jake could only just hear, 'God forgive me.'

The Earl raised an eyebrow but said nothing. He nodded to Monks and Jake was hauled up the steps and into the Hall.

The central chamber was a huge wood-panelled room with a long bench on a raised platform at the back. It was already filled with people. Earl Richard and two dusty-looking men with hook noses mounted the dais and took their seats behind the bench. From the chatter of the crowd Jake identified these men as 'Sir Thomas and Sir Daniel Noakes, the brother magistrates'. Chairs had been set up to the left of the judges' bench and the jury, a rabble of twelve freeholders, were sat down and sworn in.

Jake was positioned to the right of the bench. The chains around his neck were fastened to iron staples in the floor and his feet were rebound. There was a rustle of paper and the squeak of stoppers as people unwrapped bundles of bread and cheese and started passing around bottles. Jake was surprised that this mass picnic went unnoticed by the Earl and the magistrates. Sunlight poured through the wide windows and the stink of a hundred hot bodies filled the air. The Earl covered his face with a scented handkerchief while Jake spluttered on the stench.

'If you will, Sir Daniel,' Earl Richard said, his voice muffled.

Acting as clerk, the magistrate addressed Jake:

'You are charged, Mr Hobarron, with performing acts of conjuration and witchcraft contrary to the Witchcraft Act of 1604. How do you plead?'

'Not guilty.'

'Very well,' the Earl sighed. 'In that case, I call upon Master Matthew Hopkins to present his evidence.'

Hopkins made a deep bow to the judges and the jurors, his nose almost sweeping the floor.

'My lord, venerable magistrates, good people of Cravenmouth—I tell you now, the Signs are everywhere! In the stars, in the seas, in the great turmoil of the Age. This wicked world is coming to its END!'

A murmur of approval rippled through the crowd.

Emboldened, Hopkins stepped towards his audience, hands outstretched.

'But does that mean we lay down our arms and wait for the End of Days? No! We must fight to prove that we are worthy of our place in heaven! Good people, I know that you, like all true Protestants, have been fearless in your crusade against the enemies of God. You have smashed the gaudy windows in your church and broken the idols of the old religion!'

Rapturous roars and shrieks greeted these words. Jake saw the joy in the faces of the people and felt his heart sink. Hopkins, that master manipulator, had them eating out of his hand.

'But I tell you this,' the Witchfinder continued, 'you have but scratched the surface of the Evil that plagues this land. I name this Evil—Witchcraft!'

The crowd fell to murmuring. Hopkins's eyes blazed and he spun round and pointed at Jake.

'Here is a practitioner of the craft! Here is the Devil's true Disciple! In the Book of Revelation it tells us that such sorcerers must be thrown into the fiery lake. My friends, it is our duty to hasten this foul creature to those infernal shores!'

Hopkins's theatrics had the room enthralled, but he had not captured everyone's imagination. The Noakes brothers gave dry little coughs and said together:

'You are not in the pulpit, Mr Hopkins. Please present your evidence.'

'Gladly, sirs,' Hopkins said, and bowed again. 'I call my

first witnesses: Mary Dower, the butcher's wife; and Geoffrey and Caleb Gidd, bakers.'

Mrs Dower and the Gidds gave their evidence. Jake could not fault the beginning of their story. Some weeks ago, this strange man—a boy, really—had appeared in the square, exploding from thin air in a ball of flame. As the testimony went on, however, Hopkins began to pepper the tale with his own additions.

'And is it not true, Mother Dower, that a few days before this witch's arrival a strange light was seen in the sky?'

'Aye,' Mary Dower frowned. 'Now that you mention it, I do recall a light.'

'A comet, was it not, blazing across the heavens?'

'It was! I saw it! A great ball of flame in the sky!'

Hopkins turned to the bench. 'Others have reported seeing this phenomenon, my lord. The comet was a dark herald. An omen of the witch.'

He moved on to the bakers, starting with the father.

'Mr Gidd, is it not true that, on the morning of the witch's appearance, the first batch of bread you baked came out of the oven and was full of blood?'

'I-I cannot be sure.'

'But you have testified this story to Sergeant Monks. At the peril of your immortal soul, tell me, did not the bread bleed when you pricked it?'

'It is so!' the old man said, tears in his eyes. 'Yes, I swear it!'

'And you, Gidd the Younger—did you see this omen too?'

'Aye,' Caleb Gidd murmured, less certain than his father. 'As you say.'

The witnesses were thanked and dismissed.

'Now I will set aside Signs and Omens,' Hopkins said, 'and come to the evidence of my own eyes.'

With Monks backing him up, Hopkins told the court that they had searched the suspect for witch marks and had discovered two places insensible to pain just below Jake's shoulders. He then went on to describe how, over the course of six days, Monks and Utterson had watched Jake to see if his demonic familiars would appear.

'And did such creatures come to him?' Hopkins asked.

'Aye, sir, they did,' Monks affirmed. 'A great black rat and a loathsome spider. He named the rat Mr Smythe and the spider Miss Creekley.'

Jake realized what must have happened. Barely conscious during his torture, he had probably seen these creatures— one of the thousands of rats that plagued the keep and a stray house spider—and associated them with the demons of Sidney Tinsmouth and Mother Inglethorpe. In his delirium he had most likely called out those names. But how could he explain such a thing to the court?

'And did you not see this Mr Smythe and Miss Creekley suck blood from the suspect's body?'

'I did.'

'That's a lie!'

'The accused will hold his tongue!' Earl Richard commanded. 'You will have your chance to speak later.'

Hopkins turned to the bench.

'My lord, if I might now sum up the evidence?' He counted off the points on his fingers. 'We have the testimonies of several witnesses, each of whom saw the magical arrival of the suspect. My assistants and I have told you of the marks below his shoulders and of seeing demon familiars attend the witch. And you yourself, my lord, saw how the waters of God rejected his evil body.'

The Witchfinder swept every face in the hall. He looked to the windows where the crowd outside pressed against the glass, desperate to hear his words.

'"*Thou shalt not suffer a witch to live.*" So said the Lord, our God.'

He turned to the vicar of Cravenmouth, who had been twisting his hands together in anguish.

'Is that not so, Mr Lanyon?'

'It . . . I . . . ' Lanyon's gaze flitted between Hopkins and Jake. 'The Bible tells us that mercy—'

'Mercy for witches, sir?'

Inside and out, the people roared their disapproval. Jake could almost feel the heat of their fury as it switched from him to Lanyon. The vicar wilted before his eyes.

'Does not the Bible say that witches must be rooted out and destroyed?'

'Leave him alone,' Jake said.

'Shut your mouth, witch!' Hopkins snapped. 'Mr Lanyon, I asked you a question, sir! If this wretch is found guilty should he not hang for his crime? More! Should not he be torn to pieces and his head mounted on a pike as an example to all other foul sorcerers?'

Jake looked to the bench. While the magistrate brothers shuffled uncomfortably in their chairs and twittered about procedure, the Earl merely raised his eyebrows and waited for Lanyon's response. It was as if Hopkins had worked his own dark magic on the man. And he was not the only target of Hopkins's spell. The people of the town were now baying at their vicar like a pack of rabid wolves.

'YOU WILL SPEAK, SIR!' Hopkins roared.

Jake felt the Khepra Beetle stir. Its pincers slipped smoothly out of his brain and it began to scuttle around to the front of his head. Jake remembered Dr Holmwood's words: *As long as you're alive, as long as it doesn't sense that you're in mortal danger, the beetle will remain inside your head. It's your only way back* . . . The beetle had felt danger before and loosened its grip. Now it sensed that Jake's time was up.

'I believe that witches are evil,' Lanyon muttered, head down.

'We cannot hear you,' Hopkins hollered. 'Speak with conviction!'

'I-I believe all . . . all magic is the work of devils.'

Jake grimaced. Little stabs of pain accompanied the beetle along his optic nerve and to the back of his eyes.

'Witches are the enemies of God,' Lanyon said, his face etched with misery.

'And they must be wiped from the face of the Earth?' Hopkins prompted.

'Yes!'

The Witchfinder pointed a trembling finger at Jake.

'And this creature you see before you. If the jurors find him guilty of witchcraft should he not be hanged?'

'Yes,' more quietly now. 'Yes, he *must* be . . . '

Jake screamed.

In his surprise, Hopkins staggered back and grabbed hold of Monks for support. The entire hall watched aghast as blood exploded from Jake's nose. The red spray showered the floor and several people fainted. Those that remained conscious fell to praying and wailing.

Hopkins was the first to recover his nerve.

'Have no fear! We are in the sight of God! The witch cannot harm us!'

Monks gibbered and clutched at Hopkins's arm.

'What is it, man?'

'His nose!' the sergeant bleated. 'In God's name, what is coming out of his *nose?*'

Jake's left nostril bulged. It had been just over a week since Monks had broken his nose with the rifle butt and it had never been reset. Now the bone cracked again as the beetle worked itself free. Blades of pain rocketed through Jake's face. He fell screaming to his knees.

The hall was in uproar. Someone had opened the doors into the square and, while half the chamber ran for the exit, the crowd outside pressed to get in. The shaken voice of Earl Richard called for order, but no one was paying any attention. People called out in pain and, over the commotion, Jake could hear the snap of arms and legs being trampled underfoot. Babies cried and children shrieked for their parents.

Two black feelers tickled inside Jake's nose. A second later, they were tasting the air. Wet with blood, the head and body of the beetle followed. The insect clicked its pincers and dropped to the ground. It had begun to scuttle away when a heavy black boot descended.

'NO!' Jake cried.

He heard the crack of the beetle's body and looked up into the face of Matthew Hopkins. The Witchfinder lifted his foot. All that remained of the Khepra Beetle was a few shards of dusty old soapstone. In death, it had reverted back to its talisman form.

Defeated, Jake rocked back on his knees. Now there was no hope of him returning to his own time. No hope of him seeing his father and his friends again . . .

'Behold, it is dead!' Hopkins shouted.

Like a magical command, his words brought the crowd to order. While a few stayed back to help the injured, the rest gathered around the Witchfinder.

'What is it?' Monks asked.

'One of the witch's demons,' Hopkins said. He turned to the Earl who had joined the gathering. 'It is my last piece of evidence.'

Earl Richard nodded. 'What say you then, men of the jury? Guilty or not guilty?'

'GUILTY!' came the roar.

'The verdict of this court is that Josiah Hobarron is guilty of witchcraft!' the Earl cried. 'The sentence: death by hanging. May God have mercy on your soul.'

Hopkins stared down at Jake in triumph.

'Amen.'

Chapter 22
Revelation of the claviger

Simon had been living at the cottage for several weeks when the letter came. Apart from the odd takeaway flier it was the only thing that had been shoved through the letterbox. He looked down at the stiff, black envelope. Printed in flowing script was Simon's name and the address of the cottage. Who knew he was here? No one. He had not even told Adam Harker where he was going . . .

That final meeting with Dr Harker flashed into his mind. Adam had listened calmly as Simon described the irresistible urge which had led him to call the Demon Father. Simon had expected outrage, fury. Instead, Adam had told him that it wasn't his fault; that, in fact, *he* was to blame for not having foreseen that the Demon Father would have implanted such instincts in Simon's mind. Dr Harker had been trying to make him feel better, but the sick man's softly spoken words had only added to Simon's sense of guilt.

He tore open the envelope.

Dear Mr Lydgate

It has come to my attention, through various 'dark creature' associates, that you are currently seeking information about your mother. I am in a position to provide such information. I have a window in my diary at 11.15 this evening, and pray leave to call upon you then at your mother's charming cottage.

Your humble servant,

The Claviger

Charming? Simon sniffed the stale air. Unoccupied for years, the paint had peeled in long tongues from the cottage walls and mice had chewed holes in the carpet. All the familiar things that Simon remembered from his childhood were gone and everything was layered in thick dust. This had never been a happy house, but now it felt truly desolate.

Simon made up his mind. He left the cottage and strode down the road to the twenty-four-hour garage. Although it was warm outside, he shivered. Someone was coming. Someone who knew what had happened to his mother. He should be happy—finding out the secret of his mother's death was why he had come here in the first place. He had hoped that, by returning to the cottage, old memories might stir. Relieved to find it empty, Simon had broken in and spent his first sleepless night on the cold basement floor, staring up at the door. He remembered his mother standing in the doorway, horrified as she looked down at him. The ghost of her scream echoed inside his head. And then . . .

Nothing.

He had gone door-to-door, asking people if they remembered Mrs Lydgate and her son who used to live in the old fisherman's cottage at the outskirts of the village. Most said they did. Some frowned at Simon, clearly recognizing traces of the Lydgate boy in this troubled young man. One old lady, Mrs Grady, had blinked at him over her half-moon spectacles.

'You're him, aren't you? Little Simon? Had a hard time of it these last few years by the look of you. Why've you come back?'

Simon swallowed hard. He was surprised she hadn't shrieked in horror and run to telephone the police. The story of how Mrs Lydgate had been butchered, and how her son had then disappeared, must still be told in the village.

'I need to find out what happened to my mum,' Simon said. 'There must have been an investigation, an inquest. Do you know anything, Mrs Grady?'

The old woman had looked puzzled.

'Dear child, did something happen to your mother?'

'Yes. She . . . she was killed.'

'My God. She was a difficult woman, especially with you, but she didn't deserve that. My condolences.'

'You didn't know?'

Mrs Grady shook her head. 'After you left the village, I didn't hear from your mother again. We were never close, Simon. I told her once that she ought to treat you better and, well, after that we didn't really speak.'

'What do you mean—after we left the village?'

'Well, it did come as something of a surprise, both of you just up and going like that, not a word to anybody.'

'B-but my mother,' Simon stammered, 'she was murdered *here*. In the cottage.'

Mrs Grady narrowed her eyes and took a step back.

'Your mother didn't die here. She just left one night and never came back. Both of you just left. If she'd been killed in the village don't you think they would have found a body? Now, I don't know what your game is, but you better stop it right now.'

With that, she slammed the door. It was the same story at every house he visited. Everyone believed that Simon and his mother had quit their rented cottage and never returned. At one house a middle-aged woman, Mrs Makepeace, had looked at him sympathetically and sighed.

'I always felt sorry for you, Simon. She was such a hard woman. Very pretty and well-presented, though. And doesn't she look like *her*? It really is uncanny—'

The trill of the telephone stopped Mrs Makepeace mid-flow. 'Sorry, must get that. Nice to see you, Simon.'

All this time Simon had pictured his mother's body being found in the cottage, torn to shreds. Since regaining his memory, he had avoided reading newspapers for fear of finding his nightmares confirmed. Now he had discovered that his mother had simply disappeared. Of course, that didn't mean that he *hadn't* murdered her. Maybe—Simon shuddered—maybe after killing her, he had *eaten* the remains.

The old red telephone box stood just outside the garage forecourt. Simon rummaged in his pocket and drew out the last of the money Dr Harker had lent him. He dropped a fifty pence piece into the slot and dialled. He heard clicks and fizzes on the line—the sound of the call connecting to a phone that existed beyond the borders of reality. It rang twice before it was picked up.

Simon was ready to slam down the receiver. It all depended who answered.

'Monster Central, Pandora speaking.'

Simon let out a long breath.

'Pandora, it's me. I need your help.'

Simon sat in the gathering gloom and thought over what Pandora had told him. He had hoped that, by leaving, he would take all the danger and misery out of Rachel's life. Instead, his absence had broken her. The picture Pandora had painted of a girl, lost and abandoned, cut deep, but he was still determined never to see her again. In time, she would forget him, find someone else and build a new life. A safe life.

Rachel's torment was not the only distressing news from the Grimoire Club. Adam was now very near to death. Pandora described him as a determined corpse, propped up in bed and agonizing over each twist and turn of the *Codex Tempus*. The phantom quill had continued Jake's story, through arrest, torture, and trial. It had reached the verdict of the court and had come to a stop. In some distant time and place, Jake was waiting to mount the scaffold. Another wave of guilt crashed down on Simon and he held his head in his hands.

It was a little after eleven o'clock when he heard the crunch of feet on the gravel outside. A shadow loomed against the sitting room window. Simon sprang to his feet and went to the hall.

'Pandora? Brag, is that you?'

No answer.

Simon crept down the corridor.

He was within an arm's length of the door when it exploded inwards, striking him with the force of a steam train. He flew the length of the corridor and landed hard on his tailbone. Shaking his head against the pain, Simon saw a figure silhouetted in the doorway.

'Wh-who are you?' he groaned, pushing the broken door aside.

'My name is the Claviger,' the woman said. 'I believe you received my note.'

Simon staggered to his feet. 'You're early.'

'A lady's prerogative. And after we intercepted your friends on their way here, I thought I'd better hurry things along.'

'Pandora. Brag.'

'That would be the troll and the octopus lady? Yes, we have them.'

'If you've hurt them, I'll—'

'Calm down, Mr Lydgate. They've been knocked about a bit, but there's no real harm done. Once our business is complete my boys will release your monstrous friends back into the wild.'

Simon caught movement behind the Claviger's shoulder. Shadows in the gloom of the garden: the huge bulk of Brag Badderson slumped on the ground, Pandora beside him, her eight arms lashed to her sides. Standing over them were seven or eight men in long coats. They caught sight of Simon and smiled, their jagged teeth flashing in the darkness.

'As you see, I prepared for the eventuality that you would see through my letter,' the Claviger said. 'What gave me away?'

'It wasn't the letter. I was warned about you.'

Simon thought back to what the Oracle of the Pit had told him—*to find the truth about yourself, you must walk into a trap with your eyes wide open. Violence will be necessary, I'm afraid—you will find the keyholder a formidable foe— but after some unpleasantnessss you will know all.* After he had told Pandora about the letter, she had informed him that 'Claviger' meant 'the keeper of the keys'. She had then consulted Adam. Dr Harker had worked for many years among the dark creatures; he had heard tell of the powerful being known only as the Claviger.

'But I don't understand,' Simon said. 'You could have ambushed me at any time. Why put me on my guard with a letter?'

'I had to make sure where you'd be at a time that suited my associates. They cannot come out during the day, sunlight disagrees with them. The only risk I ran was that you might not be alone.'

'It's always handy to have back-up,' Simon said.

'You call *that* back-up? A pathetic half-breed and a stinking troll!'

'You're making me angry.' Simon squared his shoulders. 'You won't like me when I'm angry.'

The Claviger laughed. 'You've read too many comic books, boy: you're not a hero, you're a monster. In any case, I don't think you'll be turning all beast boy on me. Not tonight.'

The Claviger thrust out her hand. Moonlight glinted off the surface of a small perfume bottle. She sprayed and Simon choked.

'Hormone inhibitors,' she said. 'A little trick the Demon Father stole from the laboratories of Hobarron Tower. They'll suppress your inner beast until we deliver you into your father's hands.'

'It was all a trick.' Simon gagged. 'You know nothing about my mother. You just wanted to take me back to *him*.'

'Ah, now that's what's so deliciously ironic. I know *everything* about you, Simon Lydgate. What you were, what you are, what you could be.'

She stepped out of the shadows, a feminine figure dressed in a grey T-shirt, black trousers, and a long leather coat. Her flawless skin was as white and as perfect as a Michelangelo statue. As she came closer, Simon saw that her features were actually more metallic than stone-like: a hard, inscrutable face dominated by a pair of electric-red eyes.

'I am the Claviger,' she said, her voice taking on a mechanical hum. 'The Keeper of the Keys that unlock all secrets.'

Simon nodded. 'That's all I needed to hear. Pandora!'

Beyond the door, Pandora made her move. One hand

slipped its bonds with quicksilver dexterity. She reached into the hidden fold at the back of her dress and retrieved the blades of her ancestors. Before the guards could react, she sliced through the rope that bound her and was on her feet. Meanwhile, the apparently unconscious Brag Badderson opened his eyes and threw himself into the air. Landing on the far side of the garden, the troll retrieved his club from its hiding place in a privet hedge.

The guards pounced, but Pandora was already on the attack. Wheeling her knives, she transformed into a lethal, silver blur. Inhuman screams rang out. Arms, legs and heads tumbled and hit the ground. The three guards closest to Pandora had been scythed down like stalks of ripened wheat.

Brag Badderson was not to be outdone. He lifted his club, and Simon saw that the head of the weapon had been dipped in liquid silver. Four snarling guards rushed the troll, only to be greeted by the combined might of silver and stone. Like a troll-powered bowling ball, the club knocked them aside as if they were skittles.

'Strike!' Brag bellowed.

His joy was short-lived.

There was only one guard left: a pale-faced creature who had been standing at the fringes of the battle. Now he surveyed the crushed and butchered bodies of his comrades and his lips drew back over a set of vicious teeth. The monster hissed with rage and threw itself at the troll.

'Brag!' Pandora warned. 'Watch out!'

Brag turned to face his attacker. He pulled back his club, but it was too late. The creature flipped in the air and landed feet first, smashing his heels into Brag's gut. The troll's eyes bulged. He dropped his club, teetered backwards and crashed down onto the hard earth. Brag's face turned from pink to red to purple as he struggled to breathe. Meanwhile, the creature straddled Brag's chest like a wolf hovering over its prey.

Simon rushed forward, desperate to help his friend. He was halfway down the corridor when the iron arm of the Claviger blocked his way. Her hand gripped his throat and pinned him against the wall.

'Now, now,' she said, 'let the boys play nicely.'

She smiled victoriously, but the smirk was soon wiped from her lips. Something whispered through the air and the Claviger screamed in agony. She looked down at the silver-tipped arrow that had punctured her arm. A thread of fizzing smoke rose up from the wound. Cursing, she released Simon, who fell to his knees. Another arrow thumped into the Claviger's shoulder and sent her sprawling down the corridor.

Clutching his bruised throat, Simon got to his feet. He reached the lawn just in time to see the monster lock its jaws around Brag's neck. Although it had an arrow protruding out of its back, the thing was so enraged it did not seem to notice. Its teeth tried to pierce the troll's tough flesh but succeeded only in scraping the skin. Despite Brag's best efforts to wrestle with it, the creature managed to dodge every blow.

The archer who had saved Simon stood in the lane. She had another arrow notched in her bow but couldn't get a clear shot at Brag's attacker. Pandora had managed to slice at the monster's back but, again, his rage had made him insensible to pain. And now his frenzied attack seemed to be paying off. He had struck blood.

Simon saw the green goo ooze out of Brag's throat. It was all the motivation he needed. He ran back into the house, making for the huddled form of the Claviger. A fresh gasp escaped her lips as Simon wrenched the silver-tipped arrow from her arm. Her curses and shrieks accompanied him down the hall and onto the lawn. Pandora saw him coming and stepped back. With the arrow clenched in his mouth, Simon threw himself at the monster.

He fixed his knees around its waist and locked his right arm around its throat. A pair of red eyes turned and blazed into Simon's. He saw the green blood on its lips and his anger surged. Snatching the arrow from his mouth, Simon thrust the head into the monster's left eye. The tip punctured the soft jelly and slid back into the skull. Smoke rose up out of the eyeless socket. With a long howl of agony, the thing tumbled off Brag and lay twitching on the ground.

Simon rolled away from the slow-dying monster.

'Bl-bloody vam-vampires,' Brag croaked, lumbering upright.

Pandora slapped his lower back. 'Let's count ourselves lucky he didn't make you drink *his* blood.' She shuddered. 'Imagine it—a vampire-troll!'

Simon looked from the archer to Pandora. His face flushed an angry red.

'I told you not to—'

'Like I wasn't going to tell her,' Pandora cut in. 'I'm sorry, honey, but she had a right to know what was going on.'

Rachel slipped the bow onto her back. She walked towards Simon, her eyes hard, her mouth set.

'Rachel,' Simon gulped, 'I'm sorry about the way I left. I just—'

She grabbed his collar and pulled him into a long, deep kiss. Pandora raised her eyebrows while Brag coughed and looked at his feet. Still unsmiling, Rachel stepped back and pointed her forefinger against the bridge of Simon's nose.

'*You* have some explaining to do.'

Cross-eyed, Simon nodded dumbly. Then Rachel turned and strode into the cottage. Pandora laughed and they followed Rachel into the gloom of the corridor. They found her standing over the Claviger.

'What is she?' Simon asked.

'Part vampire, part who-the-hell-knows?' Pandora said. 'That was Adam's description, by the way. All we know is that she's very, very old, and that she has always been a close friend of demonkind. Bearing in mind the things she can do, it was a risk for the Demon Father to send her here. Still, she is one of his most powerful allies.'

'Your speculation is idle,' the Claviger said. 'You could never fathom the mind of so sublime a creature as the Demon Father. Do what you must and let this be over.'

'As you wish. Simon, you see the purse she carries on her belt? Take out the first key you find.'

The small leather purse jangled at Simon's touch. He reached inside and felt the rusty teeth of an old key. Bringing it into the light, he saw that there were words inscribed on the bronze shaft:

The Secret History of Simon Lydgate

'OK,' Pandora said. 'The next part is rather disgusting. Brag, hold her down.'

Brag secured the strange creature in the grip of his powerful hands.

'She ain't going nowhere.'

'Right, Simon, you'll find a keyhole in the back of her head—'

'What?'

'Here, I'll show you.'

Pandora combed a parting in the Claviger's hair. The black strands drew back to reveal a large weeping keyhole carved right into the creature's skull. Beyond the hole, Simon could make out the soft red shimmer of the Claviger's brain. He turned away, and even Brag Badderson gave a queasy grunt.

'Babies,' Pandora snorted. 'Here, give me the key.'

Simon gave it up willingly. He watched through wincing eyes as Pandora inserted the big key into the back of the Claviger's head. It slotted home with a wet slurp and Pandora gave it a sharp twist to the right. The Claviger's face went blank and her skin seemed to grow harder and ever more metallic in the moonlight.

'*This is the Secret History of Simon Lydgate,*' she said, her voice halting and robotic. '*Listen well, boy: you are* not *half-demon.*'

Simon felt Rachel's hand slip into his.

'*The Demon Father has claimed that you are his son. This is not, and never has been, true. Although he is connected to you, he is not your father.*'

'Then . . . my mother.'

'*Your mother was a witch. The most cunning, brilliant and black-souled witch I have ever known. Your father was a wastrel, a nobody, a piece of human garbage, much like yourself. He came begging at your mother's door and she took him in. Once she was sure she was with child, she murdered him and disposed of the body. No one came looking for him. No one cared.*'

'But why did she want a child?' Simon asked, his voice shaking.

'*It was a favour to her beloved demon. A favour to HIM.*'

'You mean the Demon Father?'

'*Even the Father of Demons has served as a familiar in his time.*'

'But why did he want a human child?' Pandora asked.

'*The Demon Father has played the long game. For years he has plotted what might happen after the Door is opened and his children have flooded into this world. They would need servants to carry out their will. A slave race to build their new dominion. Normal humans would not suffice. They are feeble-bodied, weak-willed, and they die so very easily. But if the human race could be strengthened, improved . . . All they needed was a little demon blood in their veins.*'

'My mother.'

'*The greatest alchemist and potion-maker of her age. She made a tincture of the Demon Father's blood and injected it into her baby son. For years, she continued the procedure, hoping that one day the demon's essence would bond with you. She even tried to influence your subconscious, telling you that you*' *were evil. Monstrous. And finally, it worked. The blood bonded, regressing you back to a more powerful, animalistic stage of human evolution. But you were never demonic, Simon. That monstrous side of you comes from the link that humanity once had with its near cousins—the Cynocephali.'*

'The dog-headed people,' Rachel said, thinking back to the doorman of the Grimoire Club. 'Razor told us that humans and Cynocephali were once related.'

'*A human with the strength of a Cynocephalus.'* The Claviger nodded. '*The perfect demon slave. Strong, violent, remorseless.'*

'A born killer,' Simon said. 'And she was my first victim.'

'*Who do you mean?'* the Claviger asked.

'My mother.'

The creature laughed. '*But your mother isn't dead . . . Oh, I see it now—you really have no idea, do you? Who your mother really is. What she is . . . '*

'Don't toy with him,' Rachel snapped. 'Just tell us.'

The Claviger's red eyes burned with excitement. Simon felt his soul tremble.

'*Prepare yourself, Mr Lydgate,'* she grinned. '*You are in for a big, BIG surprise . . . '*

Chapter 23
The Gallows Hour

Adam Harker gripped the telephone receiver with a shaking hand. He listened carefully to Pandora's report, interrupting only to clarify certain points.

'I see,' he said at last, 'and how is Simon?'

'Pretty shook up, as you can imagine,' Pandora said breathlessly. 'I still can't believe it. Did you ever suspect?'

'No,' Adam sighed. 'I believed whole-heartedly that he *was* half-demon. Bearing in mind the stories I'd heard, and what we saw when he transformed, it seemed the most logical explanation. I never dreamed that he'd been experimented on; that demon blood had been used to regress him back to a Cynocephalus hybrid. The Demon Father is far-sighted indeed, to have tried to create a slave race. I just pray that Simon was his *only* experiment . . . Tell me, is Simon remaining calm? There're no signs of him transforming?'

'No. Rachel's with him. They're going through the

exercises you gave him, just to be sure. And Brag's got his club handy in case Simon gets a case of the hairy.'

'And the Claviger?'

'Just sitting there. Disgusting vamp keeps saying she's thirsty. I told her to keep her eyes off our necks or I'd cut out her liver and feed it to her whole.'

'Set her loose.'

'What?'

'With the Institute destroyed, we're in no position to hold her prisoner, Pandora.'

'But she'll go straight back to the Demon Father and tell him everything.'

'That can't be helped.'

'It can if I stake her. Say the word and the bloodsucker's dust.'

'Pandora.' Adam's voice hardened. 'You're better than that.'

'Fine,' she muttered like a small child deprived of a treat. 'So, what do we do about Simon?'

'He must come back to the Grimoire Club.'

'He won't. He says that, even though he's not half-demon, he still poses a threat to us.'

'Tell him that it's vital for our safety that he returns. He cannot be allowed to fall into the hands of the Demon Father again. Tell him, now that I know what he is, I may be able to help him.'

'Is that true?'

Adam hesitated. 'I'll do my best.'

'OK,' Pandora sounded unsure. 'But I think he'll only

come if you have answers about his mother. Adam, tell me honestly, did you have *any* idea?'

Adam looked at the man sitting on the other side of the desk. 'None.'

He was about to hang up when Pandora asked her last question:

'Is there any news? Has the *Codex* started writing again? Is Jake OK?'

Adam ran his hands over the ancient yellow parchment of the *Codex Tempus*. His finger traced the last sentence on the page—*death by hanging*.

'No, Pandora, there's no news.'

He replaced the receiver in its cradle.

Dr Holmwood leaned forward in his chair. 'Tell me.'

Adam repeated Pandora's report. By the time he had reached the end, Holmwood had sucked two cigarettes down to their stubs.

'You realize that this changes everything,' he said, breathing out a lungful of grey-yellow smoke.

'Of course.' Adam held his head in his thin hands. 'I blame myself. I ought to have looked into the boy's story more closely, not just accepted the dark creature gossip.'

'It is indeed unfortunate that you were not more thorough,' Holmwood nodded, 'and that you concealed his existence from the Institute. Still, no point crying over spilt milk. Saxby has heard reports that the Demon Father and Roland Grype have left Havlock Grange and have been spotted in London. Now we have this new intelligence that makes perfect sense. He has come to see *her* . . . It is time to act.'

Holmwood heaved himself out of the chair. He shrugged on his overcoat and turned back to Adam.

'I trust the boy will survive,' he said. 'Now, more than ever, we need the power of the witch ball. Without it, this world is lost.'

'How can he survive?' Adam jabbed a finger against the *Codex*. 'The rope's virtually round his neck. You more or less put it there yourself.'

Holmwood took a deep breath. 'I'm sorry, but I still believe that I acted for the best.' He moved to the door and, with his face turned to the woodwork, said, 'I do not believe that we will see each other again, Adam. Not in this life, at any rate. I just wanted to say that, although we've had our differences, I always thought of you as a son. I may not have been much of a father, but I—'

'Goodbye, Gordon.'

Holmwood gave a stiff nod and left the room.

Adam remained at the desk while memories raged behind his eyes. He saw himself as a boy, a grimy-faced toddler being dandled on Uncle Gordon's knee. He remembered his first day at Hobarron's Hollow school, listening with rapt attention to an assembly conducted by Dr Holmwood. Other memories: his initiation into the Elders; Holmwood revealing to him the reality of witches and demons; going to the Institute leader with his idea to make a clone of the Witchfinder.

Adam gasped at the power of these memories. He realized that, although he had good reason to despise the man, without Holmwood the greatest joy in his life would never have existed. Holmwood had sent Jake to his death, and yet it had been the old doctor's power, wealth, and influence that had been responsible for giving the boy life. Surely that had deserved a scrap of thanks?

Adam turned his thoughts to the *Codex*. Staring into the grain of the parchment, he pleaded for the phantom quill to begin writing again. Somewhere in the distant past, his son's life was hanging in the balance.

'The shadows lengthen,' said Mr Lanyon. 'The hour is almost upon us.'

After the trial, Jake had been taken down into the dank cellars beneath the Shire Hall and imprisoned in a little cell filled with empty wine barrels. The thief-proof door was sturdy and the room was windowless. Jake was to be held here until the gallows were ready to receive him. With their construction almost complete, Jake had thought that his appointment with the hangman would come soon, but the afternoon had worn on and no one had come for him.

The delay was explained by Mr Lanyon. It seemed that a committee of local merchants led by the landlord of The Green Man had begged Earl Richard to hold off on the witch's execution until twilight. England's Civil War had taken its toll on their trade, and it was in the interests of the town that this unexpected festival should not be wasted. While the crowds waited for the hanging, they would eat and drink and their purses would become ever lighter. Always mindful of his popularity with the powerful merchants, the Earl had proclaimed:

'*Let the rushes be lit, for there will be gallows at twilight...*'

'Will you tell me who you really are?' Leonard Lanyon asked. 'And why you came to Cravenmouth?'

His hands still manacled, Jake sat on the floor while Lanyon hitched up his buff coat and climbed onto one of the wine barrels.

'Let's make a deal,' Jake said. 'I'll tell you who I am if you tell me who *you* are.'

The vicar's eyes flitted to the cell door.

'If you're worried, why don't you speak with your thoughts?'

The reply flashed into Jake's mind—*Hush!*

How do you do it?

My mother. Lanyon gave a sickly smile. *When I was small, I'd go out walking with her, into the fields and forest, following the roads and the streams. My father was a preacher: a man who could only find God inside the cold walls of his church. But my mother and I, we saw the goodness of the world manifest in trees and animals, in the water and the air. While we walked we would talk to each other, and yet we never once said a word. She called our talk 'the Whispers of Oldcraft'.*

Oldcraft, Jake echoed.

You know the word?

It's where all magic comes from. The ancient spirit of this world.

You mean God? Lanyon asked, and shivered, as if something troubling had touched his heart.

Maybe, Jake thought, *I don't know.*

Deep inside, Jake caught a glimpse of a hidden light

burning just beyond his reach. A secret he had glimpsed before but which always eluded him. He glanced back at Lanyon.

Sometimes I think I know where it comes from. Oldcraft. Magic. Who created it. Who placed it in the Earth. Who allowed humans to feel its touch . . . He shook his head. *So, your mother, she was a witch, then?*

That's what they called her. In the end.

They?

The townspeople. The witnesses and the magistrates. Him.

Who?

My father. It was by his word that she was condemned. They took her out to the gallows and they hanged her high. My father made me stand beneath and watch every kick, every shudder, every spasm. For long years he had used the Bible as a whetstone to sharpen his spirit into a blade of righteousness. He laid that blade at my mother's throat and thrust it deep into her flesh.

I'm sorry.

Do not say that! Silent tears rolled down Lanyon's face. *Do not apologize to me. I, who through cowardice, have trod my father's path and have condemned an innocent to the gallows.*

'You were afraid,' Jake said aloud, 'that's not a crime.'

It is. My mother's spirit tells me so. And yet even now I cannot bring myself to save you. I remember how she died, and my soul quakes at the thought of it.

Jake levelled his gaze with Lanyon's.

You wanted to hear my story? Then listen carefully.

Jake told the tale of how he had come to Cravenmouth: his life in the twenty-first century; his discovery of his true identity; his battle with dark witches and their demons; and finally his journey on the Scarab Path to find Josiah Hobarron's witch ball. By the time he had finished, Lanyon's eyes were wide and staring.

'It's madness,' the vicar said. 'Everyone knows that we are living in the final days of this world, and yet you tell me that life continues four hundred years hence?'

'Yes,' Jake said, 'but maybe not for much longer. That's why I came back. Without the witch ball, the world will fall to demonkind.'

'And the beetle that brought you here—that was the creature we saw in the hall? The stone scarab?'

Jake nodded. 'Dr Holmwood said that the beetle would only leave me if it sensed that my death was near. Mr Lanyon, if I don't escape from here, if I don't find the witch ball, then the demons will win.'

'But haven't they won already? You lost the scarab—how can you return home now?'

'I'll find a way. Maybe the witch ball will have the power to send me back. All I know is, unless you help me, then four hundred years from now the demons will break free from their prison dimension. Billions of people will be slaughtered, the entire world will fall.'

Jake rose to his feet.

'I know you're frightened, but the future is in your hands.'

He heard the sound of a bolt being drawn, the rasp of a key in the lock.

Lanyon wrenched his gaze away from Jake.

'God forgive me, I cannot help you. *I dare not!*'

The cry was taken up by the crowd.

'Hats off! Hats off!'

At first Jake thought that it was said as a mark of respect; a scrap of dignity to be afforded to the condemned man. As he saw the tall Puritan hats being batted off heads, however, he realized that it was because the people behind simply wanted a better view of the execution. The leering faces, almost inhuman in their hunger for death, made Jake's heart tremble.

He was led by Monks and Utterson down the steps of the Shire Hall and towards the baying mob. The crowd seemed to have doubled. They packed the windows and rooftops and perched on the groaning boughs of the trees like a gallery of strange birds.

At the foot of the stairs stood the gallows: a spindly man-made tree, leafless and starkly black against the sunset. The scaffold was surrounded by a ring of watchmen armed with pikes and muskets who struggled to keep back the crowd. As Jake was dragged up a rickety ladder to the gallows platform, he felt a hand clutch at his leg.

'Any last words, sir?'

Jake looked down into a dirty, eager face. The man took a quill from behind his ear and a scrap of parchment from his pocket. He licked the quill tip with an ink-black tongue.

'Who are you?' Jake asked.

'An Ordinary Man. That's to say, I write little stories for the broadsheets. Always good to get a gallows confession from a witch—helps sales immensely, don't you know.' The man winked. 'So, you gonna spill your guts or have I got to make it up?'

Monks growled like a bulldog and the Ordinary Man shrugged and scuttled away.

'Shame,' Jake smiled, 'I was just about to tell him everything. Make a full confession of my witchery ways.'

'You were?' Monks frowned.

'Wow. You really are thick, aren't you, Sergeant Monks?'

Jake flashed a grin and was bundled up the ladder. On the platform, three figures waited in the dying light: the Earl, the Witchfinder, and Leonard Lanyon. Earl Richard held a posy of flowers to his nose to ward off the stink of the square. Like a ravenous jackal tasting the kill, Matthew Hopkins's tongue flickered across his thin lips. Lanyon fixed his eyes on the wooden floor and seemed unable to look at Jake, even as the prisoner was paraded in front of him.

Having only caught a glimpse of the gallows, this was Jake's first opportunity to see how it had been constructed. The simplicity of the death machine chilled him to the core. The upright post of the inverted L stood at the back of the platform while the shorter horizontal beam jutted forward towards the square. A sturdy rope hung down from the beam to a point just level with Jake's head. He had thought that there would be a trapdoor below the noose, and that the drop of four metres to the ground would be enough to snap his neck. A clean, quick death. He should have known better. In this barbaric age, death was a hard and brutal thing, even for the innocent. For a witch it must be seen to be a lingering exercise in agony.

Instead of a trapdoor, a large rectangle had been cut out of the platform and the cart that had brought Jake from the keep had been backed into the space. Jake was led onto the back of the cart and forced to stand on the wooden box that would soon be his coffin. The manacles were struck from his wrists and his hands were tied behind his back. Monks took Jake by the scruff of the neck. The sergeant forced his head into the noose and pulled the rope tight behind his right ear.

'Ready for the drop?' he whispered.

For the first time, Jake's voice faltered.

'H-how long will it take?'

'Depends on many things,' Monks shrugged. 'On a man's will, on God's pleasure. I've heard tell of men hanged from the Tyburn Tree in London who didn't die for days. Even when the birds pecked out their eyes, still they gagged and struggled. But a scrawny little thing like you? I'd wager ten minutes, twenty at the outside.'

'And after?' Jake said, forcing the words out. 'What happens then?'

'We'll bury you under these gallows and drive an iron stake through your heart,' Monks sneered. 'Only sure way to keep your damned ghost from haunting the town.'

Due to hunger, fear, or the effects of his recent torture, Jake suddenly weakened. He stumbled across the box but managed to remain upright.

'See the tears upon his cheeks!' a voice called out from the crowd. 'The witch cries for his miserable life!'

Jake felt the single teardrop slide down his face, but the man was wrong. He did not cry for himself. As he watched the fiery sunset dip behind the black houses, his thoughts turned to the future: to his dying father and his doomed friends; to the victory of the Demon Father and the destruction of the world. Fire, death, unimaginable suffering, and every evil thing made possible by *his* failure.

A lone drummer standing at the foot of the gallows began to beat out a dirge. The heavy rhythm caught at Jake's heart. He twisted his neck and stared at Lanyon through tear-blind eyes.

'Please . . .'

Matthew Hopkins's brow furrowed. His curious gaze slipped between Jake and the vicar. Lanyon shuddered and kept his eyes on the ground.

'Make way there!' Monks shouted at the crowd.

They parted and a narrow path was made for the cart. An expression of self-importance on his face, Monks turned to Hopkins and the Earl.

'My lord,' he bowed, 'Mr Hopkins, sir—might I lead the cart?'

'You have been a faithful assistant, Mr Monks.' Hopkins nodded. 'Indeed, you shall have this last honour. Go now, put an end to the Cravenmouth witch.'

Grinning from ear to ear, Monks hauled himself down from the cart and waddled around to the front. A guard placed the reins in Monks's podgy fist. Jake felt the cart move beneath him. His bare feet slid back across the coffin lid and the noose tightened around his throat. He snatched at the air and filled his lungs. It was now or never.

Every day since his imprisonment Jake had tried to summon his magic. Every day he had failed to find it. His last desperate attempt had been in the cellar of the Shire Hall just before Lanyon had come to talk to him. Yet again he had delved deep into his soul, conjuring memories that might inspire the Oldcraft. Memories of anger and fear and dread. Now, in his dying-hour, he strove with every psychic fibre of his being to locate that hidden place where the magic was stored.

The mob had fallen silent, the drummer had ceased the dirge. The sound of Monks clicking his tongue, the rattle of the bridle, the creak of the cart, even the pad of the pony's hoof upon the dusty ground sounded out, crisp and clear in the stillness. Jake's feet slipped back another few inches across the coffin lid. He gasped as the noose hitched tighter, tighter . . .

No longer able to turn his neck, he hissed through gritted teeth, '*Pllleeeassseee.*'

The plea was addressed to both Leonard Lanyon and himself. As fear and desperation mounted, he continued his search into the dark and twisting avenues of his mind. He found . . . nothing. The Khepra Beetle, that strange creature that perceived all of time and space, had seen what was to come and had abandoned its host. There was no hope of Jake escaping his fate.

The old pony whinnied and the cart rumbled forward.

Jake's toes scraped to the edge of the coffin. His legs

scrabbled, desperate not to lose their footing. Glancing back, Monks saw that another cruel inch would do it. He slapped the whip against the pony's flank and the cart jolted forward.

Jake dropped.

The noose snatched at his neck and his body swung back and forth like a grisly human pendulum. A roar went up in the square; a ragged cheer that was troubled at its edges by a few isolated cries of horror. Behind him, Jake's hands clenched into fists. His toes curled and his knees bent as he struggled to breathe. Little sparks of pain crackled along his stretching spine. His mouth gaped and his tongue lolled over his teeth. He could hear the blood pounding in his head as it tried to squeeze below the stranglehold of the rope. In the barrel of his oxygen-starved body, his lungs fluttered like the crippled wings of a bird.

The rope began to twist in steady circles. Jake could feel the unbearable pressure of blood building behind his eyes. The pain of it blasted his vision into shards until it was like seeing the world through the facets of a diamond. The laughing, jeering, haunted and sorrowful faces of the crowd came to him in jagged pieces. He saw Earl Richard, posy still held to his upturned nose; Lanyon on his knees, eyes tight shut, praying with all his might; the Witchfinder, nodding and smiling, gratified at a job well done. Through the blood roaring in his ears, Jake heard the euphoric cry of Matthew Hopkins:

'WOE UNTO THE ENEMIES OF GOD! DEATH TO ALL WITCHES!'

A long and sickening rattle worked its way down the

length of Jake's spine. His teeth clamped together as the tarred rope burned into his neck. Still he struggled. Still he fought.

A young woman stepped forward from the crowd. Her face wet with tears, she tried to fight her way through.

'Let me catch at his legs!' she screamed. 'For the love of God, let me pull him down and shorten his suffering!'

Another woman joined her, beating her fists against the guards.

'Have mercy, you knaves!'

But there was no mercy. Not for Jake and not for the women. One of the guards raised his musket and dashed it against the first woman's head. Blood splattered the guard's face and the woman dropped to the ground. Kneeling beside her, the second woman shrieked in horror:

'You've cracked her skull wide open! She's dead! Murderer! MURDERER!'

The news caught like wildfire: one of the guards had killed a woman—butchered her—smashed her head to a pulp and was now laughing over the corpse. Even Jake, his ears filled with the dull thud of death, could hear the hollers of outrage. Fired by calls for justice, red-faced men took the clubs and cudgels from their belts and marched on the gallows. Women and even children joined them, breaking heavy branches from trees, picking sharp stones from the ground, finding weapons where they could. With their fury fixed on the circle of guards, the crowd seemed to have forgotten the witch.

The first stone struck the guard who had killed the woman

and he fell screaming to his knees. A barrage of stones followed. Three more guards dropped, their faces bloodied. Jake felt the rocks hit his legs, but against the agony of the gallows the pain was dull and distant. The rope twisted and he turned to face the platform. Always alert to danger, the Witchfinder was already beating a retreat to the safety of the Shire Hall. Earl Richard had followed Hopkins's example. The nobleman was halfway up the steps when a large brick hurtled through the air and smashed against his skull. Like the peasant woman before him, the Honourable Richard Rake was dead before he hit the ground.

Only Leonard Lanyon remained. In the chaos that had erupted, the vicar saw his chance. He took a dagger from his belt and made a dash for the gallows rope. Just before he reached it, a hand locked down on his shoulder and spun him around.

'And where do you think you're going?' Monks panted.

'For God's sake, have pity!' Lanyon bellowed.

'For God's sake, I will not.'

Monks drew back his big fist and slammed it into Lanyon's stomach. The vicar gasped and the dagger fell from his hand. Sergeant Monks took his own knife from its scabbard and pressed the tip against Lanyon's throat.

'Master Hopkins had the measure of you, sir. He told me that you were a filthy witch-lover; probably even a sorcerer yourself underneath all that godliness!'

Jake's vision dimmed. The rope righted itself and he turned again, away from Monks and Lanyon. The square was now a seething mass of people, a rabble fighting against the guards and each other. Screams and musket fire echoed on all sides and the smell of gunsmoke filled the air. To the west, the sunlight scattered in blood-red shafts while the heavens sank into a deep and desolate black.

Twilight had come.

Darkness crept from the corners of the world and Jake's pain slipped away. The noise of battle, the fear of the future, the terror of death—none of it mattered any more.

The light was waiting for him.

Jacob Harker—his true self—was going home.

Wrapped in this sense of peace, Jake looked out into the square and saw the figure coming towards him. She moved with ghost-like ease through the warring mob. The people didn't seem conscious of her presence, and yet they moved aside to let her pass. Her pace was swift and assured. Within seconds, she had slipped between what remained of the guards and was at the foot of the gallows.

Jake's legs ceased to twitch. His heart slowed. Stopped. His head fell forward and, with his last scrap of energy, he looked down on the figure in grey. The light of her soul burned around her with all the fire of the setting sun.

The girl pulled back her hood and lifted her face to him.

Jake felt his heart throb once more.

Her name creaked between his lips.

'*Eleanor* . . .'

Chapter 24
Fight and Flight

Hearing her name spoken by Jake, the girl's cool, determined expression broke apart. She looked at him with such grief in her eyes that Jake forgot the pain of his execution and felt the twist of a deeper agony in his soul. Words came to him, both familiar and strange—

My Eleanor of the May. My own sweet girl . . .

She swung herself up onto the platform, sweeping the short sword from her belt as she did so, and landing noiselessly behind Sergeant Monks. Her movements, so smooth and dextrous, stirred a memory. Jake had once known another nimble warrior with golden hair and bright wide eyes, but with his senses fading he could no longer recall the girl's name.

Eleanor jabbed her sword between Monks's shoulder blades. The sergeant squealed like a stuck pig. Then he looked over his shoulder and his expression switched from terror to amusement.

'But you're just a girl!'

'A girl with a sword,' Eleanor corrected.

She flipped the weapon and brought its heavy handle crashing down on Monks's head. The man dropped the dagger that he had been holding to Lanyon's throat and keeled over onto his back. Eleanor kicked the unconscious sergeant aside.

'The Preacher said you'd help me.' She eyed Lanyon with a trace of distrust. 'And the Preacher's never wrong, so move yourself.'

Lanyon nodded and raced across the gallows. He caught hold of Jake's legs and hauled him to the platform. Although the noose was still tight around his throat, the relentless pressure of gravity that had stretched Jake's spine was gone. Meanwhile, Eleanor took a run up and used the unwary Lanyon's back as a springboard. She rolled into the air, the sword held against the side of her body. At the apex of her leap, she struck out and, with a single blow, cut the rope.

Lanyon tightened his hold around Jake as the boy dropped. Together, they collapsed onto the platform. With Jake still struggling for breath, Lanyon retrieved his dagger and started cutting away at the noose. The rope was thick, the knots drawn taut, and the vicar's fingers fumbled with fear. Eleanor pushed him aside and went to work with her own, sharper blade. Beneath the rope, she found a raw and ragged collar of skin. Air creaked into Jake's lungs.

'M-my Eleanor of the May . . . '

'Don't call me that! Those are not *your* words.' She turned to Lanyon. 'Get him to his feet.'

Jake's heart burned. A few cruel words from this girl and he wished that he had been left on the gallows. Better to hang, to die, than to be unloved by *her*.

Lanyon tore the sleeves from his shirt and quickly bandaged Jake's throat. The three figures on the gallows stood together in the darkness after twilight. Less than five minutes had elapsed between Eleanor's arrival in the square and Jake's rescue. In that time, the fighting between the guards and the mob had reached a lull and now all eyes had turned once more to the Cravenmouth witch.

'It's the vicar!' one of the guards shouted. 'The vicar stands with the witch!'

'I can get us out of here,' Eleanor whispered. 'The Preacher has given me the means, but . . . '

'But?' Jake wheezed.

'It is a magical pathway, designed to carry only us two.'

The mood of the crowd was like quicksilver. Within the blink of an eye, they had turned from self-righteous citizens back into a superstitious mob. Seeing their chance to escape the crowd's mercurial anger, the guards spoke up.

'Mr Lanyon has always been a friend of the witch!'

'Master Hopkins told us so!'

'Aye, I've seen it with me own eyes.' This was Constable Utterson, his voice ringing through the square. 'The vicar always spoke very prettily on the witch's behalf. Now he has brought another of their coven to save the boy!'

The crowd surged forward, swords and pikes, bricks and torches, stones and halberds in hand. Their twisted mouths and narrowed eyes told their intention very clearly. There would be no trial and no tidy execution for these damned witches. The mob planned to tear them to pieces, here and now, and leave the scraps for the dogs.

'You must go,' Lanyon said. 'Leave while you still can.'

Eleanor nodded sadly. 'It's as the Preacher foretold. You are a brave man, Mr Lanyon.'

'No. I've been a coward all my life, but now I have the chance to make my mother proud.' He smiled at Jake. 'Goodbye, my brother in Oldcraft.'

The vicar turned and walked to the front of the platform. A few stray stones struck his face, but the man held his ground. The mob had started shaking the legs of the gallows and climbing the ladder when Jake made his dash. He caught Lanyon's arm and dragged him back.

'If we're going, we're going together.'

'But it's his destiny to die here,' Eleanor objected. 'The Preacher has foreseen it.'

'Yeah, well, we have a saying in the twenty-first century,' Jake licked his bone-dry lips. 'Destiny-schmestiny. He's coming with us.'

The girl's frosty expression thawed. Her hand, small and strong, went to Jake's chest and pressed against his heart. She studied his face and her voice cracked with emotion.

'It's what *he* would have done.'

Jake covered her hand with his. Their eyes met and he felt the spark of some forgotten fire in his soul. It was her and it always had been. The mover of his magic . . .

'If I may?' Lanyon interrupted. 'Whatever you're going to do, you better get on with it.'

'When I give the word, you must close your eyes.' Eleanor's gaze remained fixed on Jake. 'Do you understand? You *must not* see what happens. If you catch even the slightest glimpse, the Preacher has told me that the war with the demons will be lost before it has even begun.'

'But why? What're you gonna do?'

'No questions. Just promise me.'

Jake gave a reluctant nod.

During their discussion, the mob and the guards had climbed the scaffold and were now closing in on their prey. Scarred and limping, this half-mad horde still screeched for blood. They were within striking distance when Eleanor reached into her cloak and gave Jake the command:

'CLOSE YOUR EYES!'

A split second before he obeyed, Jake caught sight of a man standing on the far side of the platform.

Matthew Hopkins, the infamous Witchfinder General, coughed and a speckle of blood stained his lips.

'I will find you, witch!' he bellowed. 'If I have to follow you into the depths of hell, I will find you! YOU CAN NEVER ESCAPE MEEEeeee!'

A silver explosion flashed against Jake's closed lids. A rush of wind as he was lifted into the air. An electric crackle and, before the darkness reclaimed his senses, the touch of earth, the sight of trees, the hush of a forest, and . . .

Her. Eleanor. Lying beside him.

Years had fractured.

Centuries crumbled.

Time itself had shown that it could be kind.

Jacob—Josiah—had found his Eleanor again . . .

'Daybreak. We have to move.'

Jake was shaken roughly by the shoulder. He woke to find himself in the forest glade he had glimpsed the night before. A beautiful face fringed with golden, dawn-drenched hair loomed over him. He smiled, and the smile broke into every corner of his being. Untouched for so long, deep memories and feelings were rising to the surface.

As Jake blinked up at Eleanor, he suddenly realized who she reminded him of. Although they were separated by hundreds of years they could have been sisters, or even twins, for they looked about the same age: Eleanor of the May and Rachel Saxby . . . Jake sat up. A little sigh of surprise passed his lips. Of course! They *were* related. Rachel was a descendant of Josiah Hobarron, and so this young woman must be her distant ancestor too! A great-great-great-great-great (probably a few more greats) grandmother!

He laughed and the girl leaning over him smiled.

'What's funny?'

'I don't think I can explain it,' Jake said. 'It's too crazy!'

Eleanor's smile widened, and Jake saw a line of white teeth, perfect except for a slight dent on her left canine.

'Chip,' he said softly.

Eleanor's face hardened.

'Don't call me that.' She jumped to her feet and hurried

towards the campfire. 'That was his name for me.'

'Eleanor, wait.'

Jake tried to stand. He had expected flashes of agony to strike along his neck, spine, shoulders, arms and legs, but there was no pain. Not even the slightest twinge. Stunned, he rolled his head and stretched his muscles.

Jake looked at the girl slouched beside the campfire.

'How?'

When Eleanor didn't answer the man sitting on the log next to her gave a huge smile.

'Magic,' said Mr Lanyon. 'Wonderful, miraculous, spiritual, beautiful, godly magic!'

And with that the vicar leapt off the log and started dancing around the fire. He sang snippets of hymns and fragments of tavern songs, verses of scripture and bawdy ballads. It didn't seem to matter what the words were, so long as the tune could express the joy in his heart. He seemed to Jake like a sun-starved bird that had been released from its cage and given the dawn.

Jake caught Eleanor's eye. She was laughing again and clapping her hands to the rhythm of Lanyon's song. He went and sat beside her on the log and, although her smile faltered, it didn't fall away completely. At last, Lanyon tired of his dancing and took a seat between his friends.

'Magic!' he repeated and slapped Jake on the back. 'I saw it done, my boy. It was the finest, the most beautiful, the most holy sight I have ever seen. Here, let me show you.'

Tears in his eyes, Lanyon reached into his jacket pocket and brought out a sliver of mirror.

'A piece of my mother's old looking glass,' he said. 'The only thing I have to remember her by . . . But look! See!'

Lanyon held the mirror to Jake's neck. There was not a burn, not a blister, not a bruise. The glass moved to his face and showed that his nose was firm and straight.

'My back?' Jake asked, his fingers spidering along his spine.

'Healed,' Lanyon said in a soothing voice. 'There are no longer any signs of your torture, Jacob. No evidence of the bodkins and the chains. Not a single trace of that hellish witchfinder.'

Jake beamed. His hand moved over his body, seeking out the places where he had been wounded. All he found was healthy, solid flesh. Then his fingers went to the side of his head and the smile died. His ear was still missing.

Lanyon and Eleanor exchanged concerned glances.

'It seems that there are limits even to the strongest magic,' Lanyon sighed.

'The spell can heal wounds and mend bones, but if the damage is too old and too severe . . . ' Eleanor reached for Jake's hand. 'I'm so sorry, Josiah—I mean . . . '

She stood up. Unashamed of her tears, the girl walked slowly into the forest. Jake was about to follow when Lanyon caught at his sleeve.

'Let her be.'

He stared into Jake's eyes—

She has shared some of her thoughts with me. While you slept, we spoke of many things, strange and wonderful. She told me of this man, Josiah Hobarron, who she grew up with, and who she loved with all her heart. She told me of his gifts, his goodness, his fight against the hidden evils of this world. She told me of his death and of seeing her beloved frozen in a tomb of ice. And now he has returned to her . . .

Lanyon grasped Jake by the shoulders.

You look like him and you have his moral courage. Can you imagine what hopes and terrors your existence holds for her?

Jake shook his head. *I feel for her.*

Do you? Lanyon frowned. *Or are you remembering the feelings of another? You must consider that question carefully, my friend.*

The vicar held out his hand.

'Goodbye.'

Jake pulled him into a hug.

'My cowardice hardly warrants such friendship,' Lanyon said softly.

'You saved me . . . in the end.' Jake winked. 'I always knew you would. So, where will you go now? Not back to Cravenmouth, I bet!'

'No,' Lanyon laughed. 'I had always feared that my "gift" might one day be exposed, and so years ago I buried a little nest-egg near the Crow Haven Tavern on the London Road. I shall dig it up and then hide myself away somewhere in a country parish where no one has heard of Mr Lanyon and the Cravenmouth witch.'

'Good luck,' Jake said.

'And to you, Jacob Harker. My friend.'

A few minutes after Lanyon had left, Eleanor re-emerged from the forest. She looked at the vacated spot beside the fire.

'He's gone?'

'Yes.'

'He was a good man.' She kicked over the ashes, smothering the last embers of the fire. 'It's time we were on our way.'

'Where are we going?'

'To the village, of course. To the Preacher.'

'I can't,' Jake protested. 'I've got this mission, this quest, and I need to—'

'The Preacher knows all about your quest, Jacob Harker,' Eleanor said, leading the way out of the forest. 'Only he can help you find Josiah's witch ball. The Preacher sees all.'

Chapter 25
The Blind Man of Starfall

'You've got your own magic then?' Jake asked.

'No,' Eleanor said, her eyes on the road. 'What you saw was borrowed magic.'

They had been walking for the better part of a day and Jake's bare feet were hot and sore. He winced now as he followed Eleanor over a low stone wall that girdled an untidy meadow. Insects droned in the long grass and the breeze hummed through the trees.

'Then how did you teleport us away from the gallows?'

'Tele-what?'

'Um, make us vanish and reappear in the forest?'

'As I said, borrowed magic.'

Jake shot the girl a sideways look. He gave a wry smile.

'What's so amusing?' Eleanor muttered.

'You are, Chippy. You never were much good at keeping secrets.'

She glanced at him with a mixture of curiosity and annoyance.

'But you—I mean Josiah—he was always the master of secrets. Close as close could be, even when we were children. He'd tease me all the time, hide my dolls and never tell me where they were. One day I found six of them stuffed down the—'

'Well.' Jake stopped in his tracks. 'The old dried-up well in Mr Carew's lower field. You were so upset, and I—*he*—he felt so ashamed. He couldn't bear how much he'd hurt you, and it was then that he realized . . . ' Jake reached for the girl. 'He loved you.'

Eleanor flushed with anger. 'Please, don't speak about him.'

They walked on in silence. With every step new thoughts and feelings cascaded in on Jake, memories that came to him unbidden. He found the sensation both exhilarating and troubling.

In the far distance, Jake could see the shapes of men and women toiling in the fields. He heard the rattle of an oxcart and his thoughts turned to the cart that had borne him and his coffin into the square. If it hadn't been for Eleanor he would now be buried beneath the gallows, an iron stake driven through his heart.

'The Preacher sees all,' Jake quoted. 'This preacher knew that I was coming to Cravenmouth. That I would be executed there.'

'It's why he sent me,' Eleanor confirmed.

'He gave you the magic to save me?'

'Yes.'

'Then why didn't he send you sooner?' Jake thought back over the weeks he had spent in the keep. Days and nights of endless torture.

'His vision was of you on the gallows. Only in your dying moments could you be saved. He saw the woman murdered by the guard, the uproar of the crowds. The Preacher, he . . . ' the words caught her throat, 'he told me that you had to suffer at the Witchfinder's hands; only then would you be prepared.'

'Prepared for what?'

'For what will come. For the journey you will soon have to take into the land of shadows and torment.'

'What does that mean?' Jake asked.

'I'm sorry, the Preacher did not say. He may not even know. His visions are not always complete.'

'But he knows about me? He told you who I am, where I came from.'

Eleanor nodded. 'You are him—Josiah—but you are not him. You are a copy, a duplicate of the man I lost. You come from distant times to find the witch ball and then you will go away again. You have the same face and, like him, you will leave . . . '

'Eleanor?'

Jake could see the struggle as the girl forced herself to look at him.

'Will you hold my hand?'

She hesitated, just for a moment. And then Jake felt the small, strong fingers entwine with his. In that connection, memories, joys, horrors, and hopes passed between them in an unspoken thread of consciousness. They both gasped, and Jake lifted his free hand to the level of his eyes.

He clicked his fingers and a blue flame roared into life.

'Borrowed magic,' he smiled.

'No,' Eleanor said. '*Your* magic.'

They reached the far side of the meadow and Eleanor drew her hand away. Her face had closed again and in her eyes the shutters had gone up. The sound of barking dogs and the smell of woodsmoke filled the air. Jake looked down into the valley below. He saw a semi-circle of wattle and daub cottages surrounding a tiny, lopsided church.

'Starfall,' Eleanor said simply.

That was the name of the village, but another word loomed large in Jake's mind—

HOME.

A switch. A turnabout of ideas. A shifting of viewpoints.

The life of Jacob Harker became blurry while the life of Josiah Hobarron came to the fore in a thousand vivid sights and sounds. Jake's fingers played through the tall grass that bordered the road leading down into Starfall. He remembered: a boy, little more than a toddler, running through this miniature forest. Long ago days when the beetles were lions and bumble bees were dragons. Muffled by the grass, the ghost of a voice called out—*Josiah, come now, your supper is on the table. Hurry, it's your favourite.* Stewed neat's-foot. The boy licked his lips and left the lions and the dragons to their play.

The road narrowed into a cobbled lane.

'Barleyman's street,' Jake murmured. He turned to his left—'Mrs Symond's cottage,' and to his right—'the Bradburys' house.'

'You remember,' Eleanor said quietly.

'Do I?' His voice trembled. 'Or does he?'

Jake clutched the sides of his head—it was too much for one mind, too many lives for one body to contain. His dual existences burned inside him.

'Come on.'

Eleanor reached for him. At the last moment, he saw doubt flicker in her eyes and she tucked her hands under her cloak.

Jake looked at her suspiciously.

'It's hot,' he said. 'Why are you still wearing that thick cloak?'

'I . . . I have to.'

'Why?'

'He gave me the cloak. Told me to wear it, always.'

'The Preacher?'

'Yes.'

'You're hiding something.'

'No, it's just—'

'What is it? Tell me!'

Eleanor brushed past Jake and ran up the lane towards the church. She dodged between the people who had come out of their cottages to see what all the shouting was about. They turned to Jake and, in mortal dread, crossed their hearts and ran back behind their doors. Of course, Jake knew why they were so frightened. Josiah Hobarron had returned from the grave. A dead man was walking in the sunlit streets of Starfall.

As she ran, Jake noticed how Eleanor held her hand against her hip. Noticed the bulge at her belt. Whatever she was hiding from him, he could *feel* it. As soon as he had bent his thoughts on the object, his magic responded. The fire sparked inside him, licked down his arm and ignited between his fingers. From inside the cottages came shouts of surprise and terror as the blue flames erupted from Jake's fists. This was powerful magic; almost as strong as that which he had felt on the night he had destroyed the demon Door. What was happening to him? What was inspiring this formidable Oldcraft?

Only one way to find out.

Carrying the fire with him, Jake strode up the lane. Eleanor had turned down the side of the church and was now standing at the door of a two-storey thatched house. She hammered on the door and looked back over her shoulder. Jake was close enough to see that there was no fear in her eyes. He felt glad—the last thing he wanted was for her to be frightened of him. But she was anxious and, at that moment, she did not want him near her.

'Stay away!' she called. 'Jacob, please, you must *not* see. He told me to keep it hidden.'

Jake came to a stop under the shadow of the tumbledown church. He could barely hear Eleanor over the roar of the blue fire. For the last month or so he had practised and practised, delving into the most painful, hateful memories, all in a bid to reclaim his magic. And now, in the presence of this girl and the thing she had kept hidden, the power of Oldcraft had returned to him unbidden. How was that possible?

He took a step forward. In the same instant, he sensed the unearthly power of the concealed object. The raw throb of energy, the low hum of its Oldcraft song. Instinctively he cupped his palm and in some dusty part of his soul he remembered the coldness of the object in his hand. Once, long ago, he had held it. Held it, clasped it, wielded it against a terrible enemy . . .

Another step forward and the power overwhelmed him. The fire in his fists erupted into volcanic columns of light that soared into the air and pierced the clouds. Screams in the streets, the wail of frightened children, the yelps of terrified dogs. Jake staggered under the weight of his magic. Through the blue haze, he saw Eleanor press her back against the door. The earth trembled. Chips of stone and loose bricks tumbled from the walls of the old church. Birds nesting in the broken roof shot into the sky, their brittle shrieks lost against the deep rumble of Oldcraft. The summer-parched ground cracked apart and the windows of the house shattered outwards.

The glass showered across Eleanor, cutting her face and hands. She winced and a single tear rolled down her cheek. The sight of her blood was more painful to Jake than any agony he had suffered at the hands of Matthew Hopkins. He balled his hands into tight fists and directed the Oldcraft back inside himself. The columns of light collapsed and, with a final sizzle between his fingers, the magic vanished.

The earth became still and silent once more. The clouds knitted the sky back together. Jake looked from his empty hands to the girl at the door. The sight of her huddled there, bloody and bowed, struck him like a hammer blow. He fell back against the wall of the church and slid to the ground.

At the sound of footsteps, Jake looked up. He saw a man walking slowly towards him, tapping out his path with a stick. Shadowed beneath a battered straw hat, the man's grey face looked like a triangle of weather-beaten stone. Where his eyes ought to be there were two sunken sockets, the skin of the lids fused together.

The old man stood over Jake. He smiled warmly, and Jake found the echo of that smile in the darkness of his mind. Bedtime stories: *Aesop's Fables*, Bible stories, tales made up to order. Lessons in the parlour: arithmetic, calculus, the ancient Greeks, natural philosophy, the history of Oldcraft . . . demons. Games: skittles in the lane, hide-and-seek in the wood, nine men's morris played by the kitchen fire while a woman bustled around them, preparing food.

It was too much. Too many memories and emotions. The old man nodded and, with a whisper of words, passed his hand through the air. Jake felt himself slipping, the tug of sleep taking hold. He looked up at that smiling face.

'We will speak soon, my boy,' the Preacher said.

Jake's head drooped to his chest. His words came like those of a sleepy child.

'Yes, father.'

* * *

Jake woke with moonlight in his eyes. He found himself lying on a straw mattress in the corner of a small room. Pulling aside the sheepskin blanket, he saw that he had been stripped of his prison clothes and dressed in a long woollen nightshirt. His face and hands were clean, his short hair had been washed and there was the smell of jasmine on his skin. He wondered who had bathed him.

The yellow glow of a lantern crossed the ceiling. Jake got up and crept to the open window. He saw two cloaked figures on the path, one guiding the other to the door of the old church.

'Eleanor,' Jake murmured. 'Father.'

Father. The word felt right upon his lips, and yet it also struck him as a betrayal. His *real* father was Adam Harker: the man who had raised him, loved him, and who, in some distant future, was dying a slow and painful death.

Bare timbers groaned beneath Jake's feet. The latch of the bedroom door squeaked between his fingers. There were portraits on the wood-panelled walls of the corridor, but the faces were little more than milky smears in the gloom. Jake tiptoed to the stairs. He had reached the last step, and was moving towards the front door, when something warm and wet lapped against the back of his hand. He stifled a surprised yelp.

A sad-eyed bloodhound blinked up at Jake.

'Hello, Sebastian.'

The name popped into Jake's head. He scratched behind the dog's right ear and his fingers found the old scar. He remembered that day in the forest when Sebastian had defended him from a pair of ravenous wolves. The hound had saved his life . . . Josiah's life . . .

'Good boy,' Jake whispered, 'now go to your bed.'

Sebastian's jaw stretched into a wide yawn and he padded away into the darkness.

Jake eased open the front door. It was very dark outside. Heavy clouds rolled across the face of the moon and there was the smell of rain in the air. Jake could see halos of light at the windows of the church. He moved around the side of the building, keeping to the thick shadows thrown by the ancient walls. As he reached the open door and slipped into the church, the clouds broke and rain rattled across the roof.

Eleanor and the Preacher were at the far end of the church and did not hear Jake enter. By the lantern that stood on the altar table, he could just make out the strange scene. While the Preacher sat on the altar steps, Eleanor was on her knees, digging with a short-handled spade. Jake moved into the chapel's western aisle and crept within earshot.

'I've been around the village,' the Preacher said, 'spoken to every household.'

'What on earth did you tell them?'

'I didn't need to say very much. You grew up here, Eleanor; you know as well as they do that Josiah was never an ordinary boy. If anyone was to return from the dead, it would be him. I assured them that, come morning, he will be gone.'

The girl lifted her face to the light. Sweat jewelled her brow and the red scratches made by the broken glass stood out against her pale skin. Jake winced at the thought that he had been responsible for those injuries.

'We leave tomorrow?' she asked. 'But I don't think he's strong enough. He is tired, John, soul-weary. And now you wish him to journey to the House of Bones?'

'I do not wish it but it is his duty. He must find the strength to go on.'

'You were always too hard on him,' Eleanor said, bending her back to the digging, 'always expected too much.'

'You sound like my wife.' The Preacher gave a bitter laugh. 'The truth is, if I could, I would spare him this ordeal. He is my son—'

'He's not your son!' the girl snapped. 'He's . . . I don't know what he is.'

The old man laid a hand on her shoulder. 'Whatever you think, you must go with him, Eleanor. I have seen that he will need you in the dark days to come.' A weary smile creased the Preacher's lips. 'He was always lost without his Eleanor of the May.'

They sank into silence, the only sound the scrape of the spade. After a few minutes, the old man stirred. He patted the girl's shoulder and rose to his feet.

'Bury the Signum deep.'

The Preacher hobbled away down the central aisle and out into the rainstorm.

While the spade scraped on, Jake crept further into the heart of the church. Eleanor had her back turned and did not see him dart between the cover of the pillars. He had reached the end of the aisle when he saw her take a bundle from the altar and place it in the hole. It was wrapped in the grey cloak she had worn when she rescued him. She filled in the hole, patted down the earth, and slotted a stone tile back into its place in the floor. Then, bone-tired, she stumbled out of the church.

Jake raced to the hiding place below the altar steps. As soon as he dropped to his knees and laid his hands against the tile, he felt the throb of power emanating through the earth. What had Eleanor and the Preacher concealed here? Why did they want to keep it from him? All he could think of was the witch ball. While he mulled this possibility over, Jake noticed something very strange. All around the tile, small white flowers poked between the cracks. He looked around. There was no sign of the flowers growing anywhere else, just here, below the altar.

'Hyacinths.'

Jake spun round.

The Preacher was standing directly behind him.

'The flower of rebirth.' The old man's empty eyes seemed to bore into Jake. 'Well, Jacob Harker, I believe it is time we talked . . . '

Chapter 26
Secrets and Surprises

'How do you know me?'

'Despite my disadvantages,' the Preacher placed two fingers beneath his scar-soldered eyes, 'I see much. Now come away from that stone, Jacob, what lies beneath is not for you. Not yet, at least.'

The old man tapped his way back to one of the wooden pews that faced the altar and took a seat. He patted the place beside him, but Jake remained crouched at the tile. His hands flat upon the stone, he seemed to hear distant voices carried by the hum of the earth. Voices from above and below, from the future and from a past both recent and centuries old. He scraped around the edges of the stone, his fingernails scything the stems of the hyacinths.

'I said come AWAY!'

Images flashed into Jake's mind: little Josiah Hobarron, caught stealing a pie from the pantry; skipping his lessons and running away to the fair at Lowerbridge; questioning the stories of the Bible and the existence of God. On these occasions, Josiah had heard that same booming, angry voice. Like Josiah, Jake responded instantly to the Preacher's wrath. He tugged himself away from the stone and went to sit at John Hobarron's side.

The frown vanished from the old man's face.

'It is not just the appearance and the magic.' He placed a hand against Jake's cheek. 'You are like him in so many ways.'

Jake brushed the gnarled fingers away. 'I'm sorry, but I'm not your son.'

'No, and yet the resemblance *must* run deep, otherwise another would have come to replace Josiah.'

'What do you mean?'

The Preacher sighed. 'It is very difficult to explain these things to you. So much must happen before the truth can be known. There are things I *can* tell you, Jacob, and other things I cannot—because they are unknown, because they are obscure, and because some of them are forbidden.' A wry smile. 'I'm not much of a storyteller, am I?'

'Not much, no.'

'Then let me start at the beginning . . . Ah, even that is a misleading phrase—because, of course, the beginning lies far beyond the realm of human knowledge.' The Preacher's sharp ears caught Jake's frustrated sigh and he held up his hands. 'I'm sorry. For me, at least, the beginning was a mere nineteen years ago. I was then middle-aged and entering my second decade as the minister for the parish of Starfall. Such a strange name, I have always thought—"Starfall"—almost as if it was predestined to happen here.'

A moment's silence, during which the Preacher clasped and unclasped his hands. At last he shook his head, and said:

'I beg your forgiveness. Like many old men I am often given to wandering in the garden of my memories. Back to my story—as I say, the *incident* happened nineteen years ago. As with much of what follows, I cannot tell you exactly what occurred, but suffice to say that it shook the very foundations of my life and my beliefs. It was a momentous, joyful, and painful event, and I was for ever marked by it.' Again, the Preacher touched the caverns where his eyes had been. 'Such things are not meant to be seen by mortal men. I paid a heavy price for being an accidental witness. My world was darkened. But such power as I beheld is not unkind, and although I was never again to look upon my beloved wife, I was well compensated.'

He leaned to one side and breathed into Jake's ear, 'I was given sight unfettered by Time.'

'You could see into the future,' Jake said.

'The future and the past.'

'And Josiah, it had something to do with him, didn't it? It can't have been a coincidence—his magic and yours. Nineteen years ago . . . How old was Josiah when he died?'

The Preacher shifted uncomfortably. 'He was a few months shy of his twentieth birthday.'

Jake was surprised. Although he had seen Josiah's youthful face in his dreams, he had always thought of him as an older man; in fact, he was a teenager, only four years older than Jake himself.

'So, around the time Josiah was born you got your powers.'

The Preacher sat back and folded his arms. 'This is one of the things I cannot talk about.'

'But—'

'No, Jacob. I will *not* answer questions about that time. It is too dangerous.'

'OK.' Jake gave another frustrated sigh. 'But there's something I don't understand. If you can see the future, you would have seen Josiah going to the Hollow. You would have seen him dying there. Why didn't you stop him?'

'Because my vision of that event was not clear. I foresaw a *possibility* that Josiah was going to his death, but it was not inevitable. If it had been I would certainly have handed over the . . . ' John Hobarron shook his head. 'It is the past and cannot be changed. Now we must discuss the future. As you have probably guessed, I foresaw your journey on the Scarab Path and your arrival in Cravenmouth. My gift showed me that there was no hope of rescuing you from the clutches of the Witchfinder. The only opportunity was during the riot in the square. Even then I could not be sure that Eleanor would succeed, but I explained the situation to her and she was keen to try.'

'You told her who I was—what I was.'

'The parts of it that I understood, I explained. Four hundred years from now human beings had developed a process that could bring the dead back to life. Although the man himself had not been resurrected, a version of our Josiah was returning to us. She has grieved so much these last months. The chance to see Josiah again, to save him, that she could not resist.'

'You used her.'

'Her father was a respected soldier in the King's army and he taught his daughter many of his skills. She was the most formidable warrior I could send to aid you.'

'I don't think she'll thank you for it,' Jake said. 'You promised her the man she loved and all she got was me. She left her home and her child to save the life of a stranger.'

'Her child?' The frown returned to the Preacher's brow. 'What child?'

'Katherine.' Jake stared at the old man. 'Katherine Hobarron. Hers and Josiah's daughter.'

'You are mistaken—my son was never a father and Eleanor never yet a mother. I know of no daughter.'

'But that's impossible!'

Jake explained the significance of Katherine Hobarron: according to history, the daughter of Josiah went to live with her mother in Hobarron's Hollow. It was her blood, and the blood of her descendants, that had kept the demon Door sealed for almost four hundred years. How could this child not exist?

'So many strange things have happened,' the Preacher said. 'The miracle of your birth, the twinned nature of yourself and Josiah, your arrival in 1645. It is possible that Time is in flux, warping and changing around us. All of our histories must now be uncertain. Jacob, you must promise not to mention any of this to Eleanor. Her knowledge of this child could be disastrous.'

'What do you mean?'

'We do not yet know how this situation will play out. It

is clear from your understanding of history that Eleanor goes to Hobarron's Hollow and settles there with Katherine, the daughter she had with Josiah. That the descendants of Katherine will be crucial in keeping the Demontide at bay. Now it may be that this *will* come to pass, but we must be careful not to influence or prejudice the outcome. We must trust that Fate will play its hand when the time comes, and that the cards will fall in our favour.'

'But the child doesn't exist!' Jake exclaimed. 'Surely that's the end of it.'

'Perhaps . . . But come, let us move on to other, more certain things. It is time we talked about what you came here for—Josiah's witch ball.'

'You know where it is?'

'I do. In June of this year, I received a letter from Lord Tiberius Holmwood, once a member of the Crowden Coven and now the leader of the Hobarron Elders—a group of men and women dedicated to fighting demonkind. The letter informed me of the death of my son . . . ' The tears of the Preacher were in his voice for he had no eyes to shed them. 'Lord Holmwood also told me that, three days after Josiah's death, he had summoned the courage to go down into the cavern. He found the demon Door, sealed but still in existence, rooted into the roof of the cave. He also found my son, frozen in ice. But it was what he *failed* to find that disturbed him—Josiah's witch ball. You see, Josiah had told Holmwood that the ball contained great power.'

Jake stirred.

'There's something I don't understand. Did the witch ball

give Josiah his magic or was it inside him? And if it was, why did he need the ball?'

'Josiah had his own magic but the witch ball sometimes aided him and inspired his natural feel for Oldcraft.'

'But how? What is it?'

'That is what I cannot tell you. One day, if all goes well, you will hold the witch ball in your hand and you will know its true nature and purpose. I only hope that, on that day, you see it as a blessing and not the most wicked curse.'

'And that's all you'll tell me?' Jake sighed. 'All right then, go on with what you were saying about Tiberius Holmwood.'

'After Josiah left him to battle with Marcus Crowden and the Door, Lord Holmwood had ordered his men to watch the cave. Later, unable to find the witch ball, he questioned them most carefully. Each swore an oath that, other than Lord Holmwood himself, no man had gone into the cavern. During the interrogation, the watchmen had seemed strangely confused by Holmwood's simple questions, and this raised his suspicions. Using hypnosis, he asked them a slightly different question: had *anyone* entered the cavern? The response was immediate: two women had done so. What were they like? One was old and ugly. The other, younger and beautiful, had spoken to the guards. "You will forget all about us," she had crooned, "for I am Lethe, the mistress of your memories."'

Something stirred at the back of Jake's mind. He had heard that name before. His father's words came back to him:

He had three older sisters—Miss Drude, Miss Lethe, and Miss Frija . . .

'Marcus Crowden's sisters,' Jake said.

'Indeed. My guess is that their demons told the witches of their brother's fate. The demons must also have told them that a powerful object had been lost in the shadows of the cavern. Drude and Lethe then retrieved the ball and took it back to Havlock Grange.'

The Preacher reached out and grasped Jake's shoulders.

'You must go to the Grange and reclaim what once was yours.'

'But what's the point? Let's say that somehow I get the ball back from these witches—what good will it do? The Khepra Beetle is gone, the Scarab Path closed. I've no way of getting home.'

'There is a way.'

'How?'

'The box. The Pale Man used it to come here.'

Those thin, birdlike hands clutched at Jake.

'The nightmare box is your way home.'

Chapter 27
Lure of the Signum

'Tobias Quilp is *here*?'

'Is that his name? Quilp? My vision did not give me that detail.'

Jake felt anger course through his veins. Quilp must have been sent by the Demon Father to retrieve the witch ball. The very thing that Jake had travelled back in time for now rested in the hands of his mother's killer.

'Havlock Grange is a three day ride,' the Preacher said. 'You must set out at first light.'

'But why?' Jake asked through gritted teeth. 'Quilp has the witch ball. He'll take it to the Demon Father and—'

'So like Josiah!' The old man laughed. 'Your mouth is busy while your brain slumbers. Think—this Mr Quilp has been at the Grange for several weeks and yet has not returned to his own time. There must be a reason for his delay. Is there something wrong with the orb? Are the sisters reluctant to

313

part with it? Is there a problem with the nightmare box? Quilp's continued presence in this time means one thing: the witch ball is still here.'

A chance to steal back the witch ball and to use it to cure his father. A chance to revenge himself on Tobias Quilp. Hope flowered in Jake's heart, but there was a problem with this picture.

'My magic.' He turned to the Preacher. 'You want me to go after the Crowden sisters? You want me to face one of the most powerful witches in existence? I wish I could, but my magic isn't strong enough.'

Jake explained how, after he had destroyed the demon Door, the magic of Josiah Hobarron had weakened. For a long time he had tried to reignite the flame of Oldcraft but had been successful only in conjuring a weak shadow of Josiah's power. Since coming to 1645, the magic seemed to have left him completely. Jake's eyes returned to the tile below the altar. He felt again the pulsing song of the hidden object. Yesterday the magic had returned to him, stronger than ever.

'When you first felt the trace of magic in your soul, it came like wildfire,' the Preacher said, 'furious and uncontrolled. Is that not so?'

Jake remembered when he had almost drowned in the river near Dr Holmwood's house. The Preacher was right—the raw and unbridled power had overwhelmed him.

'So it was with Josiah. The first time is an emotional experience so primal that the brain has little to do with it. Oldcraft is, at its root, a power of emotion and instinct. It is only later, when doubts and logic creep in that the magic is somehow tamed. That is what has happened with you. Early on, you used your power instinctively. Later, when you faced Marcus Crowden and the Door, you had Josiah's experience to help you. If you had continued to *feel* your way into the magic it would still be strong, but you were so desperate to cling to it that you started imposing rules and structures. You conjured dead memories to inspire you, but these emotions, although strong, were not being honestly experienced. They were being summoned for a purpose, to be used as a prompt. Despite what witches may tell you, pure Oldcraft does not come to us through spell books and manipulation but through the honest passions of our heart. That is why your magic has been weak, Jacob. You must now find your way back to it.'

Jake felt the truth of these words but a sense of frustration distracted him.

'I don't have time for all that. Quilp must be dealt with *now*.' He pointed at the tile. 'That thing is like the witch ball, isn't it? When you were talking to Eleanor you called it a "Signum".'

'You overheard.' The Preacher's face turned horribly pale. 'Jacob, listen to me: something like the witch ball does indeed lie beneath that stone, but it is not your destiny to wield it, *not yet*. You must go to Havlock Grange and reclaim the witch ball from the demons before they use it to open a second Door. Jacob, please . . . '

But Jake wasn't listening. He dropped to the ground and crawled towards the stone. The power throbbed through his hands and into the hidden parts of his soul.

'I must have it,' he said. 'The power of the Signum in my hand!'

The blind man joined him on the ground and tried to pull Jake away from the stone.

'You cannot bring them together!' John Hobarron cried. 'The world still needs you, Jacob.'

'But with the Signum, I stand a chance.' Jake's upper lip curled into a snarl. 'With a flick of my fingers I can tear Tobias Quilp apart like a rag doll. Then I can bend all of time and space to my will—I can return home and save my father.'

Power like he had never felt before seared into Jake's mind. Power beyond that which he had experienced in Crowden's Sorrow. Power beyond any witch or demon. It overturned his thoughts and, in that moment, he caught a glimpse of the time before flesh. So beautiful, so distant . . .

A hand caught at his arm and tried to prise him away. Furious, he lashed out and sent the old Preacher flying down the nave of the church.

'It's mine!' Jake cried. 'It was always mine. You can't keep it from me!'

His fingers dug at the corners of the tile. Upturning with an earthy sigh, it fell against the altar steps and cracked into seven shards. Jake ploughed into the dirt—threw clods of earth aside—ripped his way down to the hidden Signum. Sweat dripped from his brow and ran into his eyes. He took a moment to clear his vision—nothing must sully his first sight of the prize.

He heard footsteps running down the aisle. Felt a tug at his shoulder—

'Stop!' Eleanor cried. 'Jake, listen to me, you must *stop*.'

He grunted and went back to digging. Her hands linked across his chest and Eleanor pulled with all her might. Jake toppled backwards out of the hole.

'No!'

He turned and raised his hand, ready to strike her down.

Eleanor's terrified eyes froze him as effectively as any freezing spell. He felt the frantic beat of his heart slow to a dull, shameful thud. He reached for her and the girl flinched away.

'Eleanor. I-I'm sorry.'

'He never . . . Josiah, he . . . '

She felt for the pew behind her and pushed herself to her feet. The fear vanished from her eyes and she looked down on Jake with such sadness that he had to turn away.

'Josiah would never have raised his hand to me. Never.'

She went to help the old preacher to his feet. For a long time no one said a word. Eventually, John Hobarron whispered to the girl and she turned and left the church.

'The Signums are there to inspire you, Jacob,' the Preacher said, 'not to consume you. For what it's worth, I have told you the truth: the witch ball and the object beneath that stone are brothers that must *never* meet. Not until all hope is lost. You must trust in yourself, my son. Believe in your instincts and in your magic.'

Jake felt the old man's hand on his shoulder. He looked up into that seeing and unseeing face.

'Believe in yourself, as I have always believed in you.'

* * *

Dawn crept over the hillside, its rays slinking across the crow-pecked fields and into the empty streets of Starfall. Standing in the sunlight of this bygone day, Jake felt the great gulf of time that separated him from his father and his friends. He remembered the harsh words he had spoken at their parting. To Simon—*I'll hunt you down. Do you understand? I won't show you any mercy.* To his father—*You haven't got any more time, Dad.* For Rachel there had been *no* words, just cruel silence. He needed to get back to them, to see them again, to hold them close and tell them he was sorry. Surely that mattered more than anything.

A mean little voice whispered to him—*More than finding Quilp? More than revenge?*

As if it sensed this dark voice, the dog at Jake's side gave a nervous whine. It nudged his leg and looked up at him with sorrowful eyes.

'Don't worry, Sebastian,' Jake said, scratching behind the dog's ear, 'he's only gonna get what's coming to him.'

Sebastian pulled his head away. The old hound threw Jake a reproachful frown and slunk back into the house.

Jake tugged his new cloak tight around his shoulders and started down the lane. An hour ago, he had woken to find fresh clothes folded on the chest that stood by the door. They had been placed there, together with a bowl of warm water, by the woman of the house. The woman that part of Jake remembered as 'mother'. After washing, he had dressed, fumbling with the ties at the knees of the breeches and the small buttons of the buff coat. Then he had gone to knock at a familiar door.

'Mothe—Mrs Hobarron? This is Jacob. I just wanted to say—'

'Go away.'

It hurt to hear that voice. He remembered a hundred scoldings and a thousand loving words.

'Please open the door,' he murmured.

'For God's sake, leave me be,' the woman cried. 'I cannot lose you again.'

Jake had left with the wailing of a heartbroken mother in his ears.

Now he joined Josiah's father at the church gate. Eleanor was busy packing the last of their provisions into the pouches of a saddlebag. Last night, after the madness in the church, Jake had returned to the house and knocked on Eleanor's door. Again, he had tried to apologize but his words had met with silence. She was equally silent now. Ignoring his 'good morning', she draped the bag over the horse's back and adjusted the straps of the saddle.

Two horses stood side-by-side in the lane, heads busy in their nosebags. The first mare was golden-brown, the second, black with a sprinkling of grey hairs. To an average rider's eye, Jake guessed that these were standard-size mounts, their withers level with his own shoulders. Eleanor removed the nosebags, placed her foot in a stirrup and swung herself onto the back of the black mare. With her eyes on the road, she asked, 'Are you ready?'

Jake swallowed. 'I've—ah—I've never been on a horse.'

They turned to him, amazed. Even the horses flicked their ears as if they couldn't believe what they had just heard.

319

'You've never ridden?' Eleanor marvelled.

'Um. No. Sorry.'

'Then how do you get from place to place in the future? Have horses died out? Do you walk everywhere?'

'I've seen it in my visions,' the Preacher chirruped excitedly. 'Glimpses of people moving at incredible speeds, twice as fast as any horse. They are encased in the bellies of metal carriages. Perhaps Jacob rides such a beast.'

'Er . . . no,' Jake said, 'I'm not old enough. Next year I can start having lessons.'

'You aren't old enough to ride these metal horses and you can't ride a normal horse.' Eleanor shook her head.

Blood rushed into Jake's face. He snatched hold of the brown mare's rein, grabbed the pommel on the saddle and tried to jump up. His sudden movement unnerved the horse. She trotted forward and Jake fell back onto the path. He groaned through gritted teeth—a sound of pain and embarrassment.

Eleanor jumped down and helped him to his feet. 'Come on, I'll show you.'

The briefest of riding classes followed. Jake was taught how to mount on the nearside of the horse and how to bounce himself into position. How to lace the rein between his fingers, how to loosen it for speed and pull it taut to stop. The pressure of his knees on the flanks was the key, Eleanor said: the tighter the grip the faster the horse would go. Like Marian, Eleanor's horse, Pepper was a mature mare and, despite Jake's fumbling, wasn't easily startled. As long as she was handled with respect, Pepper wouldn't throw him. After twenty minutes of practice, Jake had managed to trot down the lane without falling off.

'I think that's the best we can hope for,' Eleanor said, stroking Pepper's neck. She looked to the horizon and sighed. 'This is going to be a *long* journey. I'll help you where I can, Jake, but we're going to have to ride fifteen hour days to reach Havlock Grange in reasonable time.'

'Fifteen hours in the saddle,' Jake said. 'Easy.'

Eleanor laughed despite herself and mounted Marian.

'My dear, I wonder if Jacob and I might have a private word?' the Preacher said.

'Of course.'

Eleanor made a clucking sound and Marian clopped down the lane. The Preacher listened to the fading sound of hooves on stone, then turned to Jake.

'It is time to say goodbye. We shall not see each other again in this life . . . or the next.'

'What do you mean?'

'More mysteries, I'm afraid,' said John Hobarron.

'You remind me a bit of my dad. He's a pain in the backside, too.'

Jake looked down to where Eleanor waited for him.

'It's too dangerous,' he said. 'I should go alone.'

'Hasn't she proven herself to you?' the Preacher asked. 'You underestimate that girl at your peril.'

'It's not that. I don't want her putting herself in danger on my behalf.'

'Again, you sound like my son. Eleanor would plead with Josiah to allow her to accompany him on his travels.

He always refused, not because he doubted her abilities, but because the thought of her in the clutches of some witch or monster was too painful for him to bear. In the end, it was selfishness on his part. When he died, alone and helpless, she suffered more pain than a thousand dark hexes. So tell Eleanor that you forbid her to go with you.' The Preacher smiled through his sorrow. 'And I will go into the house and plug my sensitive ears.'

'Just because I look like him doesn't mean she owes *me* anything,' Jake argued. 'It wasn't her fault he died, and it won't be her fault if I die.'

'Four hundred years of progress and still men seem unable to understand the strength and the heart of women. Ah well, all will become clear before the end.' The Preacher reached up for Jake's hand. 'Goodbye, Jacob Harker.'

Jake pulled off his leather riding glove and took the Preacher's hand. At the touch of that weathered skin a fragment of memory flashed into his mind. He turned to the churchyard and there, amid the gravestones, he saw two figures looking up at the old church. A small boy and a middle-aged man, hand in hand. Jake gasped at the image: the boy looked exactly like his five-year-old self.

'*Why is the church all bent and broken, Papa?*' the boy asked.

The Preacher appeared to shiver. '*Because of the storm.*'

'*A storm? With wind and rain and lightning?*' young Josiah asked.

'*Something like that, yes. Five years ago the church was hit by ... lightning, as you say. A terrible strike that smashed through the roof and trembled the walls askew. I was in the church myself at the time and . . . '* His hands went to the hollow sockets where his eyes had been. *'It was a blessing, my child—the storm that came to Starfall.'*

Jake took a sharp breath and the ghosts in the graveyard vanished. He tried to speak, but the Preacher cut him short.

'Do not ask, for I cannot tell you.'

Jake gripped the reins and pressed his knees against Pepper's flanks. He'd had enough of mysteries.

'Murderer!'

John Hobarron had not laid eyes on his wife in over nineteen years, but in his mind he saw a vivid picture of her. Eyes raw from months of crying, Elizabeth Hobarron hurtled down the lane to meet him. She flailed her hands against his face and body, striking the old man hard. When at last she tired, the Preacher went to his wife and put shaking arms around her.

'Murderer, murderer, murderer,' she repeated, her voice a hoarse whisper.

'I'm sorry, my love,' he said, 'but I've always done what I thought was right.'

'Right for who? For our son? For that boy? You sent Josiah to his death and now you are happy to send him again.' She wailed as if her soul was being crucified. 'Last night, while he slept, I sat beside him and stroked his hair. Deep brown, just like our child's. What I would not have done to have spoken to him this dawn and to have received his kiss. But I could *not*. Not when I knew you were sending him to his ruin.'

'I have no choice, woman! The very world hangs upon the boy.' The Preacher rested his head against his wife's shoulder. 'It always has.'

'Then why not tell him all?'

Her words made John Hobarron shudder.

'Why not tell him that Josiah was *not* our son?'

The Preacher released his wife and turned his face to the church. In his world of endless night, he sensed a deeper darkness stir.

'Josiah never knew and nor shall he.' His speech had the grandeur of a sermon. 'Not until the End is near and this world stands in the shadow of nightfall. Until then, let Jacob Harker find what peace he can . . . '

Her laugh was malicious and cracked with age, but to him it was beautiful. Her scent, the stale aroma of unwashed clothes and poisonous herbs, was a sublime perfume. Her smile, seldom seen and always cruel . . .

'Beautiful,' he whispered in his sleep. 'My beautiful Esther.'

The ghost of Esther Inglethorpe haunted Tobias Quilp, as it had every night since he had learned of her death. Her murder. The dream always ended in the same way, with Quilp's fury finding its voice in the dead witch—

'They killed me, Tobias. Struck me dead without a second thought.' She stalked through the dream world. 'You are my avenger, my dark angel. Hunt them down, strip the still-warm flesh from their bones and wallow in their hot blood. The father pulled the trigger but the son stands guilty, too. Jacob Harker . . . '

Light flashed against Quilp's closed eyelids. The vision of Esther Inglethorpe began to fade.

'Be merciless, my love,' she called. 'Be cruel.'

Quilp came squinting out of the dream. He looked to the woman at the window and felt a little of his fury seep out.

'I told you I was not to be disturbed.'

'Forgive me, Master Quilp,' Lethe Crowden bowed, 'but my sister and I thought you might like to know—Frija is spinning again.'

Quilp had been lying on the four-poster bed fully dressed, Mr Pinch curled like a baby in his arms. Now he set the sleeping demon aside, strode out of the chamber and plunged down the stairs.

Taking the steps three at a time, Quilp's thoughts returned to the day of his arrival in 1645. How long ago had it been? Two weeks? Three? Four? Wrapped up in thoughts of revenge he had failed to keep track of the time. His mission had been to convince the Crowden sisters that he was an emissary sent by their brother from the future. His arrival inside Marcus's nightmare box, his intimate knowledge of their brother's appearance, character, and history had convinced the sisters of his story. He had been welcomed as an honoured guest and shown directly to the witch ball.

It had been strange, striding through the corridors of the

old-new house. Seconds before, he had been standing in the ruined shell of Havlock Grange; now here he was, in the dusty but unspoiled Great Hall. Drude had gone to a little cupboard under the stairs and retrieved a leather bag from its hiding place. Passing the bag to Quilp, the witch had said, 'Frija saw the ball in one of her visions. It seemed important and so Lethe and I travelled to the cave and stole it. A waste of time, of course.'

'Why do you say that?'

'See for yourself.'

Quilp felt inside the bag and his fingers brushed against the cold glass of the witch ball. Bringing it out into the light, he had stared into the orb's dark heart.

'But it's—'

'Dead,' Lethe nodded.

'Powerless,' Drude added.

'This is Josiah Hobarron's witch ball,' Tobias cried. 'Its magic is legendary!'

'Its power is spent,' Drude said. 'Frija's vision must have been at fault, it sometimes is. We punished her severely, of course. Still, it is rather funny.'

Caught up in thoughts of what the Demon Father would do to him if he brought the dead ball back through time, Tobias snapped, 'Funny?'

'Why yes,' Lethe tittered. 'You *and* the boy using such powerful magic to come looking for this glorified bauble!'

'Jacob Harker,' Tobias murmured. 'How did you know he was here in 1645?'

'Frija. She sees many things. The boy is presently a

prisoner in Cravenmouth, a town many days' ride from here. Frija has foretold that he will suffer at the hands of a witch-finder, but will escape and come looking for the ball. In a few weeks hence, Jacob Harker will be at our door.'

That had settled matters. If he returned to the Demon Father with this powerless orb, Quilp was as good as dead. If, however, he could bring Jacob Harker with him . . . He would lay the boy at his Master's feet and then, after the Demon Father had had his sport, Quilp would be allowed to kill him.

And so the weeks passed and Quilp waited for news of Jacob's coming . . .

Now he burst into the Crowden sisters' chamber.

'What's happened?' he demanded.

His eyes flitted between Drude and Frija. Lethe slipped in from the corridor and joined Drude at the long oak table. She began to nibble at a bone taken from her sister's caul-dron. A rib, Quilp thought, though he was not an expert in the size and shape of children's bones.

'Don't just sit there eating!' he barked. 'I said—what news?'

Drude got up from the table and took him by the arm. She led him to the veiled woman sitting at the spinning wheel.

'The cloud has dispersed, but while it held we saw the boy leaving the village of Starfall. He will be here soon. Tell him, Frija.'

The woman at the wheel turned her head aside. The chains that bound her to the floor clanked as she moved.

'You will tell him or I will be forced to boil my cauldron . . .'

Drude reached out and caressed her sister's veil, 'and hurt you all over again.'

Drude's cauldron; Frija's spinning wheel; Lethe's harp; Marcus's cabinet. Quilp had met other witches whose demons took on the form of objects, but usually familiars were more comfortable in the guise of monstrous creatures or, like Mr Pinch, malformed humans. Such things possessed the horror of the strange and the ghastly, but the Crowden demons were different. Their apparent ordinariness lent them a quiet terror.

Quilp's gaze turned to the black cabinet that stood in the corner of the room, waiting. His journey into the past had taken less than ten seconds, but ten seconds in the nightmare box had seemed like a lifetime of horrors. Soon he would have to make the return trip. The thought made him shudder.

Drude's voice returned him to the moment.

'I will do it,' she purred, 'I will heat the magical oil until it is bubbling, and then I will—'

'Please, sister,' Frija sobbed.

'Then tell him what you saw.'

'Jacob Harker,' she gasped from behind her veil. 'In two days he will be at our door.'

'And?' Drude prompted.

'Another will be at his side. A girl. He . . . he already cares for her.'

'Joyous news,' Quilp murmured.

A girl. A loved one. This was too perfect. Before he killed him, Quilp would strike at the heart of Jacob Harker. The thought fell like summer rain upon the parched soul of Tobias Quilp.

'My master—your brother—he told me that Jake's powers had dwindled since that night in the cavern. Even so, he may still be a formidable opponent.'

Drude frowned. 'There are three of us and one of him.'

'We must be sure,' Quilp insisted. 'We must weaken him *before* he reaches us.'

Drude hurried to the table. She tipped the contents of her cauldron into the empty fireplace. Bones and little hearts turned grey in the ash. Lethe watched her elder sister dash around the room, collecting odds and ends from various chests and cubbyholes.

'Dear Drude, I haven't seen you this excited for years! Not since Christmas Eve 1640 when those orphan triplets turned up on the doorstep. What a Christmas dinner that was!'

Drude set the cauldron on the table. She half-filled it with water from a jug and started throwing handfuls of herbs and other unidentifiable things into the mix. She passed her hands over the brew and muttered words, some of which Quilp recognized from spells worked by Esther Inglethorpe. Minutes later the dark green stew was bubbling and spitting. Drude filled a small glass bottle from the cauldron and tucked it into the pocket of her apron.

'I will bring him to you, Master Quilp, weak and frail.'

Drude plunged her hand into the boiling cauldron. She pulled it out again red raw and steaming, and licked the juice from her fingers. Energy crackled through the air. A phantom wind rose up from nowhere and swirled around the witch. Her hair twisted in a grey cyclone and she seemed to flicker in and out of existence. Before vanishing completely, her voice shrieked around the room—

'I will bring Jacob Harker to you on the wings of a nightmare!'

Chapter 28
The Pursuing Shadow

The first hour was the worst. Eleanor rolled her eyes and did nothing but complain about the time they were losing. As she watched Jake fall from the horse and climb doggedly back into the saddle for the fourth time, however, her tone softened. She trotted back, took his hands, and showed him again how to hold the reins properly.

'Not very good at this, am I?' Jake muttered.

Eleanor laced the reins through his fingers. 'My father was the best horseman in the shire until, one day, a musket was accidentally fired next to his head. Like you, he lost his hearing in one ear. After that he could never keep his balance on a horse.'

'Told you it wasn't my fault,' Jake grinned.

Eleanor laughed. 'Come on, we've a lot of ground to cover before nightfall.'

Navigating by the sun and by church steeples, she led them on.

It was not until late morning that Jake became aware of their pursuer. It was a feeling more than anything else—a niggle at the back of his neck, a sense that eyes were trained upon him. He looked back often and, although he sometimes caught a glimpse of a shadow moving down the dirt track road behind them, it was never more than that. He didn't mention it to Eleanor until they stopped for lunch.

They made temporary camp on the side of a hill. Marian and Pepper were busy with their nosebags while their riders ate a simple meal of bread and cheese. The ageing summer sun beat down across the hillside and into the treeless valley below. Listening to Jake's story, Eleanor brushed the bread crumbs from her lap and began searching through her saddlebag. She took out a small telescope and scanned the valley.

'I don't see anything.'

'Can I take a look?'

Jake found the view fuzzy but there was no way to focus the lens.

'All I can see is a green blur. This is a pretty primitive telescope.'

'It was my father's perspective glass.' Eleanor's words came at Jake like stony missiles. 'He took it with him whenever he fought for the king, and he died with it clasped in his hand. I can see through it clear as clear.'

Jake lowered the telescope from his eye. 'I'm sorry, I didn't know.'

'Why should you know anything about me?' Eleanor shrugged.

Jake had opened his mouth to answer, not even sure what

he was going to say, when the horses started whinnying and pawing at the ground. Birds exploded from the fringe of trees on the opposing hillside and a family of frightened deer galloped out of the forest. Heart thumping, Jake trained the telescope on the trees.

A pale moon of a face stared back at him.

From this distance, the features were little more than black scratches: two lines for eyes, the hint of a nose and an 'O' marking out the mouth. Before Jake could see any more, the figure stepped back into the forest.

Eleanor at his shoulder: 'What is it?'

'A woman. She's gone now.'

'Who do you think she was?'

'No idea, but I'm sure she's been following us. We'd better keep our eyes peeled.'

'What are you doing?!'

Eleanor's cry snatched Jake from his daydreams. He glanced down at the blur of meadow grass thrashing against the horse's legs. All he could hear was the rush of air and the hammer of Pepper's hooves against the ground. With his knees locked against her flanks, Jake felt the striving muscles of the horse as she galloped on.

Another shout from behind. Jake glanced over his shoulder and saw Eleanor kick against Marian's sides and put on a burst of speed. Jake knew that he should be desperately afraid. He had spent most of the day falling off the horse, and now she was bolting at full gallop across this overgrown meadow. Instead of tugging the rein, however, he leaned forward into a comfortable crouch and whispered into Pepper's ear, 'Yah! Faster, girl! Faster!'

Pepper snorted her agreement and jolted into a higher gear. Looking back, Jake grinned and waved at the girl pursuing him. He felt no fear, just a rush of confidence and exhilaration. While his mind had been swamped by a hundred cares and questions, old instincts had stirred and his body had responded. Without thinking, he had shaped himself along the natural lines of the horse, feeling its rhythms as he spurred it on to greater speeds. It was like magic, he guessed. The old Preacher had told him that, at its best, Oldcraft was responsive to instinct and emotion; just like the horse, neither had much use for rules and logic.

Jake had caught Eleanor by surprise, but she was by far the better rider. With her long hair flying behind her, she passed him like a comet trailing golden fire. Jake released his grip on Pepper's flanks. The thunder of hooves softened and the meadow grass came back into focus. He patted the horse's damp neck and they trotted forward to meet Eleanor.

She tried to show her anger, but amazement won the day.

'How on earth did you do that?'

'Not sure,' Jake panted. 'Pretty cool though, eh?'

'Cool? I can't see what temperature has to do with it! This morning you couldn't ride five paces without falling off, now this? Did you use magic?'

'I don't think so. One minute I was thinking about the witch ball, the next I'm galloping across a field. I think maybe I was subconsciously tapping into Josiah's memories.

His experience of riding. My dad told me it's all to do with genetic memories and . . . '

He stopped dead.

'Jake? What is it?'

Jake swung himself down from the horse and handed the reins to Eleanor. Then he ran across the hard, sun-baked ground until he came to the place where the strange flower grew. At his approach, the crow that had been picking at the flower's five pink petals took fright and flew away. A moment later, he felt the dry snort of horse breath on his neck and Eleanor's hand on his arm.

'My God,' she whispered.

Together, they stared down at the human hand that sprouted out of the earth.

Eleanor stepped forward and took a sharp breath.

'More,' she murmured. 'There are more of them.'

Just beyond the hand, the ground fell away sharply. At the bottom of a deep, narrow ditch pools of glinting red water lapped against the bodies of four dead men. Swarms of flies droned over the corpses while beetles crawled in and out of noses, ears, and mouths. A family of rats feasted on the men's eyes and gnawed their cheeks down to the skull. Twisted together, they were dressed in filthy, bloodstained clothes with tatty yellow sashes tied around their waists.

'Parliament soldiers,' Eleanor said. 'Roundheads. Probably a scout party ambushed by Cavaliers. Looks as if some kind soul started to bury them, but that the troop had to move on before the job was done.'

'They look really young.'

'Just boys,' she nodded. 'Most of them fighting for a cause they couldn't understand.'

On the far side of the ditch lay the rotting remains of a large horse. Like the weapons and the boots of the Roundheads, the horse's saddle had been taken, claimed by the Royalist soldiers. One side of the animal's face was gone and the white arcs of its ribs poked through tattered strips of flesh.

'We should finish the job,' Jake said. 'Bury them properly.'

Eleanor shook her head. 'We can't waste the energy. We still have a long ride ahead of us.'

'But these people . . . '

'There are corpses rotting in fields all over England, Jake. What do you want us to do? Bury them all?' The words were softened by a tone of genuine sadness. 'I'm sorry, but we don't even have shovels and this ground is as hard as stone. We could say a prayer if you like?'

Jake was silent for a minute, his gaze moving between the upturned faces. It felt as if, in this half-made grave, he was seeing a glimpse of the future. The bodies of the slaughtered thrown aside and left for small monsters to devour. A war was coming, and for the first time in history it would not be fought between men but between humanity and a hidden enemy.

'Yes,' Jake said quietly, 'let's pray.'

Soon after their discovery of the dead soldiers, the sun vanished behind a blanket of storm clouds. At first Eleanor had wanted to push on, but there was little point in stumbling through the dark only to find that, come morning, they were miles off course. And so they made camp. Conscious of the pursuing figure that Jake had seen, they selected a spot near the middle of the meadow, not too far from the soldiers' trench, which gave a full view of the surrounding area.

They sat under the shelter of a canvas sheet tied between two small oaks. These were the only trees within sight, and so, sitting back to back, Jake and Eleanor could watch all sides of the meadow.

Eleanor stirred the pot that hung over the fire.

'Smells good,' Jake said.

'It'll be a few more minutes.'

Jake's stomach complained and Eleanor laughed.

'I heard that!'

'I can't help it, I'm really hungry!'

'You can take your mind off it by telling me stories about the future.'

While the pot bubbled, and Pepper and Marian rubbed shoulders, Jake told tales of his own time. Everyday things that seemed like miracles to the girl: hot water at the turn of a tap; distant voices singing and chattering through little boxes called 'radios'; huge screens on which comedies and tragedies were played out; smaller screens around which a family would gather, like pilgrims around a saintly shrine; vast stretches of road on which metal carriages roared at tremendous speeds; and, most miraculous of all, metal birds that flew swifter than any eagle . . .

'Ten years ago, the Percivals—distant cousins of mine— fled this land,' Eleanor said, her voice trembling. 'They wanted to lead a more godly life in the New World. They sailed aboard the *Arbella* and reached a place called Salem, Massachusetts, where they settled. The journey was arduous, but most of the travellers survived the nine week voyage.'

'In my time an aeroplane could take you there in under nine hours,' Jake said.

'Nine *hours?*'

'That's nothing! In three or four days you could reach the moon!'

Eleanor stared open-mouthed at Jake, 'Men have been to the moon?'

'1969,' Jake said softly. 'Eleanor, are you all right?'

'Yes. Of course, I just . . . '

She glanced up at the sky. The purple hue of twilight was deepening. Somewhere out there, behind the clouds, the moon was treading an endless path, its surface as yet untouched by the outstretched hand of Man.

'Is it Oldcraft?' Eleanor asked. 'All these things, they sound so magical.'

Tears shimmered in her eyes, but Jake guessed that, if asked, she would not have known why she was crying.

'It's science,' he said. 'No one believes in magic any more.'

'They should. They live in an age of wonders.'

The rain started again, a light shower crackling on the canvas and making the fire spit.

'The Preacher said nothing of these miracles,' Eleanor said at last. 'But he did tell me *why* you had returned for the witch ball. The first reason is noble—you want to save your father. But the second . . . '

She got to her feet and walked around to face Jake.

'Tell me of this man you hunt. Tell me why you want him dead.'

Jake felt the first twist of anger. 'His name is Tobias Quilp.'

He told the story in short, brutal sentences. Quilp on the road. Mr Pinch in the tree. His mother's murder. Quilp's incarceration in Hobarron Tower and his release by the universal coven. Jake felt every hour of the monster's freedom like a knife turning in his gut.

Eleanor knelt beside him.

'You have such anger. Such rage. You mustn't let it consume you.'

'But my mum . . . '

'What was done to her was monstrous. But your anger is making her death the most important thing in her life. It's becoming your one memory of her, and that's wrong.'

'How can I think of anything else? I saw it happen. I watched him butcher her.'

'And now you want to butcher him?'

Jake hissed through tight lips. 'Yes.'

'You want to watch him writhe in agony, bleed and scream and suffer? You want to tear him apart and take *his* head as a trophy? Is that it?'

'Yes,' Jake repeated. He felt a savage joy at her words, her understanding. 'Yes.'

Eleanor stood up. Her expression was sorrowful.

'Then you really are *nothing* like Josiah.'

Jake shot to his feet. The sudden movement startled the horses and they tugged at the reins tied to the oak trees.

'What's wrong with me wanting revenge? HE KILLED MY MOTHER! How could you understand what that feels like? How could you even begin to . . . ?'

It surged inside Jake, ran down his arms and broke between his fingers. Magic. But this time of a very different kind. Instead of the blue flicker of old, a scarlet flame lit up the night. He had seen such magic before—it was the hall-mark of a dark sorcerer.

Jake stared through the magical fire and met Eleanor's gaze.

'I know, Jake,' she said quietly. 'I know.'

Unafraid, she came forward to meet him. At her approach, Jake sensed his hatred and anger fall back, like darkness retreating from candlelight. The red flame in his hand fizzled away and Eleanor wrapped her arms around him.

'I know because I lost someone, too,' she whispered. 'Josiah was my soulmate and he was torn away from me. After he died, I felt very much like you feel now. I wanted to find Marcus Crowden and make him pay. But in time I realized that was not what Josiah would have wanted. Revenge is destructive. Only justice can help us overcome grief.'

'But isn't it justice for Quilp to die?'

'On the gallows at twilight?' Eleanor asked. 'With the mob baying for his blood and you as the hangman?'

Jake didn't answer. Couldn't answer.

Eleanor turned to the fire and started ladling the soup into wooden bowls.

Jake was about to join her when the little hairs on the back of his arms bristled to attention. He peered into the early evening gloom. Wind stirred the long grass and the rain chased in sheets across the untended meadow. At the very edges of his vision, where the meadow blurred into the night, Jake could make out something white moving in the darkness.

A figure.

It was coming towards them.

Chapter 29
Army of the Dead

Jake left Eleanor by the fire and walked out alone. Squinting through the rain, he saw that the white-faced stranger had stopped at a point midway between their camp and the meadow edge. The figure stooped down onto its haunches. Its hands were busy, but Jake was too far away to see what it was doing.

He marched on.

A lisping cry, carried by the gale, reached his ears—
'*Rissssse.*'

Jake shivered. There was something horribly eerie in the sight of the woman crouching on the ground. A woman, yes, her haggard face hideous even at this distance. But it wasn't her ugliness or even that brittle voice repeating the same word over and over—*Rissssse*—that made Jake shudder. It was the apron tied around her withered body. A red-smeared apron that reminded him of the one worn by the lady butcher from Cravenmouth.

Army of the Dead

He remembered what his father had said: *They would lure orphan children to the old house with promises of food and shelter. They pretended to be kindly spinster women, but after a few weeks of fattening the kids up* . . . This was one of the Crowden sisters, Jake knew it. He wondered how many children had died at her hands. How many had been hacked to pieces by her knife and stewed in her cauldron. He imagined the sisters of Havlock Grange knee-deep in little bones, cawing over the corpses like the carrion crow had cawed over the bodies of the dead Roundheads. They were monsters, jackals, scavengers of human flesh. Like Quilp, they deserved no mercy.

Jake's magic responded to these dark thoughts. It pulsed along his arm and ignited between his fingers—flames of warring blue and red.

The witch had been so preoccupied with her conjuring that it was not until Jake had reached the ditch that she looked up. She sat on the other side of the trench, her thin, bare arms extended over the edge. In her left hand she held a glass bottle stoppered with a cork and filled with some dark green liquid. Aside from her cruel eyes, Jake could see little resemblance between this crone and the handsome Marcus Crowden. Then she smiled, and the family sneer played around her lips.

'Master Quilp told me that you had magic,' she said, 'but I do not see your demon.'

'I don't see yours either.'

'I have already taken what magic I need from my cauldron. Enough to weaken you and to kill your pretty friend.'

The witch nodded towards the campfire. Jake took a quick glance back and saw that Eleanor was now on her feet and peering in their direction.

'You *won't* hurt her.'

'Ah!' The smile widened. 'My soft-hearted sister was right—you already care for her, but does she care for you?'

Rage burned inside Jake. He repeated:

'You *won't* hurt her!'

Jake threw back his arm and pitched the magical flame at the witch. She deflected the spell with a grunt and a twist of her free hand, sending the fire dancing away into the darkness.

'No, *I* will not hurt your friend,' the crone laughed. '*They* will do it for me.'

Quick as a flash, she took a dagger from inside her cloak and sliced open her arm, elbow to wrist. Blood gushed from the wound and rained down into the ditch.

Rained down onto the faces of the dead soldiers.

'*Riiiiise.*'

The witch used her teeth to pull the cork from the bottle. Jake knew he should do something to stop her, but a strange fascination had taken hold of him. He had seen witches use their magic before—to conjure hexes, to defend themselves—but he had never seen a spell concocted from words and raw ingredients. The witch sprinkled her blood and her potion into the gaping mouths and rotten eyes of the Roundheads. It ran down their stone-cold cheeks and soaked into the wet earth.

'*Riiiiise!*

Exhausted, the witch fell back upon the ground, her injured arm clamped to her chest. Jake peered over the side of the half-made grave and saw the young soldiers sprawled together, still dead, still unmoving.

'Some magic.' Jake snorted. He began to summon a second magical flame. 'I guess your brother got all the powerful mojo.'

'You are in error, boy conjuror. See, my army awakens.'

A collective gasp rose up from the ditch.

The dead drawing breath into mouldy lungs.

Something tickled the back of Jake's leg. It wrapped itself around his ankle and tripped him to the ground. The downpour had softened the earth but the fall still rattled Jake's bones and the magic vanished from his fingers. He looked back at the thing that had tripped him. Reanimated, the buried human hand writhed in the rain.

And now more hands rose out of the earth. Eight pale palms—some with fingers stripped down to the bone— emerged over the lip of the ditch. They dug into the muddy ground and tugged at the clumps of meadow grass. Slimy with rain, the rat-gnawed heads of the four soldiers loomed into view. They moaned at the sky and their cry moulded itself into a word:

'Flesh.'

'Flesh!'

'*Flesh!*'

The dead men pulled themselves out of the grave. They lumbered towards Jake, knocking shoulders like a group of drunks staggering out of a pub. Their raggedy clothes hung in strips from their bony bodies and their fleshless feet slurped in the dirt.

'*FEE-LEEEESSHHH!*'

One of the soldiers, who in life could not have been much older than Jake, opened his mouth to repeat the chant. Worms had eaten through the muscles connecting his jaw to his skull and now the last of the skin tore away. His jawbone smashed against the ground and his teeth went skipping across the meadow. Unfazed, the soldier's long black tongue slapped against the roof of his mouth—

'*Chhlllesh! Chhlllleeesh!*'

Jake scrambled to his feet and ran back towards the camp. The soldiers were slow and clumsy but, being already dead, it was unlikely that they would ever tire of their pursuit. Still, it would not take much to outpace them, especially with the horses.

Eleanor was still peering into the darkness. She had not yet seen the troop of living corpses. At the sight of Jake, she started forward.

'We need to get out of here!' he called, waving her back. 'Untie the h—'

Hooves thundered behind him. As Jake turned his head, he heard the terrified whinnies of Pepper and Marian. The animals had sensed the thing that was coming towards them: a creature that had once been of their own kind, but that was now something *other*.

The ground trembled. Jake saw the flash of teeth and the white of rib. Frothing at the mouth, the undead horse bolted past the soldiers. Loose skin flapped behind it like party streamers caught in the breeze. The horse put a final burst of speed and the stray pieces of flesh holding its guts together gave way. Innards and entrails splashed across the ground, painting the meadow with a bright red streak.

Jake threw himself down. A second later, the horse flashed by, its hooves missing his head by centimetres. It was heading straight for the camp. There was no time for Eleanor to untie the horses and make her escape.

Jake shouted—'Get into the tree!'

He saw the agonized look on Eleanor's face. She didn't want to leave the mares to their deaths. She started fumbling with the reins tied around the trees, but the horses had strained and pulled the knots tight. She would need a knife. She rifled through the saddlebag, all the while whispering to Pepper and Marian.

'No time!' Jake cried. 'ELEANOR!'

The monstrous horse smashed its way through the camp. Sparks erupted from the fire and the cooking pot and its contents went flying into the night. The canvas shelter caught around the horse's throat and was ripped from the trees with the ease of a hand cutting through a spider web. The horse galloped in a circle, flared its nostrils, and started to pace back towards Eleanor and the mares.

There was nothing Eleanor could do. She gave the horses a forlorn glance and scrambled up to the topmost branch of the nearest oak. The undead animal snorted its frustration and reared up in front of Marian. The terrified mare shied away, but her move came too late. A hoof crashed down onto Marian's skull and she collapsed to the ground. Stunned, Jake could only watch as the skeletal horse bowed its head and started tearing into Marian's flesh.

The dull moan sounded again—

'*Fleeesh.*'

The soldiers were within a few metres of Jake. Behind them, hobbling along with the aid of a stick, the old Crowden sister.

'Don't worry, boy,' she called, 'I have mastery of my puppets. I have told them only to wound you, perhaps to rip off an arm or a leg, not to kill you. It is only the girl who will die tonight.'

Jake felt the magic pulse into his hand and he threw a fiery ball at the witch. It missed her by centimetres.

'That's it!' she cried. 'Put up a fight. It will make the game much more interesting.'

A skinless hand reached down and swiped for Jake's head. He rolled aside, leapt to his feet and ran for the camp.

'After him!' the witch instructed. 'Swift as the wind now!'

She pointed her gnarled fingers at the dead soldiers. Suddenly, they crouched forward, heads down, and started running after Jake with long, loping strides. The jolt of their feet on the ground was almost too much for their worm-weakened bodies and pieces began to fall away. Hands snapped from rotten wrists, ankles cracked and necks broke. By the time Jake reached the camp his pursuers were little more than bones strung together with shreds of skin.

Eleanor dropped down to the lowest branch, hands outstretched. Jake vaulted the dying fire and threw himself at the tree. Fear seemed to have given Eleanor supernatural strength—her hands locked like vices around his wrists and Jake was hauled into the safety of the oak. Together, they clambered to the highest branches.

Meanwhile, the undead horse was busy grazing on Marian, tearing at the tough skin with its big, bloodstained teeth. The thing chomped and swallowed, only for the chunks of meat to drop down its neck and fall through its empty ribcage onto the ground. Marian's steaming blood spread around the tree and touched Pepper's hooves. Desperate to escape, Pepper strained to free herself but the reins still held.

'We have to help her,' Eleanor said.

Jake looked from the gloating witch to her undead minions. Two of the soldiers were closing in around Pepper while the others waited beneath Jake and Eleanor's tree. Long ribbons of drool spilled over their hungry lips and made their constant cry of '*Flesh*' even more terrible.

'Enough,' Jake growled.

He climbed down to a sturdy branch that faced the soldiers and the frightened horse. Lying flat on his stomach, he held onto the branch with his left hand while, with his right, he conjured a ball of scarlet-tinged magic. He targeted the soldier closest to Pepper and hurled the hex.

The magic smashed into the man's chest and sent him toppling to the ground. Jake had already conjured a second hex, and was sighting another target, when the felled soldier *moved*.

Its legs flinched. Its hands twitched. Lifting his worm-eaten head, the soldier looked up at Jake with an expression that mixed sadness with deep, gnawing hunger. Nearby, the witch remained focused as she directed her puppets. She clicked her fingers and the soldier began to crawl across the ground. It was only then that Jake saw that his spell had blasted right through the creature, severing its spine and cutting it in half. Leaving his flinching, kicking legs behind, the soldier used his arms to drag himself back to the camp. Guts and intestines trailed behind him like the tentacles of some hideous octopus.

'Such an idiot!' Jake muttered. He swirled the magic in his palm and flicked his fingers towards the creature. 'Only one way to kill a zombie!'

The magic hit and the creature's head exploded.

Jake looked up at Eleanor and grinned.

'Gotta take out the brain!'

A flash of red light from Jake's fingers and another zombie's head was torn from its shoulders. Blood and brains misted the air. Next, he targeted the undead horse.

'The old man was right,' Jake said, summoning more magic. 'You can't think about the power—you just have to *feel* it.'

Two zombies left.

Strike.

The first dropped, its dirty yellow sash stained with fresh blood.

Jake was about to finish the job when Eleanor called out:

'Something's happening. Jake, look at the witch.'

The old woman was on her knees, hands clutched over her heart. Pain had etched itself in tight lines across her face.

'She must be connected to the zombies,' Jake said. 'Of

course! She used her blood to resurrect them and so her life-force is bound to theirs. And now there's only one left . . . '

The flame danced in Jake's palm. He eyed the zombie below.

'You can't!' Eleanor cried. 'You'll kill her.'

'But she was going to let those things tear us apart!'

Jake kept the witch in view while the magic pulsed and darkened in his hand. The blue heart of it fell back against the roar of red. His gaze played across the woman's bloody apron and he pushed his fingers towards the zombie.

'She's a murderer,' he said. 'My dad told me the history of the Crowden sisters: they were cannibals, eaters of children.'

'And they deserve to be punished. Jake, look at me.'

Eleanor climbed down to Jake's branch. She reached out and drew him close. He could feel her heart racing against his chest. Cornflower blue eyes bored into his soul.

'Let this anger go, Jake. For your sake, not for hers, be rid of it.'

'But she wanted to hurt you.'

Magic, darker than ever in his hand.

'Nothing could ever hurt me as much as the sight of you destroying that woman. Do you understand?'

'Eleanor, I . . . '

'ENOUGH!' the witch shrieked. 'I will not live by the mercy of a coward! I *will* die, boy, but in dying I will keep my promise to Master Quilp. I will take you to him.'

She screamed in agony and a dense black smoke whipped out of her hands. Before Jake could think of responding, the smoke had formed into an impenetrable wall which wrapped itself around the tree. Inside the vapour—Jake, Eleanor, Pepper, the zombie, and the witch. The meadow beyond had vanished. All around the tree, the little scrap of land trembled as if shaken by an earthquake. While Jake and Eleanor clung to the branch, the witch shrieked against the pain of her final conjuring.

Shapes began to appear in the black wall. Shadows emerging from the smoke:

A bleak woodland.

A house with blank, staring windows.

A great door with a lion's head knocker.

Jake turned to Eleanor.

'Hold tight.'

The cauldron on the table burst into flames. Its life tied to the witch, the inanimate demon was returning to its own world.

Frija's eyes snapped open. Before she could stop herself, the cloud-spinner spluttered, 'Drude is dead.'

She pointed a shaking finger at the door and, behind her veil, a smile creased her lips.

'The boy is here.'

Chapter 30
Rhapsody in Darkness

Materializing in an explosion of magical energy, the oak tree smashed against the wall of the manor house. Its branches punched through windows and its roots cracked the stone slabs outside the great door. On impact, Jake and Eleanor lost their grip and fell from the tree. The patch of soft, muddy ground that had been transported with the oak saved them from breaking their necks. Groaning, they picked themselves up and saw that the black smoke had dispersed.

Pepper nudged her nose against Eleanor. 'All right, girl, it's over now.' Long, smooth strokes against her flank seemed to calm the mare.

Jake walked over to where the witch lay sprawled on the ground. The last of her venom was frozen in her glassy eyes. She was dead. With its puppet master gone the zombie had also crumpled, the tormented soul of the soldier finally at peace.

'Where are we?' Eleanor asked.

'The home of the Crowdens,' Jake said. 'Havlock Grange.'

The house towered over them, its haughty face grey in the moonlight.

'I've been here before. Years from now, Rachel, Pandora, Brag, and me, we came to rescue Simon from the Demon Father.'

'Rachel?' Eleanor frowned. 'Who's she?'

'Rachel Saxby, my friend. Your grea—You'd like her,' Jake said, catching himself. 'She's brave, loyal, strong. She's, well, she's a lot like you.'

A sudden sense of dread made Jake shiver. Time was in flux, warping and changing around them. In the settled history of things, Rachel Saxby was a descendant of Katherine Hobarron, the daughter of Eleanor and Josiah. Yet in this version of history it seemed that Eleanor had never had a daughter. What did that mean for Rachel? Had she simply ceased to exist? And if so, why had history changed?

'What's that?' Eleanor said. 'Do you hear it?'

Haunting music, played upon the strings of a harp, reached out to them.

'It's so beautiful.'

In another time and place Jake would have agreed but here, under the shadow of this malevolent house, he shivered at each sombre note.

'Cut the horse loose,' he said. 'I want you to take her and go.'

'What?'

Jake stepped off the clump of meadow and approached the great door.

'Get out of here, Eleanor. There isn't much time.'

'Don't be a fool, I'm not leaving you.'

Jake placed his hands on the door. Smooth, solid oak. It seemed strange to think that in *his* past he had seen this door old and weathered. That the entire house had once been a ruin and would be so again. Only one thing about Havlock Grange would remain unchanged: the Evil that clung to its rotten heart. Jake could feel the strength of it now, pulsing through his fingers. So many had died here . . .

'Please, Eleanor, I have to do this alone.'

'That's what *he* said.' The girl's voice shook with emotion. 'That's what he *always* said: it's not safe, I have to do this alone. Don't you understand, I can't let it happen again? I can't let him—you—face all the horrors on your own. I need to be with you.'

Her hands pressed against Jake's.

'He couldn't take you with him, Eleanor. If you'd ever been hurt—'

'I *was* hurt, every time he left without me. And then, when I heard of his death . . . I cannot, *will not*, be hurt like that again.'

'But I'm *not* him. You said so yourself. You won't ever have to mourn for me.'

Eleanor took his hands from the door and made Jake face her.

'How could I not mourn you?'

Her lips close to his. Her fingers tracing his jaw. Her eyes making him forget the music.

'I . . .'

The door burst open.

Light flooded out from the Great Hall.

Beyond the glare, Jake glimpsed the tall, thin figure of a man standing on the stairs. His pale skin gleamed and his eyes shone from their deep, dark sockets.

'Good evening, Master Harker,' Quilp said. 'I have been waiting for you.'

At the sound of that voice, Jake forgot all about Eleanor. All he could focus on was the steady beat of his rage. He brushed her aside and stepped forward to meet his old enemy.

Mr Murdles floated towards the open door of the Grimoire Club. The early evening sunlight baked the yellow stone of the square and struggled through the body of the ghost. Murdles was wearing a new ecto-suit for the occasion; the very last in his wardrobe.

He tried to ignore the calls coming from the shadowy arcades. Fifty or more dark creatures had already gathered there. They had travelled many miles, on foot and claw, on hoof and hands, on leathery wing and scaly belly. More arrived by the minute, emerging from the teardrop doorways behind the columns. Spying the ghost that had summoned them, they called out—'Murdles! What times does the show start?'

The mood in the square was good-natured as the creatures greeted old friends and took out their picnic hampers (some of them, Murdles noticed, carried suspicious, blood-soaked lunch bags). As jovial as the atmosphere was now, the manager knew that it would not remain so for long. He glanced at the fangs and claws, the pincers and stingers. If things didn't go to plan then it would take days to clear the corpses from the square.

Razor, the dog-headed doorman, stepped across Murdles's path. He cradled the bottom of a leather purse in his huge palm, jingling the contents.

'Takings have already met your target, boss.'

'Good, good,' Murdles flustered. 'Any of them reluctant to pay up?'

Razor swung a heavy club, not unlike the preferred weapon of the troll, Brag Badderson. The end was matted with blood and hair.

'One or two,' he grunted.

'Remember, only take gold and silver coins,' Murdles instructed. 'I don't want to see any human currency. The way they run their economies, most of their money isn't worth the paper it's printed on.'

'Speaking of humans,' Razor lifted his hairy eyebrows.

Rachel Saxby and the Lydgate boy hurried down the steps of the club and towards Murdles.

'That's all I need,' the manger grumbled. Then, grinning broadly—'My dears! What can I do for you?'

'What's going on?' Rachel asked.

'Just a little event I've organized. Nothing to concern your good selves.'

'Murdles,' Simon warned.

The manager looked to his doorman for help. Razor just shrugged, slapped Simon on the back, and headed off in search of gold.

'Bloody Cynocephalus!' Murdles glanced nervously at Simon. 'No offence.'

'My canine side forgives you,' Simon growled, 'but don't try its patience. We haven't seen a soul around here for days and suddenly the square's packed to the rafters with . . . Well, whatever the hell some of those things are. So, out with it.'

'It's the Oracle,' Murdles sighed.

'Your little snakey friend in the pit?'

'I went to her a few days ago, desperate for news. You see, Mr Lydgate, I can't pay my bills. The club's almost bankrupt, and if it goes under then there will be no more ecto-suits for poor Mr Murdles. So I had to know.'

'Know what?'

'When he was coming back.'

'I'm sorry,' Simon frowned, 'when *who's* coming back?'

'Jake,' Rachel said. 'He made a deal with Murdles so that we could stay here.'

'A show of magic,' Murdles nodded. 'A show to end all shows. The Oracle told me that today's the day! Jake will return within the hour and he will keep his promise. I've sent out telegrams, notices, proclamations to every corner of the borderlands. Look.'

Murdles reached into the pocket of his ecto-suit and withdrew a rolled-up poster. Unfurled, it showed an artist's impression of Jake standing before the demon Door, magical energy rippling around him. Written above the illustration:

Rhapsody in Darkness

BY ARRANGEMENT OF
MURDLES MANAGEMENT . . .

JACOB HARKER

Destroyer of the Demon Door
Vanquisher of the Coven Master
Thwarter of the Demontide

will demonstrate his peerless power in the
square outside the *Grimoire Club* at the hour
before sunset, Sammal's Eve

'Why didn't you tell us this?' Rachel snapped. 'Didn't you
think Dr Harker would like to know that his son was coming
back?'

'The prophecy was vague, I didn't want to get his hopes
up. He seems very frail these days.'

'But you've arranged this event! You had to believe it was
true.'

'Don't you get it?' Murdles seethed. 'This is my only
chance to survive. It's the biggest gamble of my life, and
perhaps the last. In any case, I couldn't tell you because you
weren't here.' He looked at Simon and Rachel curiously. 'Are
you and Pandora still skulking around London, keeping your
ear to the ground for news? Things have changed so quickly
for the humans, have they not? In a matter of weeks, the
entire world turned on its head! I hear that Pandora's contacts will no longer see her. Powerful people are breathing

down their necks. And what of Dr Holmwood and Dr Saxby? Whoever would have thought that such important men could fall so low?'

'Come on,' Rachel said, taking Simon's hand, 'we should talk to Adam.'

Simon hesitated. 'I don't know, Rach. Maybe Murdles has a point. Adam's very weak. He can't eat or drink anything, he's drifting in and out of consciousness. Pandora says . . . ' Simon put his arms around the girl. 'She says he doesn't have much more time.'

'He should know,' Rachel insisted.

'Let's just wait and see what happens, OK?'

The great sun of the borderlands dipped in the sky and the shadows stretched across the square.

Twilight approached.

There were four figures in the hazy candlelight beyond the door: Tobias Quilp standing on the stairs, his little demon slavering beside him; a veiled woman, bound and chained at the bottom of the staircase; and a second woman, small, beautiful, sitting on a stool in the centre of the Great Hall. A harp rested between the woman's legs and against her shoulder. Jake tried to tear his gaze back to Quilp, but the song of the harp was impossible to resist. His eyes moved across the instrument—its quivering strings, its gilded wooden frame decorated with scrolls and carvings. The little witch's fingers strummed with hypnotic grace.

'Qu-ilp . . . ' Jake stumbled into the hall. 'You. I've come for you. I need to . . . '

To what? Why had he journeyed back in time? To find the witch ball, his addled mind answered. The witch ball would cure his father and give him the strength to destroy . . . Who? He struggled against the sweet lull of the music.

'Qui—'

The man on the stairs smiled down at Mr Pi— Jake shook his head—the demon's name would not come to him.

'That's right, Jacob—listen to Miss Lethe's music. Let it charm the thoughts from your mind, let it soothe all your sad and hateful memories away.'

The yellow-eyed demon laughed. It lifted a mocking talon and beckoned Jake on. He had almost reached the harpist when a weak voice called out:

'Jake. Stop. Come back.'

Something familiar in that tone. Instinct told him to trust the stranger. Looking over his shoulder, Jake saw the golden-haired girl framed in the doorway. Who was she? Her name haunted his lips but the music snatched it away. The music: it moved through his mind like a breeze, snuffing out the light of memories, leaving only darkness in its wake.

'Come back to me . . . Ja—'

The creases in the girl's brow smoothed out. The muscles in her face relaxed. Memories vanished, and with them all emotion, thought, and feeling was gone. Jake turned his back on her.

More darkness than light now. Memories closing down around him. Birthdays, Christmases, bedtimes, holidays, school trips—all of it taken by the music. And as each light was swept away, so people vanished into shadows. Eddie Rice and Dr Holmwood, Joanna Harker, Dr Saxby, the Preacher, Pandora, Lanyon and Murdles, Brag Badderson, Rachel, Simon, his father . . . his mother . . .

He must fight it, must cling to something.

The girl in the doorway.

'El-Elea—'

'Let her go, Jacob,' the harpist sighed. 'Let them all dance away into the dark.'

She turned her elfin face to him and smiled.

'Lethe,' he breathed.

Something stirred in his mind. The pages of a book. A boy with a crooked smile had once given the book a name— 'Jake's dark compendium'. No, that wasn't right. 'Dark archive'? He shook his head. It didn't matter. It was what the book told him that was important.

'Is that your real name?' he asked. 'Lethe?'

'That's right,' the witch crooned, her fingers plucking the strings.

'Lethe,' Jake breathed. 'Roman myth . . . '

'Greek,' she corrected.

'Greek. Yes. Lethe was one of the rivers of the Underworld. Anyone who drank the waters would . . . they would . . . '

Jake clutched his head. Screamed against the vanishing. The book was gone.

'Yes,' the witch smiled, 'they would.'

There was something he could do. He wasn't powerless. This was the work of magic and he . . . He was . . . What was he? Jake stared at his outstretched hands. He turned them over, as if looking for something that *should* be there.

What was he?

Who was he?

Another light snuffed out. Another memory taken.

And the music played on . . . and on . . . and on . . .

Chapter 31
Jake's Sacrifice

'Who am I?'

'My dear, how should *I* know who you are?' the lady at the harp tittered. 'Such a silly question!'

The hall in which the boy found himself was very grand. As large as an upturned ship's hull, the great arched ceiling soared beyond the reach of candlelight. The boy stared into the ceiling. Shouldn't there be rain falling through the roof? Wasn't there someone upstairs, waiting to be rescued? He tried to remember, but the music swelled and swamped his senses.

'Have a care, Lethe,' said the man on the stairs. 'My master will not thank you if the child's core memories are lost. He will want to examine the boy's magical abilities in detail.'

'Very well, Master Quilp. I will only take away those memories most precious to him.' The woman stared at the boy, as if seeing deep into his soul. 'Memories of his father and his friends. Memories of his beloved Eleanor.'

Eleanor . . .

A light reignited in the darkness.

He spun round and saw the girl in the doorway. She was reaching out to him.

'Eleanor.'

Her name left his lips and the magic appeared in his hand—a bright blue flame sizzling red at its edges. The roar of Oldcraft drowned out the song of the harp and Jake reclaimed his name from the shadows. The lights came back on inside his head, one by one: birthdays, Christmases, bedtimes, holidays, all brightening the corridors of his mind. The people who had shaped his life crowded back in, and with them came the identity of the man on the stairs.

The murderer, Tobias Quilp.

The flame in Jake's hand darkened.

'Eleanor, are you all right?' he called.

The girl nodded. Her face had lost that vacant, empty expression.

'Stay where you are.' Jake switched his attention to the witch at the harp. 'You know something, Miss Crowden? I never did like classical music.'

Lethe looked from the ball of magic to Jake's grim, determined face. Her shaking fingers left the strings.

'This was my revenge!' she shrieked. 'You killed my sister!'

'She killed herself,' Jake spat back. 'I was there. I *remember.*' He drew his hand back over his shoulder. 'Now, if I were you, I'd move away from that demon.'

Jake was about to hurl the magic when a shout from Eleanor alerted him to danger.

In a two-pronged attack, Quilp had released Mr Pinch while at the same time summoning a dark hex. The demon bounded down the stairs, its thick tongue lashing around its lips. As it ran, flecks of green mucus flicked out from the large, weeping hole that served as its nose.

Forced to turn away from Lethe, Jake sent his magic streaming towards the demon. It struck Mr Pinch with such power that the creature was plucked into the air and dashed against the wall. Pinch hit the ground and stayed there, shaking a dazed and hideous head. Jake barely had time to recover before Quilp's hex struck. It left the witch's fingers in the form of a jagged, blood-red lightning bolt.

'Know my pain!' Quilp shouted. 'Feel it!'

Jake thrust out his left hand. The lightning hit his palm and the smell of scorched skin filled the air. Dark magic juddered along the length of Jake's arm and shrieked into every corner of his body. It felt as if his blood had been turned into a river of fire and that flames were dancing in the chambers of his heart. He staggered under the onslaught of the hex.

Maintaining the lightning stream, Quilp descended the stairs.

'They told me that you had become a great sorcerer,' he laughed. 'Magic at your command as powerful as any wielded by Josiah Hobarron. It seems that such reports were exaggerated.'

As he stepped off the last stair, Quilp brought his wrists

together. The source of the hex throbbed in the bowl between his hands and grew stronger.

'Come now, show me this legendary Oldcraft I have heard so much about.'

Jake tried to lean into the lightning stream, to deflect it, but the hex was too powerful. All he could do was to contain the worst of it in his hand; a strategy that could not continue for much longer.

Lethe Crowden left her harp and skipped to Quilp's side. Pinch walked groggily to stand beside his master. The dark triumvirate looked down on Jake like cats eyeing a wounded mouse.

'You and your father have haunted my dreams these many nights,' Quilp said. 'A pair of murderers stalking my nightmares.'

'Muh-murderers?' Jake panted. '*You* are the murderer, Quilp. My mother . . . '

'*My* definition of murder is the destruction of a glorious life by an unworthy adversary. Your mother was a pathetic nobody, a scientific tinkerer without a scrap of magic in her veins. Yes, I killed her, and what did it matter? Even in the world of Man such an inconsequential life was shrugged away. But you and your father! You murdered a woman whose dark light shone with *such* brilliance . . . '

Jake could hardly believe the emotion in Quilp's voice. Could such a monster really grieve?

'Mother Inglethorpe,' Quilp shouted, spit flying from his lips. 'My Esther!'

And now Jake understood the force behind the hex. It

361

was born of love. Dark, unkind, and twisted, but love just the same.

Love—magic's most powerful spur.

Quilp joined his hands together and the source of the hex pulsed with fresh intensity. Jake felt it blaze into his flesh, reach deep and burn him from the inside out. He screamed and fell to his knees.

Cool hands touched his face. Eleanor, kneeling beside him.

'What can I do?'

'Go,' Jake hissed. 'Run.'

'The girl.' Quilp looked to the veiled lady chained at the bottom of the stairs. 'Yes indeed, your coming was also foretold by Mistress Frija.'

Frija Crowden shivered at Quilp's words.

'Before you die, Jacob, you will know some of my pain. You will lose the thing you treasure most.' The effort of maintaining the hex was beginning to show as Quilp addressed Lethe. 'A little sport for you, my dear.'

Lethe giggled and skipped back across the hall. She was within ten metres of Jake and Eleanor when she stopped and clicked her fingers. A pretty red flame flickered at the tips.

'Such a fine young girl.' Lethe's tongue slipped over her lips. 'Such sweet and supple skin. Yes, I see that I shall enjoy my lonely supper tonight.'

She swirled the magic and directed her fingers at Eleanor.

'No!'

Jake broke his defensive spell and switched all the magic to his right hand. As soon as he had relaxed his guard, the full power of Quilp's hex struck home. Jake tried to ignore the pain and focus on his conjuring. There was no point in targeting Lethe, the spell had already left her fingers. Instead, he sighted the magic itself—a flame-red orb flying towards Eleanor—and released.

Jake's burst of blue light struck the orb like one missile crashing into another. Both spells shot into the ceiling, illuminating the web-strewn darkness with flares of red and blue. While Jake screamed with pain and hit the floor, the two bolts of magic smashed through the roof. The impact shook Havlock Grange to its foundations. Tiles, dust, and debris rained across the Great Hall. Cracks splintered the walls and ran through the floor.

Shaken by the explosion, Quilp lost focus. His hex spluttered and died in his hands. Despite this, the witch smiled victoriously: one look at Jake, wrapped in a tight ball of agony, was enough to show him that the dark spell had achieved its purpose. The boy had been weakened and could now be transported back to the Demon Father. Quilp snapped his fingers. A moment later, Marcus Crowden's nightmare box emerged from one of the upstairs corridors and swept into the hall. It swirled behind Quilp, waiting, watching.

Lethe looked at Quilp imploringly. 'May I?'

'Yes, my dear. Finish her.'

Jake strived with every sinew to move but the pain was too great. He felt Eleanor's arms tighten around him.

'Go,' he gasped. 'Leave me.'

'Never,' Eleanor said.

'Such nobility. Such bravery,' Lethe purred. 'Such love.'

The witch stood over them, a bright red light in her hand. Lethal light, reflected in Eleanor's eyes.

It was then that Jake caught sight of the veiled figure, bound and chained. She was holding her manacled hands out to him in a gesture of desperation. Jake's heart responded. That secret store of power deep inside him opened its doors. Magic squeezed a path through his pain-crippled body and gasped into life between his fingers. A tiny flame flitted weakly through the air. It was seen by Quilp and Lethe and dismissed as Jake's last pathetic attempt to save the girl. A spell unworthy of their attention.

'Make her suffer,' Quilp hissed. 'Make him watch every shred of life being wrung out of her.'

Lethe pointed a finger at Eleanor. Dark magic pulsed at the tip. The girl stared defiantly at the woman, her body thrown over Jake . . .

Meanwhile, Jake's magic crept across the floor until it arrived at the feet of the witch. Frija Crowden bent her hands to the flame. At the magic's touch, the chains snapped and fell from her wrists. Frija pulled the rest of the chains from her body, straightened up, and thrust her arms into the air. Words fluttered against her veil—

'I am sorry, sister.'

Lethe's hex vanished from her finger. 'Frija . . . ?'

She turned and glared at her sister. Then, following the direction of Frija's hands, she looked up into the ruined ceiling. Part of an immense wooden beam had been sheared away by the magical crash and now hung precariously overhead. All that kept it attached to the main rafter was a thin strip of wood. Before either Lethe or Quilp could react, Frija dropped her hands and the beam was severed from the ceiling.

Quilp managed to jump aside but Lethe was not so quick. She opened her mouth to scream.

The wooden spear fell and, in an explosion of blood and gore, silenced the witch for ever. On cue, Lethe's demon harp burst into flame.

Frija hurried to Jake's side and helped Eleanor to lift him from the ground.

'Thank you,' he panted.

'You saved my life as much as I saved yours,' said the veiled woman. She looked to the stairs and the lightless corridor beyond. 'I pray now that those poor children are at peace.'

Jake reached out with his mind. He felt that, although evil still haunted Havlock Grange, its intensity had weakened. Something had departed from the house.

'They're gone,' Jake whispered. 'Flown.'

Although he could not see her face, Jake was sure that Frija was smiling. He was about to turn to Eleanor when the coldest of cold voices echoed through the chamber.

'I am not done yet, boy.'

Quilp, his lip bloody, his clothes torn, staggered to his feet. Beside him, the demonic Mr Pinch.

'At her!' Quilp commanded.

In the same instant, he directed two streams of magic towards Jake and Frija. Taken by surprise, both conjurors reacted to deflect the hexes. These spells were much weaker than the dark magic Quilp had originally used against Jake. Still, they were enough to divert attention while Mr Pinch made his move.

The demon sprinted across the hall and threw itself at Eleanor. Pinch followed the trademark attack that had served him well for many centuries: a precision landing at his victim's throat followed by a brutal, ravenous assault. During those few precious moments while Jake and Frija dealt with the hexes, Pinch unfurled his long, rapier-sharp talons. Eleanor had no time to cry out before the demon slashed at her face. A ribbon of blood folded through the air.

Everything seemed to happen in slow motion. Jake dashed the hex aside; Frija sent the magic flying back at Quilp, who ducked out of the way. The pale pink blur of Pinch's body flashed in the corner of Jake's eye. He heard the demon snicker and slurp its thick lips. Blood splashed against Jake's face.

'STOP!' he screamed.

But the demon did not stop.

It went on tearing.

Jake conjured his magic, but Frija was quicker. A streak of sky-blue energy whipped from her fingers and caught Mr Pinch around the neck. The creature shrieked as the magical lasso tightened and he was wrenched away from his victim. Frija had endured years of torment at the hands of her cruel sisters and their demons—the scalding spells from Drude's cauldron, the vicious tunes played on Lethe's harp—each torture designed to force Frija to use her gift. Now every scrap of hatred she bore for dark magic was condensed into two words—

'Die, demon!' she roared and swept her hand over her head.

Helpless in the stranglehold of the leash, Pinch hurtled towards the ceiling. He clawed at the magic but it was too powerful, even for his talons. His screams rang out like the startled squeals of a pig. Then his head smashed against one of the huge, heavy rafters and he screamed no more. Tobias Quilp cried out in horror. Even Jake, cradling Eleanor in his arms and wishing for the demon's death, winced at the sound of Pinch's skull cracking apart.

Frija closed her fist and the spell was broken. Pinch fell to earth. It was only the quick wits of his master that saved him from certain death. Quilp reached out and the demon flew into his arms.

During all this, Jake had been using his magic to heal Eleanor. He had managed to stem the flow of blood and the girl was breathing steadily. Her eyes wide with shock, she seemed unable to talk. Three wide gashes ran down the left side of her face. Pinch had vandalized her beauty and the sight of it made Jake weep.

He allowed himself a quick sideways glance. He could see Frija standing guard over them, her hands outstretched, ready to cast defensive spells. Beyond her stood Tobias Quilp, his wounded familiar in his arms. The demon's skull was a pulpy mass of bone, flesh, and dark green blood.

'This isn't over,' Quilp cried.

He had reached the foot of the stairs and the door of Crowden's nightmare box. The tall black cabinet ceased its spinning and allowed the witch to step inside. It was as Quilp took that first step that his long coat fell back and Jake saw the object tied around his neck.

The witch ball.

'Avert your gaze,' Quilp smiled. 'This is the property of the Demon Father.'

With that, he pulled his coat back over the witch ball and slammed the cabinet door.

The nightmare box turned on its axis, building steady momentum. Scarlet sparks of magical energy sizzled across its surface. From inside, Jake could hear the terrified screams of Tobias Quilp. It seemed that, even when serving a dark purpose, the box could not help but torment those that stepped within its walls. Jake could only hope that Quilp had a long, long journey before him.

Such a thought was cold comfort. Very soon now Quilp would emerge into the twenty-first century and hand the witch ball to his master. The Demontide would break, Jake's father and his friends would die, the world would be lost . . .

Frija spoke words, ancient and solemn. A grey thread issued from her fingers and swept around the nightmare box, locking it in a misty manacle. It slowed to a grinding halt.

'Quickly, Jake,' Frija cried, her voice strained. 'I cannot hold it much longer.'

'I can't.' Jake looked down at the girl in his arms. 'I can't leave her.'

'You must. I promise that I'll do my best to heal her, but you have to go.'

'But I've only just found her.' Tears prickled Jake's eyes. 'I can't lose her again.'

The nightmare box creaked and, very slowly, began to turn.

'I'm sorry, Jake, but the future of the world is in your hands. You must sacrifice . . . '

Jake's eyes blazed and his voice took on a deep, magisterial tone.

'*I have sacrificed more than you will ever know, Frija Crowden.*' He hugged Eleanor to his chest. When he spoke again it was with his own voice. 'Can't I stay with her?'

'I know you've had the dreams,' Frija sighed. 'You've seen what will happen if the Door to the demon world is opened. Devastation, despair, unending death. Demonkind triumphant.'

Magic crackled across the box. Frija's mist was fading.

'You do not belong here, Jake, this is not your time.' Regret in every syllable of the witch's words. 'You were never supposed to meet her, never supposed to love her. Your destiny lies elsewhere.'

Jake felt a tug at his sleeve. Cornflower blue eyes creased into the saddest smile he had ever seen.

'She's right,' Eleanor said. 'You have to go.'

'I won't.' He buried his face in her hair. 'He—*I*—lost you once before, I can't do it again. It's too hard.'

'Jake . . . '

'Don't you understand? I remember everything about you. My Eleanor of the May. *My beautiful girl of the spring with the promise of summer in her hair.*' Jake smiled through his tears. 'I remember, Eleanor, and I know how happy we could be.' He took her hands in his. 'Come with me.'

'She can't,' Frija said. 'She's already weak, poisoned by the demon's touch. I'm sorry, but the journey in the nightmare box would kill her.'

'There must be a way,' Jake choked.

'Listen to me,' Eleanor whispered.

'No.'

'Listen. You said you know me. Well, I believe that I know *you*, Jacob Harker. The strong, good heart of you.' She brushed her lips against the back of his hand. 'Your path is clear.'

'But I'll never see you again.'

'No,' Eleanor said softly. 'No, you won't.'

She drew him to her. Their lips met and their tears mingled. She had always given Josiah the strength he needed to do his work; to face the horrors, to vanquish evil, to save the innocent. Though it broke her heart, she now gave Jake that same loving, generous strength.

'Such sweet sorrow,' he whispered.

She smiled. 'You remember.'

'It was how I always said goodbye. And you would always laugh.'

He laid her softly on the ground. Their fingers parted.

'I found my magic again because of you.' He looked to the black box and a blue flame with a heart of scarlet ignited in his palm. The tears had vanished from his eyes. 'Now it's time to use it again.'

'Jake?' She held his gaze. 'You must never let the darkness win or I will truly have lost you.'

Jake could no longer look at her. It was too painful. He walked to Frija's side and the witch strained again to slow the box.

'Once you're inside lay your hands upon the door and concentrate on the place you wish to be taken,' she instructed.

'Surely Quilp's already done that.'

'You're a stronger sorcerer than he. Remember, I know this demon, it was my brother's familiar. It is both disloyal and greedy. It will respond to whoever wields the greatest power. Hurry now.'

'Thank you,' Jake said. 'You stood with us against your sisters. It must have been difficult for you.'

Frija Crowden shook her head. With her free hand she took hold of the corner of her veil.

'Not as difficult as you may think.'

Jake remembered how Frija's brother had torn away the dirty cloth that had hidden his face from view. In Marcus Crowden's case he had been concealing a beauty that belied his evil. As she pulled her veil away, Jake saw that Frija hid her features for a very different reason. More skull than skin, the horribly burned face of Frija Crowden glistened in the candlelight.

'Such is the evil of dark witches and demons,' she croaked.

The mist pouring from her fingers thickened. The box slowed to a near stop and the door swung open. Jake strode towards the demon, all the while sensing the magnitude of its evil. Aside from the Demon Father himself, this ordinary-looking cabinet was the foulest, darkest creature he had yet encountered.

Jake stepped inside.

A fiery wind gusted against his face. The call of a thousand despairing voices filled his head. He squinted, trying to see beyond the gale and the darkness. There was no sign of Quilp.

'Don't look!' Frija cried. 'Turn back to face the door. Do as I say, or risk losing your mind!'

Jake grasped the sides of the nightmare box. Voices again, telling him he would fail, that soon the Demon Father would stride across the wastelands of his new dominion.

And then he heard *her* voice, and his soul stirred again.

'Goodbye, Jake!' Eleanor called. 'Remember me . . . '

Turning, he caught the meanest glimpse of the girl before the door slammed shut.

Chapter 32
The Witch Ball

'Punters are getting tetchy, Boss,' Razor observed.

'I can see that, you flea-bitten mutt.'

''m just saying, something magical better start happening soon or this lot'll kick off. You do know we've got some of the Unseelie Court in the audience?' The Cynocephalus dug a toothpick around his gigantic canines and tried to appear unconcerned. 'You don't really wanna mess with dark fairies unless you can help it. Or any of the Old Ones come to that . . . '

'Shut up, shut up, shut up!' Murdles shouted.

Puzzled faces turned to the open door of the Grimoire Club, and Murdles managed a carefree smile. It only took a quick glance around the square for the smile to fall away.

Five rows deep, the covered walkways teemed with dark creatures. Thousands jostled for the best view of the square while more monsters arrived through the teardrop doorways every minute. So many creatures that Murdles had been forced to beg his fellow managers at the Lizardman Lounge and the Gore Gardens for extra doormen to control the crowds. Even in the glory days of the Grimoire, when Mulgrew the Magnificent, Savage Bones, or Letty Scrivener had graced the square, there had never been such a crowd as this. From every corner came the jingle of coins being collected.

But Razor was right, curse his hairy hide. The dark creatures were becoming impatient. The Shades of the Shadowlands whispered between themselves and kept turning their smooth, featureless heads towards Murdles. A horde of vampires sheltering under black umbrellas hissed whenever they looked in the manager's direction. And the Unseelie Court? Well, those little creatures just waited and watched in eerie silence, as the Ancients are wont to do. Meanwhile, the rest—trolls and boggarts, werewolves and warlocks, goblin and chimera, wyvern and gorgon—growled and grunted and grumbled. If the show didn't start soon then, instead of a magical display, the square would be hosting a bloodbath.

Murdles looked at the sky and shivered. The giant sun had started to set over the desert.

Fingers clicked an inch from the manager's nose.

'Borderlands to Murdles.'

His eyes focused on Rachel Saxby and Simon Lydgate. Arms folded, these humans looked almost as threatening as the crowd.

'What d'you want?' the manager snapped.

'We want to know what's going on,' said Rachel. 'The

The Witch Ball

hour before sunset, your poster said. So where is he?'

'Keep your voice down,' Murdles hissed. He floated to within whispering range. 'Truth is, I don't know where he is . . . Look, I wonder if you could do me a favour?'

'A favour?' Simon raised an eyebrow.

'It's just, *if* Dr Harker could come out and talk to a few of his friends here, explain that this really isn't my fault, I would be eternally grateful. He has such influence with these . . . people.'

Rachel and Simon exchanged glances.

'I'm sure Dr Harker would like to help—'

'Excellent!'

'If he could.'

'What do you mean?'

'Adam lost consciousness an hour ago. Pandora's with him, but . . . ' Rachel tailed off.

'Pandora, she . . . ' Simon put his arm around Rachel. Steadied himself. 'Pandora doesn't think he'll wake up again. Dr Harker is dying.'

'Oh. I see.'

Murdles looked forlornly into the square.

And then he noticed a change in the crowd.

A few of the psychics had ceased their chatter and were pointing at something as yet invisible to the naked eye. More and more of the dark creatures seemed to sense the same disturbance. A deathly hush fell across the square. Razor's ears pricked up. Simon grasped Rachel's hand. Murdles felt a shiver run through his ectoplasmic body.

Magic in the air.

Suddenly, an explosion of scarlet light blinded all but the eyeless.

When the glare fell back, Murdles saw a tall black box spinning just above the sandy ground in the centre of the square. He was about to whisper something to Razor when the door of the cabinet burst open. A thin boy wearing old-fashioned clothes and with close-cropped hair stepped out. He paced out a dozen steps, turned, and stopped, his eyes rooted on the open door.

'Jake,' Rachel and Simon said together.

A blue flame tinged with red flashed into Jacob Harker's hand.

The crowd roared.

After the door slammed, Jake had tried to clear his mind of thoughts of Eleanor. The pain of losing her would have to wait. He peered into the unending darkness but could see no sign of Quilp. Was it possible that the witch was inside the box with him, but existing inside some other dimension?

Jake placed his hands against the door. Icy to the touch, the wood crackled with magic. Through this connection, Jake caught a glimpse of the cabinet's destination: it was not moving in space, only through time, catapulting them forward to the derelict Havlock Grange of the twenty-first century.

Back to the Demon Father.

Jake pressed his palms into the wood.

Home, he thought, *take me home.*

A cruel voice echoed around him. The voice of the box—

Very well, boy, but where is 'home'?

Good question—the house in which he had grown up was now empty, deserted.

Take me to my father.

The man who stands in the shadow of death?

Jake did not answer.

Let me feel your magic and I will do as you ask.

An outraged shriek came from the shadows. Jake glanced around but there was still no trace of the witch.

'You serve my master!' Quilp cried. 'The Demon Father commands you!'

We demons are capricious creatures, Mr Quilp, and the boy's power intrigues me.

Quilp's manic screams faded away.

Now, child, the demon box whispered, *how shall we occupy ourselves during our journey? Shall I show you visions of your dead mother? Your slow-dying father? Or shall I—?*

A blue flame stood out against the darkness. Holding it aloft, Jake shook his head.

'I'd shut up, if I were you. Dimensions of suffering, endless torment, but when all's said and done you're still just an old wooden box.' The flame billowed in Jake's hand. 'And I bet wood and magical fire don't mix too well.'

You wouldn't dare.

Jake grinned. 'I've had a pretty rough few weeks, demon. Don't test me.'

* * *

Shouts, whoops, cheers, and catcalls.

Thousands of monstrous faces ranged all around him.

It was a strange scene. Why were all these creatures packed into the square outside the Grimoire Club? For now Jake put the question out of his mind and concentrated on the doorway. He transferred the ball of magic from hand to hand while his senses strained at the silence within the nightmare box.

At last, a pale presence in the darkness. The cultured voice.

'No Crowden sister to help you now, boy. No pretty little wretch to divert your attention. It's just you and me.'

The first twist of anger coiled in Jake's gut.

'Do you remember our first meeting on the road to the Hobarron Institute?'

Quilp's cadaverous face shone in the gloom. His claw-like hands curled around the side of the door.

'Less than a year ago, and you, such a miserable little child.'

The witch stepped out of the box and into the dying light. A few of the dark creatures recognized him and the whisper of his name rustled around the square. Quilp did not look once at the crowd; his full attention was focused on Jake. A blaze ignited in his palm and bathed his pallid features in a smoky red light. The enemies began to circle each other.

'Do you remember how you wailed when I took your mother's head?' Quilp purred. 'How you bawled and bleated when I cut her down and gave her to the fishes? You must remember. How could so much blood ever be forgotten?'

Anger strengthened into fury. Blades of white-hot rage sliced through Jake's mind. He saw his mother just as Quilp described her: a headless corpse falling into the murk of the canal. All it had taken was a slash of the witch's finger.

'That's it,' Quilp laughed. 'Remember her as she is—your stinking, putrid corpse of a mother. Feel the pain that I feel for my Esther.'

Something inside Jake snapped. To hear his mother spoken of in the same breath as Esther Inglethorpe brought every shred of darkness roaring out of his soul. The flame in his hand turned from blue to deepest, darkest red.

Jake looked back at his foe and grinned.

'That withered old hag?' he mused. 'That rancid old bag of bones? Is she really what all this is about? Cos, I gotta say, she was just about the most hopeless excuse for a dark witch I've ever seen. We didn't even need magic to kill her. All it took was a single bullet, smack through the brain.'

'Shut up.'

'One bullet. Just one, ordinary kill-a-human-stone-dead bullet.'

'I said, shut up.'

Jake's eyes reddened in the light of his magic. He put his head to one side and pouted his lips.

'Oh dear, have I upset you, Mr Quilp? Do you really miss Mother Inglethorpe that much?'

He strode forward, magic swirling in his grasp. His long, bleak shadow fell over Tobias Quilp.

'Then let me send you to hell too!'

Jake poured every scrap of spite and hurt, pain and

bitterness, hatred and cruelty into the flame. His brain screamed. His heart wept. Fuelled by the agonies he had suffered at the hands of Quilp and his kind, Jake crafted a spell of pitch-black malevolence. Its ferocity was shaped by the blood on the walls of Hobarron Tower; by the loss of his friend, Brett Enfield; by the slaughter of the magician Sidney Tinsmouth; by the death of his mother; by the hexing of his father; by the scars on the face of the girl he had lost. He could feel this new magic boil in the very pit of his soul and run out like poison through his veins. It scorched his fingers, burned his skin, but he did not release it until he was sure that he had nothing left to give. When the spell was done, Jake looked down into his hand and gloried in the darkness.

Even the most evil of the creatures in the crowd gasped at sight of the flame. It burned with such ferocious power that the flaming sun on the horizon seemed to dim in awe of it.

All the swagger drained from Tobias Quilp. He staggered away from Jake, tripped and fell to the ground. His own dark magic spluttered in his hand.

'Mr Quilp,' Jake shook his head, 'what's wrong with you? Scared of a little dark magic? Tell you what, I'll give you a sporting chance and let you go first.'

Quilp took Jake at his word. Whispering a few incantations, he released three feeble bolts which Jake swatted away with ease.

''S that all you've got?' Jake squatted down to Quilp's level, the dark red flame spinning in his hand. 'I'm not going to kill you, Tobias. Not just yet anyway. Let's have some fun first, shall we? I'll give you twenty seconds.'

'W-what?'

'Tick-tock, tick-tock. That's four seconds gone already.'

Quilp wiped a shaking hand across his mouth.

'I don't . . . Please, I don't understand.'

'Ten seconds gone. You're wasting valuable time, Tobias.'

'But, I—'

Jake thrust his face forward. 'Run.'

Quilp didn't need telling twice. He scrabbled to his feet and set off across the square. Howls of derision followed the fleeing witch while the crowd roared its approval for Jake. He found that he liked the adulation. Turning on the spot, he held up the crackling, spitting orb. Faces spread into wicked grins and clawed fists punched the air.

'Thataboy, Jake! Play with the witch! Make him suffer!'

'Strike him down, Jake! Do it now!'

'Slaughter him!'

'Finish him!'

'Kill him!'

'KILL! KILL! KILL!'

Jake called over his shoulder to Quilp—

'Run!'

Of course, he had no intention of letting the murderer escape.

'*Run!*'

He was just giving him the illusion of freedom. An illusion he would snatch away . . .

'RUUUUN!'

Now.

A final charge of dark thoughts and the flame billowed higher than ever.

Quilp was on the far side of the square, making for one of the teardrop doorways.

Jake licked his lips.

Targeted his victim.

Threw back his hand.

And . . .

'Jake!'

Her voice.

Jake glanced over his shoulder and there she was, running to meet him. Her skin shone and her yellow hair dazzled in the sunset. She was here. She was real. Her words reverberated in his heart—

You must never let the darkness win or I will truly have lost you.

Eleanor's hand slipped into his. In Jake's other hand, the magic immediately transformed. The red light vanished and a pure, blue flame rose up in its place.

'Thank you,' he whispered.

Reaching back, Jake hurled the Oldcraft magic across the square.

'I'm not going to hurt him,' he said, 'but he can't escape with the witch ball.'

The magic hurtled past Quilp and into the teardrop doorway. From beyond came a thunderous crack and the rumble of falling stone. The way had been blocked. Quilp panicked and tried to head for one of the other portals but the dark creatures clubbed together and would not let him pass. With no choice left, the witch ducked into the doorway he had originally chosen.

One of the larger forest trolls that had gathered around the door called out to Jake.

'Don't worry, Mr Harker, we'll keep an eye on him, make sure he doesn't find a way out. You just catch your breath. Great show, by the way!'

A ripple of applause greeted this remark. Clearly some of the dark creatures had wanted Jake to finish the witch, but few could deny that they had witnessed a real spectacle.

Jake turned to the girl beside him.

Yellow hair. Sea-green eyes. Not Eleanor of the May, but Rachel Saxby.

'Jake,' Rachel smiled through her tears. 'You look disappointed to see me.'

Jake wrapped his arms around her.

'Disappointed?' he laughed. 'Are you kidding? I never thought I'd see you again! Rachel, I'm so sorry about everything. I shouldn't have run away like that. I just—'

A boy with a crooked lip tapped Rachel on the shoulder.

'Sorry, Rach, but Jake and I need a word.'

Jake stepped back and held out his hand to Simon.

'Friends?'

'No.'

'Simon,' Rachel protested.

'Friends don't shake hands,' Simon grinned, and threw his arms around Jake. After five solid minutes of hugging he held Jake at arm's length and scowled. 'But don't you ever do that to us again, understand? Now, I think we better go and sort out that witch.'

It was cold beyond the teardrop doorway. Dust from the explosion billowed all around, but high above, where the vine-tentacles creaked, it was beginning to clear. A delighted Mr Murdles (*A triumph, Jacob! A masterpiece of magical theatre! Enough money in the pot for at least three hundred ecto-suits!*) had provided Jake and his friends with powerful electric torches which they now swept around the ceiling. Dislodged by Jake's spell, ancient chunks of stone had fallen and blocked the tunnel path that led back to Yaga Passage and London. Jake wondered whether Quilp had instinctively chosen this portal over the others. The doorway that led back to the old headquarters of the Crowden Coven.

The witch called out from the mist.

'My pet? Are you there?'

The sound of claws dragging across the ground. A pair of yellow eyes glowed dully in the dust. Rachel swept the bow from her back and notched an arrow, Simon brandished the short, heavy club that he had borrowed from Razor.

'No,' Jake held out his hand. 'Let him pass.'

Mr Pinch hobbled between the friends, eyes downcast. Every movement caused him to whimper through the ragged, wet hole that served as his nose. Not a single tooth had survived Frija Crowden's attack, and without them the gummy creature looked old and somehow pathetic. Injuries that would have killed any mortal were nevertheless taking their toll on the demon. Swollen to twice its normal size, Pinch's shattered skull swayed left and right on the spindle of his broken neck.

'You're sure it's a good idea?' Rachel asked. 'Letting him go to the witch?'

'Quilp's power is fading,' Jake whispered, 'I can feel it.'

'But why?'

'Because he no longer believes in his magic or in himself.'

The friends stayed where they were and let the dust settle.

Ghostly in the dimness, Quilp's face emerged from the mist. He seemed to be standing on higher ground. The dust fell another three metres and Jake saw that the witch was in fact perched on the low brick wall that surrounded the Oracle's pit. Mr Pinch reached out to his master, like a toddler begging to be picked up. Quilp lifted the demon and laid him gently on the wall. Then he turned to his enemy.

'Bravo, Jacob, bravo.' He clapped his thin hands. 'You have beaten me.'

The cultured voice had lost its sneer and there was nothing mocking in Quilp's applause.

'In all my years of study and practice, I have never seen such dark magic as you conjured today.'

'That wasn't me,' Jake said.

'Is that so?' Quilp tapped a long finger against his chin. 'I wonder. What is the source of that righteous anger, Jacob? That merciless rage? Perhaps one day you will find out.'

'We're not here to discuss me, Tobias,' Jake said. 'We need to decide what's going to happen to you. My dad will know what to do, but first you have to agree to come with us, quietly and peacefully.'

'You don't want to kill me any more?'

'Part of me does,' Jake admitted. 'The worst part.'

He glanced down at the hand that had conjured the darkness. *Such power . . .*

'But I can't let you go. You're too dangerous.'

Jake stepped forward. As he did so, Quilp mirrored him, taking a step back towards the precipice.

'Do you honestly think that I will let you take me alive?' The witch managed one of his old bitter laughs. 'I am Tobias Quilp, Second in Command of the Crowden Coven.'

'There is no Crowden Coven.' Jake reached out, as if to bridge the distance between them and pull Quilp back from the edge. 'Please, if you let me I can help you.'

'Help *me*?'

'It's possible,' Jake nodded. 'My dad worked with Sidney Tinsmouth. He helped Sidney reclaim his soul.'

'And you would help me do this? The man who butchered your mother?'

Jake closed his eyes and saw her. She came to him, not as the headless horror Quilp had made her, but whole and vibrant and alive. Claire Harker, his mother.

'Yes, I'll help you,' Jake breathed. 'Gladly.'

Silence in the portal. Silence in the square beyond, where the dark creatures strained to hear every word. Even the tentacles overhead had ceased their creaking.

Quilp, lost and frightened, looked back at Jake.

'Who are you?' His voice shivered. 'What manner of

mortal could stretch out his hand to so bitter a foe? You should not be. You are *monstrous*.'

Jake took another small step forward.

Quilp backed up until only the tips of his shoes clung to the wall. Below, in the unlit depths of the pit, the guardians of the Oracle waited. Jake imagined their thick white bodies uncoiling, their heads reaching up and their poisonous mouths gaping wide. The witch quaked on the precipice. He pulled back his coat and reached inside.

'I cannot destroy you, Jacob Harker, but it is still within my power to cause you pain.'

Quilp snapped the string from his neck and withdrew the witch ball.

At the sight of the dull green orb, Jake felt something stir within. It was a similar sensation to that which he had experienced in the village of Starfall. The power of Preacher Hobarron's hidden object had been identical to the surge of energy now pulsing from the witch ball. They were twins, Jake realized. Brothers.

Signums.

Jake thrust out his hand and the ball sparked into life. Brilliant green, its light flared across the cavern walls. At the sight of it, Quilp almost toppled back but managed to regain his balance.

'It answers you. How . . . ?' The witch shook his head. The time for questions had passed. 'The power contained within this talisman can send the Demon Father hurtling back into his own dimension. It can destroy any Door to the demon world. But more than that, it can restore your father to health. No sorcery wielded by man could bring him back to you now, Jacob, but with this he can be plucked from the jaws of death.'

Quilp held out the witch ball.

'My last act in this world,' he smiled. 'To strike at the very heart of you.'

He threw the witch ball to Mr Pinch, stretched out his arms, and fell back into the pit.

Jake darted forward.

'Don't!'

As Jake reached the wall, Mr Pinch staggered around to the far side, the witch ball clutched in his talons. Despite the pain of his injuries, the demon managed a low, rasping snicker. Jake shone his torch over the edge of the pit. The blue flame of Oldcraft was in his hand but it was already too late. He saw Tobias Quilp plummet the last few metres and hit the ground.

One of the Oracle's largest pets, a fork-tongued monstrosity with a scar running across its nose, bit down into Quilp's right leg. The witch screamed. Another giant serpent fastened its fangs into his left arm. The snakes lifted Quilp into the air, wrestling his broken body between them in a hideous game of tug-of-war. The once powerful sorcerer did not even try to summon his magic. He looked up and with his free hand pointed at Jake.

'Curse you!' he shrieked. 'Curse you and your fath—'

The scarred snake cut Quilp short. With a final, bone-breaking, skin-splitting tug it ripped the dark witch in two. Quilp's guts dropped out of him like the contents of

The witch Ball

a shopping bag turned upside down. The large snake then slithered into a corner, opened its great mouth and slowly began to swallow the still-writhing top half of Tobias Quilp.

Mr Pinch echoed his master's final scream. Flames erupted around his body as he was dragged back to his own infernal dimension. Jake saw the danger and ran. Simon joined him, pelting around the side of the pit. Rachel loosed an arrow in an attempt to dislodge the witch ball from the creature's grasp. They were all too late. With a final victorious shriek, Mr Pinch disappeared into the demon world, taking the Signum with him.

Ash spiralled through the air.

It was all that remained of the monster.

Jake fell to his knees. He heard Simon's roar of '*No!*' and Rachel's frustrated cry. For his part, Jake could not think, could not speak, could not feel. He just sat there, listening to the sound of the snakes feasting in the pit. It took several minutes for his senses to return.

'Jake, can you hear me?'

The gentle tones of Pandora. She was standing in front of him. Such sadness in her eyes Jake thought his heart would break.

'It's your father . . . '

Chapter 33
Twilight

The news passed around the square like an ill omen. Many dark creatures in the crowd owed Adam Harker their lives, and so they bowed their heads in mute respect when Jake passed. A few even wept at the sight of the boy: a silent, dignified presence that reminded them forcibly of his father.

Razor and Simon walked on ahead, barking people out of the way. Flanking Jake, Pandora and Rachel held his hands. He wanted to run, but thought that his heavy heart would not stand it. He might trip, fall, and never be able to drag himself from the ground again. And so he strode across the square, the last of the sunlight in his eyes.

It was in passing that he noticed the nightmare box had disappeared. Had it returned to the Demon Father? He found that he did not care.

At the door of the Grimoire Club he was met by a long-faced Mr Murdles.

'I'm so sorry, Jake. If there's anything—'

'Nothing. Thank you.' His voice faltering, empty.

He was led to the red leather door of Murdles's private apartment. Razor stayed in the corridor to make sure no one disturbed them.

'Brave heart, boy,' the Cynocephalus grunted, and turned his face away.

His friends accompanied Jake to the bedroom door and hugged him, each in turn. They spoke his name in broken voices and he felt their hot tears against his skin. Jake could not cry. Tears seemed so silly to him. So small.

'Adam regained consciousness just before sunset. When I left he was still breathing, but he may already have . . . ' Pandora gasped. 'He hung on for you, Jake. Just to see you one last time.'

Strong, proud, fearless Pandora broke down.

'He loved you too, Pandora,' Jake said.

Then he turned away from his friends and opened the door.

The dark blues and bruised purples of the desert sky shone through the big, wide window. Twilight shades, they softened the haggard face of the man in the bed. His eyes were closed, his breathing shallow. Jake knelt beside him and lifted the open book from his father's chest. Before setting the heavy tome on the floor he caught a glimpse of the title—*The Codex Tempus.*

He took his father's hand.

'I knew you'd come back to me, Jake. I read it. I was with you, you see, every step of the way.'

Adam's eyes remained closed. He drew Jake's hand to his lips and kissed it.

'I'm very proud of you.'

Jake's tears came at last. Tears that could drown the world.

'I failed you, Dad.'

'How have you failed?' Adam chuckled weakly.

'I couldn't save you. I tried so hard, but in the end I couldn't.'

Jake rested his head beside his father and felt those comforting hands stroke his hair. They were always so strong in his memories: the hands of a giant picking him from the ground and holding him as if he were the most precious thing in the world.

'You fought against evil, Jake,' his father sighed. 'Evil without, evil within, and you triumphed against it, as you always do. As you always *will*. And now, at the end of your long journey, you must face the hardest truth of this world— that there comes a time when the fighting *must* end. When twilight draws in and you must lay down your arms. That's not failure, Jake, it's wisdom.'

'I don't want to be wise,' Jake said quietly. 'I just want you to be here, with me.'

'I'll always be with you, Jake. In the light and in the darkness.'

A rattle of sand against the window. The insistence of heartless time passing by. Inside the room, a silence so deep that the little sounds could make themselves heard.

Breathing and the thud of hearts—one young and strong, the other approaching its final beat.

'Son?'

'Yes, Dad?'

'Stay with me, won't you?'

'Of course I will.'

'I feel the dark drawing in. The twilight's fading. It'll be night soon, Jacob. My son. My Finder . . . '

Chapter 34
Hellbound Hopes

Rachel poked her head around the study door. Her gaze ran over the dozens of books that Jake had pulled from the shelves.

'Are you OK?'

Jake glanced up from a huge, leather-bound volume.

'Just trying to keep busy.'

'Jake, you haven't taken a break since your dad . . . Well, it's been hours. You need to eat, rest.'

'I know,' Jake muttered. 'But I have to do this first. It's important.'

'OK, but there are some things we need to talk about. Things that have happened since you've been away. Impossible things.'

Jake straightened up in his chair. 'Give me an hour?'

'All right.'

Rachel closed the door behind her and Jake returned to his reading.

The need to find out what had happened to those he had left behind consumed him. Piece by piece, he had put together their lives from the dusty books that lined the shelves.

History showed that Preacher John Hobarron had served the village of Starfall until his death in December 1645, only a few months after Jake's departure. No cause of death was given. Mrs Hobarron had been allowed to stay at the rectory, but she had not been the only occupant of the house. A Miss Frija Crowden had been her companion.

Next, Jake turned his attention to Leonard Lanyon. The only mention of the vicar appeared in a slim book called *Great Witch Trials of England*:

Lanyon, Leonard. Involved in the famous trial of sorcerer Josiah Hobarron, who came to the town of Cravenmouth wreathed in a ball of blue fire, and who later escaped execution by mysterious means. After fleeing the town, Lanyon was tracked down by the untiring Witchfinder General, Matthew Hopkins. He had been hiding for many months in the county of Kent under the alias of Master Jacob Harker. Although tortured, Lanyon would not confess to witchcraft. Hopkins, however, had gathered sufficient evidence to convince a jury of the man's guilt, and the vicar was duly hanged on 17th March 1646.

Jake closed the book with a heavy heart and turned to Hopkins himself. The history books confirmed his vague memory of the Witchfinder's fate. Only two years after his persecution of Jake in Cravenmouth, Hopkins had died, probably of tuberculosis. Jake remembered that dry little cough and the blood on Hopkins's lips; the monster's death, although unpleasant, hardly compared to the torment he had inflicted on others.

In all of these histories Jake was unable to trace the one person he longed to find. Where was his Eleanor of the May? He guessed that she must have returned to Starfall with Frija, but there was no mention of her in the parish records. Despite this, he knew that she had lived on and that she had given birth to her child, Katherine. If she had not, then Rachel would have been wiped from the pages of history. Jake guessed that, when he had met Eleanor, she *had* in fact been pregnant with Josiah's child, but had not been aware of it. It was the only solution that fitted the facts.

He scanned all the books on the shelves. Somewhere in that long stretch of time, Eleanor was hiding.

They were waiting for him in the lounge—Pandora pacing up and down, Rachel sitting on the corner of the sofa biting her fingernails, Simon flicking through the hundreds of channels on Murdles's huge flatscreen TV.

'They've taken your father down to the cellars,' said a red-eyed Pandora. 'Razor will stand guard over him. Adam didn't leave any instructions, but I thought . . . ' She shook her head. 'It's not my decision, of course.'

'Go on, Pandora,' Jake said.

'A pyre in the square. It's the funeral rite for so many dark creatures and Adam, well, saving dark creatures was his life. And if we do it here many of those he saved will be able to attend.' Her smile was as weak as water. 'It will be a *big* funeral.'

.At that moment, the apartment door burst open and Brag Badderson came lumbering into the room. At the sight of Jake, the troll dropped his club and scooped the boy up into his arms.

'I just heard,' the troll sobbed.

After several bone-crushing squeezes, he set Jake back down.

'Thanks, Brag,' Jake panted.

Pandora snapped out of her grief for a moment and became her old, cool-headed self.

'Brag's been keeping in touch with my contacts while I was nursing your father,' she explained.

'I've just come back from Yaga Passage,' Brag grunted. 'Had to smash my way through a bloody landslide. Half the portal roof's caved in. I told Murdles that the London road needed a bit of repair, not that that old skinflint would spend a penny on it.'

'Brag,' Pandora barked.

'Oh, yeah, sorry. Well, I spoke to Drake Polidori—'

'A vampire,' Pandora cut in. 'Lives in one of the houses in Yaga. A thousand years old, so he tells anyone who'll listen.'

'Drake says that *she's* finally sent out the DREAM agents.' Brag shivered. 'They're scouring the country, bringing in anyone who fits the bill. And that's not all: they've set up a camp on the south coast. Anyone taken in by DREAM will be sent to the camp for "processing".'

'My father?' Rachel asked.

Brag shrugged. 'Sorry, I don't know. But if I had to bet the family gold on it, I'd say he's there. Dr Holmwood, too.'

Jake held up his hand. 'Whoa. Camps? Agents? Dream?'

'More like a nightmare,' Pandora said. 'A lot's happened since you've been away, Jake. Not here. Not in the borderlands, but out there, in the human world. I'm not sure how much time has passed for you, but here it's been two months since you left on the Scarab Path. Two months and everything's changed. Simon?'

Simon took up the tale.

'In a way, it started when I went looking for answers. About myself and about my mother . . . '

He told the story of how he had left the Grimoire after his dark self had betrayed Jake's whereabouts to the Demon Father. Determined to find answers, he had returned to the cottage where he had grown up. After defeating a mob of vampires sent by the Demon Father to reclaim him, Simon and the others had forced the group's leader, a creature known as the Claviger, to tell them what she knew of Simon's history. Her story had shocked everyone to the core.

First it was revealed that Simon was *not* the son of the Demon Father. His mother, who he had always thought of as an innocent, had in fact been a powerful dark witch, and the Demon Father himself had been her familiar. Together they had plotted schemes for what would happen after the Demontide. In that time of upheaval, the demons would need a slave race to help them build their new world. And so

Simon's mother had experimented on her own son, trying to produce a stronger, better human. It took several years, but eventually she succeeded in regressing Simon back to a stage in human evolution when mortal men had shared common traits with their cousins, the Cynocephali. Traits like incredible strength.

Jake stared at Simon. 'But I don't get it. Razor's one of the Cynocephali. And sure, he's a bit aggressive, but nowhere near as brutal as you were when you changed.'

'Razor is an *evolved* Cynocephalus,' Pandora said. 'His kind has had millions of years to become more civilized. What Simon's mother did was tap into the unevolved genes that humans still carry from their Cynocephali ancestors. The result was a more basic, primal creature.'

'As soon as we found out what I really was, your father started work,' Simon said. 'With this new information he could target my "inner beast" more effectively.'

He reached under his shirt and withdrew a necklace with a triangular piece of amber for the pendant. Sealed inside the amber was a purple-hooded flower.

'Aconite,' Pandora said. 'Also known as monkshood, leopard's bane, and wolfsbane. Poisonous to the Cynocephali, but trapped within the amber resin it gives off just enough noxious vibes to keep Simon's dark side at bay.'

'It was the only reason I came back.' Simon reached for Rachel. 'I wouldn't risk it unless your dad was sure that the wolfsbane would work.'

'And did it?'

'No unsightly hairiness in over two months,' Rachel grinned.

'Your dad was a genius, Jake,' Simon said. 'More than that, he was a good man.'

The sincerity in Simon's voice brought fresh tears to Jake's eyes.

'Only problem is, Razor keeps getting rashes whenever he comes near Simon,' Rachel laughed. 'But he sees it as a challenge to his machismo so he hangs around with us more than ever!'

Simon slapped his forehead.

'One more story about my "glorious Cynocephalus heritage", and I swear!'

Despite all the horrors and grief, Jake couldn't help laughing along with Rachel.

'OK, guys, let's get back on track,' Pandora scolded. 'There's something else Simon needs to tell you.'

Simon's crooked smile dropped. He switched the TV to the video channel and slipped a DVD into the player. As soon as the clip started, Simon hit the pause button. The image of a woman, dazzled by flash bulbs and standing outside a familiar front door, appeared on screen.

Jake's brow creased. 'I don't get it. What's this got to do with—?'

Simon tapped a trembling finger against the screen.

'That woman.' He swallowed hard. 'She's my mother.'

Jake's mouth fell open.

'But . . . but that's the *Prime Minister*!'

Rachel led Simon back to the sofa. Although he'd had time to process the news, the boy was obviously still coming to terms with the enormity of it.

'In his way, Simon was trying to tell us all along,' Rachel said.
'What?'

'Don't you remember after we brought him back from
Havlock Grange? He kept saying he was hearing his mother's voice. We just thought he was dreaming about her, but
actually he *was* hearing her. On the TV, on the radio. In his
confused state, Simon couldn't tell if the voices were real
or imagined. What he heard was Cynthia Croft, Prime
Minister of Great Britain, making her speeches and giving
interviews.'

'But, Simon, surely you'd seen Cynthia Croft before. Why
didn't you recognize her?'

'Think about it, Jake,' Pandora said. 'When would Simon
have had the opportunity to see her? We all know the
Cynthia Croft story. She was only elected to Parliament last
year in a by-election. Before that, no one had ever heard of
her. That's what's made her meteoric rise to Prime Minister
so amazing—in only a few months she has become one of
the most powerful people in the world. And during most of
that time Simon was a prisoner, either of Marcus Crowden
or the Demon Father.'

Rachel squeezed Simon's hand.

'So what happened to Cynthia Croft, or Cynthia Lydgate,
after she'd successfully transformed Simon?' Jake asked.

'She moved on,' Simon said. 'She'd achieved her purpose.
She knew that she could create a human-Cynocephalus slave
race, and so she had no more use for me. As a final act of
cruelty she implanted a false memory in my mind and then
vanished into the magical underworld.'

'She made you believe you'd killed her,' Jake said in disgust.

'We have no trace of her until she turned up in the town of Saltsby-on-the-Marsh a year ago,' Pandora said. 'Within a few months she'd been selected as Saltsby's Member of Parliament.'

'And around the same time that the Demon Father breaks through into this world, the old Prime Minister dies and Miss Croft replaces him.' Jake snapped his fingers. 'Of course! Dr Holmwood said that, ever since she was elected, she'd been undermining the work of the Hobarron Institute. She was working *with the Demon Father all along.*'

'And probably using magic to cement her position in the government.'

'How?'

'A hundred ways,' Pandora said. 'Charm spells, hexes, voodoo enchantments.'

'But why would the Demon Father need her to be Prime Minister?'

'Always helpful to have that kind of organizational power on your side. And now we know about her experiments on Simon the reason is surely obvious.'

Jake's face went pale. He started to connect Cynthia Croft's past with Brag's muddled talk about a camp on the south coast of England. The way was being prepared . . .

'The slave race,' Jake said slowly. 'It's starting . . . '

Simon flipped the remote control in his hand.

'You need to see this: last month's Downing Street press conference. It took the world by storm.'

Simon clicked 'play'.

Miss Cynthia Croft, her expression deadly serious, came to the podium.

'People of Britain, I come to you today with momentous news. But first I must apologize for having unwittingly misled this great nation . . . '

A stir in the press pack. The camera zoomed in on the Prime Minister.

'After the attack on the Hobarron Institute, I told you that monsters need not concern us. I was wrong. Monsters *should* concern us, for they are very real.'

The laughter that greeted this remark was soon mopped up by the Prime Minister's glare.

'I am aware that such things seem outrageous, impossible, ludicrous even, but I have been convinced of their existence. In the next hour, you will hear from the leaders of Russia, France, Germany, Japan, China, Israel, and America. They have all seen the evidence and they will all attest to the reality of this hidden world.'

No laughter now, just a confused twitter of voices. A journalist called out—

'What evidence, Miss Croft?'

'For one, the security tapes from the Hobarron Institute. The footage is now being transferred to your news rooms.'

The image flickered for a moment and then switched to various shots of the assault on the Institute. Dozens of witches plummeted from the sky, their hands filled with dark red flames. Even more striking were the creatures riding behind them: hideous, mutated demons screaming and shrieking with glee. After several minutes of destruction and slaughter, the screen blipped back to the Prime Minister.

'We've had the best audio and visual analysts examine the tape,' she said. 'Those *things* were not special effects. They were *real*.'

Another astonished voice from behind the camera—

'But . . . but they looked like—'

'Demons,' Miss Croft nodded. 'Demons and witches. After this footage was sent to us by an anonymous source, the government decided to investigate the work of the Hobarron Institute. We have found irrefutable evidence that the family of Institute leader, Dr Gordon Holmwood, has been plotting with demons and dark witches for centuries.'

'Plotting what?' another journalist called.

'The total annihilation of mankind. An event known as the Demontide.'

Jake gasped and looked back at his friends. Pandora shook her head.

'It gets better.'

The Prime Minister stared directly into the camera.

'I realize that even now some of you will not believe me. You will think I have lost my mind. Well, tomorrow you will read in your newspapers all the evidence we have gathered from our raid on the Institute.'

'What about Dr Holmwood? Where is he?'

'The good doctor and his colleague, Malcolm Saxby, were arrested this morning.' Miss Croft allowed herself the briefest smile. 'They are still being questioned.'

'Miss Croft? If all this is true, what do you plan to do about it?'

'Let me make this absolutely clear: forget terrorism, forget climate change, forget wars, pestilence, and famine—the threat of magic and demons is the most serious this planet has ever seen. These people, these *creatures*, possess incredible powers, and they have only one objective—the overthrow of humankind. Now, we have already set up a powerful new government body, answerable only to me. The Department for the Regulation, Examination, and Authorization of Magic. DREAM. But I need to stress—We. Cannot. Do. This. Alone. The British people must aid us in our fight for survival.'

'But what can they do?'

'They must keep their ears and eyes open. If they see anyone whose appearance is a little unusual or who is behaving strangely—a colleague, a friend, a brother, a sister, a mother, a father, wife, husband, even a child—they must do their duty and report them to the authorities.'

'What authorities?'

'The DREAM agents. These men and women will soon be on every street, asking questions. Please aid them in any way you can.'

Jake felt a familiar dread.

'It's a witch hunt,' he said.

'On the strength of the evidence and the threat posed, foreign governments will have their own agents in place within the week. Anyone suspected of having dark powers will be taken to internment camps and—'

'But this is madness!' a voice shouted. 'It goes against international law!'

Miss Croft gave the unseen speaker an icy stare.

'What good will your laws be when this world is over-run with demons? When your children are slaughtered in the streets by dark witches?' Miss Croft's eyes blazed. 'I give this warning to all who would stand against us—you will fall upon the flaming sword of humanity's vengeance. And to wield that sword I have appointed an expert in the wiles of demonkind. May I introduce the leader of the DREAM agents, Mr Marcus Crowden.'

The door of 10 Downing Street swung open.

Into the flood and flicker of light walked a man with the face of an angel.

His dark glasses flashed as he took Miss Croft's hand.

'Good evening, people of the world,' the Demon Father said, his voice soft and musical. 'Despite all that you have just heard, I am here to tell you not to be afraid. For *I* am with you . . .'

Clouds rolled in and masked the light of the borderlands' twin moons. The desert had vanished in the darkness, and it was only by the occasional crackle of sand against his face that Jake knew it was there at all. The friends stood on the apartment balcony, each thinking about the new world that had dawned so suddenly around them.

'The camps,' Jake said, 'that's where Cynthia Croft and the Demon Father will create their slave race. They'll experiment on the people sent there.'

'There are thousands of DREAM agents on the streets,' Brag grunted.

' "*Watch for Witches*". That's the slogan on all the posters,' Rachel said. 'Everyone wants to do their bit to help the war effort.'

'They're calling it a war?'

'A War on Witchcraft. If only they knew that a dark witch and the father of demons were their leaders!'

'There's something I don't understand,' Jake said. 'All this effort, all this risk, but for what? Let's say they create their slave race, there's still no way they can bring about the Demontide. The portal at Crowden's Sorrow is gone and the witch ball is *in* the demon dimension.'

'Maybe he plans to create another universal coven,' Simon suggested.

Jake frowned. 'Another one?'

Pandora explained how the Demon Father had used the magic of the collective covens to send Quilp back in time—a spell that had resulted in the death of everyone present.

'But the creation of a second universal coven would be impossible,' she continued. 'Sure, there are plenty more covens around the world, but the DF cherry-picked the most powerful ones last time. Anyway, the others will have heard what happened to their predecessors. These witches may want the Demontide to break but they're not going to risk their own necks for it.'

'What if a demon on the other side used the witch ball to

open a Door into the *human* world?' Brag asked.

Pandora stared at the troll. 'You know something, Brag? That's a fairly intelligent point!'

Brag beamed.

'But the Demontide doesn't work like that,' Pandora continued. 'A Door can only be opened on this side.'

'Then how——?'

'Hello? Anyone up there?'

Murdles's head poked through the hatch that led up to the balcony. He spied Jake and floated through the roof.

'Ah, Jacob, excellent. I just wanted to thank you again for your sterling efforts today. I—ah—' The manager tugged at the lapels of a brand new ecto-suit. 'I owe you my life.'

'Don't you mean your "death",' Simon corrected.

'Very witty, Mr Lydgate. Anyway, I thought you would like to know that everything has been arranged for tomorrow. We will give your father a fine send off.'

'Tomorrow?' Jake sighed. 'So soon.'

His friends gathered around him.

'All right, Murdles,' Simon grunted, 'off you pop.'

The manager bowed and was almost at the hatchway when he turned back.

'I knew something else had brought me up here. I'd forget my head if it wasn't glued ectoplasmically into place! This came for you by the last phantom coach.'

Murdles took a scarlet envelope from his pocket, bowed again, and disappeared down the hatch. The thick, expensive paper burned Jake's fingers as he tore it open.

Hellbound Hopes

Dear Jacob,

My spies on the borderlands have already informed me of your great battle against my former favourite, Tobias Quilp. Many congratulations, dear child, on a notable victory.

Please also accept my most sincere condolences on the passing of your dear father: Dr Harker was a wise, brave man, if a little sentimental.

It may be of some comfort to you to know that, although you have lost your father, I also lost something precious today. The witch ball. My spies tell me that Mr Pinch has returned home with the orb. The only difference between us, Jacob Harker, is that I will soon retrieve my prize. I will find the one among millions with the power to pluck it from my old realm and return it to me. But your father? I'm afraid that there is no bringing him back.

But to more serious matters. You must now be aware that I am in control of your government, and that all hope you had of interfering in my plans is lost. Take my advice, boy conjuror, and disappear. If you do not give me cause, I will not pursue you.

With fond regards
DF

Jake handed the letter to Pandora.

'This is not good,' she murmured, passing it to Rachel.

'No,' Jake agreed. 'It's brilliant!'

He burst out laughing and a rich blue flame erupted in his hand.

'He's lost it,' Brag shrugged. 'Can't blame him, I suppose.'

'But don't you see what he's done?' Jake shouted happily.

'He's gloating,' Rachel said.

'Exactly!'

'He's taking the p—' Simon grunted.

'Precisely! And he's told us everything we need to know,' Jake laughed. 'Everything we need to stop him. Those camps, they're not just for the slave race experiments, they're to find someone. Someone very special.'

'Who?' Pandora frowned, turning the letter over, as if searching for a clue she had missed.

'A witch.'

'What?'

'The Demon Father's looking for a witch.'

'But he knows dozens of witches,' Simon protested. 'My mum, for one.'

'Ah, but those witches *already* have their demons. Pandora, correct me if I'm wrong, but when a witch summons a demon, that's it. No exchanges or refunds, that's their demon for life.'

'That's right.'

'And once summoned, demons can't travel back and forth between the human and demon world. They're stuck here until their witch dies.'

'Right again. Not that they'd want to go to and fro— escaping the demon dimension is half the reason why they agree to serve as familiars.'

'But where does that get us?' Rachel asked.

Jake grinned, barely able to contain his excitement. 'Read the letter again. The Demon Father is using the DREAM agents, not only to get experiment subjects, but to find *one among the millions*. Translation: a *potential* witch. One who's not yet summoned a demon.'

'And?'

'I think that, when he finds that "one in a million", the Demon Father will force the witch to summon one demon in particular. One of the most evil, vicious, depraved demons that ever existed.'

Rachel's eyes widened. 'You mean . . . Mr Pinch!'

'That's the boy!' Jake shouted. 'And Pinch won't be coming alone. He'll bring the witch ball back with him.'

'Great,' Simon shrugged. 'So what are we gonna do about it?'

Jake gave his broadest grin yet and juggled the magic in his hands.

'We're going to fight. We're going to play the Demon Father at his own game and we're going to win.'

'I don't want to sound pessimistic,' Rachel said, 'but how on Earth are we going to do that?'

'We're going to the demon world,' Jake shrugged.

'WHAT?' cried Brag, Pandora, Rachel, and Simon in unison.

'We're going to smash our way into the demon dimension.'

Jake concentrated his magic into two sizzling blue streams.

'We're going to hunt down Mr Pinch and take back the witch ball.'

The streams became columns in Jake's hands.

Magic powered by love and hope. Love for his friends and his father.

Love for Eleanor.

The hope that he would see her again.

Magic roared into the sky, split the ominous clouds and allowed the moonlight to shine through.

'Buckle up, boys and girls!' Jake cried. 'Next stop, the demon world!'

Then: 1645
The Home of Demons

'My dear, I have made a terrible, terrible mistake. My visions were not clear at the time and . . . well, our guest has shown me the error of my imperfect sight.'

Preacher Hobarron nodded at the lady sitting opposite him.

'The fault was not yours, sir,' Frija Crowden said. 'The future is always hazy, and *his* future more than most. But now we must set things right. For the boy and his friends, the cataclysm is fast approaching.'

Eleanor looked from the blind preacher to the veiled lady.

'I don't understand.'

The three of them were sitting in the cosy parlour of the Starfall rectory. Outside, a bitter December wind howled around the house and shook the windows. Spots of snow drifted down the chimney and made the fire sizzle. Before she had been called to the parlour, Eleanor had been with

Pepper in the stables. Since returning to Starfall, she had spent much of her time with the horse, brushing her down, taking her out for long rides across the meadows. Being close to Pepper reminded her of Jake. The memory of him sitting awkwardly in the saddle was the only thing that made her smile. It had been nearly four months since she had lost him.

She caught her reflection in the dark pane of the window. A scarred face full of sorrow.

Preacher Hobarron went to the large travelling trunk kept at the back of the room. He turned the key in the lock and brought out a grey cloak covered with morsels of earth. Eleanor recognized it at once. It was the cloak she had buried beneath the altar of the church. The preacher hobbled over to Eleanor and laid the hidden treasure in her lap.

'You must take it to him, my dear.'

Eleanor stared at the old man.

'To Jake? But how?'

'We will see to that,' Frija said softly, 'but do you agree?'

'Yes,' the word leapt from her lips.

'There may be danger,' Preacher Hobarron advised. 'Your life will be at risk.'

'I don't care. When can I leave?'

Hobarron gave a weary smile and Frija bowed her head. 'Now.'

Eleanor grasped the bundle and shot out of the chair. Her face flushed with excitement. She was going to see him again. Her Josiah . . . Her Jacob . . .

'Wife? Are you there?' the Preacher called.

The parlour door opened and Mrs Hobarron bustled into

the room. She managed a curt nod at Frija but did not look once at her husband. She had a leather saddlebag in her hands which she draped over Eleanor's shoulder.

'Provisions for your journey. Some food and clothing, nothing much.'

Eleanor knew that Mrs Hobarron's 'nothing much' would probably amount to a feast and, in all likelihood, an entire wardrobe of clothes. The old woman bent Eleanor's head and kissed her gently.

'Always been like a daughter to me, you have.' She looked over her shoulder and cast her husband an evil stare. 'A good, gentle girl, who deserves better than to be the object of clever plots.'

'But I want to go,' Eleanor said, 'I need to.'

'Then more fool you!' Mrs Hobarron burst out crying and fled from the room.

'Put the object inside the saddlebag, Eleanor,' the Preacher instructed. 'Miss Crowden has cast a masking spell that will keep it concealed from Jacob until the time is right.'

'What do you mean?'

'There is much I have not told you,' the Preacher sighed. 'About Jacob and about Josiah. On the night Josiah came to Starfall, the one that brought him swore me to secrecy . . . '

'Brought him?' Eleanor gasped.

'Josiah was *not* our child.'

'Then whose was he?'

'That I cannot say. I gave my word that his identity would remain a secret.'

'Did Josiah know you weren't his father?'

'No. Had I known his true mission in that cavern, I would have told him. Alas, my visions were at fault.' If the Preacher could have cried then this was the moment for his tears. 'Jacob is Josiah reborn,' he continued, voice gruff with emotion, 'though he was conjured from the dust of Josiah, his core identity is the same. But like Josiah, he *cannot* know who he is until all hope is lost. To know beforehand would ruin everything. The witch ball and what you hold in that bag is the key to his identity and to the destruction of demonkind. He will need both Signums, but only when the time is right.'

'But how will *I* know when the time is right?'

The Preacher's face turned as hard as stone. 'Oh, my dear, you will know.'

Frija Crowden rose from her chair. She took a little leather pouch from her pocket and gave it to Eleanor.

'A charm to keep you safe, my dear. A thank you for helping me find a new home.' She kissed Eleanor through her veil. 'Farewell.'

Eleanor tucked the pouch into the saddlebag and turned to the Seers.

'How do I travel?'

'With hope,' the old man said. 'This is very tricky magic. We will bend our thoughts and powers towards the boy and, with luck, you will arrive at a time and place where you can intercept him. Now, I want you to concentrate on the fire.'

Eleanor went to stand in front of the little fireplace. From behind, she heard a stir of words, foreign, beautiful, and somehow menacing.

'Do not look back,' Frija hissed. 'The source of the magic should not be seen.'

A flurry of snow wafted down the chimney and the flames in the grate sizzled. Suddenly, they reared up like a dozen yellow snakes. Eleanor's eyes misted in the glare. All the colour seemed to fade from the flames and she caught a glimpse of shapes moving within the fire. Shadows within shadows, darkness everlasting. Her heart quickened. As much as she longed to see Jake, part of her was now reluctant to enter this future world.

A scream cut the air. Preacher Hobarron in agony. She began to turn when Frija called—

'Keep your eyes on the fire, Eleanor.'

'Ye-yesss,' the Preacher cried. 'I was aware of the risks, my d-dear. This is my choice.'

The flames spilled out of the fireplace and singed Eleanor's face. She tried to back away but remained rooted to the spot. Stunned, she realized that the fire had not burned her. That, in fact, its flickering fingers were as cold as ice. They billowed around her in a ragged circle of cool, grey light. In the final moment before the flames engulfed her, Eleanor peered back over her shoulder.

Frija was leaning forward in her chair, a stream of mist issuing from her hands. Next to Frija, Preacher Hobarron had slumped forward. His face was waxy and unmoving.

The fire rose up around Eleanor. Frija and the dead preacher, the parlour, the rectory, and Starfall itself disappeared into darkness. Everything she had known fell away from the girl as she crossed into new and terrible dimensions.

Alien skies wheeled overhead; strange stars rose and set around her. She closed her eyes against the horror.

When at last she opened them again, the floor was solid beneath her feet. A hard, stone floor, cold and damp. She appeared to be in a chamber of some kind, but it was too dark to see the walls.

'Who's there? Who has come to find me?'

That voice. There was something familiar about it. A voice from her own time. 'M-my name's Eleanor,' she stuttered.

A figure moved in the dimness. Shuffled forward with the gait of an old man. 'El-ean-or. That is a *human* name, is it not?'

'Yes.'

'But there are no humans here. I see to that . . . '

He came forward into the light, and Eleanor recognized him at once. Mad eyes rolled in his head and he clutched his haggard face like a man trying to tear the skin from his skull. There were drops of red in his straggly beard and old brown stains on his filthy shirt.

'Witchfinder,' Eleanor gasped.

Matthew Hopkins coughed up a mouthful of blood.

'That was what they called me,' he grinned, the blood spilling over his lips. 'Witchfinder General. I killed so many, many, many, many, many. That is why I am here.'

'Where?'

The madman cocked his head to one side.

'Do you not know? Can you not guess?'

He sidled up to Eleanor and whispered in her ear.

'Hell, my dear. This is hell. The home of demons . . . '

Many thanks to my brilliant agent Veronique Baxter and editors extraordinaire Jasmine Richards, Clare Whitston, and Kate Williams for helping to shape and reshape this book.

I must also acknowledge the invaluable assistance of Vicki Malkinson and her knowledge of all things equestrian.

My heartfelt thanks go to the ever-resourceful librarians at Skegness Library for helping me to find a path into the seventeenth century.

As ever, I must also acknowledge my friends and family whose love, support, and patience makes writing possible.

Finally, thank you to all the bright and brilliant people at Oxford University Press who have worked their own special magic on Witchfinder—here are a just a few of them: Molly Dallas, Lou Brown, Nicola Atkinson, Katie Hovell, Anna Baldwin, and Harriet Bayly.

About the author

William Hussey has a Masters Degree in Writing from Sheffield Hallam University. His novels are inspired by long walks in the lonely Fenlands of Lincolnshire and by a lifetime devoted to horror stories, folklore, and legends. William lives in Skegness and writes stories about things that go bump in the night . . .

THEN – circa 29,000 BC –
Where Demons Dwell

'She's just a child, a baby—why must you do this?'

'Because I am hungry.'

'I have meat in my shelter. All the reindeer flesh you can eat.'

'But I have told you, I cannot live in this world on animal meat alone. I must have my fill of human flesh or I will fade back into the shadows. Is that what you want?'

'No, my child!'

'Then let me eat in peace.'

The baby in the demon's arms started to cry, a high-pitched mewling that set his teeth on edge. He ought to silence her. Snap her frail neck and then feast, but the demon wanted the blood to be as hot and as fresh as possible.

Perched on the bank of the wide river, the demon lifted the baby to its jaws. So weak, so fragile. How could these pitiful mortals hope to survive in such a cold and ruthless

cosmos? To destroy them—to *eat* them—was really a kind
of mercy. The woman squatting beside the demon shivered;
a delightful tremor that made him smile. Not only were they
weak and fragile, they were sentimental!

The baby flailed her plump little limbs. Her hand latched
onto the demon's lower lip and turned his smile into a
grimace. His tongue slavered and his needle-sharp teeth
grazed her fragile fingers and moved up to her tiny wrist. He
would soon strip the meat from this young carcass. Then, when
the feast was over, he'd fling the bones into the great river:
a watery graveyard that had already washed away the
leftovers of six sumptuous meals.

The demon crammed the baby's arm into his mouth,
ready to bite down . . .

'I SEE THE MONSTER! HE HAS THE CHILD!'

Three men crashed through the trees on the far bank.
Spears raised, they glared at the woman and her demon.

The monster reacted with lightning speed. He dropped
the baby onto the soft earth and darted into the forest.
Behind him, he could hear the fading cry of the infant and
the woman's breathless pursuit.

'Where are you, my child? Answer me! The hunters are
crossing the river!'

And now her words became ragged with fear—

'*Please,* my little Pinch, they are going to kill us!'

The demon hurtled on into the lush green depths of the
forest. A low-lying mist lapped around the trees and the creature's powerful body cut through it like the prow of a ca-
noe through still waters. Foraging animals scattered before

him and the insects hidden in the long grass ceased their chirrup-song.

Gradually, the forest began to thin out, the trees became more stunted and patches of cold sunlight broke through. Up ahead, he could see a landslide of immense boulders that had smashed its way into the forest, felling small redwoods and providing a rugged slope to the foot of the mountain. Within seconds, he had reached the first boulder and scrambled over the scree. At the base of the mountain, Pinch craned his neck and tried to gauge its height, but the summit of the red-rock giant disappeared into a crown of wispy white clouds.

Pinch filled his lungs and began the climb. His talons found niches in the rock and he swung himself from crevice to crevice, moving with monkey-like agility. The demon was beginning to tire when he caught sight of a ledge jutting out from the rock face like a petulant lip. Exhausted, he clawed his way onto the little plateau.

Birds nesting on the ledge took one look at the demon and exploded into the sky. They climbed high, wheeling and shrieking. Anyone in the forest valley below would be certain to notice their panicked flight. Pinch scampered back to the edge and peered over.

The river blinked up from between the trees. Somewhere down there the womenfolk had herded the children into the safety of their reindeer-skin huts. Pinch imagined them sitting in circles, holding hands and praying for the safe return of the hunters. Those fearless men had tracked and killed every danger that had ever threatened their camp: hungry wolves and ravenous cave lions, even the cannibal tribe that had made its home in the next valley. All the same, Pinch knew that they had never faced a creature such as he.

A dark spirit summoned forth by one of their own.

The demon's gaze swept around the plateau. It was a wide ledge bound on three sides by the mountain *Ayyuk*, named in honour of the falling night and of the 'Great Giver'. At the centre stood a beautiful statue almost as tall as Pinch. Carved from mammoth tusk, it depicted the Great Giver in the form of a tribesman—a tall, long-limbed figure, his bone-white hands pressed against the earth.

Pinch snorted and shook his head. By some accident, he had reached the place most sacred to the tribe. They called it the 'Watching Eye'. From here, so the legend went, the Great Giver saw all of creation and judged everything in his view, good and evil.

A sudden fury took hold of the demon. He snatched up the idol and threw it with all his might into the forest below. The white god shimmered in the late-summer sun before vanishing into the whispering ocean of redwoods. *Down you go*, Pinch thought, *out of the light and into the darkness*. He allowed himself a brief smile before turning back to the mountain. The sheer walls were impossible to climb, even for the dexterous demon. What was he going to do?

'Pinch? Answer me!'

At the sound of the woman's voice, Pinch sought shelter in the only place he could: a rough collar of juniper bushes that ran in a semi-circle around the plateau. He snuffled, breathless as that strange emotion—fear—ran through his little body. For a short time, he had known freedom and, more importantly, the sense of being whole again. No longer a thing of shapeless shadow, he had felt solid earth beneath his feet and the sharp mountain wind against his face. He had breathed the air, drunk the water, eaten the flesh. After eons in the airy darkness, he had been grateful for his liberty and his crude form. But now Pinch sensed that his time in this world was almost up.

The hunters were coming.

'My little child! Where you?'

The woman clambered over the ridge, a whisker away from Pinch's hiding place. Her words were rough but he had been her companion for almost a year and had developed an understanding for the tribe's brutish speech. Now he automatically translated it into his own, more refined demon-tongue.

Half-crouching, his mistress wheeled around the ledge, eyes alert, ears straining. As tough as a rhino's hide, her bare feet padded across the rocky ground. She swept her head low and the reindeer horn pendants hanging around her neck grazed the earth like limp fingers. She called out again, spittle flying from her lips, the indecision plain on her face—should she continue the hunt for her beloved 'child' or should she flee? Already she could hear the thunder-step of her pursuers and the clack of their spears.

'Where? Where?' she cried. 'Cannot lose him again. Cannot. But where my child? Where my little man? Where my son made alive again?'

Pinch drew back, the bracken folding around him like a bearskin blanket.

The hunters arrived in a wave. They broke over the ridge and fanned out around the sacred plateau. With a shriek of terror, the woman stumbled back against the cliff wall. Fifteen faces stared at her, square eyes narrowed, high foreheads crumpled. The men were dressed in reindeer hides decorated with bright feathers and painted shells. Blue thunderbolt tattoos blazed across their cheeks and rippled down their powerful forearms. Each hunter held a spear, a formidable weapon fashioned from a mammoth's thighbone.

The leader of the tribe came forward. He walked with calculated grace, every muscle in his battle-scarred body turning and tensing. He wore a diadem of bones around his head—the crown of a seasoned warrior. His sad eyes looked from the woman to the mark in the dust where the idol had stood.

'Where the Great Giver?'

The woman shivered. 'Don't know.'

A leathery squeak as the hunters' hands tightened around their spears. Some cried out in grief: this traitor to their tribe had desecrated The Watching Eye, their most sacred place.

'Where the monster?' the leader said, stepping to within striking distance of the woman. 'Where the dark child?'

'Don't know,' she whispered.

'You are wise-woman. Daughter of the daughter of the daughter of she who first saw the Great Giver. You are teacher and worker of the sacred gift. You are speaker and mover of Oldcraft.'

'Oldcraft is for good,' one of the tribe barked. 'Not evil, so said the Great Giver.'

'Our people were told, warned.' The leader nodded. 'Not to let evil into hearts. Not to let it turn the magic dark. Why you bring the monster here?'

'Not "monster"!' the wise-woman shrieked. 'My child!'

The leader pressed his fingers to her lips.

'All knew you missed your Pinch. When starving wolves found him alone in the woods, we grieved with you.'

He turned to one of his hunters, took the warrior's weapon.

The hunter bowed and stepped back, away from his leader and the killing ground.

'Cried with you, prayed with you, even begged the Great Giver to look after the boy's soul in the grey beyond, though He told us He had no knowledge of that place. That none of his kind did. We felt your pain, my sister, and saw how it made you bite and snap at us like a crazed dog. How it turned your thoughts to bleak winter. But this thing you brought to our camp—'

'Not thing! Please, brother, hear me: his face and form was made ugly by my poor magic. He told me that I had bad skill and could not shape him. But this "monster" *is* my little Pinch. My child. Your sister-son. He heard my crying in the grey place where all our ancestors go. Heard the prayers of his mother for him to return. My strong Oldcraft brought him back to us.'

'No, sister. What came to you was a thing of lies and death. Would your good child Pinch have returned here and made his mother's magic like poison? Would he have murdered so many of our little ones? No. It is the thing the Great Giver warned us of. It is *demon*.'

'I do not believe——!'

'Your belief does not matter. Now, tell us where the de-mon is.'

The leader brought the tip of the spear to rest against the throbbing artery of his sister's throat. A rustle of feet as the hunters gathered around. Anticipating the kill, some of the younger tribesmen smiled, but the older ones, weary from a lifetime of blood, merely nodded in acceptance. Although she was sister to the leader her crime was the gravest their people had ever known and execution the only punishment. Chosen children of Oldcraft, they had a duty to stop this evil before it spread throughout the known lands. If not, then how many more demons might come out of the darkness?

'Guide us!' the cry was taken up by the tribe. 'Guide us to the demon!'

'Not demon,' the wise-woman said, her voice as barren as winter. 'Son. He told me, promised me——*son*. Please, brother, he said he was my Pin——'

The leader struck home. His spear pierced flesh, grazed bone, split rock. Pinioned against the mountain, the wise woman kicked and wriggled, her hands loose around the bloody spear. The younger hunters roared their approval, a victory call that was soon silenced by their leader's bellow.

'SHE WAS MY SISTER!'

He turned back to the woman.

She was trying to speak.

'Pi . . . Pin . . . '

The wise-woman pointed a shaking finger. In her dying moments, she had glimpsed the shape in the juniper bushes.

'Pin-ch. M-my Pin-ch . . . '

The demon had been summoned by this woman and his life-force was tied to hers. Now Pinch felt the last flickers of that force die out. Fire erupted around his body. He was going home. In a final act of cruelty, the demon locked eyes with the witch who had given him his form and freedom, and slowly, slowly shook his head. A gesture that meant only one thing—

I lied.

The scene before him—the furious hunters, the grief-stricken leader, the betrayed and slow-dying witch—flickered and vanished. As the fire faded, Pinch felt himself being drawn through the dimensional rift and back to the demon prison. Leaving the solid world of the tribe behind, he had expected that his body would melt away to its old shadowy form, but here he was, on the cusp of the demon realm, still possessing the crude shape that the witch had conjured for him.

The creature now known as Pinch smiled. He would go straight to the Shadow Palace and beg an audience with the Demon Father himself. He would tell of his adventures: of the woman whose bitter cry had pierced the walls of the demon dimension and drawn him to her. He would tell of the tribe's magic, of its superstitions, of its 'Oldcraft'. And then he would outline his plan.

These mortals had the power to release demonkind. If their hearts were dark, if they hated and envied, if they lusted for power and vengeance, then their minds would be open to demonic influence. Let us prey upon their weak natures,

Pinch would suggest. When they cry out in pain and fury, let us answer them and pretend that it is only through us that they can work their magic . . .

He arrived in the murk and silence of the demon realm and hurried to the palace gates. Without sun or moon or stars in the empty sky it was impossible to gauge time here, but it could not have been many minutes before Pinch was standing in his master's presence.

Once, long ago, the Demon Father had possessed a form, wondrous and terrible. Then the war had come, and the trap had been set, and demonkind had been relegated to things of shapeless shadow. Even the Demon Father had managed to maintain only the crudest of forms: a pair of hideous, blood-soaked eyes that hovered above his insubstantial throne.

Breathless, Pinch bowed before his master and began his story.

The Demon Father did not possess a mouth, but when Pinch reached the end of the tale, a cold, booming voice echoed around the chamber.

'Oldcraft . . . Is it possible that one of the Three could have gifted the mortals their magic? They called the mountain *Ayyuk*. Nightfall.' A brief silence, and then the terrible eyes focused on Pinch. 'Your plan is admirable, my child, but your ambition is too limited. Temporary freedom will do for now, but my eyes see far. The mortals you have described are a primitive breed, but gradually they will evolve until their knowledge and their magic reaches a pinnacle. There are clearly weak points in this world of theirs, portals into our dimension, otherwise the woman's magic could not have reached here and drawn you to her. One day, when the time is ripe, the mortals will use their magic to open a great door into our prison. A door large enough for all of demon-kind to pass through.'

'But that may take centuries!' Pinch cried.

'Thousands of years,' the Demon Father corrected, 'but we have been imprisoned here for millennia and we have learned patience. I promise you, my child, one day the Time of Demons will come. One day the Demontide will dawn!'